THE LOVE MATCH

Also by Michael Taylor

EVE'S DAUGHTER

THE
LOVE MATCH

Michael Taylor

Hodder & Stoughton

Copyright © 1999 by Michael Taylor

First published in Great Britain in 1999
by Hodder and Stoughton
A division of Hodder Headline PLC

British Library Cataloguing in Publication Data
A CIP catalogue record for this book
is available from the British Library

ISBN 0 340 75129 0

Typeset by Hewer Text Ltd, Edinburgh
Printed and bound in Great Britain by
Mackays of Chatham PLC, Chatham, Kent

Hodder and Stoughton
A division of Hodder Headline PLC
338 Euston Road
London NW1 3BH

To the memory of Marie Vanes

With grateful thanks to Ian Pethick, David Elvidge, Marion Davies, Carolyn Caughey and Jill Bright, all of whom have given tremendous help and encouragement.

Chapter One

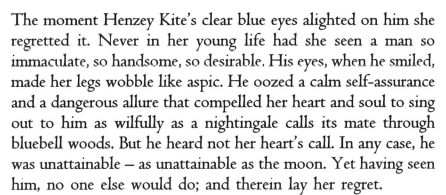

The moment Henzey Kite's clear blue eyes alighted on him she regretted it. Never in her young life had she seen a man so immaculate, so handsome, so desirable. His eyes, when he smiled, made her legs wobble like aspic. He oozed a calm self-assurance and a dangerous allure that compelled her heart and soul to sing out to him as wilfully as a nightingale calls its mate through bluebell woods. But he heard not her heart's call. In any case, he was unattainable – as unattainable as the moon. Yet having seen him, no one else would do; and therein lay her regret.

The girl at his side matched him perfectly. She was strikingly beautiful. Henzey had spotted her once before; a week ago, on the evening she first met Andrew. She was called Nellie, and she was Andrew's sister; but Andrew had not introduced them. Everything about Nellie was exquisite, especially her dark hair, which was impeccably styled and framed her lovely face. Her skin was flawless, her clothes fitted to a stitch and her figure was inspiring. Yet everything about her was sublimely understated to the point of rendering her demure. Men would die for Nellie Dewsbury. She stood out like a fine-cut diamond in a tray of gaudy baubles.

And Henzey wanted to be just like her.

Realising that she was staring at them both, Henzey turned away to appraise the fine set of framed watercolours that hung on the wall behind her. She must find time to do more watercolours herself; a change from the pen and ink and charcoal drawings she'd been doing lately. Just fancy if she were in a position to paint *him* and capture *his* calm self-assurance. The thought sent a warm flush of blood through her veins. But then she would spend her time just looking at him, ogling him, and doubtless get little painting done.

Standing unaccompanied, holding a glass of lemonade Andrew had brought her earlier, she noted how many people in that elegant drawing-room were in fancy dress. One young man arrived dressed like Rudolph Valentino as 'The Sheikh', another like Al Jolson in *The Jazz Singer*, and one masqueraded as an ancient pharaoh, obviously influenced by the recent excavations of Tutankhamun's tomb. Couples began dancing to the strident sounds of a jazz band emanating from a gramophone standing in a corner. Henzey looked doubtfully at the highly polished wood-block floor, which was at the mercy of so many skidding, twisting, leather-soled shoes.

Sipping her drink, Henzey was aware that the party was growing noisier. All around her, people were shrieking with laughter. Clipped accents proliferated, sounding as foreign to her as the strange, rolling American cadences she'd heard in the talkies. She'd often imagined that people who spoke 'posh' would be stand-offish, so she was surprised at how friendly they were, towards each other at any rate. They were totally uninhibited, prepared to do things to make fools of themselves that she would never contemplate. Three young men took everybody's attention when they held an impromptu competition between themselves to see who could dance ragtime best to a scratchy version of 'Alexander's Ragtime Band'. A diminutive young thing in a long, blue dress elected herself both partner and judge for each. Henzey watched their tomfoolery and laughed.

'Who's this raven-haired girl here?' she overheard somebody behind her say. 'The one with the Egyptian bob. She's absolutely too divine.'

His chum replied, 'Sorry, old man. Never seen her before.'

She turned to see who had spoken, naturally believing they must be referring to Nellie. When it was obvious that the two young men were discussing herself, Henzey smiled, flattered. Blushing, she cast her eyes down.

'Wouldn't mind having a tilt at her. Love her dress.'

The dress had been bought specially for the party; black, with a low waist, short and straight. Save for the low back, it gave her a boyish appearance; the height of fashion. A matching headband and a row of long, black beads afforded the finishing touch. She looked beautiful, and respectable enough to be visiting the home of a wealthy family, her mother had affirmed with pride.

'See how it falls over the cheeks of her backside? She's an absolute peach.'

'Faint heart ne'er won a fair lady,' said the first. 'Introduce yourself, man . . . Go on, before somebody else snaps her up. Sweep her off her feet.'

Henzey wished fervently that Andrew would return to her side. But the young man's approach was thwarted nonetheless; a tall, willowy girl had been edging towards her unwittingly, and overheard the boys' comments. She was wearing an expensive-looking, sleeveless, white pyjama suit with a green snake embroidered on the front, poised to strike. She carried a long black cigarette-holder in one hand and a half-empty champagne flute in the other. Her head was wrapped in an unusual cloche hat, styled like a turban.

'At the risk of ultimately dying a spinster,' she articulated close to Henzey's ear, as if to impart a great secret, 'I would go so far as to say that some of these young men have a tendency to overrate their own merit.'

'Oh?' Henzey replied with an interested smile.

'You must have heard what they said just now? . . . They must believe they are some sort of rare species. Frankly, I blame their mothers. They've doubtless drummed into them that they're worth their weight in gold. Such sentiments should have been directed at their elder brothers, surely? – those spared by the war.'

'I'm sorry.' Henzey could hear Andrew's voice booming boisterously on the other side of the room, and she was trying to listen to him at the same time. 'I didn't quite catch what you said.'

'I said, these boys have such high opinions of themselves.'

'Oh, some of them, maybe,' nodded Henzey. 'One of my friends made me laugh the other day. She reckons all they're interested in is getting their hands up your frock. I wouldn't know, myself. I've only ever had a couple of boyfriends, and I certainly wouldn't let anybody do that.'

The girl was already laughing. 'I say! I wouldn't have put it quite like that personally, but your synopsis has a ring of truth. You a local gel?'

'Born and bred. My name's Henzey Kite. I'm with Andrew, and he's getting more drunk by the minute, by the looks of him.'

'Margot Hartford-Giles.' She offered her hand, and they shook. 'Delighted to make your acquaintance, Henzey. So you're with Andrew, are you?'

'If I ever get to see him again. My sister Alice is here as well somewhere with Andrew's friend, George. Do you know George?'

'Know George? George is my brother, though that's not something I should be crowing about. So, that little girl I saw him plying with drink is your sister, eh? She looks very young.'

'She is. I'm supposed to keep my eye on her.'

'It's George you should keep an eye on, my dear – Andrew too. They're like all the rest. They believe they're a species of rare bird that should be kept in a gilded cage and have their feathers perpetually preened. If only they could rid themselves of this pitiful delusion.'

'If only they could see themselves, some of them.'

Margot drew herself closer to Henzey's ear and lowered her voice. 'Frankly, you wouldn't believe some of the things my friends say about men.'

'But they're not all as bad as you say, are they, Margot?' She risked another glance at *him* with the fascinating allure, in time to see him leaving the drawing-room with the equally fascinating Nellie. 'My brother's all right,' she continued, her eyes following them. 'He's fifteen and never had a girlfriend. He's good to our mom, though, and kind to his horse . . .'

'Oh, does he ride?'

'Ride? Oh, no. He's a milkman. The horse pulls his float.'

'Oh, I see.' Margot turned her head to conceal her amusement.

'Mind you,' Henzey continued, uninhibited by their cultural distance, 'sometimes he tries to make everybody think as he's better at everything than me and our Alice and our Maxine, but his brain ain't quick enough. He thinks too slow.'

'Like all men.'

'He's all right really, though.'

'But it proves my point, Henzey.'

Margot took a gulp of champagne and Henzey swigged her lemonade. Increasingly, it seemed as if she was not part of her surroundings; a peculiar sensation, as if she were in a dream and observing, but detached from the party.

'They're all different, I suppose,' Henzey said chattily and smiled.

'Oh, they fall into all sorts of categories. Do you know – in London, those on the social scene go out to dances practically every night of the season? Not any dance, mark you. Only *very* carefully selected ones. They owe it to themselves, you see, to be seen only at the right places. They get to know everybody on the social circuit, get to know everything about them – how much money they have, whom they hope to marry, even whom they've slept with.'

'Slept with? You don't mean . . .?'

'Oh, please, don't be shocked. That sort of thing's par for the course these days, my dear. Whilst they'll sleep with absolutely anybody, these socialites only fall in love with heiresses. But at least they are polite, which these days has to be admired. Immaculately dressed too. Most wear pristine white gloves so as not to mark your best silk dress with sweaty hands. Very commendable, what? Even their socks are beyond criticism, I'm told.

'Then there's the academic. Utterly boring. Can you imagine anything more tedious than discussing a collection of specialist books on the impact of treacle on furry worms, for instance?'

Henzey chuckled. 'What a lark, Margot! You must get about a bit. What other sorts are there?' She was beginning to enjoy Margot's dissertation on today's young men.

'Well, I suspect the nightclub goon is worthy of mention.'

Henzey laughed. 'The nightclub goon?'

'You know the type. Tries to make himself look exactly like Ramon Novarro, or Ronald Colman. Hair sleeked down with hair-oil, perfumed like the inside of a whore's handbag. Frankly, I fail to understand this fixation for emulating such people. Mind you, Henzey, the nightclub goon was doing the Charleston long before the rest of us had even heard of it. I must confess, I've panted with nightclub goons on many a dance floor.'

'What about those with cars?' Henzey asked out of self-interest, for Andrew had a car.

A man nudged Margot, placed a cigarette in her cigarette-holder, and deftly lit it with a silver lighter as she put it to her lips. He smiled, looked Henzey up and down, and just as deftly moved on without a word. She drew on the cigarette as though her life depended on it, exhaling smoke in great billows. Henzey was reminded of a fiery dragon.

'Frankly, the youth with a motor car is the worst of the lot. Absolutely reeks of engine oil. Usually got a horrid, grubby bandage on at least one finger. Conversation's rather limited too – to carburettors and magnetos usually. And the only thing he'll ever drive you to is drink. All he ever reads is motoring magazines, and his favourite pastime is to disappear into a smelly garage for hours on end with an equally smelly chum to hot the blessed vehicle up.'

'What about his girlfriend?'

Margot sucked earnestly at her cigarette-holder again. 'I should say the jolly old girlfriend has to be rather slim to fit in the damn thing – like you. But whatever car he's got, he'll scare you rigid with his driving.'

At that, Andrew came along with a fresh pint of beer in his hand. 'Ah, I shee you two have met,' he said with some difficulty. 'Margot is George's shishter, you know. Up from Windsor for the weekend.' He went to put his glass to his lips and slopped some over himself, which he tried to pat away with the flat of his hand.

'Charming gel you have here, Andrew,' Margot said. 'Henzey and I are confidantes. Her opinion of men concurs generally with my own. What was it you said, my dear? Men are only interested in getting their oily hands up our frocks. That was it, more or less, was it not? I trust it's not true of you, Andrew.'

Margot laughed like a donkey, and Henzey chuckled in-fectiously at Margot.

'I've come to drag her away from you, Margot,' Andrew said, a little wobbly on his legs. 'I want to show her off to Nellie.'

'Ah, Nellie. So be it. I'll circulate.'

Henzey was still chuckling, but stiffened a little at hearing Nellie's name. She was longing to get a closer look at her hair, and how she applied her make-up. Still holding her empty glass, she turned to follow Andrew. He led her into the breakfast room, and there she saw Nellie and her godlike companion talking and laughing with a group of people, some of whom she recognised from the roller-skating rink.

But Henzey was feeling hot and light-headed. Her thoughts were becoming unfocused. 'Andrew, would you get me some more lemonade first, please? I'm feeling a bit peculiar.'

He took her glass biddably, and was soon back at her side with a refill. She took a long drink, hoping it would clear her head. The last thing she wanted was to go down with a bout of flu.

'Are you ready now?'

'Yes, I'm ready.'

'Helen, I'd like you to meet Henzey. Henzey . . . Helen.'

'Nice to meet you, Henzey,' she said with a smile.

Henzey smiled back. 'Nice to meet you, too, Nellie.' She tried to take in Nellie's technique with make-up, but the handsome companion was proving a greater attraction. Her eyes swivelled towards him, and she smiled coyly in anticipation of the introduction. His eyes lit up in response, and Nellie witnessed the exchange.

'Excuse me,' she said severely, drawing Henzey's attention again. 'Was I not introduced as Helen?'

'Helen? . . . Oh, sorry. I thought everybody called you Nellie.' She blushed deeply at her blunder.

Nellie smiled, but too sweetly for it to be sincere. 'Only family and close friends call me Nellie.' Then her expression changed to frozen marble. 'You've reached the status of neither . . . nor are you ever likely to, unless I'm very much mistaken.'

Henzey's head was swimming, and Nellie's aggressive attitude unnerved her. It seemed so unnecessary. She began trembling with embarrassment and disappointment.

He looked at Henzey with some sympathy. 'That's a bit unkind, Nell.'

'Oh, er . . . this is Billy Witts. Nellie's . . . er, Helen's boyfriend,' Andrew said meekly.

She looked at Billy Witts again, but this time in bewilderment. Her smile had disappeared, her blue eyes told of the hurt and humiliation she felt inside. Floundering, she looked to Andrew for support. But no support came. He was too drunk to think straight. People were milling past Henzey, and the noise from the party seemed strangely overpowering. She was feeling queasy, hot, and her legs were shaking now.

'Please excuse me.' She turned away and heard Billy remonstrate with Nellie.

Andrew caught up with her. 'Take no notice of her, Henzey. She's probably jealous of you.'

'Why should she be jealous of me? I've done nothing. All I did was call her by the name everybody else calls her by. She's rude, your sister, and I thought she was so nice.' Tears flooded her eyes. 'I don't feel very well, either.'

As she walked unsteadily past the kitchen, something clicked ominously in her mind. Something. She wasn't sure what. It had some vital significance, but she could not pinpoint it in her perplexity. In the hall, she sat on the stairs and put her head in her hands trying to remember, trying to overcome the unaccountable swimming sensation in her mind.

Andrew said, 'I'll get you another glass of lemonade, shall I?'

She wanted water, but she could not form the words to say so. Lemonade would have to do. She closed her eyes and her head seemed to spin. With a start she stared around her and shook her head violently in an attempt to stem the awful sensation of giddiness. But she was so thirsty as well. Something was radically wrong. She must be ill. Andrew returned from the kitchen with another full glass and handed it to her. She quaffed the lemonade, staring vacantly.

'I say! Are you all right? You look jolly pale.'

'Oh Andrew, I feel terrible. I'll have to get some fresh air. I think I'll have to go home.'

He took her glass, put it down on the telephone table and helped her to her feet, as well as he was able in his own inebriated state. 'Not yet. Come on, I've got a better idea. You can lie down on my bed and I'll open the windows for you.'

'Oh, I couldn't go to your bedroom. What would people think?'

But she was incapable of further resistance. Andrew held on to the banister with one hand and, with his other arm around Henzey's waist, they lumbered awkwardly upstairs. He struggled to open the door to his bedroom. When at last he did, they entered and both slumped onto the bed. It finally dawned on her that she must be drunk. But she was by no means certain. She'd never been drunk before.

'Have you put anything in my drinks, Andrew?' she asked, not without some impediment. 'Andrew, have you put anything in my drinks?'

'Oh, just a drop of Russian vodka.' He sounded pleased with himself. 'Just a teensy-weensy drop. George and I thought it would looshen you up a bit . . . help you enjoy the party.'

'Oh, what you do that for?' She sounded so disappointed. 'I promised my mother . . .'

She passed out.

In her dream she was turning, revolving, spinning in a black velvet sky. Stars whizzed round her at a fantastic rate, making her dizzy, and all she could hear was a high-pitched whistling in her head. She was searching, searching, but for what? In her dream she was desperately searching for something as she spun round and round, like a top gone berserk. But she could not remember what it was. The shrill whistling grew louder the dizzier she got. A burden of responsibility was hanging heavy upon her, she was aware. But the spinning, the endless turning, the stars racing by, the searching . . . this anxiety. If only she knew what she was seeking. It was making her feel sick.

An overwhelming need to vomit forced her to consciousness again and she sat up. She was surprised to see the hem of her dress round her waist and Andrew lying beside her, his hand stroking the bare flesh of her thighs between the tops of her stockings and her knickers.

'Let's have your clothes off, there's a sport,' he was saying. 'Let's shee you in the buff.'

She slapped his face with as much indignation as she could muster and, with an extraordinary effort, staggered off the bed. She opened the door and lurched from the room, stumbling. Just in time she found the bathroom, vacant for once, and retched into the lavatory. She shuddered at the awful bitter taste in her mouth. Almost at once, her head cleared. Again she heaved . . . And again. Her eyes were streaming . . . yet miraculously she felt better. But the spark of anger she'd felt was being fanned into a roaring flame by the thought of Andrew's stupidity. What a downright cad to even think of lacing a girl's drinks with vodka when she believed all along it was just lemonade! Had he and George done it just so they could take advantage of her and Alice?

Alice!

It was then she realised why she was so racked with anxiety. She stood up. Her mind was clear. She washed her mouth and wiped the tears from her eyes, then cursed her own slowness of mind. 'Alice! Oh, Alice!' If anything had happened to Alice . . . She thrust open the bathroom door and stormed out. The door to Nellie's room, the ladies powder room for the evening, was shut. Seeking Alice, she shoved it open angrily. It almost hit Nellie, who was just coming out.

'Hey, I think "excuse me" is the expression you're looking for, Miss.'

Henzey ignored her only because she had something more important to attend to. She rushed to the next door on the landing and thrust it open. In the darkness of the room she could just make out two people in bed. Instantly, they parted.

'Is that you, Alice?'

A girl's voice answered warily, 'Hello, Henzey.'

'Alice, you damn fool! What the hell d'you think you're doing?'

'Just talking.' There was annoyance in her voice.

'Get up, for God's sake!' But the sight of George in bed with her sister was too much. Henzey burst into tears, shaking with anger and disappointment at this lesson in human nature. 'George, George! D'you know how old she is? . . . *Do* you?'

'Sixteen, she told me. You were there, at the roller-skating rink.'

'I'll tell you how old she is,' she sobbed. 'She's fourteen. D'you hear what I said? *Fourteen.*' Tears were streaming down her face.

'Christ, I had absolutely no idea. She said she was sixteen.

You heard her.' He turned to Alice. 'You told me you were sixteen, didn't you? I distinctly remember.'

Alice shrugged, unconcerned. 'I don't see what all the fuss is about.'

Henzey was weeping copiously, tired, and drained of emotion. But she marshalled enough ardour to tell George what she thought of him. 'Fourteen, sixteen, what's the difference? Neither makes you any better. Neither makes you a knight in shining armour, specially after you've deliberately tried to get her drunk. I bet you think you're really clever. I bet you and your stupid pals will have a good laugh over this, won't you?' She took a deep breath to help regain her composure. 'Alice, come on. We're going home.'

While Henzey waited outside the door, wiping away her tears with the back of her hand, Billy Witts appeared at the top of the stairs. 'Hey, what's going on?' he asked. 'Somebody says there's trouble up here.'

Henzey burst into tears again.

'What's the matter, my flower?' He sounded genuinely concerned. 'What happened?'

'It's my sister . . . in there with that . . . that swine George . . . I'm taking her home. What time is it, please? We're supposed to be home by twelve.'

'It's about half past eleven. Andrew brought you, didn't he?'

'He did, and some use he is, as well. He's as bad as that George. He's as drunk as a rat. Look at him in there.' They both peered through the open door into Andrew's bedroom. He was sprawled out on the bed, oblivious to the world. 'If he's supposed to be a gentleman, give me a rough miner any day of the week.'

At that moment, Alice appeared at the bedroom door, bleary-eyed, her best dress crumpled, her hair tousled.

Billy said, 'I'll take you home. How far is it?'

'Not far. But we wouldn't want you to get into trouble with her ladyship.'

'I said I'll take you home.'

Henzey shrugged, feigning indifference, but he took it as her acceptance. Once outside, he let them into his car parked in the street, and they drove off.

'So what happened back there? I could see there was something wrong. What was all the fuss about?'

Henzey explained more fully what had happened at the hands of Andrew and George.

'Did George put anything in your drink, Alice?' she asked.

'I dunno. Maybe he did,' she answered. 'I only had two. I feel all right – I think.'

'I'm livid at that George, Billy. He must have tried to get her drunk. He took her to that bedroom, and she's only fourteen. I daren't begin to think what went on.'

'Nothin' went on.'

'Something went on, Alice. I could tell by the state of you.'

'Nothin' went on worth *mentionin'*. We was kissin', that's all. What's wrong wi' kissin'?'

'You said you were talking. Either way, you look as if you've been dragged through a hedge backwards. Your frock looks as if it's been put through the mangle all crooked and you should see your hair. 'Tis to be hoped Mother doesn't catch sight of you.'

Billy said, 'Course, he don't come from round here, that George. He came up from Windsor with his sister and her young man, just for Andrew's party. He's one of his university mates at Oxford.'

'Well the sooner he clears off back, the better.'

Nobody spoke for a while, till Henzey said, 'So how long have you been courting Nellie, Billy?'

'About two years, I reckon,' he replied.

'Mmm . . . Where does she get her hair done?'

'That hairdresser in Union Street, I think.'

Billy smiled to himself. What little he'd seen of this girl he liked. She was not sophisticated like Nellie, but she was no less beautiful. There was something refreshing about her, even in her distressed state. He perceived within her an earthy passion, something indefinably basic, elemental. She had no airs and graces, yet she possessed undeniable self-esteem. She was like him; a born survivor with the potential to be a cut above the rest. There was hidden promise in her clear blue eyes, her red lips, so kissable, and her long, shapely legs. He changed to a lower gear as they turned into the Market Place, and glimpsed the few tantalising inches of her thighs that were visible as her short dress rode up her legs in the seat next to him. Pity she was so young. But with such potential all she needed was the rough edges knocking off her. She could be moulded into something really special.

The town was deserted. Henzey peered through the car window now at George Mason's shop, and tried to push to the back of her mind all the questions her workmates would ask on Monday about the party. They were expecting her to be practically engaged to this wealthy Andrew Dewsbury she'd told them so much about. Now she would look such a fool. They were expecting a love affair at the very least. They had even called her Cinderella when she told them she had to be home by midnight.

'I'm not looking forward to work on Monday,' she said absently.

'What on earth's made you think of work?' Billy asked.

''Cause we've just gone past the place where she works,' Alice proclaimed, pointing. 'At George Mason's just there.'

'You have to turn right here up Hall Street,' Henzey said. 'Anyway, how come you don't sound like the Dewsburys and all that crowd, Billy? The first time I caught sight of you I thought you'd talk really posh, like them.'

'I'm just an ordinary chap, who happens to be courting somebody who does talk posh. I can put it on when I have to.'

They travelled on in silence, listening to the thrum of the big Vauxhall's engine as it reverberated between the red-brick terraces in Kates Hill's narrow, inclined streets. Eventually they turned into Cromwell Street.

'Is this where you live?'

Henzey peered out. Iky Bottlebrush was mopping round the floor of his fish and chip shop before he went to bed. 'Here's fine, thanks. It's very nice of you, Billy.'

'It's the least I could do. Andrew was in no fit state to bring you back, was he? And I should hate you to think all blokes are the same. By the way – what did you say your name was?'

'Henzey.'

'And your surname?'

'Kite.'

He flashed her a broad smile. 'See you around some time, Henzey Kite.'

They clambered out of the car, shut the doors behind them, and crossed the street to walk the last few yards, stepping over the inky puddles that punctuated the pattern of damp cobbles. Smoke was curling into the dark, navy sky from the rows of chimneys that were lined up like soldiers on the slate roofs of the terraced houses. A dog barked in the next street, and a key turned in a lock, shutting out the night for someone. Under the light of the gas street lamp, Henzey stopped to inspect Alice again, and tried to smooth away the creases in her dress with the flat of her hand.

'Hope and pray Mother's not back yet,' she told Alice as they walked on. 'Hope and pray she's still out with Jesse.'

'Oh, I don't care, Henzey. We din't do anythin' . . . More's the pity.'

'What do you mean, more's the pity? You ought to be ashamed. Would you have let him?'

'I let him kiss me.' She shrugged. It was of little significance to Alice. 'We kissed with our mouths open . . . *And* he stuck his tongue in me mouth.'

Henzey shook her head in disgust. 'Yuk!'

'It was nice . . . I let 'im feel me Phyllis and Floss as well.'

'Oh, Alice, you didn't!' She stopped walking, both for effect and to allow this alarming piece of information to sink in.

'Why not? What's wrong with that? . . . Come on, slow-coach. What yer stopped for?'

'It's just not right, Alice. A girl your age. You should think more of yourself. What if you got into trouble?'

'We din't do *that*, if that's what you'm thinkin'.'

'Well, the way you're talking, nothing would surprise me.'

'No, I only let 'im feel me Phyllis and Floss – only for a minute or two. Nothin' else.'

Henzey sighed heavily, more troubled than Alice could appreciate, but resumed walking. 'I blame myself. I should never have let you out of my sight. I should've known they might try to get us drunk . . . God, my head's spinning again now . . . Oh, I hope I'm not going to be sick again.'

'Mine is a bit now as well, an' I only had two. Is that how drink makes you feel?'

'Oh, Alice, I despair of you . . .'

They turned into the entry on tiptoe, lest their footsteps announced their return. The door to the brewhouse was shut and the house was in darkness. At least Herbert, and Maxine their younger sister, had gone to bed. Henzey lifted the door latch and entered. Embers slipped in the black-leaded grate, prompting a flurry of sparks to shoot up the chimney, but affording sufficient light for her to see where she was going. She felt on the mantelpiece for a spill, and kindled it in what remained of the fire. As it flared, she reached for the oil lamp that resided on the windowsill and lit it, trimming the wick to give less smoke. The old black marble clock said five to twelve. She turned and saw that the door to the cellar was shut. She rounded the old horsehair sofa her father always used to lie on, reached out and lifted the latch as quietly as she could. Her mother's coat was not hanging there. She breathed a sigh of relief.

'Upstairs, quick,' she whispered. 'She's not back yet. And, in the morning, when she asks how we got on, say we had a smashing time.'

'I had a smashin' time anyway.'

Chapter Two

The back room at George Mason's grocery store in Dudley Market Place was where the female staff ate their sandwiches and made pots of tea. It was small and whitewashed. The glass on the outside of the tiny iron-framed window, that afforded it some daylight, had not been cleaned in two decades, but a pair of second-hand chenille curtains had been hung at it years ago. A couple of creaky chairs with fraying squabs furnished it, along with a torn seat from a charabanc that had been involved in a road accident. A brass tap rhythmically dripped cold water into a stone sink and, on top of a scrubbed wooden draining board, stood a gas ring, a black enamelled kettle and a selection of odd cups and saucers. In this room, secrets were revealed, souls were bared and an infinite amount of gossip was examined and disseminated.

Talk was usually about men. Henzey wondered how some of these girls she worked with got themselves into the cumbersome situations they confessed to, and decided they must be as immature as the boys they associated with. For instance, poor Rosie Frost, one of her workmates, had become involved with a young lad who was wanted by the police for burglary. He was lodging with Rosie and her widowed mother, using it as a safe house, abusing their good nature. At one of their dinnertime discussions, Rosie confessed she was having his child.

'And do you love him?' Clara Maitland asked. Clara was thirty, a childless widow, and a fine-looking woman, who was indifferent to the advances of optimistic suitors. She was well-fleshed but not overweight, her figure unsuited to the will-o'-the-wisp, boyish look that was in vogue; Clara had feminine curves and wore affordable clothes that tastefully accentuated them.

'No, can't say as I do,' was Rosie's half-hearted reply.

'Then you're a very silly girl, Rosie. Does your poor mother know you're pregnant?'

Rosie shook her head and looked guiltily into her lap.

'How do you girls get yourselves into such awful trouble? You must want your head looking at, Rosie. Get rid of him; that's my advice. Get rid of him . . . How old are you?'

'Eighteen.'

'Eighteen, and pregnant by a wanted criminal. My God! Wake up, child, and make something of yourself, and do it while you've still got the chance. Then when you've done that, try and find yourself somebody decent. Life'll be a lot easier, take it from me. A lot easier.'

Rosie sighed heavily. 'It's easy to say find somebody decent. But who? Anyway, if I am pregnant, it's me own fault.'

'Your fault? I'd have thought he'd had a part in it, Rosie,' Clara suggested wryly. 'It takes two, you know. Some men are all too keen to take advantage of girls. They promise you the earth. You should've been firmer with him. You should have said no. You should've told him you'd have no truck with doing things you ought not to be doing unless you're wed. You should've told him, if he wanted *that*, he should give up his burgling and make a decent, honest living by working, like the rest of us have to, and then marry you. Good God, what's the world coming to?'

Clara was in full flow, but she took another bite from her sandwich and munched it while she waited for the reaction of her younger workmates.

'I'd never marry 'im, Clara,' Rosie said, and licked jam off her fingers. 'I've been a proper fool, but I'm stuck with it now.'

Clara flicked breadcrumbs from her apron. 'Well, the doctor can't get rid of it for you. It'd be more than his life's worth. But I daresay there's some old women who know how, if that's what you wanted. It's always risky though.'

'No, I'm gunn'ave the child, Clara.'

Edie Soap, whose real name was Edie Hudson, had been listening while she filled the kettle and put it on the gas ring to boil. She sat down on the charabanc seat.

'And you, Edie,' Clara said, 'just mind what you're doing with that Arnold Jennings.'

Edie adjusted the fall of her apron and opened her sandwich tin. 'Doh thee fret, Clara,' she returned, in her deep voice. 'I'n sid enough o' that Rosie's plight. I'm keepin' me legs crossed an' me drawers on. Me fairther'd kill me if 'e thought I was lettin' any chap interfere wi' me. Besides, I'm afeared. Our Araminta says it 'urts vile the fust time. 'Er says it doh 'alf mek yer yowk.'

Clara smothered a chuckle. 'It can be a lot of pleasure with somebody you love.'

'Arnold's younger than you, isn't he, Edie?' Henzey commented as she stood up to stir the tea in the pot.

'By a year. I've took to 'im a treat, but the trouble is, I doh think I can stand 'is moods for long.'

'What makes him moody?' Henzey asked.

'Sayin' no to 'im,' Edie answered. 'He's like a bear with sore arse.'

'Well, you know what some of these young men are like,' Clara warned. 'They only care about themselves. Things are different now to how they were before the war. A lot different. There are more girls than boys now, so to some extent boys can take their pick. Trouble is, because of it, the boys expect the girls to be easy. Well, don't be . . . You mustn't be.

'I remember years ago my mother telling me about one of her friends, Bessie Hipkiss. She was in service at a really well-to-do house in Birmingham. Anyway, she fell in love with the master's son, and they had an illicit affair for a while. Long enough for him to put her in the family way, anyway. But when poor Bessie asked him what they should do about it, he said the child couldn't possibly be his and sacked her for her trouble. She was broken-hearted. All she'd got were the wages they sent her away with and the clothes on her back – and nowhere to live. As it happens, she remembered my grandfather and came straight to him for help. Her parents knew him well when they were alive, you see. She didn't want to be a burden, though. She just wanted the chance to make her own way. It turned out that he'd got an empty house – he was quite well off and owned some property – and he let Bessie have it for nothing. It was only a little back-to-back in Flood Street, and you know what a slum it is down there. Damp as the Dudley Tunnel, it was, and overrun with vermin. But she was glad of it. The trouble was, when she gave birth, she didn't have just one child, did she? Oh, no, not Bessie. She had twins – both boys – and like peas in a pod my mother always said.'

'Twins?' Henzey exclaimed. 'Just imagine being in all that trouble, then having twins.'

Clara nodded. 'She did her best to rear them, but she was poverty-stricken. Anyway, she fell ill and, when they were just two years old, Bessie died of consumption, poor soul.'

'Oh, that's terrible. All because the father denied all knowledge . . . What a rogue! So what happened to the poor little lads?'

'As it happens, Henzey, they were all right. My grandfather, being well respected in Methodist circles, found a nice family who took in one of them. Trouble was, they were poor, and they could only afford to take the one.'

'You mean they were split up?'

'I'm afraid so.'

'So what happened to the other?' Henzey's eyes were misty with tears by this time. She was deeply touched by the story.

Clara shook her head. 'We never knew for sure. My grandfather took him away, but he wouldn't say where, though we'd got a good idea. He reckoned he was sworn to secrecy. He just said the boy was going to be all right. My mother was certain sure he took him back to the house Bessie came from – to the boys' father – to make him face up to his responsibilities. Bessie had told him who the father was – from a rich family, anyway. But I never heard anything else about either of those two children since. Sad, isn't it?'

'When did all this happen, Clara?' Henzey asked. 'How long ago?'

'Well I was only a child meself when Bessie died. It'd be about 1902. Those twins would be about twenty-eight now if they're still alive.'

'Grown men. It'd be interesting to know what happened to them, wouldn't it?'

'I'd dearly love to know . . . But listen, I've told you girls this story to point out what can happen if you're easy. Men will always take what they want, and then, when they've took it, they'll be off like a shot unless you handle them right. Keep your man interested by being just a little bit elusive. That's what I always say. Before you give yourself to a man be sure he's in love with you. Or better still, wait till you're married.'

'Elusive?' Edie queried. 'What the bleedin' 'ell's that mean?'

'It means, be a bit mysterious, Edie. Don't be at his beck and call. Let him worry about what you're up to. Let him think you're up to no good sometimes when he's not around. Give him a hint occasionally that you might be interested in somebody else. It works wonders.'

Henzey glanced from one to the other, trying to gauge the girls' reaction to Clara's sage advice. 'You *do* seem to know a lot about men, Clara,' she said. 'I wish I did.'

'I'm thirty, Henzey, and I know what I'm talking about. I'm not sixteen, like you. I've been married and I enjoyed married life, and no man will ever replace my husband. I loved him dearly – I still do.'

'Are you saying we're all too young to be messing about with chaps, Clara?'

'No, I'm not saying that at all. I'm saying you're too young to be doing what you do in the marriage bed, but see as many young men as you like. Have some fun, but save yourself for one.'

Henzey said reverently, 'Oh, Clara, you are sensible.'

'I try to be. But what about you, Henzey? Have you seen that Jack Harper since you told him you were going to that party?'

'I've seen him, but only from a distance. He doesn't speak to me now . . . Has he been in the shop?'

'Why? You missin' 'im?'

Henzey nodded glumly. It had been more than two weeks since that party; two weeks during which she had all but forgotten Billy Witts, dismissed Andrew Dewsbury and his petulant sister from her mind, and started thinking again about Jack Harper.

'No, we ain't seen 'im,' Rosie said. 'I'd 'ave noticed 'im. I think 'e's bostin'. I think you'm daft, Henzey, for givin' 'im up, just for the chance o' goin' to a party with some lads you didn't even know. Just 'cause they was well-to-do.'

'Yes, yer know what well-to-do lads'm like,' Edie agreed. 'Just remember the story Clara just to'd we about that Bessie and her twins. He was a well-to-do chap what got 'er into trouble.'

'Listen,' Clara said, crunching into an apple. 'The tea'll be cold. Who's going to pour it?'

'I'll do it,' Henzey volunteered, and got up from the charabanc seat.

Henzey had made a sad error of judgement in allowing Andrew Dewsbury to take her to his party. It had been as much to the detriment of Jack Harper too, her regular escort, as to herself. Jack had always mooned over her like a lovesick fool, but she'd been prepared to put up with that, since he was generally pleasant company if a bit insipid. Maybe she should make the first moves towards reconciliation. His absence was feeding her guilt, and her guilt was clouding her true emotions, like disturbed sediment muddies clear water. She was starting to believe she was in love with Jack. Her mood was cheerless, disconsolate. Evidently he was upset with her, and she could hardly blame him. And she missed him more than she thought possible.

'Yo' could always goo round to the Midland Shoe shop and try and catch 'is eye,' Edie suggested. 'He wun't ignore yer there. Specially if 'e thought yo' was gunna buy a pair o' shoes off 'im.'

The others laughed at that.

'Never,' Clara said decisively. 'Never run after a man, no matter how much your heart might be aching. Promise me you won't, Henzey.'

Henzey shrugged, and handed the first cup of tea to Clara. 'I just think it's my fault. I think I was rotten to him . . . I think the first move should come from me.' She turned away again to serve the second cup to Rosie.

'I'm sure he'll get over it. In no time he'll . . .'

The door opened unexpectedly, and Arnold Jennings' face appeared. 'Henzey, there's a chap outside askin' to see yer.'

At once her heart jumped and she coloured up. 'To see me?' It was too much to hope that it might be Jack.

'Talk of the devil . . .' Clara said confidently.

'A stroke o' luck, if yer like,' Rosie affirmed. 'Save yer runnin' after 'im, eh?'

Henzey put her cup of tea down on the draining board and stood up, smoothing the creases out of her apron. She flicked her hair out of her eyes, and smiled with anticipation at the others, her heart pounding now. It was a God-sent opportunity to make it up with Jack, just as they'd been discussing it. She walked through the door and through the stockroom, her heart in her throat. When she entered the shop Phoebe Mantle, one of the other girls, nudged her.

'Here, Henzey. That's the chap out there.' She pointed outside to a man who had his back towards them. 'He came in askin' for yer. He said he'd wait outside. He's a bit of all right, I can tell yer. Who is he?'

Henzey looked up and peered through the window. 'Good God!' she exclaimed. Her feelings a mixture of apprehension and delight, she went to the door, suddenly conscious of her working clothes.

In the street the cold October air clung to her. It was a grey day and threatened rain. The red brick façades of the buildings around her looked shabby under their film of grime, the legacy of more than a century's emissions from the foundries, forges and ironworks. People were ambling along unhurriedly from store to store, gazing covetously into shop windows; some stood and gossiped; a woman tugged impatiently at the hand of a grizzling, unwilling child, and scolded him.

'Fancy seeing you,' Henzey said, smiling. 'This is a surprise. What brings you here?'

Billy Witts scratched the back of his neck casually. 'Just passing. I thought I'd call to see if you were all right after your spot of bother at the party the other week.' His voice was rich and mellow, and his easy drawl, neither broad nor particularly cultured, sounded attractive to Henzey.

She felt herself blushing. 'Oh, don't remind me.' She rolled her eyes sheepishly. 'We were both all right, thanks. It's nice of you to come and ask, though. Did it go off all right after?'

'I believe so. To tell you the truth I didn't go back after I dropped you off. I went home. Nellie was in one of her moods and she's best left alone when she's like that. I'm not really one for parties meself, specially the sort that Andrew and his mates throw. Course, he's gone back to Oxford now. And so's George.'

'God help Oxford, that's all I can say. So how's Nellie? Or should I say Helen, since I'm neither close friend nor family?'

He smiled at her jibe and shrugged. 'Oh, she's all right.'

'You don't sound too sure.'

He gave an evasive little laugh. 'Yes, she's as all right as she'll ever be. I was concerned about you and your sister, though. She looked a bit the worse for wear, your sister. You both did, to tell you the truth. Did you get into trouble with your mom and dad?'

A black and white mongrel appeared and sniffed at her apron. She bent down and stroked its neck, then it trotted contentedly across the street to the market stalls. 'We were lucky, Billy. Our mom always goes out on a Saturday night and, by the time she got back, me and Alice were in bed. As far as she was concerned, we had a great night.'

'And your dad? Was he still up?'

'We haven't got a dad, Billy.'

'Oh. Sorry for mentioning it, Henzey. Trust me to put me foot in it. Really, I'm sorry.'

'Oh, it's all right. You weren't to know.'

'Anyway, fancy those two gawbies spiking your drinks. You're best off without the likes of Andrew and George.'

She tutted diffidently. 'I know that now, but when somebody asks you out, you expect them to behave like gentlemen. You expect to be able to trust them a little bit. Or am I just being naïve?'

'I think you were unlucky. Haven't you got a regular sweetheart, Henzey?'

'Not since the party.'

'Get away with you! I can scarcely believe that. Somebody as lovely as you? Men must be falling at your feet.'

She gave a dispirited little laugh. 'Flattery will get you everywhere, Billy. I *was* going out with somebody but, because I wouldn't go to the Palais with him on the night of that party, I haven't seen him since. Shame really. I wish I'd gone with him now. I expect he thought I was mucking him about.'

'Never mind, Henzey. Just keep smiling. You've got a lovely smile, you know. It's your fortune, believe me.' His eyes lingered on her face for a second or two. 'Ah well, I'd best be off. Give me regards to your Alice, will you? You never know, I might pop and see you again some time.'

'Oh, any time, Billy. Any time you're passing. It's grand to see you again.'

Henzey could hardly believe Billy Witts had actually called

on her. She could hardly believe he remembered her at all. Her heart danced, wondering why. Could he be interested in her? If not, why had he called? As he walked away, she admired his physique. He was tall, slim and athletic-looking. Henzey liked tall men. At five feet six in her stockings, an inch or two taller in her heels, she was bound to. She especially liked tall men who were clean-shaven, devoid of moustaches, tattoos and other adornments she considered superfluous. Billy Witts qualified nicely. Always he was immaculate. He was courteous, too – to her at least – and that implied far more masculinity than brashness or well-developed muscles. Any woman would fancy him. When he smiled, his eyes creased and twinkled, and she felt she would be able to trust him with her life. He was about twenty-four, she reckoned. Funny, though, but every new man she fancied seemed to be significantly older than the one before.

Seeing Billy Witts, so unexpectedly, lifted Henzey from her melancholy over Jack Harper and clarified the murkiness. But it also stirred up the loathing she felt for Nellie Dewsbury.

That feeling was intensified when one Tuesday – it was the 16th of October – Henzey and Clara Maitland went to join the crowds for the official opening of Dudley's new Town Hall. Stanley Baldwin, the Prime Minister, was there to perform the opening ceremony. All the local dignitaries were present, and the two friends had insinuated themselves into a good place to view the proceedings, lining the steps to the new entrance. Over the heads of the crowds they could see a cavalcade of cars approaching. There was a buzz of excitement as, one by one, the cars pulled up. At last Mr Baldwin stepped out with the Mayor of Dudley and Lady Mayoress, to some cheers and, predictably, some jeers. Four cars later, a man with a ruddy complexion alighted with his wife and another, younger, trim-looking girl. Henzey saw, to her great surprise, that it was Nellie Dewsbury.

Henzey nudged Clara urgently. 'Look! There's that Nellie

Dewsbury I told you about,' she whispered. 'That must be her mother and father.'

As she swanked up the steps, Nellie caught sight of Henzey just a few feet away and gave her a look that would have withered a lesser mortal. Then she stuck her nose in the air and strutted uppishly into the Town Hall.

'I see what you mean,' Clara remarked. 'Snotty devil, isn't she?'

'I hate her. Oh, I *hate* her. Did you see her? Did you see how snooty she was?'

'She'll get her comeuppance, Henzey. That sort always do.'

Henzey smiled, her annoyance abating. 'I wish I could let her know that her Billy's been to see me. That'd nark her good and proper.'

Billy began calling regularly. At first it was no more than once a fortnight, but soon his visits became more frequent. They would chat for only a few minutes, then he would depart. He rarely spoke about Nellie, but Henzey was beginning to sense that there was something amiss with that relationship. Why else would he keep calling on her? Yet he never once asked her out, even though she was convinced he liked her. And she was dying to be asked; not least because of the opportunity it presented to wreak revenge on Nellie. Nellie's unkind words at the party still haunted and hurt her, especially as she'd previously admired the girl so much.

Henzey began to look forward to Billy's visits and, as each one approached, she would make a special effort to look good. If he was a day or two late she would fret, forever glancing through the front windows of the store, and would smile with pleasure and relief when she saw him arrive outside. Her workmates recognised her infatuation, and she suffered endless teasing.

'Nice frock you'm wearin' today, Henzey,' Edie Soap commented one morning in December as she was restocking shelves with blue bags of sugar. 'Billy due?'

'How should I know?' she answered sheepishly. She had just struggled in from the stockroom with a fresh tub of cheese and was cutting it, ready for it to be displayed. 'I never know when he's coming. He just turns up.'

'I reckon 'er's took with 'im,' Edie said to Rosie and Clara. They were making neat parcels of groceries for those customers whose orders were to be delivered.

'I'd be took with 'im, an' all,' Rosie answered. 'I wish 'e'd come an' see me.'

'Come on, Rosie,' Edie said. 'He'd have no truck wi' you and your big belly.'

Henzey smiled, and wished she could assume some claim over Billy. But she could not. He only ever came and talked to her. She could not say he was hers, and it was looking as though she never would.

Clara picked up a Christmas pudding from the shelf behind her and nestled it into the box she was packing. 'What's he do for a living, Henzey? He always looks smart. His suits aren't cheap, are they? And you only have to look at his shoes to know he spends a lot of money on his things.'

Henzey shrugged. 'He works for himself.'

'Not as a chimney sweep,' Rosie said.

'Nor as an iron puddler,' Phoebe Mantle offered.

'He's an agent,' Henzey informed them coolly. 'He sells things. To the motor-car factories. Things like electric motors for windscreen wipers . . . and things with adenoids in . . .'

'You mean solenoids?' corrected Wally Bibb with a chuckle. Wally was the manager and, while trade was quiet, he had no objection to their chatter.

Henzey laughed with the others at her mistake. 'Oh, all right. Solenoids . . . He sells things with solenoids in to the car firms, like Morris and Austin and Clyno . . . and Vauxhall.' Henzey thought the list sounded impressive.

'He must make a tidy penny,' Clara said.

'I think he's quite well-off,' Henzey replied with

satisfaction. 'He told me once he'd got a fortune put by in stocks and shares.'

'Trying to impress you, was he?' Wally suggested cynically, sharpening the blade of his carving knife.

'I don't think so, Mister Bibb. Why should he want to impress me? I'm nothing to him.'

'He's got no side on him, I'll grant you that,' Clara said. 'He's not one of those snooty toffs.'

'He's not a toff, Clara. Well, not born a toff, at any rate. He comes from one of those terraced houses in Abberley Street up by Top Church. His family are just ordinary folk. But he's done well for himself in the motor industry from what I can hear of it.'

'And the best of luck to him,' said Clara. 'How old is he? Twenty-five?'

'Twenty-four.'

'Young to have done so well. He'll end up a millionaire at that rate.'

'Or a bleedin' pauper,' Wally muttered cynically. 'Anyway, I thought you said he'd got a fancy bit. I thought you said he was knockin' off Councillor Dewsbury's daughter.'

'Oh, her,' Henzey replied with disdain. 'He's courting her for the time being, yes. But I don't think it'll be for much longer. He doesn't seem *that* taken with her.'

Wally scoffed. 'That's what he tells you, Henzey. Whatever he tells you, take it with a pinch of salt.'

Wally annoyed her sometimes. It seemed as if he was jealous of any man she was interested in. And to add fuel to these beliefs, she often caught him staring at her, which made her feel uncomfortable. Sometimes she could sense he was looking at her; at her breasts, at her hips, her legs, her waist. It was most disconcerting. But she could never be interested in Wally. He was in his mid-thirties, married, with several children; she wasn't sure how many. He had short, stubby fingers, a big droopy moustache and greasy hair that smelled of rancid lard; and the hem of his apron dusted his shoes when he walked. He was interested in photography and, once, he asked Henzey if he could take some pictures of her on the Clent Hills, but she refused. The idea of him gawping at her through the back plate of his field camera while she posed, not knowing what dirty thoughts he might be thinking, did not appeal.

'Well, I don't really expect nothing, Mister Bibb,' Henzey replied, trying not to show her indignation. 'I can never expect to have the likes of him, so I don't suppose I'll be too disappointed.'

'But you can dream, Henzey,' Clara encouraged. 'You can certainly dream.'

Billy Witts was no academic, and his repartee was rarely sparkling, but he exuded a presence that was sufficient to compensate. This was especially so in business, where he proved to himself that it was no detriment to be endowed with more brawn than brain. As a freelance sales agent for manufacturers of motor-car parts and accessories, he had nurtured many contacts in the trade and had fared remarkably well. Recently he had obtained contracts for all his agencies. Morris Motors had contracted to buy a new American type of window-winding mechanism, and Austin a new headlight that used a solenoid to dip the reflector. Vauxhall were fitting a high-frequency electric horn from a continental firm he represented, instead of the usual hand-operated bulb horns. A company from Birmingham with whom he had connections, called Worthington Commercials, which had recently gone into the business of producing three-wheeled vans, were promising to place orders. All this business netted him a tidy sum and would continue to do so for as long as the equipment was purchased. The motor trade was thriving, he told Henzey and, judging by the ever-increasing numbers of cars on the roads, she reckoned it must be true. Billy still lived with his mother and father but he had notions of changing all that soon enough.

Billy Witts was quietly taken with Henzey. She was an

enigma; different to all the others. Whenever he saw her he couldn't take his eyes off her beautiful face. It was amazing that a girl so young, and with such exquisite looks, was so modest; she was not in the least conceited. If anything she underestimated her potential, yet at the same time she possessed tremendous self-esteem. Every time he saw her he expected her to say that she had started courting and he knew that, when that day arrived, he would kick himself for not being the lucky one to have snapped her up.

Just yet, though, he could not quite fit her in. Ideally, he would need to sever relations with Nellie and, even though things with her were at a critical stage, he was loath to do it just yet. Nellie was sullen, self-centred and demanding, and Billy was finding her possessiveness increasingly stifling, for he enjoyed other women besides from time to time; but her family was rich. At first, of course, he found it flattering that the lovely daughter of a wealthy industrialist and town councillor was head over heels in love with him. Gradually, however, her shortcomings were eclipsing her virtues. Compared to Henzey she had no virtues at all.

But one thing ensured his continuing interest in Nellie, and that was sex. It had become their mutual obsession; an art form; the only enduring feature of their liaison. It was like a drug, and his other women paled in comparison. Such a circumstance was not unique in the liberal atmosphere following the Great War, when torrid affairs were deemed acceptable, especially among the wealthy. But he was actually growing to dislike Nellie, and yet he could not keep his hands off her. The relationship was thus rendered tolerable, but as unstable as nitroglycerine.

His heart, however, was with Henzey. But, because she had to be lacking in sexual experience, he hesitated to involve himself. Whenever he encountered her he was entirely confused: he would behold her girlish innocence, study her striking face, her youthful figure, her wholesome demeanour and end up telling himself that she was as close to perfection as he would ever find. So after weeks of soul-searching, convincing himself that there was no future in a future with Nellie, he finally made up his mind that somebody in his position really ought to have a girl as lovely and unspoiled as Henzey Kite on his arm, for all to admire.

Chapter Three

On Wednesday, 27th March, Henzey waited eagerly for early closing. Billy Witts had arranged to meet her at last, and promised to take her to the Station Hotel to celebrate her seventeenth birthday, which was tomorrow. She was wearing her best coat, and had taken a new skirt and blouse to work to change into. When the shop closed, she had duly changed, made up her face and gone out eagerly to meet him.

The fact that he continued to call on her – always during working hours – had been tormenting her. He was patently interested in her, and it had spawned her greater interest in him. Every time he appeared she would think that this must certainly be the day he would ask her out, but every time he left her, saying: 'See you soon, then, Henzey.' And this relentless teasing was driving her mad, fuelling her fixation. She cared deeply for him now; her infatuation and curiosity had matured into love; but that love remained frustrated, unexpressed, because he'd allowed no outlet for it. It was unthinkable that love of such intensity as hers might be ignored. So she dared to hope that this one occasion – this sole dinnertime tryst – might just be the trigger to fire him into romance.

At ten minutes past one, the appointed time, Henzey and Billy met by his rakish 1926 Vauxhall sports tourer parked in the Market Place outside Boots the Chemist. He greeted her for the first time ever with a kiss on the cheek, which made her tingle inside, and he told her how lovely she looked. As the swish motor car pulled away, envious passers-by witnessed her happy, smiling face that was hiding a deal of nervousness.

'So how's it feel to be on your last day of being sixteen, Henzey?' Billy asked as they drove past the open market.

She turned to look at his handsome face, scarcely able to believe that she had him all to herself, alone, in the privacy of his car without the staff of George Mason's winking and nudging each other as they looked on. 'Oh, it's another year closer to being twenty-one.'

They pulled up on the front apron of the mock Tudor building known as the Station Hotel, an imposing structure, overlooking the railway station in the cutting below. Evidently Billy believed she looked old enough to take into a public bar.

He took her hand and led her into a comfortable and well-furnished saloon. There were men in there, businessmen, she presumed, by the look of their fine suits and starched white collars and cuffs. Some spoke to Billy, and some merely nodded, but she noticed how they all watched her. She sat on a settle that was finely upholstered in dark green moquette and Billy went to the bar, returning with a bottle of champagne and two lead crystal flutes.

Henzey flinched as the cork popped and hit the ornately plastered ceiling, and she laughed at her own nervousness. With a practised skill he filled the two glasses slowly, allowing the bubbles to subside.

'I expect you've done that lots of times,' she suggested.

'But never before with you, Henzey. This is just our own private little celebration, and a chance to talk to you properly. I've been meaning to for ages. Bottoms up! Happy birthday for tomorrow.' He raised his glass.

She did the same, and the bubbles tickled the end of her nose. 'You're not trying to get me drunk, like your daft brother-in-law, are you, Billy?'

'Hey, hang on a bit. That's two things you've just mentioned that I ought to get straight with you. First, I ain't trying to get you drunk – that's not my style – and second, Andrew ain't me brother-in-law. Nor ever likely to be.'

Curiosity set her pulse racing.

Billy casually took a Black Cat from his silver cigarette case, tapped the end down, put it between his lips and lit it. When he exhaled his first cloud of smoke he began twirling the champagne flute on the table, momentarily gazing into it. Nellie was becoming insufferable when she had her clothes on; hard work these days. It was even worth considering forfeiting her share of the Dewsbury fortune; worth considering forfeiting the possibility of a seat on the board of the Castle Iron Foundry. Henzey was far more agreeable. Her lack of sophistication and unassuming manner were refreshing, and far more suited to his own temperament.

'Me an' Nellie have been going through a bit of a rough patch,' he said at last. 'I've decided to finish with her – give her up. We couldn't go on like we have been. It was a waste of time.'

Henzey looked into her glass, too, watching the bubbles, like tiny stars, rise to the surface. She said, 'I bet she's heartbroken.' She wanted to say more – a lot more – and a thousand questions begged to be asked.

'Heartbroken? Maybe she is, maybe she ain't. She'll get over it, whether or no.'

'How do you get on with her mom and dad, Billy?'

'All right, I suppose. Her mother gets a bit above herself sometimes, but old Walter Dewsbury's a down-to-earth Black Countryman.'

'It's funny, I imagined him to be ever so posh being a councillor. Like Nellie and Andrew.'

'Blimey, no,' he scoffed. 'Walter's a foundryman. Have you ever heard of a foundryman with airs and graces? Calls a spade a spade, does Walter, and swears like a trooper. He talks broader than me.'

'Oh, you talk nice, Billy,' she assured him. 'But how come the son and daughter are so lah-di-dah?'

'It's how they've been educated. They've been to private schools. Cost a fortune an' all, I imagine. But still, Walter's made a lot of money over the years. He could afford it.'

Henzey sipped her champagne and shuffled prettily on the settle, her back gracefully erect. Billy watched her, admiring the way she held her head. He noticed her neck, so elegant, her throat so pale, her skin so clear, the soft fullness high in her cheeks provided by a delicate bone structure; that ultimate beauty that would never fade. Her thick hair yielded a fine lustre, and its colour was a rich dark brown, with an occasional strand of red, like a random thread of burnished copper, glistening as it caught the light. Long, dark lashes enhanced her soft, blue eyes and, when she smiled, intensifying the delicious contours of her lips, he yearned to kiss her. This girl was irresistible, he told himself, and he was a fool for trying to resist. Never in his whole life had he known a girl so lovely, and yet so natural.

'I'd like to take you out Sunday, Henzey.'

Her heart missed a beat, but she smiled brightly. 'Oh, that'd be nice. Thank you, Billy. Where would we go?'

'I thought a ride out into the country. I could call for you after dinner. The nights are drawing out a bit now, and we could stop on the way back for a drink in a nice country pub.'

'Oh, Billy, I'd really like that. What about Nellie, though?'

'Well, I hadn't intended inviting her, to be truthful.'

She laughed self-consciously. 'I didn't mean that.'

She blushed a virtuous shade of crimson and lowered her eyelids as she regarded her drink. Inside, her heart was dancing and, for a few seconds, she did not know what to say, though a hundred things she could say flashed through her mind. The trouble was, nothing seemed really appropriate to how she felt.

Billy took Henzey home in the middle of the afternoon. As they said their goodbyes he handed her a small package, beautifully gift-wrapped, which he'd taken out of his pocket.

Not to be opened till tomorrow, he said. But even more than receiving this gift she was elated that she was going to see him again on Sunday. She could barely think straight. It was a dream come true. Oh, she loved him all right. And this time she knew there was no chance of getting bored like she had with Jack Harper. How could she possibly get bored with Billy knowing that her arch-rival, Nellie Dewsbury, might still be vying for Billy's affection? The fact that Nellie would do all she could to hold on to him was a challenge she would meet head on and parry, no matter what it took. Henzey vowed that as long as she drew breath she would do everything in her power to possess Billy. She had had two boyfriends before, so she had learned a thing or two about men.

Over and over in her mind she relived the two hours they'd spent together in the Station Hotel's lounge bar. She felt much closer to him now. The thought that she would have him all to herself on Sunday left her trembling with anticipation. Soon she would be able to express this frustrated love that had been smouldering within her heart for so long. She imagined romantic evenings over candlelit dinners, visits to nightclubs in Birmingham, to theatres and art galleries. She imagined picnics on hot summer days, in green meadows dotted with daisies and buttercups in the Worcestershire countryside. There would be walks in parks among beautiful flowers and shrubs, and garden parties at the smart homes of his well-to-do friends. It would be a whole new world. And she must get out her sketchbooks and pencils at the earliest opportunity and draw him, since that too was a sublime expression of love.

On Saturday evening, the Kites sat around the table after tea. Alice went upstairs to get herself ready to go 'chapping', while Maxine, Henzey's youngest sister, decided she would go to bed early to read Thomas Hardy's *The Mayor of Casterbridge*. Herbert, her brother, went up the yard to the privy, but saw no point in taking the *Sports Argus* with him as it was too dark by now to read it, with nowhere to stand the oil lamp. So Henzey and Lizzie, her mother, were left together, ready to clear the table and start the washing up.

'Are you going out with Jesse tonight, Mom?' Henzey asked.

'We might go to the Shoulder of Mutton a bit later.'

Lizzie began clearing the crockery, stacking it together as she sat. 'Our Alice told me earlier that "The Bean" might be shutting. Did you know?' 'The Bean' was the firm in Dudley that made Bean Cars, and Henzey had not been present when Alice announced its impending closure. It was all too obvious what it implied. 'They're selling no cars,' Lizzie went on. 'They reckon they're too dear. Folks can't afford them. She'll be out of a job.'

Henzey took the teapot and drained it into her own and her mother's empty cup, remembering how they had struggled for years to make ends meet; how her mother had had to find work to keep them from starvation. After Henzey had found a job at George Mason's things had improved enormously and, since Alice had been employed at Bean Cars, and Herbert had begun working in Jesse Clancey's dairy business, things had become even better.

'There's a job going at George Mason's, Mom. Rosie's leaving to have her baby. If Alice sees Wally Bibb he'll very likely set her on.'

Resigned to a long conversation, Lizzie settled back on her chair again and watched Henzey add milk to the two cups, ready for another cup of tea. She said, 'It'd be better than nothing, our Henzey. You can't pick and choose these days with so many out of work. Will you put a word in with Wally Bibb for her?'

Henzey shook her head, recalling how he was continuing to look at her so lecherously. She did not want to be beholden to Wally. She wanted to owe him no favours. 'I'd rather not. It's best if she goes herself and doesn't even mention I'm her sister. He'll take to her all right when he sees her. He enjoys a bit of glamour round him.'

'What's the best time to catch him?'

'If she goes in her dinner break she'll catch him.'

'Then let's hope she can get the job. It'd be nice for you, as well, having our Alice working beside you. Her wages have come in handy. I don't know what we'd do if you lost your job as well, our Henzey.'

'You wouldn't have to worry about things like that if you and Jesse got married, Mom. It's time you did.'

Lizzie sighed. 'Yes, perhaps it is. It's his mother, though — old Ezme. I should be back where I was before looking after your father, except I'd be nursing her instead. I didn't mind so much with your father. It was hard work, but at least I was married to him. But I'm hanged if I'll nurse old Ezme. The thought of having to look after her puts me right off. She never could stand me, and she never could stand my mother before me. There's no love lost between us, Henzey. If we all had to live under the same roof as Ezme, it would be Bedlam.'

'It wouldn't bother me very much, Mom. Maxine would be at school, and the rest of us would be out at work all day.'

'But I wouldn't be. Not if I was married to Jesse. I'd have to be at home.'

'Couldn't you just grin and bear it? She might not live that long.'

'Ezme'll live forever, just to spite me.' Lizzie sighed. 'Oh, we'll see. Who knows what the future might bring?'

'What's the matter, Mom? You seem fed up?' Henzey had thought for some time that her mother seemed depressed.

'Oh, it's nothing.' She smiled in an effort to look brighter. 'Just one of my moods . . . Now then, madam . . . who's this Billy who sent you a card for your birthday? I've noticed you mooning over him for ages.'

Henzey smiled coyly. 'I can't keep anything from you, can I?'

'I was a young girl myself once, our Henzey. I know what it's like being in love when you're young.'

'D'you remember that party Alice and me went to ages ago? I met him there.'

'Oh? And what's he like?'

'I think you'd approve. He's twenty-four . . .'

'Twenty-four?'

'Yes, twenty-four, handsome, steady . . . and very well-off . . .' Henzey smiled challengingly. 'Anything else you want to know?'

'I think twenty-four's a bit old for you.'

'Well, I don't think so, Mom. I like men older than myself. Younger chaps are too stupid. Look at Jack Harper, and he's twenty-one.'

'Jack Harper,' Lizzie repeated reflectively. 'I see what you mean.' She picked up her cup and sipped her tea, holding it in front of her with both hands, her elbows on the table.

Henzey said, 'Anyway, what about Jesse? He's nine years older than you. You haven't heard me mention that he's too old for you.'

'Yes, but that's different . . . So is this Billy working?'

'Works for himself. He's got plenty money, like I told you. *And* a nice car.'

'Well, he must have plenty money to be able to buy you pearl necklaces.'

Henzey smiled again. 'You noticed it, then?'

'I could hardly miss that glistening round your neck like I don't know what. Are you taken with him?'

'I like him a lot,' she said quietly, looking down at the table cloth. 'I've liked him a long time.'

'Then you'd best let me meet him. When are you supposed to see him?'

'Tomorrow. We're going for a ride in the country.'

'Well, just mind what you're doing, our Henzey. You're only just seventeen, remember.'

That last Sunday in March was a blustery, wet day. The month had come in like the proverbial lion and was going out like one.

Once out of Stourbridge and on the road to Kinver Henzey noticed how the winter-yellowed meadows were taking on their spring greenery, bright even under the dark, rolling clouds. Trees swayed boisterously, and the wind boomed against the canvas hood of Billy's car. The windscreen wipers struggled to maintain visibility in the squalling rain. It was not ideal weather for a trip into the countryside with a new beau, but one that she had eagerly looked forward to, rain or shine. The weather did not matter; the fact that she was with Billy did.

In Kinver, Henzey was still intrigued by the houses hollowed out of a sandstone rock face on the outskirts of the village, though she had seen them before on her Sunday school trips as a child. People still lived in them, and neat they looked too, with nets at the leaded windows and brightly painted front doors. The main street was deserted as they drove through it. Any Sunday afternoon in summer it would be teeming with folk ferried in by the Kinver Light Railway, which was really just a tram that looked like a charabanc on rails. The village was noted for its public houses but, by this time, they were shut for the afternoon, and those who had been supping in them earlier were doubtless all having their after-dinner naps by now.

Once through the village, Billy parked the car under some trees on a patch of ground off a narrow lane overlooking Kinver Edge, a natural beauty spot. Drops of water fell from the bare branches above and drummed intermittently on the motor car's hood. Henzey wiped the inside of the misted window with her gloved hand and peered out at the landscape, unspoilt, despite the ravages of the wind and the rain.

'Let's go for a walk,' she suggested.

'We'll get soaked.'

'Oh, Billy, we've got our hats and coats. Come on, let's have a look round.'

She stepped out of the car and pulled the collar of her coat up round her neck, and her pretty cloche hat more firmly on her head. The rain on her face, the tranquillity of the woods, the

41

meadows and the smell of damp grass, were like a tonic. After the constriction of rows and rows of houses, of factory chimneys, of the crowded, jostling town centre where she worked, she allowed herself to wallow in this expanse of rurality. But, above all, she found herself walking with Billy's arm around her waist. She nuzzled her head against his shoulder momentarily and looked up into his eyes as they walked back down the hill they'd just driven up. He caught her glance and smiled.

'Did you go out last night, Henzey?'

'No, I stayed in . . . I told my mom about you . . .'

'Oh?'

'She wants to meet you.'

'Honest? What have you told her?'

'Oh, that you're twenty-four, that you've got a car, that you work for yourself in the motor industry . . . that you're always smartly dressed . . .'

'And what did she say to that?'

'She says you're too old for me.' She grinned at such a ridiculous notion, and he laughed.

'Oh? And what do you think?'

'I think boys my own age are immature . . . What about you, Billy? Did you go out last night?'

'I went to the Tower Ballroom at Edgbaston.'

'Not with Nellie, though?'

'No, not with Nellie. With the usual crowd.'

But Henzey knew that Nellie was part of the usual crowd. 'Was Nellie there?'

'Oh, yes, she was there.'

Henzey felt a bitter pang of disappointment, like a stab in the heart, but she tried not to let it show. An image flooded her mind of Billy dancing with her, of Nellie clinging to him. Did he take her home afterwards? Did he kiss her good night? She was longing to know, but she tried desperately to let him think she was not particularly concerned. So when did he intend telling Nellie that he was seeing somebody else? The thought of waiting

– of waiting days, weeks, perhaps even months – for him to pick his moment, horrified her. She'd assumed he would give up Nellie straight away. That would be the honourable thing to do. That's what she would do. But she was judging Billy by her own standards. If she wasn't careful he would have her dangling on a string like some mindless puppet. He would still be seeing Nellie, and she'd be just a bit on the side. Under no circumstances could she allow that to happen; her self-esteem was far too high. She had to show him she was worthy of more. She had to let him see that she would not be so manipulated. Oh, she wanted Billy desperately, but he had to come to her in his own time, under his own steam, because he wanted to. It must also be on terms that suited her. So, she had to be the stronger attraction.

At the bottom of the hill they turned right into another quiet lane overhung with trees and ivy. It was steep, narrow and winding, with the village church at the top, its ancient bell-tower overlooking all like a sandstone fortress. Rain was spattering their faces as they walked huddled together.

'Let's not talk about Nellie,' Billy said, uncomfortable with the subject.

'I don't want to talk about her anyway.'

He detected a note of scorn, of detachment in her voice. He did not wish to alienate her. Best to justify last night's encounter and be done with it.

'Henzey, I know I told you I'd finish with her, and in my own mind I have already. It's just that . . .'

'It's just that you haven't told her yet.'

'Right. I haven't told her yet . . . I haven't had the heart to tell her. But I shall. As soon as it's right.'

She shrugged dismissively, but her mind was awhirl. 'It's up to you, Billy.'

'Last night was arranged ages ago, not just with her, but with the folks who were with us. It was an engagement party, see? Friends . . . Look, I don't feel anything for Nellie now. I'd much rather have been with you. Just bear with me, eh? . . . Can you bear with me? . . . You've got to understand, Henzey, that I feel nothing for her. It's just that I don't want her to do anything stupid.'

'Billy, I'm not making a fuss, you are,' she said, though there was a hell of a fuss going on inside her head. 'I'm not worried about Nellie, so you don't have to account to me for what you did. If you still love her, all well and good. If you don't, you don't. I'm looking no further than that. I like you, Billy – a lot – but I don't intend to compete with her, so don't expect me to. If you still want her, have her. That's all right by me.' She had learnt never to declare her true feelings this early in the game.

'One thing I like about you, Henzey, is that you've got your head screwed on good an' proper. Anybody would think you were as old as me.' He put his arm round her again and gave her a hug.

Yes, this was the way to handle Billy: pretend to be indifferent, then offer him some bait and keep repeating the process. He was not going to be easy to handle, that much she could already discern, but the challenge made him all the more interesting.

Within a few minutes they were at the village church. They walked down a path that led to the lychgate and the church-yard. Billy suggested they have a look at the inscriptions on the gravestones. They held a fascination for him, he said. As they ambled through, noting the names and the dates, making little comments about them, Henzey conjured up images of those people all those years ago whose names and dates of death she read; images of their homes, their families, habits, fears, loves, heartbreaks. They had lived and breathed, had been flesh and blood, and now they were all but forgotten. How had they lived? What mark had they made on their community? How had their lives affected those who came later? Had they been happy?

This last question was the most important. For to live and be unhappy made living pointless. For a few moments she pondered whether happiness was God-given, or whether you have to strive for it. Indeed, she felt she knew the answer. Already she had seen enough of life to know that people often make their own happiness and their own unhappiness. It's up to each of us to make ourselves and each other happy, she told herself. Nobody can do it for us. And if we turn out to be unhappy, usually we have nobody to blame but ourselves.

These thoughts she did not communicate to Billy. They were deep, and she did not know him well enough to speak of such things. He would probably be inclined to think she was mad. Besides, he was one of those elements likely to influence her future happiness. It all depended on her. It all depended on whether she, when the time came, made the right decisions to ensure her own future happiness.

From inside the church they could hear children's voices singing.

'Sunday school,' Henzey said with a smile. 'Don't they sound angelic?'

They moved on, looking at the gravestones. Henzey's feet were getting colder and wetter all the time. She shivered, and Billy laughed.

'What's so funny?'

'I bet when you agreed to come out with me for a Sunday afternoon spin you didn't reckon on spending it in a soaking-wet churchyard.'

She chuckled. 'Oh, anything for a lark.' She looked around her, at the rain, still falling, splashing off the graves. She listened to it trickling down the drainpipe of the church and exiting over a drain. 'I'd like to come here again some time, Billy. You remember I said I like drawing and painting? Well, I'd love to do some watercolours of this place. Would you bring me back one day when the weather picks up? You know, if . . .' If they continued to see each other was what she wanted to say, but the words would not come out.

'Course I would. That'd be interesting for me as well. I've never known anybody before who paints seriously.'

Suddenly the wind whipped up and the rain became torrential. Billy suggested they shelter inside the church till it eased off. As they entered quietly, one or two of the children turned round to look at them. Their Sunday school was just drawing to a close and the teacher was telling them to say their prayers every night when they went to bed, and that she would see them all again next Sunday afternoon. Henzey and Billy sat in a back pew while they filed down the aisle on their way out. Those children, whose parents could afford to buy them raincoats, donned them. Henzey smiled at each of them and waved her fingers in goodbye as they departed.

It was a gesture that touched Billy. There was a warmth in this Henzey Kite he'd never witnessed in anybody else. She seemed the essence of kindness and pleasantness. In the same situation, Nellie would have glowered at the children. She would have been impatient for them to be out of her sight. This girl beside him was so very different. As the Sunday school teacher closed the door behind her, Billy put his arm around Henzey's shoulder and drew her to him. When she looked up at him, her eyes bright, her face wet from the rain, he kissed her full on the lips, tenderly, gently.

While she enjoyed it she contemplated the strangeness of this first romantic kiss taking place in a church, and she panicked at the realisation, breaking away.

'What's wrong?'

'We shouldn't, Billy. We shouldn't be kissing in church.' She feared the heavenly host might see and hear, and wreak immediate vengeance. 'It isn't right.'

'It ain't wrong either.'

He kissed her again, defiantly, more ardently this time. Every time, as she tried to pull away, laughing and uttering feeble excuses, his mouth followed hers till she resigned herself to his kisses and enjoyed them the more. She shut her mind to the sanctity of the church and, when he eased her down so that she was lying on the pew, she was surprised, both at his forwardness and her own passiveness, for she offered no resistance. His caresses were mesmerising. She was unable to resist. Indeed she did not want to resist. He unbuttoned her wet coat as he kneeled between the pews on a hassock, his lips still on hers. She felt his hand slip inside her coat and to her waist, to her hip. Her arms were around his neck, then she held his face as she heard herself sigh with pleasure at his touch. He kissed her wet eyelids, her flushed cheeks, her forehead, and then again touched her lips with his own, as gently as a butterfly settling on a flower. Then, to her horror, he thrust his tongue into her mouth, and she tasted him with some shock . . . But it was not so bad . . . It was quite nice really . . . In fact it made her feel all weak inside, and so much closer to him. Never before had she been kissed like this. Jack Harper never kissed her like this.

But they were in a church. The door was unlocked, open to anybody. The world could have walked in. The vicar might come in. God, what if the vicar walked in and saw her wantonly draped over his pew? There must be some law against this. At the thought of divine retribution she struggled and managed to sit up.

Billy ran his hand through his hair, for want of something to do with it, and smiled. 'Blimey, you don't 'alf kiss nice, Henzey. I got really carried away there.'

Feelings of guilt swept over her; not guilt for kissing Billy; not guilt for merely enjoying it. The guilt was for enjoying it inside a church; for the possibility of being caught. And yet, for the very same reason, it generated an undeniable exhilaration. And it was a good omen, surely, to be kissed like this in church?

'Let's go outside, Billy. It doesn't feel right kissing you in here.'

'It feels all right to me.'

He stood, pulled his coat to, and offered his hand. As Henzey stood up and faced him, their bodies touched and he kissed her again, lingering over the sensuality of her lips, so soft, so accommodating. She wanted him to keep kissing her all day, to feel his body against her; sensations she'd never experienced before. They shuffled out of the pew, and still their lips were touching. They moved towards the main door of the church, parting for a second to look where they were going. They stopped to open the heavy door, then walked out into the rain, looking hungrily into each other's eyes. Henzey leaned against one of the sandstone buttresses. Her arms went round his neck again as the rain teemed down, running in rivulets down her face, upturned to receive more delicious kisses.

She allowed his hands to wander inside her coat again, fleetingly over her bottom, her thighs. Willingly she would have lain in the soaking grass with him, but when he felt her breasts, even though her heart pounded, she deftly moved his probing hand away in case he might think her cheap. His right thigh docked between hers in another sortie, and she sighed vocally, inducing him to kiss her even more passionately. The rain drenching their faces did not matter, nor did their cold feet in the wet grass. The wind blowing and gusting so rudely was hardly intrusive. But, to Billy's surprise and disappointment, Henzey broke off their embrace and moved away from the buttress.

'My God! To think Nellie's had your kisses all to herself.' She took his hand and invited him to follow her. 'Shall we go, Billy? Else we'll never dry out before I get you home to meet my mom.'

Chapter Four

That Sunday night Henzey walked down the entry with Billy Witts to bid him good night. It was half past ten. He had stayed for Sunday tea, for supper and had enjoyed the company and the hospitality of the Kites.

'Nice of your mom to invite me to your house next Saturday night,' he said.

'If you're sure you want to come.' She was happy that her mother had proposed a belated birthday party for her. 'But I won't expect you if you're going to see Nellie.'

She was standing facing him, her arms folded. In the dimness of the entry he saw the catchlights in her eyes. Never before had he seen eyes so beautiful, with such a look of gentleness and honesty, as at that moment in the half-light. He took both her hands and held them down by their sides. Their bodies touched and, as he leaned his head forward to kiss her, to taste again her lips, her heart beat faster. Whilst he had been sitting in the house, talking, laughing with the family, confident and at ease, he was still contemplating their afternoon out. He liked this girl; she was so refreshingly honest, and he realised that Henzey would never commit herself until she was certain that Nellie played no further part in his life. He also perceived that when – if – she did commit herself it would be whole-heartedly. That commitment would be his for the taking.

It presented him with a great dilemma. He had in mind his intense sexual encounters with Nellie, and how much they meant to him.

'I should be finished with Nellie by then,' he whispered, unsure of the truth of his own statement; but he kissed her convincingly enough. 'I'll see you Tuesday night, eh?'

She shook her head, slowly, deliberately meeting his eyes directly. But if he'd been able to read her expression accurately in the darkness he would have read her look of uncertainty. She wanted him for herself so much, that to enforce such a refusal was breaking her heart. Heeding Clara's advice was decidedly painful.

'Why?' he asked. 'Are you doing something else?'

She shook her head again. 'I'm not going to see you till Saturday night,' she whispered coolly. 'Not till you've finished with Nellie. That'll give you plenty of time to sort things out, if that's what you decide to do. Then you can tell me what happened, and how she took it. If you don't . . . well . . . you won't turn up here, will you? And I shall understand, Billy. At lest we'll know exactly where we stand.'

She was aching to hug him tight, to give him her love, but how much better to lose him now than to hurl herself headlong into an affair that might end in heartbreak because she was too soft in the beginning. Billy had to know she was not going to be a pushover. She had her standards, and she intended to implement them. A week gave him plenty of time. If he failed to do it there would be little point in carrying on, for this new affair would deteriorate into a charade. She was certain she had given him enough of a glimpse of how things could be. She could do no more. The rest was up to him.

On Tuesday dinnertime Alice found time to present herself in front of Wally Bibb at George Mason's. He offered her a job at a shilling a week less than she was getting at Bean Cars, but she accepted it gladly, since it was almost certain that she would not have a job in the office there much longer. Shop work was not exactly what Alice wanted. Her heart was set on the glamour of being a private secretary to some suave company director, but it would do till such an opening came along. When Henzey asked Alice later what she thought of Wally, she said that she'd probably have to watch out, because he kept looking at her bust.

'Oh, I daresay he was trying to see where it had got to,' Henzey quipped, and dodged as Alice went to swipe her playfully.

Henzey had kept out of the way while Alice was interviewed. Afterwards Wally asked her if she was any relation, since he reckoned Kite was not that common a name. She admitted Alice was her sister, and Wally made some sarcastic comment about there being safety in numbers, which seemed to amuse him.

But her mind was not on Alice, nor Wally, nor George Mason's. As the week wore on, Henzey was becoming disconsolate, certain that Billy was out enjoying himself with Nellie Dewsbury. Each night as she lay in bed thinking, she would imagine them together. She pictured them laughing, holding hands, kissing. As sleep escaped her, and the night induced more disturbing images, she saw them making love with all the passion and commitment of a latter-day Romeo and Juliet. The more she thought about these things the more she convinced herself that it was so, and the less chance she believed she had. She yearned to be with him again, to hear him laugh, to feel his lips on hers, to hold his hand, to feel his manly arms around her. If only she had agreed to see him on Tuesday night she might not be tossing and turning now, unable to sleep. If only he would call at the shop tomorrow. He would only have to smile at her and she would know. She would know immediately that all was well. But she did not know, and it was torture. This uncertainty was creasing her and she still had this night to get through, and then two more to follow.

She was certain she had driven Billy away with her feigned

indifference. How could she have been so cock-sure of herself? How could she have been so arrogant? She could no more dictate to Billy Witts what he should do than he could dictate to her. Now she was angry with herself for ruining the best opportunity ever to find happiness, with a man who really suited her, a man she admired in every way. She liked him so much. No. It was more than that; it was much more than that. She loved him. Even more than *that*; she loved him desperately.

As they left the shop on Saturday evening after work, Clara Maitland and Henzey stepped out into the bustle of market traders packing away their wares, and across the street to Clara's tram stop. The days were getting longer, and it was still light, but the overhead wires, from which the trams drew their power, were swinging in the wind that was yet vigorous.

'I haven't seen that Billy all week, Henzey,' Clara said, avoiding a handcart. 'Hasn't he been to see you? It's unusual. Have you upset him?'

'If I have I never intended to,' Henzey answered, her eyes misting.

'Oh?'

'I haven't told you, but I went out with him last Sunday afternoon. He stopped for tea and for supper and my mother invited him to our house tonight for my birthday . . . But I don't expect he'll come.'

They paused while a man loading sacks of potatoes onto a lorry blocked their way. He apologised for holding them up, and they walked on.

Clara said, 'I suspect he hasn't been to see you just to make you think about him all the more. Absence making the heart grow fonder, and all that. I wouldn't think much of him if he accepted your mother's invitation, then didn't have the grace to show up.'

'Oh, I don't think it's just that, Clara . . .'

'What then? There's something else?'

'Well, I thought he'd given that Nellie Dewsbury up. At least that's what he led me to think.'

'And he hadn't?'

'No. So I told him I wouldn't see him again until he had. I told him only to come tonight if he'd finished with her.'

'Well, good for you, Henzey. He sounds a bit of a cad after all.'

'I suppose I've put him off. I suppose he thought I was a bossy little madam. Did I do the right thing, d'you think, Clara?'

'Exactly right. You've let him know you weren't going to be manipulated, or swept off your feet.'

'Oh, but I'm swept off my feet, all right, Clara. I'm swept off my feet good and proper.'

'And that's what makes it hard for you, eh? Did your mother like him?'

'She must've. She invited him tonight . . .'

'Well, if he doesn't come you'll have lost nothing, Henzey,' Clara said resignedly. 'You'll have escaped a lot of heartbreak. That's the best way to look at it.'

But that was not the way Henzey wished to look at it. She had her heart set on Billy Witts. Come the evening, Henzey contemplated him as she undressed herself, ready to put on her new frock, just in case he did turn up after all. If he did come, it would be to claim her, and she knew he would be far more demanding than Jack Harper had been. Jack was never any trouble to keep at bay. Only occasionally would she allow him to kiss her. But she was much more of a woman now. Her natural awareness of things sensual and erotic was infinitely more acute, and her emotions were intensifying, accelerated by her enduring hopes and dreams of being Billy's girl. As she recalled how he had taken her in his arms and kissed her, her heart beat faster and her body seemed to glow.

It occurred to her that she might not want to keep Billy at bay at all. Her new adult emotions were less ambiguous, more profound. She was contemplating more and more what it would be like to go all the way with a man. Of course such things were for marriage and not before, and she understood that, but still she couldn't help wondering. She closed the door to the bedroom and sat naked on her bed. With her eyes closed she gently squeezed her breasts, imagining Billy to be doing it, and an unfamiliar warmth of desire lit her up. She stood up, and for the first time seriously scrutinised her own slender body in the tall mirror standing in the corner. Her breasts were firm and supple, and she saw how her nipples had awoken in response to her own sensuality, each standing proud like a small, pink raspberry on a smooth, cream blancmange. She stroked the skin of her stomach. It was silky smooth. Her face was fine-featured and strikingly beautiful, though she considered her nose too long and her eyebrows too thick. She twisted sideways and turned her head to inspect her body in profile. Her waist was tight, her neck elegant, her stomach gently rounded. Her legs were long, well shaped and unblemished, and her buttocks protruded neatly. Without even trying she possessed the sort of figure every modern, young woman was striving for.

By this time Henzey was earning eleven shillings a week and could afford to buy a nice dress and decent shoes occasionally. That day she had been shopping and bought a pair of silk French knickers, and a blue, waistless dress the same colour as her eyes, in crepe de Chine, loosely fitted at the hips. It was barely knee length, and her flesh-coloured silk stockings enhanced the shape of her legs. Her lustrous, dark hair framed her face, and she rounded off the whole effect with a long string of glass beads and a dab of her mother's Chanel No. 5 behind each ear. When she emerged into the scullery even Herbert commented on how lovely she looked.

On tenterhooks, she helped her mother with final preparations while Alice and Maxine changed into their Sunday best. The closer the hands on the clock moved towards half past seven, the more she trembled inside, praying silently that he would arrive, but resigned to the certainty that he would not. When her mother spoke she failed to hear, her thoughts only with Billy. Lizzie smiled to herself at her daughter's preoccupation, and understood; she had been there herself.

But prompt at half past seven she heard a motor car pull up outside the house. Her heart pounded with anticipation as she ran into the front room where the table was laid out for a meal. She peered through the lace curtains. It was him. It was Billy. She breathed a sigh of profound relief and smiled, keeping her fingers crossed that everything had gone the way she wanted.

'Here, I've bought you some flowers,' he said, producing a bouquet of roses from behind his back when she opened the door to him. He smiled at her expression and placed a kiss on her cheek, which made her blush since her mother witnessed it. But everything was all right. He had come to claim her after all.

'Oh, Billy. Red roses. Oh, they're beautiful. You shouldn't have, but thank you ever so much. Aren't they beautiful, Mom?'

'You'd better put them in some water right away.'

The evening went well, and Henzey was pleased to see that her mother seemed less tense than she had been for some time, more able to enjoy herself. Jesse, too, was bubbling with even more humour than normal. It was good to see them so happy.

Afterwards, in Billy's arms, as they stood in the entry as he was about to leave, Henzey said, 'It would mean a lot to me to see my mother and Jesse get married. I've dreamed about it for ages now.'

'They seem well suited.'

'Oh, they are.'

'That Jesse seems a genuine sort of chap. Is he anything like your dad was?'

'In some ways. Except my dad used to get upset with people. He was so intense sometimes – very serious. Other times he was just the opposite – soft as a bottle of pop. Jesse never gets frustrated or upset like my dad used to. He's proper half-soaked. Good as gold he is with us, specially considering he isn't our dad. He thinks the world of our Herbert.'

'It seems to me he thinks the world of all of you, Henzey. I think your mom's lucky to find somebody like him.'

'I think he's lucky to get my mom.'

He gave her a hug. 'That as well. She's a lovely-looking woman for her age, your mom. I can see who you get your good looks from.'

Henzey shrugged. 'Everybody says I'm like my father. I loved him, Billy. He was a lovely man. I did some drawings of him when he was alive. I can show you them one of the days.' She forced back a tear. This was not the time to weep after so pleasant an evening. 'So what about Nellie?' She had been dying to ask. 'You finally broke it off with her?'

'Last Monday night. I went round to their house, and we went for a drink at the Saracen's Head. We talked things over and decided to part friends. She took it better than I thought she would. I think she was half expecting it.'

'Any regrets?'

'No regrets, Henzey. No regrets at all. I'm happy if you are.'

'Oh, Billy, I'm happy,' she breathed, and snuggled into his open coat like a kitten seeking warmth. 'You'll never know how happy.'

He gave her a hug. 'I've been dying to see you all week. D'you know, most o' the time I couldn't even remember what you looked like. Daft ain't it?'

'So why didn't you come and see me? I'd have been glad to see you. I was dying to see you.'

'I dunno, really. It was a sort of punishment for me. A test, in a way, denying myself the pleasure of seeing you. I knew it'd be all the sweeter when I did. The waiting made me all the more anxious. I haven't felt like that for years. It was a sort of perverse enjoyment.'

She wallowed luxuriously in his embrace. 'Mmm. I know what you mean. It's been the same for me, Billy.'

'Anyway, I'm certain of one thing, after it all.'

'What's that?'

'That I'm in love with you.'

She trembled inside at his unexpected confession of love, while he bent his head and kissed her on the lips, a long, lingering kiss.

At length, he said, 'Shall I see you tomorrow? We could go for a ride out into the country like last Sunday. The weather's due to pick up. What do you reckon?'

'If you promise not to take me round any more churchyards.'

Henzey had never been so happy. At last she had the love of Billy Witts. Boys like Harold Deakin, Jack Harper and Andrew Dewsbury paled into insignificance. But she had known them to good advantage; even Andrew Dewsbury. They had given her the experience she needed to know how to handle men. Everything had been in preparation for this love of her life at the ripe old age of seventeen, and she knew it. Now she could not imagine life without Billy. He was her life all of a sudden.

But there was something else afoot.

'Me and your mother are gettin' married on the 28th of April,' Jesse announced one evening, with Lizzie at his side.

Henzey, utterly surprised, embraced her mother and then Jesse. 'All my wishes are coming true,' she said, weeping tears of joy at the news. She had Billy Witts and soon her mother would be Mrs Lizzie Clancey. 'Oh, wait till I tell Billy. He'll be that pleased. How's Ezme taken the news?'

Lizzie smiled. 'Let's just say she's come round to accepting it. She didn't at first, but she does now.'

The next time the rent man called Lizzie gave notice that they wanted to vacate their house by the 4th May, which would give them ample time to shift everything to the dairy house, their new home. Henzey suggested to her brother and sisters that for the first few days after the wedding they should continue to sleep in the old house, thus giving their mother and Jesse a brief honeymoon alone.

And so the ceremony took place at St John's church, Kates Hill, at twelve o'clock, after matins. It was conducted by the Reverend John Mainwaring who knew the bride and groom well. Lizzie looked significantly younger than her thirty-nine years and quite radiant in her short cream satin dress with its fashionable uneven hemline. Maxine was the only bridesmaid and Dr Donald Clark, Jesse's lifelong friend, was best man. Henzey wore a new short straight dress in cinnabar red with the row of pearls Billy had given her, and Alice, a beige flouncy dress and a borrowed fox fur. They all looked exquisite, enhancing the reputation they were rapidly acquiring of being the best-looking girls in the parish. And that reputation also included Lizzie in the eyes of a great many.

Later that evening when the hangers-on had left and Alice, Maxine and Herbert had drifted back to number 48, Billy Witts announced he ought to leave, too. It was after midnight and he'd got to be up early next morning. Henzey duly fetched her best hat and coat from the hall and gave Jesse and her mother a good-night kiss.

'It's been a happy day for me seeing you two married,' she confessed. 'I know you'll be happy.'

Lizzie wrapped her arms around her. 'Thanks, my flower. You don't know how much that means to both of us.'

'Good night, Mom. Good night, Jesse.' Henzey took Billy's hand. Billy raised his free arm in a gesture of good night and they left the newly-weds to their first night together.

As Henzey and Billy walked across the street, Lizzie watched them from the front room window of the dairy house. She watched as they stood by his car holding each other in a clinch for about five minutes, pecking at each other's lips occasionally, looking into each other's eyes and laughing.

'Are you coming to bed, Lizzie, or are you gunna stand ganning on them pair all night?' Jesse called from the bedroom, after settling his mother for the night.

Lizzie dragged herself away from the chink in the curtains and climbed the stairs. 'I just wanted to make sure Billy hadn't gone in the house with her at this time of night.' She kicked off her new shoes with relief and slumped onto their new, supple bed. 'If they do, I'll know they're up to no good. I just don't trust that Billy, Jesse.'

For Henzey it had been the happiest day of her life. For once she lay alone in bed – in Lizzie's big bed – wide awake, thinking over what had happened that day. Life really was going her way now and she had every reason to be happy. Not only was her mother married to a man they all loved and respected, but she herself was deeply in love with a well-set-up young man. Who knew where it might lead eventually? Best not to dwell on it, but she fostered a few hopes and wishes already. Love was new, exhilarating and, every time she even thought about Billy, her pulse raced and butterflies stirred in the pit of her stomach. She would not see him tomorrow – she didn't on a Monday – but he had promised to take her to meet his family soon and, on Saturday night, they were due to go to the Tower Ballroom by the reservoir at Edgbaston. She did not know yet what they would be doing on the other nights of the week, except on Wednesday, which was May Day. Doubtless they would join the throngs in the castle grounds that day and go for a drive into the country in the evening. She didn't mind what, just so long as she was with him.

Henzey rolled onto her left side in the bed and shuffled herself comfortable. Yes, she really had got the better of Nellie Dewsbury. Whatever heartbreak Nellie was going through, somehow it served her right. Whatever that horrible girl was feeling she was only reaping what she had sown.

With these thoughts running through her head she was as far from sleep as it was possible to be. She sighed and closed her eyes again, and her thoughts meandered to her family. They, too, were settled. Herbert was doing well in Jesse's dairy business, and Jesse had suggested they become partners when he was twenty-one. Already they were considering taking on other men and expanding the business. In an atmosphere of increasing economic gloom, it was fortunate that they were doing so well. Alice was coming fifteen and seemed to have settled in at George Mason's. Henzey had taken her under her wing to some extent, showing her what to do and putting her right if she erred. She had also warned her about Wally Bibb whom she did not trust. Maxine was excelling at school, though that was to be expected, for they were always being told that she was the brightest girl in the class and she should go to university since more of them were accepting girls. But Maxine was set on music and her ambitions lay no further than her cello.

At last Henzey felt sleepy. She turned over to her other side and smiled contentedly again as she curled up in the big, wide bed, all warm and snug. Soon she was dreaming of Billy Witts.

Henzey happily fell into the routine of seeing Billy Witts about three times a week. She had met most of his family, who were very nice to her. At weekends they went dancing at the Tower Ballroom in Edgbaston; one night in the week they usually went to the cinema and twice already he had taken her to posh restaurants. On Saturday mornings, while she was at work, Billy liked to play golf and, on summer Sunday afternoons, he usually played cricket for St Thomas's church team. She had accompanied him to a couple of matches. The many of his friends she had met seemed to like her as far as she could tell, and a girl-friend of one of them, Marjorie Lycett, told her how glad she was that Billy had finally ditched that snotty Nellie Dewsbury.

When Billy brought Henzey back home to the dairy house at

night he would swing his Vauxhall through the wide entry and into the yard and stop the engine while they said good night. And sometimes it would take them a whole hour. Henzey knew that it would have been so easy to get carried away with Billy, for he always left her longing for him, breathless and tingling all over; but happy, for he wooed her with fine words.

She wanted him. He lit her up like a firecracker whenever he touched her, but she dare not make the running and he certainly seemed in no hurry, however passionately they kissed. But she never allowed herself to become preoccupied with such thoughts. Rather, she enjoyed being in love, with all the attention and sweetness it brought, and was content to let such physical matters take their course. Besides, she did not want to get into trouble, like Rosie Frost. She wanted no guilty conscience that she had gone against her mother's wishes. Sex should be confined to the marriage bed; and she was happy to wait.

Then one Wednesday in the middle of May, when Henzey had come home from work, she went upstairs to change. Her mother was half-undressed in her bedroom, posing in the cheval mirror at the side of her dressing table. The door was open and as Henzey walked by she caught sight of Lizzie in profile. She stopped to talk, leaning against the door jamb, and saw how much weight Lizzie had gained.

'I was just trying on this new frock,' Lizzie said, pointing towards a heap of floral patterned voile. 'Jesse and me have been invited to a Masonic do on the first of June. He reckons they might invite him to join. He's that proud. It's his life's ambition now to be a Mason.'

'Coming up in the world, eh? Come on, then. Let's see your new frock. I bet you've had to have a bigger size again. You're really putting weight on, Mom. It must be contentment.'

Lizzie took the dress and slipped it over her head, adjusting it as it fell around her body.

'Mother, it looks like a maternity frock,' Henzey commented innocently. 'You're not that fat.'

'No, not yet I'm not,' she sighed. 'But I soon shall be.'

'Not if you watch what you eat.'

Then it dawned on her.

'God! You're not pregnant, are you, Mom?' Henzey sat down on the bed and looked at her mother.

Lizzie turned away self-consciously. 'Yes, I am, our Henzey.'

'But you shouldn't show yet.'

'Henzey, I'm four months.' Lizzie walked over to the window and stared out across the field behind the house and the vast industrial landscape that was spread out before her.

'But you've only been married a fortnight . . . You mean you got married because you *had* to?'

Lizzie did not reply.

'And all the time you're preaching to me to mind what I'm doing? That I'm only seventeen. My God! You're no different to any common little slut that gets into trouble having it up against the mangle in the brewhouse.'

Never before had Henzey spoken to her mother like that, and she half expected a slap across the face for her trouble. Yet no slap came. For long seconds Henzey was silent while she tried to collect her thoughts. Abruptly, she stood up and turned away from Lizzie, biting her bottom lip in anger and distaste. Then, just as abruptly, she sat down again. Her mother – her own mother – had been having sex with Jesse before she was married . . . And at her age . . . It was disgusting. It was absolutely disgusting. It came as such a shock that Henzey felt she'd been punched in the stomach.

Lizzie remained at the window, looking out.

Henzey shook her head slowly in disbelief, then spoke again, quietly, composed. 'What am I supposed to say, Mom, when folks start making jokes about my mother and the milkman?'

Lizzie remained silent.

'And how d'you think our Herbert's going to feel when his mates start laughing behind his back, making sarcastic com- ments?' Henzey continued. 'Dear God, what sort of an example d'you think you've set our Alice and Maxine? Come to that, what sort of an example d'you think you've set me, after all your preaching and finger wagging? Good God, Mother! I can hardly believe it.'

Lizzie continued to look outside with glazed eyes. Everything Henzey said was true. Every example she cited, as to the consequences for the family, she had herself considered. It was as if their roles had been reversed, as if Lizzie was the errant, wayward daughter and Henzey the fraught and angry mother. Lizzie felt ashamed. She was thoroughly ashamed. She had no wish to alienate her daughter over this, nor any of her family. What she needed above all was their understanding and their support, but particularly from Henzey.

Henzey saw her mother's shoulders shaking and, at first, she thought she was laughing in defiance. Till she turned round and she saw the tears streaming down her agonised face. Lizzie took a handkerchief from a drawer in her dressing table and wiped her eyes. Then she sat on the bed by Henzey's side and turned to face her, taking her daughter's hands.

'Don't be judge and jury, our Henzey,' she wept. 'But for the grace of God it could be you pregnant.'

'Then, Mother, for the grace of God I'd have to call the child Jesus,' Henzey replied indignantly, 'because it'd be another virgin birth.'

'Oh, our Henzey, I knew it'd be like this when you found out. I wanted to tell you from the outset, but like a fool I decided against it.' She wiped away another flush of tears. 'I hoped you'd understand. It's not as if Jesse and me are kids. We love one another and we wanted one another. We haven't stalked out like a tomcat and a tabby to do it behind the miskins and then run off. It's meant something to us – try and understand that. Don't forget, either, that we aren't too old for that sort of thing, even if you might think we are. We would've got married whether or no. My being pregnant has only made it happen sooner.'

'Maybe I shouldn't have expected you to be a saint,' Henzey

said quietly, 'but I never dreamed you'd get pregnant. My own mother. It's so damned *stupid* . . . And at your age.'

'Well, I confess I hadn't counted on it, our Henzey. And I'll confess to you that at first I didn't want the child. But I'm stuck with it, nevertheless.'

'Does Jesse want it?'

'Oh, he's happy about it. He's like a dog with two tails. Can't you tell? He reckons we won't get a look in when it's born. He reckons you girls'll bring it up.' She looked up at her daughter beseechingly, tears again filling her eyes, which now were showing signs of puffiness. 'Henzey, I don't need your condemnation, I need your support. It'll be hard enough as it is without me feeling you despise me. Try to imagine yourself in this position. You'd want my support if it was you that was pregnant.'

'If it was me that was pregnant, Mother, I'd consider it my just desserts.'

But it was not in Henzey's nature to be hard, least of all with the woman who had carried her, fed her, sacrificed everything for her and brought her up against all odds. Especially when she was crying. Always she'd hated to see her mother cry. It reminded her of when she was a child, how she would be filled with anxiety at the sight of Lizzie weeping over her poor, invalid father. It was the same now. Already she was regretting the harsh words. She began weeping herself and opened her arms to Lizzie. They held each other tight, letting the tears flow unabated. Lizzie needed Henzey's encouragement, she needed her love and not least her friendship. Henzey could no more refuse these things than she could walk out of her life.

There was instantly a new bond; a new kind of love; a mutual respect that had not manifested itself before. They both felt it. Henzey sensed her own maturity and, for the first time, realised her mother's fallibility. Lizzie was merely flesh and blood, prone to all its weaknesses and likely to be submitted to its derision unless they outfaced this thing together. And Lizzie realised that her daughter was no longer a child; she was a woman and could be addressed thus. Why had she overlooked it all this time?

Henzey spoke again, softly, tenderly. 'What about the others, Mom? What shall we tell them? And when?'

Lizzie blew her nose. 'I'm only really worried about our Herbert now. He's the one who'll feel it most, like you say. He's sixteen in a week or two, and he'll be ever so sensitive to it. I hope he won't be awkward, because Jesse will never stand that off him. I'm not worried about the other two. They'll think it's lovely to have a baby round the house.'

'Then why not ask Jesse to have a word with Herbert. He'll take it from Jesse more easily. He's got a way of explaining things.'

Lizzie agreed. 'Come to think of it, he can tell our Alice and Maxine, as well.'

'I'll tell them if you like. Oh, I'm sorry I was so horrible to you, Mom, but it was such a shock. You can't imagine. I never dreamed . . . I promise I'll help all I can. What other folks think doesn't matter, does it? As long as we're all happy. I mean to say, you're married now anyway and everybody knows you were about to get married. It'll be nice having a baby round the house. Oh, I shall be able to take it for walks and buy it little coats and little shoes. Me and Billy will take it for rides into the country, so's it can have some fresh air. You're right, Mom, you won't get a look in.'

'I suppose you'll spoil it rotten,' Lizzie said, smiling now through her tears.

'Oh, I expect so. When's it due?'

'Donald Clark's given me the first of October.'

Chapter Five

Polling day was always more like a carnival than the serious election of a new government, and the one in 1929 was no different. Children were not at school, and they followed the candidates around, creating a din, banging draw tins and dustbin lids with sticks, and each getting a penny for doing it. This was designed to get the people out to vote. Coloured rosettes were in abundance, pinned on coats everywhere; red, white and blue for the Conservatives, yellow for Labour. Folk had put posters in their windows hailing one or other of the candidates, and even shop windows and pubs advertised their favourites. Carts and their horses were decorated in the colours of their owners' political persuasions, as were any available lorries and vans. They toured the streets, some urging people to vote for Cyril Lloyd, the Tory candidate, others for Oliver Baldwin, the renegade Labour son of the Conservative Prime Minister who, the previous evening, had held a political meeting in the Board School at Kates Hill.

Spirits were high, people were loud in acclaim of their preferred contender and even louder in their revilement of the opponent. Newspapers were full of electioneering, praising one party, denigrating another, and had been for weeks. Today, the people would decide it all, one way or the other. The trouble was, it would not be known who would form the government till some time tomorrow. Meanwhile, the public houses fared remarkably well out of it.

Billy collected Henzey at about half past eight that evening after taking his mother and father to vote. The weather was picking up encouragingly and, because of the lighter evenings, they decided to go for a ride out to Baggeridge Wood where it would be peaceful and quiet, away from the palaver of electioneering. Henzey was looking forward to having Billy all to herself for a while. He was feeling guilty, however; he wanted to take her home early and informed her of it as they sat in the car under a tree watching the sun go down over Wolverhampton.

'Oh, Billy, why?' she said, with bitter disappointment. 'I thought we might go to the Town Hall after to hear whether Cyril Lloyd or Oliver Baldwin won the Dudley seat.'

'I can't, my sweetheart, sorry. I'll have to pick my father up from the Gypsy's Tent just after ten. He'll be legless. He's the same every polling day.'

'But I can wait in the car while you fetch him. Then we can take him home together.'

Billy sighed inwardly, wishing to show neither his frustration nor his guilt. 'No, I'd best drop you at home first. God knows what sort of state he'll be in. I don't want you to see him like that. His language will be foul, especially if he's had a rough time with his Labour mates – he's ever likely to spew up in the car. I'm sorry, my angel, but it's for the best. Besides, I suppose I'll have to stop and have a drink myself. I won't be able to get away that quick.'

'Well, it's hardly been worth seeing you. If you'd said so before I wouldn't have bothered. I could've gone to the Town Hall with Florrie Shuker, or our Alice. Or even with Jesse.'

'And how long have you been so interested in politics?' There was sarcasm in his voice.

'I'm not particularly interested in the politics,' she said, 'but it's a nice atmosphere, with all those people late at night waiting to hear who got in. I just thought it'd be nice to be a part of it –

with you, Billy. Still, it doesn't matter.' She sighed disconsolately. 'Your family comes first.'

Henzey was acutely hurt. The men at work had been talking about going to the Town Hall later. It was a lovely idea and she'd been certain she could persuade Billy to take her, too.

'Henzey, if I don't get my dad home he'll probably be set upon, just for wearing a red, white and blue rosette. It's a rough area and, besides, when he's had a drink he wants to fight every bugger, especially Labour folks.'

That bit was true. But it was only half the story. The other half he had no intention of confessing. Billy still possessed a jacket belonging to Nellie Dewsbury and he had already arranged to return it to her that night. Earlier, she called at his house to see him, to ask when he could return it. He was not at home, but his mother innocently agreed an arrangement for him to deliver it to her on the night of polling day, as Nellie had suggested. Billy knew that Walter Dewsbury and his wife would be involved in the electioneering, so they would not be at home, and he recognised at once the intention in Nellie's scheming. He was unable to resist what was a very tempting offer, especially as he had been celibate for so long.

Henzey saw little profit in arguing. In accepting his excuses she resigned herself to losing that battle and Billy delivered her home. It was a quick good-night kiss and off he went. She entered the house forlorn, pouting and disheartened, but never doubting his fidelity. The thing that upset her most was that it would be another two whole days before she would be with him again. Now she would not see him till Saturday night when they went dancing.

Henzey opened the door to the dairy house.

Something was wrong. Whether it was a manifestation of her discontent or her cheerless mood playing tricks, she could not tell; but there was a strange atmosphere. Normally this new home of theirs was vibrant since they moved in, embracing them like a benign, old uncle, who had once lost them and suddenly found them again. It was a happy house, but now it felt cold, empty and peculiarly sad. It was something she could never have defined. Just a feeling, but a weird feeling.

She heard lowered voices upstairs, and called out, 'Yoo-hoo!'

Lizzie answered. 'Henzey? Is that you?' She came to the head of the stairs, looking anxious. 'Thank God. Is Billy with you?'

'No, he's gone.'

'Damn. We could have done with him to fetch the doctor. Looks like Ezme's had another stroke.' She walked downstairs towards Henzey, her voice still low. 'She's in a bad way, Henzey.'

'I can fetch Donald. It's only five to ten. I'll be all right.'

'Let's hope he's still sober. I'd ask our Herbert to go, but he's out God knows where. Alice and Maxine should be back any minute. You'd better go, our Henzey. But be quick. And be careful. You know what they're like on election night. If you see any fights walk on the other side of the horse road.'

So Henzey went out again. As she rushed down Cromwell Street, she saw Alice and Maxine coming the other way with two boys. She explained what had happened, that she was on her way to fetch the doctor. Seeing it as a way of staying out later, Alice agreed to accompany Henzey. Maxine said she would let their mother know where Alice was.

'How come you'm 'ome so early?' Alice enquired.

'Billy had to go early to fetch his father from the pub.' Henzey tried not to sound concerned.

'Oh . . . An' 'ave a drink 'imself, I daresay.' Alice's tone was tinged with cynicism.

'I daresay. That's up to him. I can't dictate what he should or shouldn't do.'

'Yer can try. I would. If he tried to get rid o' me early I'd play hell up. You'm too saft with 'im, Henzey. Yer let 'im boss yer about an' everything'.'

'No, I don't.'

'Yes, yer do. Just 'cause he's got a motor and a pocketful o' money, he thinks he owns yer. He thinks he's everybody.'

'I think you've got a tainted view, Alice,' Henzey said, ruffled by Alice's observations, even though she recognised that there was an element of truth in what she said. 'He doesn't think he's everybody at all, and he certainly doesn't own me.'

'Well, he could if he wanted.'

'No he couldn't.'

'Yes, he could – easy . . . Have yer slept with 'im yet?'

'Alice! Course I haven't slept with him. What do you think I am?'

'Nor let 'im do anything' to yer?'

'No!'

'Never?'

'No, never.'

'Huh! You'm a bit slow. I thought you was potty about 'im . . . Or is it 'im what's slow? Mind yer, I'd want 'im slow. I wun't want 'im to touch me. I think he's a smarmy sod. He gives me the creeps.'

'Good,' Henzey replied indignantly. 'For goodness' sake, Alice, if you can't say anything nice about him don't say anything at all. Keep your opinions to yourself . . . Quick – let's cross over the road . . .'

Two grown men, the worse for drink, tumbled out of the Fountain public house fighting. Had they been sober they would merely have agreed to differ. As fists flew the pub emptied as all the patrons followed the men outside, cheering and jeering, inflaming the situation. Somebody smashed a glass, and in an instant, most of the other men seemed to be involved, flailing their arms like persons drowning.

'Quick, let's get out of the way,' Henzey said to Alice, and they both ran, diffusing their argument.

Soon, they were back home, riding into the yard in Dr Donald Clark's Morris. Henzey could smell drink on him. Even she could tell that it was a bad time to call Donald Clark out when he'd had three or more hours of solo drinking. Yet his brain and his body seemed immune to the effects of whisky. He drove his car capably enough and his speech, though limited to just a few monosyllables, did not sound slurred. Henzey felt sorry for him. Why should a man so patently intelligent try and dissolve his brain in alcohol? What was it that drove him to it? What demons lurked inside his head provoking him to consume the stuff at every opportunity? From what was he trying to escape? What was he trying to blot out from him mind?

They entered the house and Donald stumbled on the first step as he went to climb the stairs. Quickly he righted himself and went on up with his bag while Henzey remained downstairs with Alice and Maxine.

Henzey heard hushed voices upstairs again. Soon, Donald came down with Lizzie and Jesse. After a few minutes they heard him saying good night and Jesse thanked him over and over for coming out to his mother. Then they walked into the sitting-room where the three girls were already seated, waiting for news. They heard Donald's motor car start up and move off.

'How is she?' Henzey asked.

'She's bad, poor soul,' Jesse replied quietly. 'She's sleeping. Somehow, I don't think she'll pull through this as easy as she did the last one.'

Lizzie said, 'You can never tell with a stroke, Jesse. She might be as right as rain tomorrow.'

Jesse shook his head. 'But then again she might not.' He sat down on the sofa and sighed heavily. 'Fetch us a bottle o' Guinness in, Lizzie. I could murder a drink.'

'I'll get it,' Maxine said. 'Mom, would you like one?'

'Yes, go on then, our Maxi. It'll help me sleep.' She looked at Jesse. 'This means we won't be able to go to the Masonic do on Saturday. Had you forgotten it?'

'Bugger me! You'm right, Lizzie. And I've really been looking forward to that. I don't suppose they'll be in a rush to ask me again if we don't show up at this one.'

'Oh, course they will,' Lizzie consoled. 'It can't be helped, your mother being poorly. Anyway, you can always go without me.'

'Don't be daft, Lizzie. I couldn't go there without you. Not on Ladies' Night.'

'There's nothing to stop you both going, Jesse,' Henzey said. 'Billy and me could stay in and keep an eye on Ezme while you went out. If anything were to go wrong Billy could always drive down to Donald's and fetch him.'

Jesse and Lizzie looked at each other, seeking consensus. Lizzie knew how much going to the Masonic Lodge on Saturday meant to him. He did not want to miss it, and if there was a way they could both attend he would take it gladly. Lizzie nodded and Jesse shrugged his consent.

'I imagined you'd want to go dancing,' Lizzie said.

'Well, we would normally, but it's not important. Billy won't mind.'

In any case, after giving precedence to his family tonight, he could hardly complain if she made a similar appeal on Saturday. Vindictiveness did not urge her to arrange it, since she felt not one ounce of malice. She could help Jesse and, in so doing, might feasibly make Billy realise that he had hurt her by dumping her at home so early. Perhaps he should be made to realise that.

'Henzey, you're a treasure,' Jesse declared.

'Well . . . as I'm such a treasure . . . can I go to the Town Hall and wait for the election result?'

'Not on your own you won't, madam,' Lizzie answered. 'And neither Jesse nor me can go now, on account of Ezme.'

Jesse said, 'Didn't her Uncle Joe and Aunt May say they were going? She could go with them.'

'She could, but then she won't want to get up for work in the morning.'

'I shall be up like a lark.'

'As long as that's a promise. If they're not still at home, they'll be up the Junction. Put your hat and coat back on.'

Uncle Joe and Aunty May lived next door to number 48, where the Kites used to live before moving across the road to the dairy house. Henzey found them in the Junction as her mother had suggested. They were about to go to the Town Hall with Tom the Tatter, who had his best suit on with a grubby old cap and a dirty, white muffler. Phyllis Fat and her husband, Hartwell Dabbs, had decided to go too, as had Colonel Bradley, who was really a woman but cursed and drank like a hammer driver.

'Ain't yer courtin' tonight, our Henzey?' May asked.

'I've done my courting tonight, Aunty May. Now I'm going out to enjoy myself.'

May chuckled at Henzey's apparent indifference to courtship.

They walked steadily to the town, through the Market Place, where one or two revellers were sitting on the empty market stall trestles, some with their heads in their hands, the worse for drink. Others were singing noisily.

By the time they reached the new Town Hall, all lit up with electric lights, a sizeable crowd had gathered. There were intense debates between some on the vices and virtues of the main parties. Half a dozen constables broke up a brawl between a Labour supporter and a Conservative supporter and then their indignant wives, who were pulling each other's hair out in handfuls. Others laughed at the political fervour of some of their fellow citizens.

'Just look at them daft buggers,' Tom the Tatter said from under his cap and unkempt hair, which always seemed as one single unit.

'What they arguin' about, I wonder?' May said.

Hartwell replied, 'I 'eard 'em. The Labour chap was on about gettin' rid o' the peers.'

'Why, the saft sod. There's ne'er a pier in Dudley. Where's 'e think 'e is? Soddin' Blackpool? Yo' can tell 'e ai' a local mon.'

The Town Hall clock struck midnight.

'Shouldn't be long now,' Colonel Bradley commented, looking up at the sky as if the darkness might yield a clue as to any likely change in the weather. She took a hip flask out of her jacket pocket and took a slug of whisky. 'Come and stand by me, young Henzey. You'll get a better view here.'

Henzey did as she was invited.

'I shun't get too excited yet,' Phyllis Fat crowed. 'There's still some more dignit'ries what ai' in yet. 'Ere's some more on 'em now by the looks o' things.'

Three limousines pulled up. Henzey, standing on the steps of the art gallery opposite with Colonel Bradley, noticed the Mayor and his family alight from the first car. The second one disgorged Councillor Walter Dewsbury and his wife. Next out of the same car, to her surprise, came Andrew Dewsbury and she shuddered as she recalled his birthday party. She waited and craned her neck to get a look at Nellie, but Andrew was the last person to get out of the second motor car. Nellie obviously had better things to do. The third vehicle deposited somebody Joe maintained was Alderman and Mrs Hickinbottom.

Another quarter of an hour passed before the Mayor, with Councillor Dewsbury, Alderman Hickinbottom and half a dozen others, stepped out onto the balcony above the Town Hall entrance. One man started to blow into the huge microphone in front of him. After they'd all shuffled into suitable positions the returning officer looked round, nodded, blew into the microphone again, then announced the count. Oliver Baldwin had taken the Dudley seat for Labour and there was raucous cheering.

Next day revealed how the general election ended in stalemate. Labour won most seats but the Conservatives polled most votes. Stanley Baldwin remained at 10 Downing Street and it was hinted that he would reshuffle his cabinet. Because it was up to the Liberals to decide who should govern it was far from over yet. Many reckoned that the lowering of the voting age for women from thirty to twenty-one, the 'flapper vote', had helped Labour.

*   *   *

On Saturday evening Billy arrived at the dairy house to collect Henzey. He wore a navy-blue three-piece suit, white shirt and Paisley tie. As Henzey opened the door to him he handed her a bouquet of roses and kissed her.

'To say sorry for last Thursday night. Am I forgiven?'

'You didn't have to bring me flowers, Billy. They are beautiful, though. Thank you.' He stepped inside. 'Before you say anything else, I've got a confession to make – I went to watch the election results after with Aunty May and Uncle Joe.'

'Oh?'

'At least I've got an idea what our new MP looks like. I wish you'd been there, though. I saw the Dewsbury family, but Nellie wasn't with them.'

'Oh,' he grunted evasively, then followed her into the sitting-room. He sat down next to Alice, who had her nose in a book. She greeted him summarily. 'Aren't you ready yet, Henzey?'

She shook her head.

'How long shall you be?'

'We're not going anywhere, Billy. Leastwise I'm not. Mom and Jesse have already gone out and I have to look after Ezme. I don't mind if you still want to go out without me, though. Let me just go and put these roses into a vase, then I'll explain.'

Herbert was out with Edgar Hodgetts, his pal, and Alice and Maxine both said they had arranged to meet a gang from Oldbury at the roller-skating rink. Henzey returned with her blooms in an earthenware vase, which she put on the table. She sat down beside Billy on the sofa and explained more fully what had happened.

'You don't mind do you, Billy?'

'Oh, I can hardly mind after what happened on Thursday. So how is the old dutch?'

'She's ever so poorly. Doctor's been again today. Anyway, how was your dad on Thursday? Was he drunk, like you said he'd be?'

'As a bobowler. It's good job I went to fetch him. Mind you, he's been drunk ever since he heard the result.'

'Would you like a drink? I'll get you a bottle of beer from the kitchen if you like.'

He said he would, so she fetched a bottle and glass and poured it for him. He took a long drink, then put his glass on the floor at the side of the sofa while she took the empty bottle out. She came back sipping a glass of sherry.

'Might as well have a drink myself, even if we are stopping in.'

She sat beside him again. He stood up, took off his jacket, threw it over one of the armchairs and sat beside her again companionably.

'I've missed you this last couple of days, Henzey. I really have.'

She snuggled up to him. 'Ooh, tell me again.'

He chuckled. 'I have, honest. I've really missed you. I've been thinking about you all the time. I don't mind that we're stopping in tonight. At least I'll have you to myself.' He took another quaff of beer.

Henzey took a sip of her sherry and smiled contentedly. 'You know, I like this house,' she commented, looking round her. 'It's so much bigger than the one we lived in over the road, isn't it?'

'Your mother's got it nice.'

'Oh, it'll be even nicer in time. You should see upstairs now.'

'I've seen upstairs. Well, I've seen the new bathroom.'

'You should see the difference now. Come up with me and have a look. I've got to go up and have a look at Ezme again, anyway.' She took another sip of sherry and put it on the table as she rose from the sofa. Billy followed her upstairs.

Henzey gently opened the door into Ezme's room and walked over to where she lay. The old lady seemed to be sleeping soundly enough, but grunted once.

'God, she looks pale,' Billy whispered.

'Poor old soul. If I ever get like that I hope they'll put me down. I never want to suffer. I'm too much of a coward. I remember my dad . . .'

Billy took her hand. He led her out of the room and out of the mood. 'Nice, big landing,' he said brightly. 'Now show me your room. I've never seen your room.'

She feigned primness. 'My room? Hey, I'm not sure that's quite the proper thing for a young lady to do,'

'Oh, it'll be all right, Henzey. I shan't disgrace you by being indiscreet.'

She laughed and, still with her hand in his, she led him along the landing to the room at the end, overlooking the back of the house. It was small and, in it, was a new single bed with a pale blue bedspread, a dressing table covered with an assortment of make-up and bottles of perfume, and a tall cane whatnot standing in a corner bearing a cyclamen in flower. The walls were painted in a cool, pale blue and the woodwork was white. A photograph of her father as a very handsome young man hung on the wall opposite her bed.

'I say, this is really nice,' Billy enthused. 'Did you pick the colours yourself?'

She sat on the bed, looked around her, and nodded. 'I like it. It's all my own. A whole room to myself. I can still hardly believe it.'

He sat beside her. 'It's cool, like you.'

'What is?'

'Blue. It suits you. Reflects your personality . . . and it matches your eyes.'

She flashed a smile at him for the compliment. 'Think I'm cool, do you? D'you mean cold?'

'No. Definitely not cold, Henzey. Not you. Cool. Sometimes a bit aloof. Like when I got here and you said I could still go out by myself if I wanted. As if you didn't care.'

'Oh, Billy, is that how I seem?' She looked at him earnestly, and she wrapped her arms around him. 'Billy, I do care. Maybe more than it shows. Maybe more than is good for me.'

He saw the love shining unmistakably at him through her soft, sincere eyes, and he kissed her. His lips felt so good. It would be forever impossible to have a surfeit of his kisses. She could happily kiss him till eternity. She offered no resistance when he pressed her backwards so that she was lying on the bed; no resistance at all. Gently he rolled on top of her, their lips still touching, and she realised the joy of having his weight upon her. After a while they broke off their kiss and his lips first brushed her throat and her neck, as light as the touch of a feather, then lingered at her ear. As she felt his warm breath she experienced sensations up and down her spine that she could not control. She could feel him pressing against her, urgently, and her heart beat faster at the pleasure of it all. They kissed more, lingering, savouring each other's lips. He rolled onto his side and she shuffled to face him, smiling trustingly. His knee slid evocatively between her thighs and she liked the feel of it. But the familiar mental barriers arose inside her head like intruding demons.

With no hesitation Billy unfastened the buttons at the front of her blouse and she knew that from this moment, unless she stopped him, there would be no turning back. The familiar fear of getting into trouble taunted her, though she desperately wished to fight it. Now Billy's hands, so smooth, so caring, were inside her brassiere, gently fondling her breasts. It was such bewildering pleasure. As she felt his mouth on hers again she thought of her mother, and what would happen if she allowed herself to give in to her physical desires and got into trouble as a result. While she desperately wanted to be whisked along on this tide of passion, she wrestled with the years of indoctrination. She was being pulled one way by apprehension, the other way by yearning. It was like a tug of war.

But desire was gaining the upper hand.

Her blouse was all undone, the shoulder strap of her underslip was halfway down her arm and her brassiere was loose. She wriggled and thought she was going to burst with ecstasy when Billy's tongue settled on one of her nipples, teasing it unmercifully as it hardened. He undid the waistband of her skirt and opened it up with his delving, free hand. Her underslip was up, baring her midriff, and he nuzzled his face into her soft belly, venturing lower and lower with his mouth. Before she knew it, her skirt was off, slid under her bottom and down her legs. His hand stopped to explore the smooth, bare flesh above her stockings before he kissed her there, too. Her heart was pounding hard, and her breathing was in faltering gasps. She wanted him. God, how she wanted him, feeling his warm, gentle kisses all over her body, tingling, tantalising, so scandalously tempting. What on earth would her mother have to say if she could see her now, down to her underwear, her underslip around her waist, her brassiere there, too, and Billy sprawled over her, kissing her thighs?

It was then, with thankfulness and relief, that she remembered there need be no guilt anymore. She had been freed of it. There could be no more threats. Her mother had condoned this sort of thing by her own example. Her mother had behaved like this, also lured by love and by desire; by her own admission; before she was married.

So could she.

She sighed vocally at both the realisation and the astounding sensations Billy was inducing.

'My angel,' he breathed, pushing himself up the bed to face her and to lie alongside her again. 'Have I shocked you?'

She groaned earnestly, and the spittle in her mouth thickened. 'Shock me a bit more, Billy. Shock me a bit more.'

'Henzey, I want you.' His voice was as soft and warm as his kisses. 'God, how I want you.'

She sighed at the clean, manly smell of his skin. She sighed even more as he slid her knickers down her legs. 'Oh, Billy, I love you so much.'

As she lay there afterwards she did not know how she felt. Maybe she had expected too much. Maybe she was expecting some magnificent, automatic fireworks display or something, but none came. Billy lay beside her, quiet, still. She could feel the sweat on his forehead as she stroked it while he fought against sleep. She began to feel cold so she pulled up the bedclothes. Her emotions were half delight that she had given herself, that she had committed herself fully to the man she loved so much, but they were also half disappointment. Billy seemed satisfied but where was the satisfaction for her? Still she felt unfulfilled, hungry after what should have been a feast. She was still aching to be loved, still tingling inside. She turned to Billy and he opened his eyes. They kissed briefly and he smiled, his arm going around her, his hand gently squeezing a cheek of her naked bottom. She loved him beyond her wildest imaginings. The feel of his skin against hers was a delight she had never known before, never properly imagined.

'What time is it?' she asked.

'About nine, judging by the light. We don't have to get up yet, do we?'

'Alice and Maxi won't be back before half past ten.'

He kissed her again, more fervently this time. 'Jesus Christ, I love you, Henzey Kite. I didn't know how much till just now.'

She pushed herself against him. Within a few minutes he wanted her again.

There *was* a fireworks display after all. Her eyes were closed but she saw bright lights, dancing, shooting everywhere, cascading in plumes, soaring, bursting, lighting her up, making her smile and gasp and sigh profoundly at the beauty of it all.

At last she understood. At last she knew what total pleasure was, what real love was. At last she understood why she had always felt so empty and unfulfilled when they had merely kissed passionately before. At last she was a woman, utter and complete. At last she understood why her mother, and so many others like her, had so easily fallen into the oldest of nature's traps. Who could blame them? Never had she experienced anything like this. Never had she dreamed that there could be anything so sublime. It was a revelation. And she knew already that she was addicted.

Outside, the light of that first day of June had dimmed. All was quiet except for the sound of a distant motor car and the plaintive barking of a dog on Cawney Hill. She got out of bed, picked up her clothes from the floor, and got dressed. She woke Billy. He, too, slid out of bed and stood, holding her tight before she rearranged the sheets and blankets. While he dressed she tiptoed into Ezme's room. The curtains were still open and the grey dusk afforded just enough light to see that the old lady still lay undisturbed, exactly as they had left her before they went to bed. Henzey took a match and lit the oil lamp on the bedside table, for Jesse had not seen fit to disturb her with having gas-lights fitted in her room while she was so unwell.

In its glow Ezme's complexion was like wax. Henzey touched her face with the backs of her fingers, half expecting her to react. But there was no reaction. Ezme's face felt cold as clay. She was dead.

Chapter Six

Ezme Clancey was buried on the 7th June 1929, the same day that
Ramsay MacDonald announced the Cabinet that was to form
the country's second only Labour Government. The very same
day, Jesse tactfully explained to Herbert that Lizzie was going to
have his baby, though Herbert had guessed as much, since his
mother's belly was swelling appreciably. At first he was piqued
and told Jesse that it was indecent at their age, but he accepted it
well enough when Henzey asked him why on earth he should
resent it at all. Lizzie told Alice and Maxine, but they were
predictably excited.

Billy celebrated his twenty-fifth birthday the day afterwards, a
Saturday, by taking Henzey out to dinner at the Grand Hotel in
Colmore Row, Birmingham. They were joined by some business
friends, Harvey and Gladys Tennant, a couple in their late
forties, and Neville Worthington with his very attractive wife,
Eunice, who was in her late twenties. Henzey estimated that
Neville was in his mid-thirties. The event was a double
celebration. Billy had just invested five thousand pounds in
the firm that belonged to Harvey, Tennant Electrics, which
manufactured small electric motors. The investment meant that
the firm could expand by broadening their range, to meet the

new demand for small electric motors to drive windscreen wipers. Billy was to become a sleeping partner, and he would have a greater incentive to sell their products to the big motor manufacturers. He could not fail to make even more money.

Neville Worthington was the eccentric owner of a family firm producing commercial vehicles, and Billy had recently won a contract to supply Tennant Electrics' wiper motors to him. He thus felt inclined to nurture the relationship with this new client, and saw this occasion as an ideal opportunity. It turned out to be a very successful and interesting evening for Billy. Henzey, however, was overawed by the extravagance of their guests, by the way they spoke so beautifully, and by the obvious trappings of wealth. She was all of a sudden immersed in another world, far removed from the whitewashed scullery walls, the blackleaded grates and the dilapidated brewhouses of Cromwell Street. But her outward appearance would have fooled anybody; she was wearing an expensive, red, silk pyjama suit that Billy had chosen and paid for; and she looked the very epitome of feminine beauty and sophistication.

She was, however, a little subdued. Seated at Billy's right, with Neville Worthington to her own right, she gazed with eager interest at the haddock with shrimp sauce that had been set before her. She watched Eunice Worthington, waiting for her to take the lead, to ascertain what cutlery she should use for this course.

Talk at first was about Ramsay MacDonald's new Labour cabinet.

'The only glimmer of hope,' said Neville, 'is that there are no radical extremists there. At least he seems to be attempting to maintain some credulity.'

'Except for that woman he's appointed Minister of Labour,' Harvey Tennant scoffed. 'I mean, a woman in the cabinet, for God's sake . . .'

'You mean Margaret Bondfield,' Eunice said evenly.

'That's her. I mean, really! She's a damned trade unionist.'

'Chairman of the TUC,' Eunice added.

'Precisely. What does she know about government? What does she know about the problems facing employers and factory owners like ourselves, eh, Neville? She's a troublemaker, mark my words. Neither your business nor mine will prosper while the likes of her are in such elevated positions. Baldwin should have held on to the reins, I maintain, and parleyed with Lloyd George for the Liberals' support. Frankly, I rue the day women were given the vote.'

Billy astutely perceived tension arising from this political discussion. Eunice Worthington had said little, but he could tell she was a suffragette in spirit and would be at odds with Harvey if the debate was allowed to progress. He wished to avert trouble. 'How did you do at Epsom, Neville?' he asked astutely. 'Did you back the winner?'

'Trigo?' Neville replied. 'No. Didn't even see the race, Billy. Still dining. Met Peter Bennett of Lucas down there.'

'What? *The* Peter Bennett? The Managing Director?'

'Joint Managing Director, isn't he? . . . Thought so . . . Talked for ages. Missed the race completely.'

'I see that Douglas Fairbanks' son has married,' Gladys said irrelevantly, directing her comment at Henzey, who so far had said little, guessing that it would bring her into the conversation.

This was more in Henzey's line. She took advantage of the prompt, and swallowed her piece of fish. 'Yes, and he's only nineteen,' she replied as if she were an authority. 'That girl he's married, though, Joan Crawford, is much older. Twenty-three according to the paper.'

'Do you not condone a man marrying a girl some years older than himself, Henzey?' Neville asked, evidently preferring this conversation.

She looked at him, with his unfashionable long hair and thick, full beard, and their eyes met momentarily. In that brief instant she saw such an appealing look of soulfulness in his eyes. 'Well, I just can't see what contentment she would find marrying a boy so much younger than herself, that's all,' she remarked. 'I prefer men a bit older than me. Younger men always seem so childish.'

'I see. You seem to have a very mature outlook for someone so young. So . . . how long have you known Billy?'

Neville was regarding her keenly; it seemed he could not take his eyes off her and she found it disconcerting. 'Oh, quite a long time now, but we've only been courting about three months.' She smiled politely, then finished her last piece of fish, placing her knife and fork together neatly on her plate, ready for it to be collected. She still felt the urge to gather everybody else's empty plates and stack them in a heap, as she had done on a previous visit to a restaurant. But Billy had told her firmly not to demean herself again by doing the waitress's job.

Henzey was not sorry when dinner was finished and they retired to the hotel's lounge to take coffee. She made for one of the settees which, with another similar one and a couple of armchairs, were grouped convivially around a low, round table. She hoped that Billy would settle beside her, but Neville was too quick and eased himself into the same settee before Billy had even thought about it. Fortunately, Neville was affable and Henzey found him easy to talk to. They spoke politely about this and that and she asked him about his family. He had been married to Eunice for four years and had a young son, he told her as a wine waiter approached seeking orders for brandies.

'You're a lucky man, Neville,' Henzey commented, 'having a lovely child and a beautiful wife who, I imagine, thinks the world of you.'

'Yes, I am a lucky man to have a lovely child . . .' He paused deliberately. This lack of acknowledgement of Eunice made Henzey curious, although she ventured no further comment. He continued: 'Have you and Billy talked of marriage?'

She shook her head and smiled. 'After three months? Anyway, I'm too young yet.'

'Sensible, Henzey. Very sensible. Lately, I take a dim view of marriage.' He spoke quietly, intimately, only to her. 'I see so many people unhappily bound by its restrictions. I see so many people hurt by the consequences of marital foolishness.'

'Oh, that's a shame. I've never looked at it like that. I've only ever known people happy in their marriages. Where they love each other I mean, I suppose.'

'Oh, love's a different thing altogether, Henzey. You mustn't think I take a dim view of love – I certainly do not. To love passionately and be loved back in like manner is a gift of God. But marriage isn't always like that. Romance can quickly disappear from marriage. It can end up a sham – as nothing more than trying to be nice to each other for the sake of peace and quiet. If you'll pardon me for being blunt, it can degenerate to a few quick thrusts between the sheets every now and again just to show willing, instead of the romance and passion you enjoyed before, that you never dreamed would slip away so insidiously.'

Henzey blushed. 'I think that's a cynical view, Neville.'

'Maybe it is . . . But real passionate love is something quite different, wouldn't you say? Real passionate love is what makes life worth living. Without it we might as well be dead.'

'I suppose.' She felt his eyes burning into her again, and she felt uneasy. It was evident that he found her appealing, and now he was sounding her out; assessing his chances, it seemed. Perhaps love was lacking from his life, inducing him to say these things.

The wine waiter returned with a tray of brandy glasses, each with an inch or so of the deep amber liquid swishing around.

'What I miss more than anything in my marriage, Henzey,' he said after he had taken a glass and sipped it, 'is love. I mean real physical, ardent, energetic love . . . The sort of love that leaves you breathless and utterly exhausted. But totally satisfied.'

She avoided his eyes. What was he trying to say? She glanced guiltily at Billy but he was too deeply engrossed in conversation with Eunice to notice. Henzey felt naked under Neville's eyes and felt inclined to cross her legs. It would be an appropriate thing to do. But, to her surprise, Neville's words did not offend her. Rather, she found them stimulating. It was a change to hear a man be so direct about love and passion without sounding either sloppy or apologetic.

'You know, you're a fine-looking girl, Henzey. I hope you don't mind me saying so . . .'

She looked at him and smiled. 'No, I don't mind you saying so at all, Neville. I'm very flattered.'

'I look at you and imagine you to be a very passionate young woman, you know. You have that look about you . . . I don't mean to offend . . . It's just that I do find you extremely attractive. Extremely attractive. Billy's a jolly lucky chap. I hope he appreciates you.'

She shrugged, and smiled. 'I hope so, too.'

Neville Worthington picked up his bottle of Exshaw's No. I, his favourite brandy, poured himself a last one and took it upstairs to his bedroom. He sat on the bed and loosened his bow tie with his free hand before taking a sip and placing the glass on his bedside table. As he bent over to untie his shoelaces he sighed heavily. Henzey Kite was occupying his mind. He wanted her, and such ardent desire for a woman had not taken him like this since his first encounters with Eunice. He sighed, kicked off his shoes and stood up again to put away his bow tie and unfasten his cuff-links.

'Don't forget to put your shoes in your wardrobe, Neville,' his wife said as she drove a brush through her stylishly cut hair.

'In a minute, when I'm undressed.'

'. . . Otherwise you'll fall over them and wake me up if you have to get up in the night.' Eunice was at her dressing table in her white silk pyjamas. A shopful of beauty aids stood randomly on top of it. She took one small dainty pot, dipped her fingers into it and proceeded to rub a creamy substance over her face. 'No doubt you'll forget them altogether.'

'Well, if I do happen to fall over them and wake you in the night, rest assured I shall not tumble into your bed and interfere with you, Eunice, either deliberately or in error.'

She made no reply. Neville removed the coins from his trouser pockets and let them tumble onto his tallboy. Then he undressed himself, and took his clean pyjamas that the maid had placed on his pillow while he was out.

'I enjoyed this evening, Eunice. Didn't you?'

'Towards the end. Not during the meal.'

'Actually, I found it all rather stimulating.'

'I suspect you found talking to that young girl rather stimulating. More so than talking to that other woman. What was her name?'

'Henzey.'

'Not Henzey, the older woman.'

'I've forgotten.' He pulled his pyjama trousers on.

'Strange how you can remember Henzey's name but not that other woman's.' Eunice began removing the cleansing cream with a damp face towel.

Neville tied the cord of his pyjamas. 'It's hardly strange, my dear. You also remembered it, evidently. Anyway, Henzey was by far the more interesting of the two.' He sat on his bed again and reached for his drink.

'And by far the more attractive.'

'That as well.'

Eunice turned to address him. There was an earnest look on her face. 'But Neville, you'd never attract a girl like that until you altered your style.'

'Oh, and I thought she seemed quite taken with me.'

Eunice laughed scornfully. 'You fool yourself, Neville. Look at your awful beard and your disastrous hair. Do you realise I have never, in all the years I've known you, seen you without that damn beard? You had it when we were first introduced, and you've had it ever since – all through your Oxford days.'

'So what? That's me. That's how I am.'

'But you're only twenty-nine, dammit, and you look forty-nine. Young ladies nowadays go for the smooth, clean-shaven look in men – short, neat haircuts. I mean, look at that Billy fellow she was with . . . he's fashionable . . . typical of the type of young men women go for. I can understand why she finds *him* appealing.'

'Surely girls prefer someone more masculine?'

'On the contrary, girls today prefer a more feminine-looking man . . . Not that he's feminine . . . Not by any stretch of imagination.'

'And some girls try to look like boys with their flat chests and short haircuts. It's a strange world we live in.'

Eunice continued peering at her moistened face in the mirror of her dressing table. 'The point I'm trying to make, my darling Neville, is that if you altered your style *I* might find you more attractive. What is it that compels you to want to look so . . . so *eccentric?*'

'It's how I want to look, no more, no less. It pleases me. I dislike shaving. I dislike having my hair cut more than is necessary. And anyway, people remember me all the easier for it. And that's good for business.'

'But you look like somebody from the last century. It makes you look so old. Whom are trying to emulate, for God's sake? Leon Trotsky? It's not as if you have a poor physique. You have an excellent physique.'

He pulled back the covers of his single bed and slid between the sheets. 'I'd like to invite that Billy and Henzey over to dinner one evening. Can we fix a convenient date?'

'I . . . I think not. I have no wish to entertain them here.'

'You said a minute ago Billy was very appealing. Do make up your mind, Eunice.'

'What I said was, I could understand why that young girl found him appealing, unlike that other man, that Harvey. He's an old-fashioned, bigoted, high Tory. Please don't embarrass me by inviting them here. If you wish to meet them alone at a restaurant that's up to you. But please don't involve me.'

Neville lay back and closed his eyes, urgently seeking a mental image of Henzey. 'As for Harvey and his anonymous wife,' he said, 'I hadn't intended asking them.'

Neither spoke more. Neville sighed unhappily and snuggled down in his bed. He ventured no further conversation, remaining silent, trying to sleep. But sleep eluded him for a long time after Eunice had slid into her own bed and turned out the light. He tried to imagine the young Henzey Kite lying naked in bed with him; the feel of her warm, soft skin against his; her silken mouth; his thigh gripped lovingly between hers; her arching back as his tongue drove her wild, probing her secret places; her appreciative sighs as he thrust hungrily into her. His throat went dry just thinking about it.

But eventually the erotic fantasies were eclipsed by more mundane thoughts. Meeting Henzey Kite also focused his mind on the shortcomings of his marriage; shortcomings he regretted, but was unable to change in the short term. His marriage used to be very satisfactory, but now it was a compromise; an arrangement; a result of the marital foolishness he had spoken about to Henzey. He wondered how long it might survive in this hideous state. Eunice was a beautiful woman, and desirable. They lived together without sleeping together, and though there was seldom any open hostility between them, mainly for the sake of their son, neither was there any visible affection. Yet there was a glimmer of hope. Eunice had said that if he chose to shave off his beard and have his hair cut decently she might find him more attractive. She had said that before, but why should his beard and his hair make any difference? She married him with his beard and his hair, why should she despise it now? He would divest himself of it as a last resort; only if absolutely necessary.

For Neville took refuge behind his beard. It was protection; a disguise to prevent recognition. He wore it just in case; just in case one particular person were to recognise him first. He knew it was ridiculous, an idea conceived in his youth that had developed and intensified over the years. He had never confided his thoughts to Eunice about it, hence she saw him merely as somebody completely out of step with fashion, unaware of the real unease fixed illogically inside his head; unaware of the unease that coerced him to be the way he was.

This nagging doubt, which dictated his appearance, was generated by the knowledge that he once had a twin brother. He could not remember him, he did not even know his name, but the odds were that he was still alive, and possibly round the next corner if he had not emigrated. That being so, Neville wanted the advantage; he wanted to be able to recognise him first, without being recognised himself. It was an irrational notion on the face of it, but important to him. In the event it would allow him the choice of turning away or making himself known, depending on what he perceived in the man.

Neville only knew what Magdalen Worthington, his adoptive mother, had told him: that he was the son of his father, Oswald Worthington, by one of the housemaids of the time called Bessie Hipkiss. Neville believed that Bessie had died in abject poverty when he and his brother were but two years old and that his twin had been taken into the care of a Christian family of very moderate means in the Black Country, while he was subsequently delivered, as a last resort, to the large, elegant house of his father. The intention, apparently, was that his father should rightfully be made to face all responsibility for him. The trouble was, by that time his father was dead. It was fortunate indeed that Oswald's young widow, Magdalen, was still grieving, and was more than happy to accept the return of anything that was her husband's, especially a son, albeit by another woman. She took Neville in as her own and doted on him, ensuring that he had the very best of everything, including the best education money could buy.

As he turned restlessly in his bed, dissatisfied with the state of his marriage, Neville's thoughts turned to his real mother and he wondered what she was like. He would dearly love to know more about her, to see a photograph of her. But how to go about finding out? Who, twenty-seven years after her death, would remember somebody as insignificant as Bessie Hipkiss? Who would possibly remember a particular housemaid put in the family way by a male member of the family that employed her, out of the hundreds of such beguiled and unfortunate young women who littered society? If only she could have lived a year or two longer so that he might have some memory of her, however vague.

And this brother, sight of whom Neville was so apprehensive about . . . He longed to know him. He longed to be able to talk to him about their mother, about how he felt now at their being parted then. Sometimes he felt as if he was only half a person, that there was another half somewhere, waiting to make the whole. It was a strange feeling. He would love to know whether his brother felt it, too. Some day he might meet him. He would know him immediately; they were identical twins after all, or so he'd been led to believe. He hoped that when that day came he would like the man; that any differences in their circumstances and upbringing would not render them entirely incompatible.

Chapter Seven

By the end of July, the government had announced plans to increase unemployment benefit, and forty-eight countries had signed the Geneva Convention on the treatment of prisoners of war. Lizzie was even bigger, but at no time did she suffer the things normally associated with pregnancy, such as morning sickness.

From the point of view of business, Billy Witts began to worry; he was finding it ever more difficult to achieve lucrative deals, due to the general economic climate. But he and Henzey had been making love regularly for two months, which helped take his mind off his finances. Lovemaking concentrated Henzey's mind on their relationship. It was the ultimate expression of her feelings for Billy and, often, she pondered Neville Worthington's words about energetic love that made you breathless and exhausted. It did not apply to Billy and her, but she reckoned things must be approaching something akin. At least she thought so.

She had finished half a dozen watercolours and three pencil sketches of Billy besides, the best of which she'd had framed and were now hanging on her bedroom walls. For years, Henzey had yearned for some hero; not necessarily Billy, but just someone to come along and sweep her off her feet. The vision of him haunted her in the cool April rain, in the golden August sunshine and in the thick pea-soupers of November. She did not miss such a hero to any great extent. She could have comfortably existed without a male companion. She'd been perfectly content to open doors herself, pull on her own coat, without any masculine courtesies. In any case, on a practical level, doing things for herself was by far the fastest way.

Her hero physically existed as a brief manifestation in Jack Harper, but never could she be interested in the man who would moon over her as he did; who might declare his feelings before she had decided hers, like he had. Never could she fall for a love-sick lap dog that bored her with predictable soppiness. The reason Billy fascinated her in the first place was because he kept her guessing. Because he resisted her for so long she was intrigued, and that intrigue turned to fixation, and then to love.

In love, she was profoundly sentimental. The glow of romance fired her imagination with thoughts of just the two of them in their own house; of cosy evenings, snuggled roman-tically together before a homely fire. At no time did she ever consider the raking out of that fire; not the blackleading, the ironing, the cleaning or any of the unromantic chores of daily living. And she was dying to tell Billy her dreams. But she dare not. At least not yet.

As far as she was concerned, Billy was faultless. He was hard working, generous and passionate. Never did she tire of looking at his handsome face, of enjoying the tingles when he touched her. He had money to indulge her, not that she expected much, but what she got she appreciated. He loved to see the joy on her face whenever he took her shopping and bought her expensive new clothes. He wined her and dined her, showed her off to his well-to-do friends and business associates at dinner and garden parties. Mentally, she put Billy on a pedestal, expecting him to live up to her image of perfection. What she never thought about, indeed, typically, what she overlooked, were his imperfec-tions and his weaknesses.

Billy's whims and fancies changed with the wind. He could be charming – his compliments always sounded so sincere, especially to women – but he was inclined to sarcasm, moods and irritability if things did not go all his way. He was as changeable as the weather. One day he was warmly romantic, openly weaving dreams; the next, aloof, impatient and critical. Always, he had an unwitting urge to disguise his true intentions, to conceal his motives. Money was his god; he worshipped it and he kept his financial position entirely to himself. He forever sought companionship, male and female, and would have resented any move to curb it. He was full of good intentions but because he was also impulsive, many of his well-intended promises ended up broken. Henzey thus found he was frequently late calling for her, or having to make last-minute changes to their plans, even abandoning them. These things were part of his nature and, at no time, did he knowingly make Henzey suffer because of it, since he was in love with her in his own mercurial way. Simply, he was easily diverted.

Billy saw Henzey as capable, with an independent streak. Her conversation was bright and never boring but, when she spoke, she expected him to listen. His circle of friends found her disarming and, on such occasions as she was in their company, her manner was always impeccable. In the matter of attention and recognising her artistic abilities, she demanded a lot from Billy and wallowed in his appreciation of her creativity. But usually she gave double attention in return.

In the exalted company they often kept, she was becoming more aware of her accent and was determined to lose it. Each day she listened to herself speaking and, each day, she heard herself utter some word or phrase that she realised she could improve upon. So, gradually, a general smoothing off of those rougher-sounding edges began to creep into her everyday speech.

Billy often detected jealousy in Henzey if another woman smiled at him fancifully, though he knew she would never admit to it. Thus, he learned quickly never to pay another woman a compliment within her hearing. It was not in his own nature to be jealous, but she would have resented it as a slur on her integrity if he ever showed the merest hint of jealousy; she could be trusted implicitly and he should know that. Indeed, he never had any reason to feel jealous. Henzey was generous to a fault, with what money she had, with her time, but particularly with her love. And though she appeared capable and confident to the world, Billy soon understood that if the world was unkind to her, that composure would evaporate and she would be as defenceless and vulnerable as a kitten.

This was demonstrated in early August after he called for her one warm evening when he'd been away at the Morris works at Cowley for a couple of days. She jumped in the car and they drove off with the hood down to find some secluded spot. They ended up near the Staffordshire-Shropshire border, at a deserted but beautiful area, called Enville Common. Even though she had not seen Billy for a few days she barely spoke a word during the half-hour journey.

'What's the matter then, Henzey?' he asked. 'You're quiet. Who's upset you?'

He went to put his arm around her, but sensed her recoil. It was almost imperceptible, but it was there, and it was distinctly unusual. At first she didn't answer, so he asked her again. She shook her head slightly and he saw her eyes fill with tears. She needed to cry, he could see that, but she was fighting it, trying, as ever, to be strong.

'If I tell you, you'll go mad,' she said at last, and turned her head away to look unseeing at the thicket of young silver birches glistening in the oblique, yellowing sunlight.

'Then you'd best let me go mad, and get it over with, eh?'

'Do you promise not to be angry, Billy?' Her expression was intense.

Two flies, one chasing the other, settled on the dashboard of the car and he flicked them away absently.

'How can I promise anything if I don't know what you're about to tell me?'

It suddenly dawned on him that maybe she was trying to tell him she was pregnant. A lump came to his throat and he felt suddenly hot. Oh, Jesus. Yes, he had put her at risk, but surely he had been careful enough. Surely . . .

'Because something's happened . . . and it isn't my fault.'

'All right. Whatever it is, it ain't your fault, I'll accept that. Now will you tell me what it's all about?'

She looked directly in front of her, her back erect, her hands primly on her knees. She began to weep. 'I'll have to leave George Mason's. I've said nothing to nobody. I wanted to tell you first, Billy. When I tell my mother, she'll go mad.'

Billy felt himself sweating. This was the last thing he needed. He could do without more problems at this time. 'Come on, what is it, for God's sake? Why have you got to give up your job?'

'Because of Wally Bibb.'

He breathed a sigh of relief. 'What about Wally Bibb?' He leaned against the car door, his arm resting on the back of his seat, bent, so his hand could support his chin as he watched her.

'He's had another go at me — made another pass at me, I mean. I was in the stockroom and he came up behind me and put his hands down the front of my blouse and in my brassiere. I struggled, but he got his arm round my waist as well and started kissing my neck.' A tear rolled down her right cheek. 'It was horrible, Billy. It made me feel horrible and dirty. It's not the first time he's tried and I can't stand it anymore. I can't stand him messing with me and having to look over my shoulder every minute I'm there, just to keep out of his way.' Her sense of loyalty was such that she was feeling guilty that Wally had touched her; as if she were the one who should be blamed.

'Oh, ain't he a flippin' pest!' Billy said sympathetically. 'He wants locking up.'

A pause.

'Is that all you can say?'

'What d'you expect me to say? I'm certainly not very pleased, I can tell you.'

'Well, what are you going to do about it?'

'What am I going to do about it? I'm not going to do anything, am I? You're the one who's doing something about it by leaving . . . and finding another job, presumably.'

She shook her head and took a small handkerchief out of her handbag to wipe her tears. 'I'm speechless, Billy. If you were me and I were you, I'd go and punch him on the nose for messing with my girl.'

'Oh? And what would that solve? The man's just perverted. He's more to be pitied than blamed. Just tell him you're leaving on Friday after you've been paid, and be sure to tell him why. That'll have much more effect.'

Henzey sighed, a great shuddering sigh. How could he not want to protect her from the depraved groping of Wally Bibb? She expected him to be nettled, at the very least, that Wally had succeeded in sliding his hands around the hallowed flesh of her breasts, where only he, Billy, was allowed. She could not understand why it did not incite him to absolute outrage. It would her if she were a man. She needed the reassurance of his love and of his protection, and felt that only some sort of retaliation would convince her of it. Perhaps he didn't love her as much as he said he did?

'Then that says to me as you don't care.'

'That's nonsense, Henzey, and you know it. You know I care, but me going to see Wally would serve no useful purpose at all. Even less being violent. Why, it'd bring me down to his level, don't you see that? The best way is what you suggest – leave, and find yourself another job. Let him see as you won't be messed with – that you're capable of makin' your own decisions – that you're strong enough to get out of there on a matter of principle. That's far better than having me or anybody else fight your battles. And it'll give you more self-respect and satisfaction. Anyway, you'd soon get another job, somebody as conscientious as you.'

She sighed again, half in exasperation, half in resignation. For a while she was quiet but, as she pondered his words, they made more sense. Perhaps she had been hasty and unfair in expecting him to jump at Wally Bibb. She leaned over and rested her head on his shoulder and his arm went about her.

'I'm sorry,' she whispered. 'I'll have to stop being such a cissy, won't I?'

They sat in a silent embrace for a long time while she dried her tears and watched the shadows of the trees grow longer, the warm, evening sunlight turn to a deep orange then to the shifting greyness of dusk. Billy lit another cigarette. Wood pigeons cooed as they settled for the night and magpies still squawked rowdily, as if to deny the others rest. While he smoked, Henzey relived a thousand times the abhorrent groping of Wally Bibb and compared them to the welcome caresses of Billy. What was it that made her relish the touch of one man and detest the touch of another? Was it because the one was uninvited, speculating that a stolen caress might turn her head? Or was it simply that she loved the one and loathed the other?

The unsettling of her emotions had driven out thoughts of romance that night, but as Billy began to hug her now and nuzzle her hair, she began to feel a warm stirring within her. He perceived it at once and kissed her softly on the lips. Eagerly, she responded, and her tension evaporated with every second of that embrace. Then he broke off to reach for the blanket lying on the back seat of the car. That action was a signal; the sort of signal a dog might respond to when shown its lead; a signal that meant it was time for lovemaking. Wordlessly, slavishly, she climbed out of the car. Billy placed the blanket on the dry grass at the side of the car in the murky dusk, and sat on it. When he stretched out his hand to her, she took it and sat beside him, smiling submissively.

They lay down and made love.

Henzey took the train from Dudley, following the Great Western line to Snow Hill Station in Birmingham, by way of

Dudley Port and Hockley. She did not heed the drab, industrial landscape that slid past the window of the compartment. Instead, she pondered the circumstances that had forced her to leave her job at George Mason's. She should have given a week's notice, but so adamant was she that she would not return to work again with Wally Bibb after that Friday, that he gave her a week's money in lieu and hoped there were no hard feelings. The other girls were sorry to see her go, but understood her reluctance to continue working there. It was a wrench for her, too. She had been close friends with them all, especially with Clara Maitland, but she could no longer tolerate the situation. Wally was making it impossible. All the time she had to be on her guard lest he stalk up behind her when she was working alone in the stockroom or in the office. It was an atmosphere she resented. Clara Maitland had even tried to talk to him about it, but he was contemptuous of her voicing any opinion and told her to mind her own business.

The train finally steamed into Snow Hill station. Henzey alighted, looking fresh in a printed cotton, sleeveless dress. The locomotive hissed deafeningly as she walked past it and she was glad to be up the wide steps from the platform and onto Colmore Row in the warm sunshine. In Corporation Street, she took a tram to Aston Cross, conscious of the bustle of the city.

She had imagined that a factory making sauce would not be a very grand affair, but the one that faced her, the one she was headed for, seemed enormous. Around it were shops and scores of other factories, large and small. Beyond them, she could see rows and rows of red-brick terraced houses, street after street, branching off from Aston Cross in all directions. It was like Kates Hill, but on an infinitely larger scale. Not only that, she could smell the rich, pungent smell of vinegar and spices, and it made her feel hungry.

This outing had resulted from an advertisement in the *Evening Mail* stating that there were a few vacancies for hard-working girls to operate new machinery at I IP Sauce Limited, at Aston. It promised above-average rates of pay. Applicants were to apply in person to the Personnel Department. Henzey had no job, and nothing to lose. She was shown to a waiting room where she sat with another girl of similar age, who was called in for her interview before they'd had a chance to get acquainted.

Ten minutes later Henzey herself was called, interviewed, and told she could have a job on a bottle-capping machine at twenty-two shillings a week if she could start on Monday. She could, and was instructed to report to a Mr Harman in Personnel at eight o'clock on Monday morning. Henzey could scarcely believe the pay. At Mason's she was earning thirteen shillings a week. Even taking into account train and tram fares she would still be lots better off, and she would have her Saturdays free. This had to be better than working in a shop with the manager trying to grope you at every turn.

On her way home, Henzey stopped for a cup of coffee at Lyon's café in Corporation Street, then called in Lewis's store to treat herself to some alluring new underwear and new shoes. She felt she could afford it. Never had she been in a store like it. The choice and quality of goods was astounding and she could have happily spent a week in there, just browsing. As it was, she spent more than she intended. But, as the afternoon wore on, she became anxious to get back home to tell everybody about her new job and the unbelievable wages.

Henzey started her new job on Monday, 19th August 1929. By coincidence she found herself travelling on the same train as her best friend from school, Florrie Shuker, who used this train every day. Since Billy had been courting Henzey, the girls hadn't seen much of each other and there was plenty of gossip to catch up on. Yes, Florrie had heard she was courting serious, but so was she now, to a chap called Oliver Priest, who was a toolsetter. They were planning to get engaged on Christmas Eve, Florrie's eighteenth birthday. Henzey could claim no such good fortune, however. The girls chatted incessantly till the train stopped at Hockley, where Florrie had to get off to go to Lucas's where she worked. They looked forward to travelling to Brum together every morning.

And then, the day they had all awaited with such a mixture of feelings came to pass. Henzey arrived home from her bottle capping on the evening of the 2nd October to find the house in turmoil. Jesse greeted her at the door, beaming. Her mother had given birth to a boy, seven pounds nine ounces, at ten past four that afternoon, and both were fine and beautiful. Henzey rushed upstairs eagerly to see the baby, to hold it for a little while and to give her mother a hug. They had decided to call him Richard.

Jesse was without doubt the proudest father that had ever lived. Until he and Lizzie had fallen in love he had given up all hope of ever being wed, let alone fathering a son. He would have been perfectly content simply as the stepfather of Lizzie's four children by Ben Kite. But this was another red-letter day in his life; a bonus more valuable than anything. For days, he went around euphorically, a smile fixed on his face. He told each and every customer, proudly, that his new wife had presented him with a son, and he gave them all an extra measure of milk in celebration. On the Friday night he went to find his friends in the local pubs and bought them all drinks before he stumbled home, contentedly drunk, plaiting his legs like a sailor on shore leave.

Getting up early and catching a train to work soon became a matter of course for Henzey and, before she knew it, autumn was upon them in all its red and gold glory. The mornings became progressively cooler and there were heavy dews. Most mornings she bought a newspaper from Wyman's at Snow Hill station, to read in her dinner break, but one morning, the 25th, a Friday, all the newspapers screamed a similar headline. Each and every one carried news about something they called the Wall Street Crash. When she saw Billy that night she asked him the significance of it and he said that nobody would know how it might affect Britain till the London Stock Exchange opened on Monday. He seemed very depressed about it, though.

Monday came, and feeling the first shock waves from the New York Stock Exchange, London share values plummeted. On Tuesday, Billy informed Henzey that he had lost almost every penny he'd ever made.

'I'm ruined,' he said, as they sat in his car in the yard at the dairy house. 'Unless I can pick up some commission soon I shall even have to sell the car. The prospects are bleak. Some of the deals I've already negotiated are in danger of being cancelled outright.'

'Oh, Billy, I'm so sorry,' she sighed. 'I've got a bit saved. You can have that if you need it.'

He smiled at her. Of course, she would give him everything she had and more. He knew that. But what she possessed, compared to what he had lost, was nothing. He was a worried man. Money was all. Money was the means to the finer things in life. He might have had a lowly upbringing, but money had given him a taste for refinement. Money had given him self-respect and the admiration of others. Money had elevated his social status, so that he now moved in higher circles. Money had brought him to the attention of some beautiful, wealthy women, some of whom he had enjoyed, others he was still enjoying. Eventually it might have brought him power, for he was ambitious to do well. There were those, of course, who envied him his new wealth and who denigrated him, saying that he must have trodden others underfoot in acquiring it. He dismissed their allegations with scorn, however.

'You're a kind soul, Henzey,' he said, and stroked her cheek, 'but what you've got ain't about to pay off my debts, nor restore what I've lost. I'm talking about thousands of pounds, my angel. Thousands. That five thousand I invested in Tennant Electrics was money I borrowed on the strength of my stocks and shares. Now those stocks and shares are worthless, but that five thousand still has to be paid back. If we can find no work for the factory, it'll go bankrupt. And so shall I.'

'So how much have you lost in stocks and shares?'

'Enough for us to get married in quite some style.'

'Married?'

'Enough to buy a big house . . . no, two big houses, and go on honeymoon for six months on one of those world cruises. Oh, and plenty more besides. Now it's bloody-well gone. The bleedin' lot, bar about five hundred quid. God, a paltry five hundred quid. It means starting all over again. But the way things are, there's a fat chance of that, I don't think.'

He had never mentioned marriage before and perhaps he should not have done so now, since it was merely a convenient way of illustrating how much he had lost. But it set Henzey's heart fluttering.

'I didn't know you were thinking of marriage, Billy,' she said quietly. 'You never said.'

'I know I never said, Henzey, because you're too young. Oh, in a couple of years, maybe, but not now. Not the way things are. I couldn't support you now.'

'But things'll pick up, Billy. Anyway, if we did get married I could support you. I work. I've got a good job. Other girls my age get married and still work.'

'Usually because they have to, Henzey. I wouldn't want that for you. I wouldn't want you to work if we ever got married. I'd want to be able to keep you comfortable, like a lady.'

She squeezed his hand. 'I wouldn't mind roughing it, Billy. I had to rough it before when my father was alive and so ill. We had nothing then, but we managed. I could do it again. At least we'd have each other.'

He shook his head. 'You're a treasure, Henzey. If I couldn't manage the best for you, then I'd subject you to nothing less.' He looked at his watch. 'Look, I'd better go. When shall I see you?'

'Tomorrow, if you like.'

'No, not tomorrow, my angel. There's some business I need to attend to. I'll see you on Saturday, eh?'

'Not till Saturday? I shall feel like a nun if I don't see you till Saturday. Shall you play golf on Saturday morning?'

'I doubt it. Not this week.'

'Come for your tea, then?'

'No, let's say half past seven.'

'Have I got to dress up to go dancing?'

'Yes. Bugger the expense. We'll go dancin'.'

For weeks Henzey secretly pined for what she thought was a missed opportunity to become Mrs Billy Witts. It started her thinking how he might be enticed into it after all. She considered asking him outright to marry her, so confident was she that she could afford to keep him if his business did not pick up. But she knew what he was like. He would run a mile. If there were to be any proposals Billy would be the one to make them, and only when it suited him. He was certainly not above being kept, that she also perceived, but there was no way she could hope to keep him in anything like the manner he wanted. He liked to smoke, cigars usually, to drink spirits; he could hardly give up his car, since that would be defeating his ability to find work. So his car had to be run. Then they would need a house to live in, so they would have to rent one. It would need to be furnished nicely and that, too, cost money. They would have to eat and Billy would never be happy with bread and dripping. He would still want to hobnob with his wealthy business friends and that would mean keeping up appearances. In short, he liked to spend freely.

What she failed to understand was that Billy was still drawing some commission for contracts previously negotiated. The motor industry was not closed down altogether because of the Depression. Merely it had slowed down. He was still earning some money, though at nowhere near the same level as before. That, however, was not enough.

Something else Henzey did not know was, that after the Crash, Billy had formulated a plan, and a contingency plan besides, to ensure his personal financial survival. Both were already well in hand and paying some early dividends on the nights he did not now see her.

Jesse had been right about how the girls would feel with a baby in the house. Each wanted to be the child's mother. While Lizzie fed him they would sit at her side mesmerised, watching the infant sucking gently at her breast. They took it in turns to change his napkins and to bath him, and debated at length whose likeness he had inherited. Herbert, Alice and Maxine all thought he resembled Lizzie. Henzey saucily said, while the child was lying naked on the table, exposing all, that right now he must look a bit like Jesse, then darted out of the way, laughing, before her mother could catch her.

If Richard awoke in the night, which he did every night for the first few weeks, the whole household would get up and rush around in disarray. Alice and Maxine even suggested that the crib be placed in their room so that they could tend to the baby in the night, and so give their mother a rest. Lizzie reminded them though, that they might have some difficulty feeding him if he was hungry. It was certain that this child was not going to be hard work with all the help that was available. Richard's brother and sisters were going to spoil him terribly, but Lizzie was happy. If anything, she felt guilty at having been so selfish early on in her pregnancy when she had regarded the prospect of another baby with horror.

Henzey adored her little half-brother. She took a delight in holding him over her shoulder to help get his wind up after he had been fed, and more than once had a shoulder flecked with vomit. She rocked him in her arms and sang softly to get him to sleep and, when he was asleep, was reluctant to put him in his crib. There was something wonderful about the smell of a new baby, and she could not define exactly what it was. All she knew was that it was appealing. She was also entranced by his tiny fingers, his tiny toes and the smooth, soft flesh of his little fat legs. And it seemed that there was something mysterious, if not sensual, about the way his lips suckled his mother's nipple. Secretly, while she watched, she wondered just what it was like to suckle a child, since it did not look unpleasant in the least. If she and Billy were to get married, when times were better, that would be her priority – a baby. She would love to have a baby in the security of marriage, in the contentment and comfort of their own love nest.

Chapter Eight

Billy called at the dairy house to collect Henzey one Saturday evening in January. He tapped on the verandah door before opening it and, having heard his car, she rushed out with her usual admiring smile to greet him. He, however, could scarcely look her in the eye. Lizzie was still at the sink washing crockery and his greeting for her was but a token raising of his hand. As soon as Henzey saw his expression she knew something was not right. She detected in him impatience and, worse, indifference. His attire was incongruous with what she believed was their destination, for he was wearing a formal dinner suit with cummerbund and bow tie, when she expected to be going dancing. As usual she looked striking, this time in a blue velvet, strapless dress, the same colour as her eyes; a dress that she had bought herself the previous day.

He looked her up and down. 'You look very nice.' His tone seemed to suggest that he found it unusual.

'Thanks. So do you.' She smiled again, but with uncertainty, trying to read what was on his mind. Things had been strained since the stock market crash and his moods had been mercurial. 'Are you taking me out to a restaurant, since you're wearing a dinner jacket?'

He shrugged, non-committally.

'I wish I'd known. I wouldn't have had any tea if I'd known.'

He glanced at his watch. 'Come on if you're ready. There's not much time.'

'I'll just grab my coat.'

'Have you got your key, madam?' Lizzie asked. 'I doubt if we'll still be up by the time you get back.'

Henzey kissed her mother goodbye. 'It's all right, I've got it.'

Out in the yard, in the bitter, winter wind, Henzey and Billy climbed aboard the car. She held her collar tight to her neck and shivered at the miserable, damp cold as he turned the Vauxhall around and drove out onto Cromwell Street. She looked at him earnestly, trying to read the grim expression on the handsome face she loved so much. He sensed her gaze but drove on coolly without acknowledging it; without saying a word.

By the time they arrived at the crossroads, where the Station Hotel overlooked the railway station, he still had not spoken.

'What's the matter, Billy?' Her plea was from the heart. She could stand neither the silence nor the indifference any longer. 'What's wrong? Please tell me what's wrong.'

He looked one way, then the other and, as the road was clear, instead of turning right as he would normally have done for Birmingham, he drove straight on, down the station drive.

'Where are we going?' she asked. 'Why are we stopping here?'

Above the rattle of the engine they heard a whistle blow in the station and a locomotive rasping asthmatically, its dense column of surging steam scattering in the wind as it strained to pull away from the platform and enter the long tunnel that exited at Blowers Green station a mile away. The carriages clanked together as the slack between the couplings was taken up.

Henzey reckoned it was time Billy answered her. 'Billy! Why don't you say something to me?'

He pulled on the handbrake and switched off the motor. 'All right . . . I've got something to tell you, Henzey.' He looked straight ahead through the car's windscreen and lit a cigarette. With increasing apprehension she watched him. Smoke from his cigarette drifted up, silhouetted against the light from the station. Some, appearing to escape his first inhalation, was sucked back into his tight-lipped mouth. Her heart was beating fast. Something monumental was about to unfold. He exhaled a great fog and drew on his cigarette again, intensely, as if buying time to choose his words extra carefully. She waited, her eyes watching his face, and shivered again with cold. 'I didn't want to say anything while we were at your house,' he said, his breath a mixture of steam and smoke that punctuated his words. 'But I have to tell you it's all over between us.' He glanced briefly at her to note her reaction.

She gasped, suddenly trembling, and stared blankly ahead at the windscreen that was starting to mist up, trying to grasp the meaning of his words. Only since Christmas had this unthinkable possibility crossed her mind, so sure was she that they would eventually wed. But events since had suggested that such an outcome was not a foregone conclusion. Their relationship had changed so much since the stock market crash. He'd seemed increasingly uninterested in her, aloof, and sometimes even terse, which had hurt her beyond measure. But, always believing unequivocally that she had his devout love, she silently forgave him and told herself his financial worries were the cause of it, and she should dutifully, subserviently understand.

'I see,' she said quietly, her heart pounding, her mind awhirl with shock and profound disappointment. 'No, that's a lie. I don't see, Billy . . . Why? . . . Why should it be all over between us? We love each other. I don't understand.'

'Because it's over.'

'But I thought you loved me. You've told me often enough.'

'Oh, I did love you, Henzey. I still do in a way, I suppose.'

'You suppose? Well if you suppose you still do, why do you say it's all over between us? I don't understand.' He remained silent and she prompted him for an answer. She could hardly let it rest there after all. 'Tell me, Billy. What's brought all this on? I think I have a right to know.'

'I'm about to tell you. But you're not going to like it . . .'

'Just tell me, Billy.'

'I'm getting married, Henzey.'

'Married?' she cried with incredulity. 'Married? Married to who?'

'To Nellie.'

She gasped, as if she'd been punched in the stomach. 'To Nellie Dewsbury?' Then she smiled in realisation. 'I don't believe you. You're just trying to kid me, aren't you? You're just testing me, to see how much I can take . . . Aren't you?'

He sucked ardently on his cigarette again and opened the quarterlight to let out smoke that was filling the car. 'No, I'm not testing you, Henzey. It's true. I'm getting married to Nellie. It's all arranged.'

In horror, she buried her head in her hands, trying to make sense of this calamity. 'Billy, you don't even like her. You said so yourself. So why are you marrying her? It doesn't make sense. It doesn't make any sense at all.'

'I'm marrying her because she's pregnant.'

'Oh, God! Are you saying you got her pregnant?' She watched him, waiting for his reply. But he said nothing. 'How do you know it's you that got her pregnant? It might have been somebody else.'

'No, it was me all right.'

He looked sad now, very serious, and she at once wondered whether marrying Nellie might be something he regretted having to do. It gave her renewed hope.

'Just because she's pregnant, it doesn't mean you have to marry her. You don't have to get married to her if you don't want to. Don't you understand that?'

'Henzey, it's not just because she's pregnant,' he sighed. 'I do happen to love the girl.'

'But you just said you still love me, Billy. How can you love us both? It's either one or the other.'

He shrugged, pulling on his cigarette. 'I've always thought a lot of you, Henzey, and I've enjoyed our times together. But before I was in love with you I was in love with Nellie . . . And we had a good time of it really. In the end she was the stronger pull.' He shrugged, as if further explanation was irrelevant.

'So you've been seeing her on the nights you didn't see me?'

'Something like that.'

'And you've made her pregnant . . . I can't believe it.'

'Oh, she's pregnant all right.'

'And that's why you're marrying her?'

'And because I love her.'

'You could marry me, Billy. You know I want us to get married. I've always wanted it. And I'd be a good wife to you, you know that. Better than Nellie Dewsbury. Anyway, how do you know I'm not pregnant? Or doesn't it matter if I am?' She thought she saw him smile, almost mocking, and felt deeply hurt by it.

'You're not pregnant, Henzey,' he scoffed. 'I know that much. If you are, it's not mine. I've been very careful with you. Very careful.'

At this insinuation she felt tears well up in her eyes, but her indignation forced them back. How could he think such a thing? 'Then let's hope you're right. Let's hope I'm not pregnant. But you've got a nerve suggesting it wouldn't be yours.' If only she *were* having his baby. Next to losing him, it was the greatest disappointment of her life that she was not, for then she would have some hope to cling to, something to fight Nellie Dewsbury with. But he was right; she was not pregnant and she was as certain of it as he. He had been very careful lately. So why on earth hadn't he exercised the same due care with *her*?

He held his wrist up to the light from outside and looked at his watch. 'I'll have to go.'

'Go then,' she said with a feeble attempt at indifference. But her heart was screaming out for him to take her in his arms, to tell her that he was just testing her after all. 'So where are you going all dressed up like that?'

'To a dinner party at the Dewsburys. I'm late already.'

'To celebrate your engagement I shouldn't be surprised.' Tears prickled her eyes again but she forced them back. In a sudden spurt of defiance she opened the car door and let herself out. 'Have a nice time,' she called, scarcely able to believe she'd torn herself away as she slammed it shut again.

It was biting cold, but as she began walking back up the station drive she hardly noticed it. She was hardly aware of where she was going, of what she was doing. She was, however, aware of him drawing alongside her in his car; of him opening the window and leaning over towards her.

'Get in, Henzey. I'll take you back home. Come on, get back in.'

'It doesn't matter,' she replied not yet fully comprehending why all this had happened. She tried to sound hurt and haughty, but all the time she was longing to get back into the car, to be with him. Only her injured pride was preventing her. 'You're late already. I don't want you to be even later on my account.'

'Come on. I shan't ask you again.'

She wanted to say that if ever he needed her he should send for her, that nothing should keep them apart, certainly not Nellie Dewsbury. But she could not bring herself to say it. Deep down she was aware he did not deserve such an offer.

'Come on, it's the least I can do.'

His voice seemed a long way away and she felt that her heart had spiralled into a deep chasm of loneliness, as if she were the only person left in the world, as if nobody cared for her, or ever would again. He didn't want her anymore but he was calling her back, as if giving her a lift home would appease his guilt.

'Oh, Billy,' she cried, very sadly, and felt tears that could no longer be stemmed stinging her eyes. 'The least you can do now is leave me alone. *Please?*'

He drove off.

*　　*　　*

It was about half past seven when she got out of bed. She put on her dressing-gown and stood shivering at the window that overlooked the back of the house and the field. Dawn was breaking, but daylight was still a drab, grey hour away. She heard Richard's infant voice as he cried to be fed, then a bump as her mother got out of bed to suckle him. Then all went quiet while his hunger was satisfied.

That dismal morning there was within Henzey a pain so deep that it seemed to emanate from some part of her too remote to have experienced feelings before. Never had she known such despair. There seemed to be an aching, throbbing void where her heart should be gently beating. She felt empty and desolate. Mentally she'd had no time to come to terms with this anguish. All her dreams had been shattered, all her hopes destroyed. Her life was in ruins and was not worth the living. It had crumbled, and lay in ashes.

Vacantly, she gazed out. Had she been able to see herself in the darkness she would have seen how pale she was, how her normally sparkling eyes were puffy and red. She took her saturated handkerchief and wiped her nose. She had cried so much, alone in the night, that she must surely have no more tears left to cry. Was it her own fault for thinking him so godlike and perfect? Had she been a fool for trusting him in the same way that she herself could be trusted? Because she trusted him so well, had she not brought this dark, sinister shadow of disillusionment upon herself? Maybe she had. But it was the principle of trust that mattered. It was that fundamental, basic ethic and its apparent lack of relevance to *him* that had really shaken her. He took her trust and betrayed it as if it never existed; as if it was of no significance whatsoever. This was the galling part. This was what really hurt deep inside. After her believing him to be perfect, he was not. Far from it, he had many faults, and would that she had recognised them long ago. His shortcomings would never have restrained her love, but an awareness of them might have enabled her to make some allowances, or given her at least some insight into the sort of deeds of which he was capable. She had her faults, too, and many they were, but betraying a trust was not one of them.

There was the possibility, of course, that this was all a horrible dream, that not a minute too soon she would wake up and all would be as it should be. But no. This was no dream. Nor even a nightmare. For nightmares ended. This trauma could go on forever.

She heard her mother cooing contentedly to the baby, then Jesse coughed and murmured something. A door opened on the landing; Jesse's bare feet padded on the oilcloth when he visited the bathroom; the bathroom door shut, quietly; intermittent trickling as Jesse's lengthy pee alternated between the sides of the pan and the water contained in it; then the amazing sound, as of somebody ripping a piece of best barathea, as he broke first wind of the day; the cistern flushed.

Henzey ignored the habitual sounds of morning and continued to look out of the window with this intolerable ache in her heart. Dawn was breaking so painfully. The happiness of the last ten months had vanished overnight. Now all she possessed of *him* were memories. Now she could only *imagine* him caressing her. He might as well have never existed. Never again would she thrill to his touch, nor feel the excitement of his kisses, nor indulge the yearning for his love. And that longing would take years to diminish, if ever.

Always she had commenced lovemaking with little thought for the likely consequences, such was her commitment to him. If she had become pregnant, then so be it; marriage would have been the remedy. At least that's how it had been until yesterday; or, rather, that's how she believed it had been. But what if she were pregnant after all, now that he had gone? What if she found out in a few weeks' time that she was indeed carrying his child? If only! She would endure it gladly. It would be nothing compared to this heartbreak. A child would at least be a part of him; a souvenir of that love which would doubtless last her lifetime. She searched her memory for occasions since her last monthly bleeding when she might have been at risk, but either he, or providence, had ordained that there were none. He had been extra careful. Each time they made love lately, he had used a sheath. In the beginning, of course, he had not, but lately, for some reason, which she had never questioned, he had.

An early blackbird stalked the stunted, winter grass of the field in search of his breakfast. He tapped the turf with his beak as if it were a trapdoor, then tugged at a worm when it answered. If only it were always that easy to get what you want, Henzey thought.

She became aware of the clammy cold creeping over her skin and she shivered. Her bare feet were like ice on the oilcloth, and her fingers were numb. She huddled inside her dressing-gown and quit the cheerless, misty view in favour of her bed. The bedclothes were still warm and she hunched under them again, desperately pining for her lost love, profoundly miserable, until she fell back to sleep and dreamed more of *him* and Nellie Dewsbury.

It was five to ten when her mother came into her room and woke her, carrying a cup of hot tea. Lizzie put down the tea at the side of the bed and flung open the curtains. Henzey stirred and frowned at the invading light.

'Come on, madam, rouse yourself,' Lizzie said. 'It's nearly ten.' Henzey sat up drowsily, reluctantly, and yawned, her hair bedraggled, her eyes still puffy and red. 'Whatever's the matter, our Henzey? You've been crying.' Henzey reached down for the cup of tea, asked how Richard was, avoiding her mother's eyes. But Lizzie was not to be sidetracked. 'What's the matter, my flower? Why've you been crying?'

Henzey sipped her hot tea and savoured its sweet warmth. It was like a warming elixir to her dry, dingy mouth, good to the taste, somehow regenerative. She gave a deep, shuddering sigh.

'Oh, it's *him*, Mom.'

'What about him?'

'We've finished.'

'Finished?'

Henzey nodded in confirmation and shrugged, sad-faced.

'Oh . . . I thought you'd come home early last night. Well, I can't say as I'm sorry, our Henzey. I was never that keen on him. He was too fly for you, my darling. Anyway, what happened? D'you want to tell me?'

'He's been seeing that Nellie Dewsbury again – the one he used to court before me – Councillor Dewsbury's daughter. He's put her in the family way.' She sighed again.

'He's what?'

She placed her cup of tea down, still avoiding her mother's eyes. 'Oh, you heard me right, Mom. She's in the family way.'

Lizzie's face was a mask of resentment. 'Oh, my flower, what a dirty trick. I can see you're hurt, our Henzey. I am sorry.' Despite her dislike of Billy, Lizzie could not help but sympathise with her daughter, since it had been obvious all along that she was besotted. And yet she felt a great relief that he was out of her life.

'Of course I'm hurt, Mom. I idolised him. I trusted him.'

'I know,' she said comfortingly. 'And I daresay the hurt will last a month or two. But it won't last forever, believe me. We've all been through the mill, our Henzey, and we all have to go through it at some time or other. If we had no bad times we wouldn't appreciate the good times. I went through it enough with your father. More than three years of torture I had with him away in the war, God bless him, not knowing whether he was dead or alive from one day to the next.'

Henzey nodded. Having tasted real love herself she could at last appreciate the torment her mother had suffered. 'Did it make you cry, Mom?'

'Our Henzey, my heart would break a hundred times a day. Every time I thought of him, imagining him shot, lying dead in some filthy, muddy trench; frightened to answer the door in case it was a telegram.'

She shook her head in sympathy, trying to imagine it. But it did not make her own situation any more tolerable. It did not make the raw wound in her soul any easier to bear.

Henzey broke down again in a flood of tears. 'It doesn't help knowing he's been lying with her in her bed when I trusted him. He knew how I felt about him, Mom. Why did he have to do that? Wasn't I good enough for him?'

'Not good enough for him? Huh! Too good, I should say.' Lizzie put a consoling arm around Henzey's shoulders and felt her shake with sobbing. 'There's worse could happen. What if you were pregnant yourself?'

'You need have no fear.'

'Lucky for him then, else there'd be hell to pay. He'd think his father's firecoal had come.'

Henzey saw it differently. Had she been pregnant she might now be making plans for her own wedding, instead of being tormented by Nellie's. They were silent for a few minutes while Henzey wiped her tears and blew her nose, trying to regain some composure.

Lizzie tightened her lips in agitation. What Billy had done came as no great surprise, but it sickened her all the same. She said, 'I knew he'd bring you heartache. At first he seemed all right, but it didn't take me long to see what he was really like. Count your blessings, my girl, that you're free of him. He'll be no good to any woman, and that includes Nellie Dewsbury. If one woman isn't enough, twenty aren't too many. You're best off without him, take it from me.'

'But I love him, Mom.' The tears flowed again with renewed vigour. 'I love him and I can't help it. And I was that sure he loved me . . . I still believe he loves me. I really can't understand why he's done it.' She wiped her eyes again to stem another flood of tears. 'He always said he loved me. I know he meant it.'

'He told you he loved you 'cause you looked good on his arm, my flower. If he really loved you, why did he do that? Why's he been having it off with Councillor Dewsbury's daughter?'

Henzey shook her head. 'I don't know why. I wish I did.'
'I bet I know.'

Henzey looked up at Lizzie through a haze of tears. 'Why
d'you reckon he's done it then?'

'Money. It's obvious. You've got no money, our Henzey. The
Dewsburys have.'

Henzey pondered hard her rejection while Lizzie continued
to console her. In the beginning they, Henzey and he, were so
engrossed in each other that the prospect of a child would merely
have accelerated a marriage, of that she was sure, even though the
possibility had remained unspoken. A love child would have
been so romantic, too; so romantic that they could have overlooked any social denigration. But why had he started to see
Nellie again? Was it really money? Was it because he was broke
and needed her to get back in the financial swim? If so, there had
to be the intention on his part of making her pregnant. That, in
turn, must eliminate the possibility of him fathering a child
elsewhere, since if she, Henzey, also became pregnant it would
foil his plan and thus his future. Perhaps that was why he had
begun to use those French letters.

It was beginning to make sense.

Ever since the stock market crashed last October she might
have seen this heartbreak coming, but she was not of a cynical
enough nature to have spotted it. To insinuate himself with
Nellie and her family was the only way he saw of securing his
financial future, and to put Nellie in the family way made his
position rock solid. Henzey began to wonder whether he realised
it was a short-sighted view, recalling what he had told her of her
moods and tantrums. Perhaps she had been the biggest fool that
ever wore a pair of shoes for believing she could compete with
Nellie. Nellie came from a wealthy family; had had a privileged
education; boasted incomparable looks and elegance. So, despite
her failings, she still had plenty going for her.

And now she had him back again. *Him*, whose name she
could not even bring herself to think about anymore, let alone

say, so acutely did it distress her. To crown it all, he told her that after this last ten wonderful months, when he professed his love countless times, it was Nellie he was really in love with after all.

Last night she had been too shocked, too dazed to cry. It was not till she had walked back home and immediately gone to her room, that she shed the first tear. But God alone knew how long it would be before she would cease crying.

She could have been happy with him forever. He satisfied every emotion, every itch, every craving. No other man could ever take his place. Even now, after what he had done, she still loved him hopelessly and would gladly take him back if he renounced Nellie. The child he would still have to maintain, but she could even countenance that if she could only have him back. Perhaps she should have let him know that. But last night she could not think. It had all been too sudden. It had all been totally unexpected.

Lizzie said, 'Well, he's really shown himself up for what he is, our Henzey. Perhaps you don't see it right now, and perhaps you won't see it for a month or two, but take it from me, you'll get over it and you'll thank God above for sparing you a life of misery with him.'

'Instead, I'm due for a life of misery without him.'

'But he's no good for you and you're best off without him. You're sensitive, our Henzey, and he's a fly-by-night. He didn't deserve you. Let him have his rich fancy piece. But one thing's for sure — he'll get his comeuppance one day. You know what they say — marry the miskin for the muck and be poisoned by the stink of it. Money won't make him happy, our Henzey. You'll see — before long you'll meet a nice young chap who'll look after you. Somebody decent, somebody more your own age.'

'I don't want anybody else, Mom,' she wept. 'Specially my own age.'

'Come on. Dry your tears and come and have some breakfast. The others all had theirs an hour ago.'

'All right. But please don't tell anybody yet what's happened. I'll tell them myself in my own good time.'

'My flower, they'll only have to look at you to know there's something amiss.'

Chapter Nine

Three months after Henzey's break up with *him* the heartache was still as intense, but the depression she had grown used to as her tolerance of it increased. She thought about him constantly and had lost weight, fretting and pining. Only now was she coming to terms with it. She reached her nadir when she saw his wedding photograph and a report of the event in the *Dudley Herald*. She cried buckets over that. It should have been herself in the photograph.

Many men at the HP sauce factory had asked her out, including one or two of the married ones, but she politely turned them all down. She was not interested in other men. The only man she wanted was *him* and now he was wed to her rival. It even occurred to her that maybe Nellie might miscarry, and then he would return to her arms and all would be as it was, so certain was she that he had truly loved her and not the girl he'd married. It even crossed her mind that she could have an extra-marital affair with him. That would serve to spite Nellie as well. But, as time wore on, Henzey dismissed that idea; it had to be all or nothing; and gradually she was resigning herself to the certainty that it must be the latter.

She avoided going to the Palais in Dudley, to the roller-skating rink, or anywhere that she might see him with his new bride, though friends had offered to take her. But the last thing she wanted was to see him under those circumstances. If she could see him alone, that would be different, but to see him out with *her* on his arm would only bring back all the heartache. It just wasn't worth it. So most nights she stayed at home and drew, and listened to the wireless.

'Have you seen anythin' o' Billy lately?' Florrie Shuker asked Henzey.

They were waiting among a host of other people at Dudley Port station for the train to take them into work. It was a bright but nippy morning in early May, with white clouds easing themselves across a pale sky. A chill breeze blew through the station like it would through a corridor.

'Nothing at all.' Henzey turned her back to the breeze. 'I wouldn't want to see him now, either. I've got used to being without him this last three months. If I were to see him again it would upset me.'

'D'you still love him, then?'

'I suppose I do. Even after what he did across me. But at least I can see clearly enough what a rotter he really was. I'd have been a bit more wary if I'd known what he was really like. I'll never get caught like that again, I can promise you.'

'What about other chaps, Henzey? Ain't there nobody else as yer fancy?'

Henzey pulled the collar of her coat up to shield herself from the funnelling wind. 'Oh, I can look at a man now and think how nice he is. For the first two months I couldn't even do that. Every time I looked at somebody I'd compare him with *him*, and then turn away, moping. So I'm making *some* progress.'

'What about goin' out with other chaps? Has anybody asked yer?'

She shrugged. 'One or two. But I'm not interested. If I went out with anybody I don't think I'd be very good company. It wouldn't be fair. I'm still a bit raw, Florrie.'

In the distance they heard the harsh, rasping breath of the approaching locomotive, which was hauling the train that would take them to Birmingham. Those nearest the edge of the platform instinctively moved back a step, while those standing at the rear shuffled forward. Henzey turned and saw the white plume of steam from the engine's funnel and heard its hoarse gasps slowing as it decelerated. As it drew closer and grew louder she braced herself, putting her fingers to her ears to shut out the deafening hiss and roar. This hideous noise as it rumbled past her was the only part of the routine of working in Birmingham that she dreaded. The buffers clanged randomly as the coaches nudged each other before coming to rest. The doors were opened, and a few passengers alighted with their pleasant 'Good mornings', followed by an orderly boarding by those waiting.

Every morning brought Florrie and Henzey into a compartment with somebody fresh, and this morning was no different. When they first started travelling, the sight of complete strangers sitting with them usually inhibited conversation, but now, seasoned commuters, it made no difference and conversation flowed as if there were no other people about. Florrie, sitting directly opposite Henzey, took off her gloves and put them in her bag. Unconsciously, she stretched her left hand out on her lap and gazed fondly at her engagement ring while they waited for the train to start, till she realised it was a tactless thing to do in front of Henzey. But Henzey had not noticed. She had caught the eye of a smartly dressed man of about forty-five who wore a bowler hat, a dark grey overcoat over pinstripe trousers and an immaculate, white collar with a sombre, maroon tie. He smiled at her from the facing seat, though he was at the opposite end to Florrie. Henzey was used to men smiling at her. She smiled back politely as a whistle blew outside and the train steadily pulled away.

'Oliver's got a mate he works with, who ain't courtin',' Florrie commented, continuing the conversation they'd begun outside. 'Why don't yet let us fix y'up with 'im for Saturday night? The four of us could go out together, dancin' or somethin'. He's ever so nice. He'll do anythin' for a lark. You'd like 'im, Henzey.'

'Oh, I'd rather not, Florrie. You might think he's nice, but I might not.'

'Oh, go on. It can't do no 'arm. It'd be a change for yer. It'd do yer good to get out, wun't it? An' anyway, you might like 'im after all. Even if yer don't, there's nothin' lost.'

Henzey shook her head. 'Thanks for the offer, Florrie, but I don't feel like meeting anybody. Not yet. Ask me in another month or two. Perhaps I'll feel a bit more like it then.'

'I tell you what,' Florrie went on, undaunted. 'Say you'll come out with us an' I'll tell yer somethin' as might be to your advantage.'

Henzey laughed and glanced self-consciously at the well-dressed man. He was still looking at her, fascinated. 'Oh, Florrie, you're not going to give up, are you? What could you know that might be to my advantage?'

'Say you'll come out with Fred an' Oliver an' me, an' I'll tell yer. You'll kill me if I don't tell yer, but I don't care. You've got to promise to go out with us first.'

Henzey was intrigued. But she had to earn the knowledge she was being offered, and earn it in a way she was not altogether prepared for.

'And if I do promise, then you'll tell me?'

'I'll tell yer straight away. It's somethin' you'll be really interested in, honest.'

'To do with what?'

'Never mind what it's to do with. Just say as you'll go out with Fred.'

It was turning into a game and she was enjoying it, like they used to when they were at school.

'Fred who? What's his surname?'

'Parker. Fred Parker. Honest, Henzey, he's ever so nice. I know you'll like 'im.'

Henzey's curiosity got the better of her. 'All right, then.

Saturday night, but no strings, no promises. Just don't expect me to fall in love with this Fred Parker. Now what is it that I should know that's going to change my life, eh?'

Florrie leaned forward as if to impart a great secret. 'I 'appen to know as Lucas's, am gunna tek on a few workers in a new bit o' the factory at Great King Street where I work. You said to let yer know when there was any jobs goin', didn't yer?'

The man opposite seemed to take a great interest in what they were saying. He said nothing, of course, but Henzey sensed his curiosity; and he had ceased smiling.

'Honest? What's the work?'

'I 'eard as we've got a new order from Ford's to make dynamos and starters, so they'm settin' up a new shop.'

'Yes, I am interested, Florrie. What's the wages?'

'On piecework you could earn over thirty bob a week, I reckon. An' they'm a good firm to work for, an' all. They don't 'alf look after yer.'

'What do I have to do to be considered?'

'I'd just go along to the personnel department if I were you. They'll ask you to fill an application form in, I expect. Then it's up to you.'

'But I've never done work like that — assembling. Is it hard?'

'I'd never done it when I started, but it's easy. You get really quick in no time.'

'Will you be working in that department, Florrie? It'd be nice if we could work together.'

'I work in a different department makin' headlamps. Trouble is, there's talk of short time. Anybody who gets laid off in other departments ought to get jobs makin' these dynamos. That's only fair, in't it? So I should look sharp, Henzey.'

'I don't know what to do. There's still full-time working at the Sauce. It'd be daft to leave and find myself on short time in a new job. I like my job really.'

'I bet most o' the folks on this train am goin' to Lucas's,'

Florrie said. 'It's a massive place. I bet there's ten thousand or more work there.'

'I'll see if I can finish work at dinnertime. I'll call at Lucas's this afternoon. I can at least find out what's on offer.'

Henzey turned to look out of the carriage window to her left. Again, the man in the dark grey overcoat caught her eye. He wore a smile but was looking straight ahead at a photograph, in a frame below the luggage rack, of the promenade at New Brighton.

'Now we've got that out the way we'd better arrange about Saturday night, hadn't we?' Florrie said.

As dinnertime drew closer, Henzey feigned sickness and told her supervisor that she felt unwell. The supervisor agreed that she did not look too good, which brought a wry smile to Henzey's face. If she didn't feel any better by the time the hooter went, she was to go home. So she found herself in the bustle of jostling people, all leaving work at the same time to go to their dinners or do some shopping, or even taking advantage of the break to do a spot of courting. There was a queue for the tram. When it arrived she managed to get on it and stood on the rear platform the whole way, holding tightly on to the rail. In the city centre she wandered up and down Corporation Street looking in shop windows to kill time, entering the occasional store, and ended up buying a new skirt and blouse.

Just before two o'clock she took another tram to Hockley and walked to Great King Street, lined on either side with houses and little shops with canvas awnings pulled out over the windows. Henzey was torn between her present job and the prospect of a new job at Lucas's. Both had advantages. The Lucas factory was easier and cheaper to get to, being just a short walk from Hockley station. To get to HP she had to travel on to Snow Hill, then take the tram to Aston. But at HP she was more certain of full-time work, when many were being laid off due to the Depression.

The Lucas factory was an imposing pair of five-storey buildings, split symmetrically down the middle by Great King Street, yet linked by a footbridge. Henzey approached the twin façades with increasing curiosity. She looked at it all in awe, and thought it might be rather nice to be a part of all this; to be just a small fish in a very big pond. Many times she had heard from Florrie of all the social activities that went on, and decided it might be an appropriate time to join in one or two. So the prospect of working there began to appeal.

As she reached the factory she stopped, looking around her, wondering where to go. A commissionaire with a friendly smile appeared and asked if she was lost. She told him she was seeking the Personnel Department and he pointed to the main entrance. After thanking him she set off again. Inside, a smartly dressed girl, somewhat older than herself, asked if she could help.

Henzey smiled. 'I've called about a job. I think I'm supposed to go to the Personnel Department.'

The girl looked her up and down. 'Do you have an appointment?'

'Oh, no. If I can't see anybody today I thought I might be able to get an application form.'

The girl looked her up and down and smiled mysteriously. 'Just a moment, please.' She picked up the telephone at her right hand, dialled a number, and after a few seconds said, 'Mr Cherrington, I think the young lady you were expecting has arrived . . . Yes, she's here in reception.' Then, to Henzey: 'What's your name, please?' She told her. 'Henzey Kite, Mr Cherrington . . . Very well.' She put the telephone receiver back in its cradle and asked Henzey to take a seat. Mr Cherrington would be along in a few minutes.

'But nobody's expecting me,' she said. 'I think you've made a mistake.'

'Well, if I have, make the most of it, Miss Kite,' the girl said with a wink.

She did as she was bid and sat on one of the fine leather

upholstered chairs in the corner of the large reception area, and looked about her. The walls were clad in dark panelled oak, and a portrait, an old photograph, of the bearded Joseph Lucas, the founder of the company, hung almost facing her, looking very severe. In glass cases many of the company's past and present products were exhibited. People came and went, dashing between offices, from one side of the road to the other, and she wondered if there really were ten thousand people employed here. It seemed an awful lot.

As she looked about her, contemplating the irony of working in a firm making car accessories when it was also *his* line of business, Henzey didn't see a tall man of about forty-five walk towards her wearing pinstriped trousers and black jacket, immaculate white shirt and collar and a sombre, maroon tie.

'Miss Kite?'

He startled her a little.

'Oh . . . Yes? . . . Sorry, I was looking at all those things in the glass cabinets.'

He smiled, and she returned the smile. She had seen that smile before. It was the same benign smile she'd seen in the train that morning. Its owner offered his hand, genteelly.

'Very glad you came, Miss Kite. I've been looking forward to meeting you all day.'

'You heard my friend and me talking in the train this morning.' She put her hands to her face. 'Oh, I'm so embarrassed.'

He laughed kindly. 'I couldn't help but overhear. So you thought you'd come and see if Lucas Electrical is all it's cracked up to be, eh? Well, I'm in charge of recruitment. Come to my office, eh? We can have a chat and you can tell me all about yourself. Bring your shopping bag with you . . . You've bought something nice?'

'Just a new skirt and blouse,' she said, following him.

He led her outside, across the street and along one side of the building, into his tidy, well-laid-out office. He invited her to sit in the chair facing his desk and, when she was seated, he sat down himself. He took a form from a drawer, a fountain pen from his inside pocket, and looked at her while he unscrewed the cap.

'I was so sure you'd come after I heard your conversation in the train that I described you to the ladies in reception,' he confessed. 'I must have given them a fairly accurate description, eh?' He smiled again. 'Anyway, we had a little bet between ourselves as to whether or not you'd turn up. Happily, I won, didn't I? I shall be two shillings better off as a result. Now, Miss Kite. You're obviously interested in working here. Tell me a bit about yourself. First, your address.'

She told him, and he began writing it all down. She answered all his questions candidly about her previous employment; why she had left; her schooling; her hobbies; about her family.

'Let me tell you a little bit about the job,' he said when he'd finished writing. 'Your friend was right when she said we're due to open a new department to manufacture dynamos and starters for Ford. Incidentally, I don't know your friend. You can't possibly hope to know everyone in a factory this size, of course.'

'Yes, I see that.'

'This new department will be a self-contained factory in its own right, but I'm not certain that handling dynamos and starter motors will quite suit a girl like you. They're heavy, you know, and whilst winding the armatures is not such heavy work, it requires some experience. I take it you've not had to wind any armatures before?'

She shook her head and smiled, and he smiled too.

'What about your friend? What department does she work in, do you know?'

'She assembles headlamps, if that's anything to go on.'

'Pioos, Morris, Standard Motors, Wolseley, Hillman, Rover, Humber, Riley?'

'I don't know.'

'What's her name and we'll look her up?'

'Florence May Shuker.'

Mr Cherrington picked up the telephone on his desk, dialled a number, and requested Florrie's file. To Henzey, he said, 'If I can find you a job working with her, would you like that?'

'Oh, I would. But I've not done that sort of work before. I don't know if I could do it.'

'It's easy enough. It's the sort of work that suits girls — naturally more adept at it than men, although there are some men working on the headlamp lines, and very good they are, too. It's clean work and you can earn good money. Lucas are proud to pay some of the best rates in Birmingham, you know, but in return we expect loyalty and dedication to the job.'

'Oh, I'm very conscientious, Mr Cherrington. But Florrie — Miss Shuker — says the factory might go on short time. How much money could I expect to make then?'

'It depends how nimble you are at your work, but working a full five-day week you could earn up to thirty shillings. On four days, which seems likely in the present economic climate, about twenty-four shillings if you're good. Unfortunately we've shed a few people in that department already but, on top of that, others have left to get married, have babies and so on, which quite honestly you can't account for. Consequently, we're actually short of girls there. We've cut too near the bone, in other words. Strictly speaking I shouldn't be recruiting anybody, but I can make out a perfectly good case for it. As far as I'm concerned, Miss Kite, you're exactly the sort of girl we like to recruit here: neat and tidy, obviously loyal, conscientious, as you say, and a very pleasant and unassuming personality, if I may say so.'

Henzey smiled demurely. 'Thank you, Mr Cherrington. It's kind of you to say so. I think I'd like to give it a try. I'm sure I could fit in. Florrie — Miss Shuker — says there are a lot of Black Country girls here. You must be from the Black Country yourself, as you were on the train this morning.'

'Oh, I live in Sedgley. You know it?'

'Yes, we go through it on the way to Wolverhampton.'

Somebody knocked at the door and entered. A woman of

about thirty-five handed him a folder. 'Florence May Shuker, Mr Cherrington.'

'Thank you, Miss Smart.' Miss Smart departed and Mr Cherrington studied the file. 'Your friend works on the Morris line. That is actually rather understaffed. When could you start, Miss Kite?'

'A week on Monday, if that's all right.'

'Perfect. Come in with Miss Shuker a week on Monday. She can take you to your department manager. He'll be expecting you. In the meantime I'll write confirming your appointment.'

She thanked him, stood up to go, and he came quickly from behind his desk and opened the door for her.

'Goodbye, Miss Kite, and the best of luck. I shall certainly keep an eye on your progress. Oh . . . and the best of luck with Fred on Saturday night!'

'Oh, that won't amount to much,' she said, blushing.

Indeed, Saturday night was not a great success as far as Fred Parker was concerned. He turned out to be an affable sort of chap, and was considerate. He had been sufficiently primed about the traumas in Henzey's recent life to expect no great success with her, but he liked her all the same. When he asked if he could take her out another time, just the two of them, she politely excused herself. He did not appeal greatly to Henzey, although she enjoyed the evening at the Palais in Dudley. There, she saw many of the friends she hadn't seen for a while, some of whom were principally *his* friends. It was little comfort to know they all considered *he'd* made a big mistake in forsaking her for the unmentionable Nellie. Marjorie Lycett, one of the girls she'd got to know well, told her she was best off without *him*, and even congratulated her in finding out about *him* before it was much too late. That made her feel a bit better, and she began to believe at last, that there was some truth in what everybody was saying.

✳   ✳   ✳

Lucas's was the start of a new way of life for Henzey, and a new way of approaching work. The work force was extremely loyal and everybody worked hard. She found it stimulating to be a part of such a well-organised establishment, especially so in view of the thousands of people who worked there. In no time she got used to assembling headlamps for Morris cars, earning as much as Florrie who had been doing the job for considerably longer, and she was quickly accepted by the other women on the line.

The works canteen was not the only place they spent their dinner breaks, since Henzey would enthral her new workmates by drawing pencil sketches of them in the works itself. It became a feature of dinnertime and people would book up, sometimes a week in advance, to have their portrait done. As a subject sat facing her, a group of ten or even twenty would gather behind her, watching the likeness develop, greatly admiring her talent.

Gradually, Henzey's fame spread throughout the factory and she was asked if the joint managing directors, Peter Bennett and Oliver Lucas, known affectionately as 'The Bing Boys', could sit for her. Henzey said of course she would be privileged to draw them and arrangements were made accordingly. The portraits were to be done in the Board Room and each could only allow an hour at most, due to their busy schedules. It transpired that she needed only about forty-five minutes to complete each of the two astonishingly accurate drawings, and the two chiefs were so thrilled that they promised to arrange an exhibition of her work in the canteen.

Thereafter, some of the lesser management, in their turn, requested the same for themselves. So when time permitted, Henzey obliged, and she got to know many of the departmental managers and foremen because of it. Her artistic talent was turning her into quite a celebrity.

Then, one dinnertime in early September, she received a more unusual request. A deputation of girls from the Product Development Department asked if she would draw a portrait of their manager, Will Parish. It was soon to be the sixth anniversary of his appointment to the position. The only problem was that the portrait was to be a surprise, so there was no question of him being able to sit for her. All the girls could offer were a couple of photographs, one of him alone, just head and shoulders; the other, not so new, showed him smiling happily with a pretty young woman on his arm. Henzey accepted the challenge but asked if there was some way she could get a look at him in the flesh, to assess the structure of his face and detect any mannerisms that might help to represent him more accurately on paper.

'Why not come with us now to our workshop?' one of the girls suggested. 'He's eatin' his sandwiches in his office. If yer pretend you'm payin' a social call on us he won't twig it, an' you can get a good look at him.'

So they set off briskly through the factory, Henzey having slipped the photos into the pocket of her overall. When they reached the department they all gathered round a copy of *Woman and Home*, which one of the girls took from her basket and pretended to discuss some new fashion idea that was illustrated. Henzey carefully placed herself so that she could look directly into the office to get a good view of Will Parish who, by now, had finished his sandwiches and was reading a newspaper. She was concerned that she could not get a proper look at his eyes while they were cast downwards, but the girls' persistent giggling drew his attention. He looked up at them, smiling with curiosity. Henzey detected a soulfulness in his eyes that seemed vaguely familiar.

'What are you lot up to?' he asked good-naturedly.

'Nothin', Will,' one of them, Sarah Ball, answered. 'We was just lookin' at a picture of a girl in a bathing costume. Want to 'ave a look?' She raised the magazine up to him so he could see it.

'Oh, very tasty,' he said. 'Fancy you lot looking at pictures of girls. I'd have thought Jack Buchanan would've been more up your street.'

'We don't need photos of the likes of 'im when we've got you to look at all day, Will,' Sarah laughed. 'You'm a lot more 'andsomer than that Jack Buchanan.'

There was an instant chorus of agreement that turned into laughter.

'I've never heard such flannel. You all after a rise?' He smiled again and returned to his newspaper.

'Seen enough?' Sarah whispered to Henzey.

Henzey nodded. 'He seems nice.'

'Oh, he's real nice, is Will,' Sarah replied as they all trooped out. 'He's a smashin' gaffer. We think the world of 'im. D'ya think you can do 'im all right now?'

'I'll do my best.'

When the girls had left her and she was sitting on the line next to Florrie she thought about Will Parish. There was something about his eyes that was hauntingly familiar and it was bothering her. There was such a look of sorrow in them; or was she just imagining it? Oh, superficially he seemed happy enough but, deep down, she perceived something more. She took out the photographs from her pocket and looked at them again. Yes, there was a sort of sadness in his eyes shadowing the warmth of his expression, even when he smiled, which she must try to capture in her drawing. She slid the photos back into her overall pocket and continued with her work, her thoughts still with him.

'You'm quiet, Henzey,' Florrie commented after an hour.

'I was just thinking.'

'Not about that Billy Witts again?'

'No, not this time, Florrie.'

Chapter Ten

Henzey was not entirely satisfied with her first effort of the drawing she'd been commissioned to do of Will Parish. Somehow the expression she had captured lacked the openness she perceived when she saw him in the flesh. She had rendered the eyes too deep-set, the expression too cold, soulless. It bore a resemblance, but it was not right. So she turned to a clean sheet in her sketchpad to begin again.

Alice drifted downstairs and into the room. She looked a picture in a sleeveless dress of green cotton. Over her arm was a matching green jacket. Her hair nowadays was fashionably cut in the shingle, with little flat curls at the nape of her neck. She was sixteen and a fine-looking girl. Jesse glanced at her and thought that, apart from the hairstyle, she was the image of her mother at the same age; even her eyes had the same look of vitality and devilment. She seemed to have quickly grown up into a young woman; a canny, wily young woman at that, seemingly wise to the world and its ways.

'Jack Harper tonight again, is it?' Henzey taunted, looking up from her work.

Alice blushed. 'So?' There was defiance in her voice.

'Twice last week, once the week before, and last Saturday night.'

'Oh! You been keepin' a tally, then?'

'Well, we can't help but notice, can we, Mom? Serious is it? You'll have me jealous, our Alice.'

'You had your chance,' Alice retorted acidly. Jack Harper was hers now. She felt like telling Henzey to keep her distance, not to encroach.

'Oh, don't be so touchy. I was only pulling your leg. I was never that taken with him, but I'm first to admit he's decent company – even if he is a bit old for you.'

'Oh, hark who's talkin'. Billy Witts was nearly old enough to be your father.'

Alice was convinced that ever since Henzey had broken up with Billy she would be glad to get back with Jack Harper. It was a misapprehension, distorted by her own heightened emotions. Just because she was besotted with Jack herself and had been from the moment she first saw him, she believed Henzey couldn't fail to be also. Thus, she was possessive, resentful, feeling the sort of mistrust you would expect from an earnest rival, not a devoted sister.

Henzey chuckled, unable to take Alice's fervour seriously. 'It seems we all like older men, Alice. Even mother. Look how content she is since she married Jesse.'

Lizzie, rocking Richard in her arms, tutted at her daughters. 'Try arguing a bit quieter,' she said in a hushed voice. 'The baby's nearly asleep now. For God's sake don't disturb him.'

Henzey moved round, trying to position herself so that more light fell on her drawing. She sighed, got up from the table and turned up the gaslight. 'That's better. I can see what I'm doing now.'

'Who's that you'm drawin'?' Alice enquired, relieved that perhaps it was a new boyfriend she had mentioned nothing about yet. She peered inquisitively at the photographs from which Henzey was working.

'He's from work. The girls who work for him want to surprise him with it.'

'That his wife?'

Henzey was shading the area under the bridge of the nose. 'I expect so.'

'Shame,' Alice exclaimed cynically. 'He looks just the right age for you.'

'Hadn't you better hurry if you're meeting Jack Harper? You know how he frets if you're late.'

'Oh, shut up, Henzey,' Alice snapped. 'You'm only jealous.'

Alice was all too aware that her older sister knew all about Jack's quirks. Alice wanted to find them out for herself, however. Part of the joy of being in love with somebody was watching how all their ways unfolded, like reading a novel and seeing the story develop. It was irritating being told beforehand how he would behave, like somebody telling you how the story ended when you were just getting into it.

Alice had suffered her young girl's infatuation for Jack ever since Henzey first brought him home to meet her mother. Now, at last, he was paying attention to her. Since she had been working at George Mason's they had stopped to talk a few times while she walked past the shoe shop where he worked. An observer would have beheld more than a spark of interest between them. Three weeks ago they had arranged to meet and Alice had been thrilled. But she was so sensitive to Jack's past association with Henzey, that she turned him into a stumbling-block between herself and her sister, impeding their usual accord. But it was only in Alice's mind. Henzey was as yet unaware of Alice's increasing fear and resentment. Certainly she would not wish to fuel it, even if she had known about it. If she had not been so concerned with other things she might easily have spotted it.

'I'm off now, then,' Alice said. 'Ta-ra.'

'Mind your time in, madam,' Lizzie remarked. 'Half past ten and no later . . . And mind what you're up to.'

Henzey smiled to herself and recommenced her work. She placed a faint cross on the page as a guide for this new attempt at this Will Parish, inclining it a little more this time; a trick she'd learnt that would help to give it more vitality; the line from left to right was the axis for the eyes. The eyes were the most important feature; get them right and everything else would fall into place. The right eye: yes, draw the top eyelid just a little heavier and not quite so arched; now faint creases at the outer corner . . . Better. The eyeball; just over half the iris visible below the eyelid; some delicate shading below that top eyelid; the lashes, long for a man. Oh, yes, much better. Those faint creases at the outer corner again: perhaps not quite so faint. Yes, a little more pronounced; that emphasised the look of sincerity. The eyebrow; going straight from the centre; slanting down slightly as it reached the side of the face. Yes, that's it . . . That's it. Nice eyes for a man; eloquent; expressive. And so familiar. So strangely familiar. Now the left eye; build it up in the same way. Another look at the photograph . . . no, there's no perfect symmetry, but there rarely is in a face. A few pencil strokes; the half-circle of the iris; leave a highlight . . . Yes, it's coming. Tone down the white of the eye more. Yes . . . Oh, yes. She smiled to herself. There was no joy quite like the joy of self-satisfaction at getting something absolutely right.

Now the nose; another look at the photograph; where does the nose fall in relation to the mouth and the eyes? Right. A couple of faint lines to show where the mouth must be. This is a fine nose; not too big, not too small; straight, which somehow gives him the look of someone highborn . . . Yes, this is going well. Now the mouth . . . masculine, sensuous curves; lips, neither thick nor thin, but right for the rest of the face; the bottom lip slightly fuller than the top one . . . a clean-looking mouth. She always admired a clean mouth in a man and here was no exception. These lips she could have enjoyed kissing. God, had it been so long since she'd been kissed? . . . He was almost smiling; a melancholy smile, as if hiding some inner, deep-rooted emotions.

It was all coming together nicely. The forehead; dignified, patrician, straight almost to the hairline, and only then did it begin to sweep back. . .The cheeks; cheekbones high; highlights here, hollowed slightly below that, which made him look lean and athletic . . . The chin; proud, noble, strong, complimenting the set of the mouth . . . Now the hair; slightly wavy, swept back, no parting; capture that sheen; a full head of hair . . . The ears; fine, like the nose, well shaped, neither big nor small.

Henzey had learned, through all her years of drawing, that real beauty emanated from features that were of moderate size. Too big a nose, too small a mouth, bulging eyes, chin too weak or too prominent, all marred a person's looks. Each element of the face had to be without extremes. And yet, that in itself was not enough, for all those separate elements had to combine together well to provide beauty. None of us could choose our face, nor its arrangement, save for accentuating this or enhancing that with make-up – so long as you were a woman, of course. You had to accept what God gave you and make the best of it.

But, as she looked at this portrait she was finishing, she suddenly realised that it was as handsome a face, by those rules, as any she had ever seen. It did not strike her thus when first she saw him, but now, having studied it intensely, it did. In her eyes it was an astonishingly beautiful, manly face.

Henzey heard the verandah door open and the scuffing sound of Jesse wiping his feet as he returned from settling the horses. She looked up at her mother. Richard was now fast asleep in her arms, settled at last.

'Shall I take him up for you, Mom?'

'You'd best not for fear of waking him. I'll take him up myself in a minute or two. How's your picture coming on?'

She held it up for Lizzie to see. 'I think it's one of the best I've ever done. I'm ever so pleased with it.'

Sarah Ball and the other girls from Product Development were delighted with the portrait of Will Parish and they wanted to know how much they owed Henzey. She declined any money, but they pressed five shillings on her that they'd collected. Her brother, Sarah said, made picture frames and he was going to frame this one for them. Henzey said she would like to see it when it was done, so they invited her along to the presentation.

On the day of the presentation, Florrie said she was going to the canteen for her dinner with other girls from the line, because cottage pie was on the menu and she loved cottage pie. So Henzey made her way alone to meet Sarah and the others. When she arrived, Will was eating his sandwiches in his office, reading his newspaper, oblivious to their plot. While they waited, they stood around, talking, laughing with some of the men of that department, highly qualified engineers mostly. Eventually, Will finished eating and Sarah went to his door and asked him to step into the workshop.

She said, 'We've got something for you, Will.' From a drawer in a cabinet at her right, she drew out a flat, rectangular parcel and offered it him. 'Here, it's from all of us, the men as well. Happy anniversary.'

He scratched his head self-consciously and took it, smiling that melancholy smile Henzey had succeeded in capturing. 'Well, thanks. Fancy you lot remembering this anniversary.' He removed the paper, fearing that a joke of some sort was being perpetrated. But when he saw it was a framed drawing of himself he held it up in front of him and looked at it intently. Then, still smiling, he looked at the girls. 'It's fantastic. Even I can see it's like me. Did that girl from Lighting do it, who did "The Bing Boys"?'

'Yes,' Sarah said. 'And she's here.' She introduced Henzey.

Will regarded her for a moment. 'It's a magnificent drawing, Henzey. I shall always treasure it. It's quite a talent you have. Thank you for drawing me so accurately. But how did you do it? I obviously didn't sit for you, did I?'

Henzey blushed at being spoken to for the first time by this man whom she had secretly, intimately pondered. She hoped he did not have the ability to read her private thoughts, especially as she had thought how nice and kissable his lips were. Being so closely involved with a good-looking male subject sometimes made her feel like that. But this was a married man.

'The girls gave me two photos to work from, but I did come to have a look at you one day.' Her face reddened more with her confession and she laughed self-consciously. 'I think I was lucky to be able to draw you so accurately.'

'It strikes me you're too modest, Miss. It's more accurate than any photograph. I look at this and think you must have seen into my soul. It's uncanny. Anyway, I understand they're putting on an exhibition of your work in the canteen in a couple of weeks.'

She nodded. 'Mr Oliver Lucas arranged it through Mr Cherrington in Personnel. All the folk I've done portraits for have agreed to let me borrow them for the exhibition. I've got some other work, watercolours and things I've done at home over the past few years, that I'll include as well.'

'Then you must also include this.'

'Well, I'd love to if you don't mind. I think it's one of my best. Thanks for the offer. Thanks ever so much, Mr Parish.'

'You're more than welcome. First, though, I'll have a day or two with it at home – just to admire the quality of your work.'

She thanked him once more and went on her way. Will Parish watched her go. Sarah said, 'She's a nice girl, in't she?'

'Mmm, she's lovely.'

That night, at home, Henzey went to her room and looked through her old sketchbooks to decide which pieces of work, if any, would be suitable for her exhibition. Among the very old ones were drawings of her father she had done when she was little more than a child. She lingered over them, recalling the happy times she'd spent with him. He would sit for her, holding an expression for ages, till he grew tired and would ask how long she was going to be. Only another minute, she would say, then press on, trying to get this or that right. Although most of these drawings were not technically good, and hence, unsuitable to show in the canteen, they were priceless, because when she looked at them she relived such precious times. There were sketches, too, of all the family. Watercolours of streets on Kates Hill and lots more besides that she could include. There were charcoal drawings, not very good; pen and ink drawings of Jack Harper – Alice could take her pick of those. One of Stanley Dando, her mother's second cousin – her heart skipped a beat when she saw it, for she always secretly fancied her Uncle Stanley. Then an ideal portrait of Uncle Joe came to light in which his rough and ready, but good as gold character, was evident.

Some drawings of Billy Witts came to light, including the one that had been hanging on her bedroom wall, and her heart seemed to turn a somersault. But the drawings she had completed of Will Parish were still fresh in her mind and she could vividly remember that look of honesty and that sad, haunting smile of his.

Then, when she compared the portrait of Billy, something really surprised her; she knew she had drawn him accurately, but there was no equivalent look of tenderness, of compassion, of openness that she had captured in Will Parish. Rather, the expressions she caught in every picture of Billy suggested guile, conceit, and self-regard, as if he believed the world was interested in looking only at him.

But only now did she recognise it; only now, when she made this comparison.

How strange! His true character had been evident all the time in her own drawings. From the start, she had represented him on paper as he really was. Why hadn't she seen him as he really was when her subconscious evidently had? It was there for all to see. It was in the eyes; the eyes, which enable you to see out but allow others to see in, deep into the soul. If only we knew how to interpret what we saw.

Billy Witts. *Him.* Still, after nine months, she yearned for him. Oh, he was a rotter, for sure, she accepted that now. But she had loved him with all her heart. She loved him now, if she was honest with herself. No doubt she always would. If he appeared at the verandah door tonight she would fall into his arms, married or not. She would never get him out of her system. But it did not hurt anymore and she could laugh again, even though she still wanted him enough to deny the advances of any other man. Even now she recoiled if another man touched her. But for some months she had been able to look at men and actually quite fancied one or two. So maybe she was getting over it. The trouble was, she did not want anybody else. She did not need anybody else. Her love was still focused and it would take either an extraordinary man to re-focus it, or a great deal more time to heal her broken heart.

From all the older work she picked out about twenty that she thought reflected her current ability. The rest would come from the pictures done of people at work; and they were more appropriate since they would be of more interest to her audience. But all these pictures needed mounting in some way. Certainly she could not afford to have them all framed, but some sort of mount for each was vital. It would be tedious doing it, but it ought to be done.

Having sorted her work to her satisfaction she went downstairs. Jesse was telling Lizzie that he had been to price a van for the business, but there was nothing really suitable so he had decided to buy another horse and float instead. And would she remind Herbert to take the accumulator for the wireless to be charged up? It was too heavy for any of the girls to carry.

Lizzie said she would. 'And I'd best go across the road and see how Beccy Crump is. I wouldn't be surprised if she's broken her arm. That's the trouble with falling down those steep stairs in those houses. She was in such a lot of pain. It's really knocked her about. I took her some dinner and a cup of tea earlier, but that new family, the Tomlins, who've moved into our old house, have been nowhere near. They're about as much use as a yard and a half of pump water.'

'Have you sent for the doctor?' Jesse asked.

'No, but I ought to. I'll send for him tomorrow. I reckon she'll have to have her arm set in plaster. May's going round in the morning, but I said I'd go and see to her later.'

'I'll go,' Henzey offered. 'About what time, though?'

'No later than ten. The back door'll be open.'

Henzey looked at the clock. It was half past nine. 'I'll go now,' she said. 'I can have a chat with her. There's no point trying to do anything more with these pictures tonight.'

Outside, the sky was clear and the bright, three-quarter moon seemed to afford more light than the feeble street lamps. As her mother had said, Beccy's back door was not locked. It was seldom locked. As Henzey entered in the darkness she heard the cat mewing. She picked her way over to the hearth and felt on the mantelpiece for a box of matches. She lit the gaslight and announced with a shout to Beccy that she was in the house. The cat rubbed itself against her legs, so she squatted down and stroked it, whispering soft words. It purred contentedly. Its bowl, lying on the floor by the fender, was empty. From the pantry at the top of the cellar Henzey took the jug of milk and sniffed it. It was fresh, so she rinsed the bowl out in the brewhouse, returned and filled it with the milk. 'There,' she said. 'I bet you were thirsty with nobody to look after you all day.' The cat lapped it straight away.

Henzey lit an oil lamp and took it upstairs to light her way. Beccy greeted her from her bed when she reached the top of the scrubbed stairs.

'I've come to say good night and tuck you up, Beccy. How's your arm?'

'By God, it's givin' me some gyp, young Henzey. I'm sure I'n bosted it. 'Ere, look. It's all swelled up like a great big polony.'

'Ooh, it looks ever so painful. We'll get the doctor in tomorrow. It'll need setting.'

Beccy nodded her consent. 'I'm clammed to jeth an' all. Not a thing's passed me lips since your mother come in earlier an' brought me a pork sandwich. I thought May would've bin round afore now. I could bost a conga eel an' a few chips.'

'May's coming in the morning, Beccy. But I'll fetch you some fish and chips from Iky's, if you like. Would you like me to make you a cup of tea first?'

'Yes, I would, my flower. God bless yer.'

So Henzey went down again and made them both a cup of tea, boiling the water on a portable gas ring.

When she returned, Beccy said, 'Henzey, cost 'elp me get me stays off, my wench? They'm a-diggin' into me summat vile. After I fell over I dai' feel like gettin' 'em off. Me legs was all of a wamble. But I'll 'ave to get 'em off now afore they squeege the life out o' me. Trouble is, I cor' undo 'em with just one 'and.'

Beccy pushed the bedclothes back and lifted up her night-gown with her good hand. Henzey was amused to see that she was still wearing an enormous pair of thick navy-blue bloomers over her stays, big enough to accommodate herself and her mother. She tugged them down, half a yard of material at a time it seemed, and they both started to laugh at the absurdity of the situation. Beccy struggled to raise herself to make it easier, till Henzey had them round her ankles and off. Breathless with laughter they undid her stays, peeled the rigid garment off, and Henzey watched the old lady's belly find its normal roundness, like dough rising, stretch marks and all. Beccy had a good scratch round with her good hand and blew her cheeks out with relief, while Henzey removed Beccy's garters and rolled her stockings down.

'Look at me, young Henzey, I'm like a little tunky pig,' she chuckled.

'Are you sure you still want the conga eel and chips, then?'

'By God, I do. There's no point me worryin' about me figure at my age. Hark, yo'll find a shillin' in me puss on the mantel-shelf downstairs.'

So out Henzey went. When Iky Bottlebrush knew the order was for Beccy, typically, he wouldn't accept any money; he'd heard about her fall and was anxious to know how she was. Ten minutes later, when Henzey unwrapped the conga eel and chips, they smelt divine and she couldn't resist pinching one or two as she passed them to Beccy.

'Best I'n ever 'ad,' the old lady declared as she finished the last bit. 'He knows how to fry fish an' chips, that Iky . . . Henzey, my wench, if yo' goo downstairs yo'll find a bottle o' stout on the shelf the top o' the cellar steps. Tek the top off for me, will yer, an' bring me a glass? It'll 'elp me sleep.'

Henzey gladly did as she was asked. She stayed till Beccy had finished the stout and used the jeroboam. Then she tucked her up in bed, gave her a kiss on the cheek and went back downstairs. She let the cat out, put the light out, and shut the door behind her. Then she walked back to the dairy house. It was nearly half past ten.

She was just about to open the verandah door to go in when she thought she heard a voice. It sounded like a child whimpering, being hurt. Ramsbottom and Clement were restless in their stables; they were blowing and she could hear them clomping about fretfully on their straw. Henzey stopped and listened. There was the sound again. It was certainly not the horses. It was a girl's voice, moaning soulfully, coming from the direction of the old brewhouse. Henzey took off her shoes so as not to be heard, and walked silently in stockinged feet up the yard to investigate. After a few yards she stopped in her tracks. The moonlight presented her with a sight she never expected to see in a thousand years. Jack Harper had his back towards her, his trousers round his ankles. Alice's bare legs were wrapped about him, her skirt up round her waist, her bare backside cupped in his hands, evidently relishing every moment. She was pressed against the back wall of the brewhouse for support, while he thrust into her like a rampant stallion.

No wonder the horses were restless.

Chapter Eleven

For days Henzey could not rid herself of the image of Jack Harper and Alice in the moonlight. It was not that she cared for him, but she cared deeply for her younger sister, despite the animosity that had come between them over him. The first opportunity to caution her on her foolishness presented itself the following Saturday. Henzey had been shopping in the town in the afternoon and, just prior to closing time, had gone into George Mason's to say hello to Clara Maitland and the rest of her old workmates, so as to catch up on gossip. It seemed a good idea to wait for Alice; while they were walking home she could broach the subject. Jack Harper was there to meet her, too, as welcome as a blue-bottle on a pork chop as far as Henzey was concerned, but he soon left to catch his tram. The girls walked without speaking for five minutes, though it seemed like an hour. Till Henzey broke the strained silence.

'Our Alice, there's something I want to say to you, if you promise you won't get the wrong idea.'

'Oh? What about?' Alice swapped the string bag full of groceries she was carrying to her other hand.

'I called to see Beccy Crump the other night, before she had her wrist in plaster. As I came back through the yard I saw you and Jack against the old brewhouse door.'

'You have to say good night somewhere.'

'Course you do. But do you have to say good night with his trousers round his ankles and your skirt up round your waist?'

'What are you talkin' about, Henzey?'

'Oh, spare us the pretence, Alice.'

'You're jealous, that's all.'

Henzey sighed with frustration. 'Alice, I'm not jealous, I swear. What you do is your own business, but don't you think you ought to be a bit more careful where you do it? What if Mother had seen you, or Jesse?'

'They wouldn't have done. We'd have heard 'em.'

'But you didn't hear me. And you didn't hear me because you were too engrossed in what you were doing. I heard you grunting and groaning and I thought it was a child or somebody, hurt and in trouble. That's why I went to see what it was. That's when I saw you. Why should *you* hear anybody?'

Alice shrugged nonchalantly. 'You'm right. What I do is me own business. An' next time don't stand an' watch. Who d'you think you are? You make me sick lately, just 'cause you used to go out with some flash creep with plenty money. An' he was only too happy to get rid of you when he knew what you was really like. But you ain't too proud to watch me an' Jack, are you?'

The reference to Billy jilting her was hurtful but Henzey tried not to let it show. Alice had changed beyond recognition. She was no longer the soft-spoken, shy little girl she had known all her life. Now there seemed to be an unbridgeable gap between them; a gulf too wide to cross. Her usual sullenness apart, she showed no hostility to any other member of the family and she was reasonably affable with the staff of George Mason's. It had to be because of Jack Harper and what Henzey had meant to him in the past. It had to be jealousy. There was no other explanation.

'Alice, what's got into you? Why are you so resentful towards me?'

'You keep pokin' your nose where it ain't wanted. Why don't you mind your own business? Just because you ain't got nobody now.'

Henzey's anger flared. Alice's arguments were puerile and contemptible.

'I haven't got anybody because I don't want anybody. And I've got no interest whatsoever in your pathetic Jack Harper. As far as I'm concerned he's yours and you're welcome to him. He's welcome to you, as well, and all your snide remarks. But let me tell you this for your own good, whether you take any notice or not. I know what you're like. You've been nothing but a wanton little trollop ever since I caught you with that George at Andrew Dewsbury's party two years ago. I was sick with worry for you then, but I don't give a damn what you do now. But spare a thought for Mother and what she might have to go through. If you're not careful, you'll get pregnant. You could even catch the clap. So just be careful, for your own good.'

Alice looked at her with scorn. 'Do you think I'm so stupid as to get pregnant? Do you think I don't know how to stop gettin' pregnant? Do you think I don't know about the clap and the pox? You think you know everythin', Henzey Kite. But I'll tell you what – you ain't got a clue about one thing.'

'Really! So what don't I know?'

'Oh, just that George wouldn't have been the first,' she said indifferently.

'I'm not surprised. You sound as if you're dying to tell me who was.'

'I am . . . It was Jack.' She smiled vindictively. 'While you were goin' out with him.'

Henzey laughed with contempt. Alice was lying, of course, trying to stir up trouble. It was becoming more and more evident that she was capable of such things. But, even if what she said were true, Henzey couldn't have cared less.

Not another word passed between them as they walked home, but somehow Henzey's anger evaporated. Alice was still just a young, impressionable, immature girl, despite her sexual precociousness.

*   *   *

Two days before her exhibition was due to be shown in the works canteen, Henzey received a message from her supervisor that Mr Cherrington in Personnel wanted to see her. She duly left her post and made her way to the offices. When she knocked on his door he called her in, and they exchanged pleasantries.

He said, 'About your exhibition in the canteen, Miss Kite — do you have all the work available that you want to show?'

'All but one,' she answered. 'Mr Parish said he would let me borrow one I did of him, but so far I've heard nothing.'

'Should I remind him for you?'

'Oh, no, thank you. I don't want to press him. He knows the exhibition's on. If he wants me to have it he'll send it, I'm sure.'

'Fair enough. Now — the only time available to set it up is Saturday morning. It'll be quieter then. Is that convenient?'

'Oh, yes. I can get here at my usual time.'

'I'll arrange for a couple of lads from the Maintenance Department to help you. They will have all the materials and tools.'

And so Saturday morning arrived and, true to his word, Mr Cherrington had arranged for two lads from the Maintenance Department to be there. They looked after the mechanics of hanging the pictures while Henzey chose where and how they should be positioned. Her drawing of Will Parish had still not arrived, and she was bitterly disappointed.

'Yo 'int bin t'our shop to draw any o' we,' the taller and more confident lad, called Matthew, remarked. He then clouted his thumb with his hammer and uttered a string of expletives that were largely unintelligible to Henzey. The thumb evidently began to throb, and he sucked it for a few seconds, a frown on his face. His pained expression was incongruous to the image he was evidently trying to cultivate, with his hair well greased with Brylcreem and the Ronald Colman moustache. Henzey smiled to herself. 'Y'oughta come, ya know,' he continued, smiling cockily again, trying to ignore his thumb. 'We got some roight charicters in minetenance, oi can tell ya.'

'I bet,' Henzey said. 'But I only do these drawings in my spare time. I don't think I'd have time to do everybody in the Maintenance Department.'

Matthew glanced knowingly at Arthur Warrender, his younger colleague, and winked. 'Well ya can do me any toime ya loike, gal. Even better out o' wairkin' hours, eh? Tell yer what — I'll tek yer owver the Lickeys tomorra if ya loike, an' ya could do me then, eh? The Lickeys'd mek a smashin' backdrop for a pikcha.'

'A nice idea,' she replied, hiding her true thoughts. 'I bet you'd be a great subject.'

Slowly the pictures went up on the walls, liberally inter-spersed with innuendo from Matthew, aided and abetted by Arthur. It all quietly amused Henzey.

The canteen was open to serve those who were working on Saturday morning and, when their break time arrived, she bought Matthew and Arthur a cup of tea each to wash down their bacon and egg sandwiches. They sat together, and Henzey was sub-jected to a further barrage of suggestive comments and not a few overblown compliments, especially when more of their work-mates arrived.

The door opened on the other side of the canteen and she turned to see who it was. At once she stood up.

'Mr Parish! I thought you'd forgotten. I didn't expect to see you this morning.'

He smiled as he approached, carrying a flat parcel. 'No, I hadn't forgotten, Henzey.'

'As you can see, we've made some progress.'

'Well, I thought if I waited till you were putting the exhibition up I might be able to help. I seldom come in here to eat, so it's likely I would've missed the whole thing . . . So here I am, come for a private showing. I hope you don't mind.'

'Of course I don't mind.'

'Here's the drawing. I hope I'm not too late with it. I hope you can still find space.'

He handed her the package while the two lads looked at each other, indignant that their attempts to impress this jewel were being threatened. Matthew thought he was entitled to Henzey's full attention during his break and his face bore a look of resentment that someone else was now encroaching.

Henzey opened up the parcel and laid it on the table. The two lads peered at it bumptiously.

'That '*im*?' Arthur enquired of Matthew with a nudge. He nodded at the drawing, then at Will.

'No, don't be darft. It's too good-lookin' for 'im.'

Henzey seethed at their insensitivity and appalling manners. 'I'll fetch you a cup of tea, Mr Parish. Why don't you all introduce yourselves while I'm gone?'

While she went to the counter, Will indeed introduced himself as the manager of Product Development and told them how well he got on with their boss. Matthew picked up his mug, told Arthur they were to get on with their job straight away, and downed his tea quickly.

Will Parish stayed to help and his presence seemed to temper the brashness of the two younger helpmates. He stood, admiring Henzey's work, and remarked how much like the subject this or that drawing was, and asked how long it took to do this or that watercolour? It was mid-day when they finished hanging the pictures. Henzey thanked them all, took her coat from the back of one of the chairs and declared that she was going home.

'Wharrabout Sund'y, then,' Matthew reminded Henzey as he picked up his toolbag to go.

'Oh, I don't think I can, after all,' Henzey replied with a plausible smile, donning her coat. 'Some other time, maybe.'

Will smiled as the two young men left. 'A conquest, eh?'

She laughed. 'I might call it that if I were interested. He's not really my type.'

'It wouldn't do for us all to like the same type, I suppose . . . Which way are you going, Henzey?'

'Hockley station.'

'D'you mind if I walk with you? Hockley station's on my way home. Perhaps you'd let me take you for a cup of tea first? Away from here, I mean . . . if you've got a minute or two to spare.'

She looked at the clock. 'Well, my next train isn't due for a while.'

'Is that a yes?'

'Yes, all right. Thank you.'

'Good. I know a smashing little place in Great Hampton Street, not far from the station. We could get a bite to eat there, too, if you're hungry.'

'I'm sure that would be very nice,' she answered affably. 'As long as you won't get into trouble with your wife.' She turned to take one last look at her work, expecting him to reply to this comment, but no reply came. So to disguise what she imagined must have sounded like prying, she quickly said, 'My first exhibition. A moment to be proud of, I suppose. Doesn't look too bad, does it, Mr Parish?'

'I'm really impressed. I recognise most of these people. It speaks volumes for your ability. And by the way, please call me Will. Everybody else does.'

As they walked along Great King Street they made small talk, about the weather, about the worsening economy in general and the effect it would have on Lucas's in particular. He mentioned some of the new products they were developing in his department.

'Sorry, Henzey. I'm talking shop,' he said, realising that he might be boring her.

'Oh, I don't mind. You make it all sound very interesting. It must be an interesting department to work in. All these new-fangled things.'

'Oh, there's always something new coming up.'

They entered a café on Great Hampton Street, a bustling road that led directly into the city, and took the only vacant table. The place was clean and inviting. The walls were decorated with a pale blue, patterned wallpaper, clean blue table cloths adorned the tables and net curtains, tied in the middle, embellished the large window like a row of white sheaves. Henzey declined anything to eat, so Will ordered just a pot of tea for two. She said he was not to go without something to eat just because she didn't want anything, but he claimed he could wait till he got home.

'Where is home, Will?' she enquired.

'Ladywood. Ten or fifteen minutes' walk from here.'

'I don't think I've ever been to Ladywood. Is it nice?'

He laughed. 'I wouldn't call it especially picturesque, although it has its interesting bits. There are some nice churches. St John's is a lovely church. I got married there. I sing in the choir there, as well. Then there's the Monument in Waterworks Road – that great tall tower. Have you seen it? Built as a folly, it was. There's the reservoir as well – it's quite pretty round there in summer.'

'The reservoir? That rings a bell. And the tall tower. Is that where the Tower Ballroom is?'

He nodded.

'Oh, I have been to Ladywood, then. I've been to the Tower Ballroom lots of times. But I thought that was in Edgbaston.'

'Part of the reservoir is, I think. I expect they say the ballroom's in Edgbaston to make it sound more posh.'

An elderly waitress delivered their tea and Will thanked her.

'So where do you live, Henzey?'

'Dudley.'

His eyes lit up. 'Fancy that. I was born in Dudley.'

Henzey lifted the lid off the pot and stirred the tea. 'But you don't have a Dudley accent,' she said.

'Well, neither do you.'

'Oh, I do.' She laughed, comfortable with this Will Parish. 'When I say something like, "I don't think I've ever been to Ladywood", for instance, my voice goes up at the end of the sentence. See?'

'But it's not pronounced.'

'I suppose you can't help the way you speak, but I became very self-conscious of my accent, especially when I was among the people I was mixing with. So I made a real effort to try and change it. Occasionally I lapse, though – especially if I fly into a temper or something.'

'So what sort of people were you mixing with? If I'm not prying, of course.'

'Well, I used to go out with this chap called Billy Witts. He worked for himself, selling to the motor industry, and did quite well till the stock market crashed . . . But that's another story . . . Anyway, he knew some wealthy and influential people and he used to take me along to meet them. Dinners and garden parties and things. Some were really posh, really classy, and I felt so out of my depth that at first I'd hardly speak because of my accent. Then I decided I was as good as them and I realised I could speak nicely too, if I really tried.'

'So this Billy is in the past?'

'Yes. We split up . . .' She smiled self-consciously. 'I'll pour the tea now, shall I? . . . Why are you smiling?'

'The tea. Don't you think it'll still be a bit on the weak side? She's only just brought it.'

'Well, let's try it anyhow.' She lifted the pot and poured a few spots into Will's cup to assess the colour. 'Does that look all right?'

'Perfect.' He was aware she was embarrassed, that she did not want to speak about this Billy Witts. 'No doubt you have another young man now – a lovely-looking girl like you.'

She filled his cup, feeling her colour rise. 'No. I don't really want anybody, either. To tell you the truth I'm still smarting a bit over him. But you won't want to hear about that.'

'No, not if you don't want to talk about it.'

'Oh, it's not that. I mean I don't want to bore you.' She filled her own cup, then added the milk.

'I doubt if I'll be bored, Henzey. I'd love to know about this Billy. You must have loved him dearly.'

'Yes . . . I loved him too dearly . . . Far too dearly.'

She opened up her heart about Billy Witts, about his ways, his foibles, how she felt about him, how he had lost his money and how she came to regard him as a rat. Will Parish listened intently, his eyes fixed on hers, hypnotised.

'So, you see,' she explained, 'to get back into the money, he made this Nellie Dewsbury pregnant. Now they're married and have a little daughter. It hurt me a lot at the time, I can tell you.'

'Good God, I can well imagine. But do you reckon he's happy now?'

She shrugged with indifference. 'It's not my concern. He wasn't happy with her before.'

'He's a fool, Henzey.' Will sipped his tea, then added: 'As a dog returneth to his vomit, so a fool returneth to his folly . . . *Proverbs.*'

She met his eyes and smiled. 'Oh, he had his reasons which were valid enough as far as he was concerned. It just seemed very callous to me.'

'You're still very loyal.'

'Soft, more like. Anyway, enough of Billy Witts and me. What about you? I don't know anything about you, except that you're married and live in Ladywood. And here I am, baring my soul as if I've known you all my life.'

'Well, may I correct you on one thing, Henzey? Unfortunately, I don't have a wife any longer. She died five years ago . . . In childbirth.'

Henzey felt greatly embarrassed. 'Oh, Will, I'm so sorry. Me and my big mouth. I wouldn't have mentioned it . . .'

'You weren't to know. Don't worry. I'm over it now. But like you, at first I was devastated.'

'How old were you then?'

'Twenty-five. I'm thirty now.'

As Henzey held her teacup in front of her with both hands she studied Will's face again. There was that pleasant but melancholy smile. No wonder there was an innate sadness in his soft brown eyes. He must have suffered dreadfully. Who knows what heartache he must have endured? Who knows to what extent he'd been scarred inside? And she had been bemoaning her own insignificant suffering at the hands of Billy Witts. She felt such a fraud. Her troubles were nothing compared to his. Her heart went out to him. He seemed such a genteel person; so pleasant, so affable, so inoffensive. Why did the most awful things seem to happen to the nicest people? What had he done to deserve such grief?

'What about the baby?'

'It was a boy. Still-born.'

'Will, I shouldn't have asked such questions. I had no right.' She put down her cup and shuffled uncomfortably. 'I didn't realise, Will. I'm ever so sorry.'

He reached out and touched her hand, briefly, as a reassurance that it was all right. 'Please, Henzey, don't apologise. I'm quite happy to talk about it. Everybody believes it's a taboo subject, so I never get the chance. At first that was understandable, but nobody ever mentions Dorothy now. I welcome the opportunity to talk about her.'

'I'd love to hear about her, Will.'

'Well . . . Dorothy was the sun and the moon and the stars to me. I adored her. Still do. She was a teacher, two years younger than me. We met at a wedding and I think we both fell in love straight away.' He laughed a little as he recalled it, that laugh expressing more than a thousand words. 'She was the sister of a friend of the bridegroom. We were introduced and we spent the rest of the time there in each other's company. Afterwards, I walked her home and we arranged to meet again. I was afraid of losing her so, just to make certain she would turn up, I gave her the fob watch I was wearing on my waistcoat, which actually belonged to my father. I wanted it back of course. It was just my way of ensuring that I saw her again. The watch was gold and I remember thinking, "If she doesn't turn up, I'll be in such a pickle with the old man".'

'But she did.'

He smiled. 'Yes, she did. And from then on we began to see each other regularly. She was at Dudley Training College in the beginning. She left shortly after and found a job teaching infants at the Osler Street School, just round the corner from your Tower Ballroom. We married in January 1923. I was already working at Lucas's then, so it seemed logical to find a house in the Ladywood area, which we did. Two and a half years later, she was dead.'

Will sighed and that sad, soulful look returned.

'I won't ask if you were happy,' Henzey said quietly. 'You obviously were.'

He nodded, looking into his teacup. 'We were very happy in the short time we had together.' Then he paused and looked into her eyes. 'But who knows whether we would always have been happy? People change, don't they? You can marry and be very happy but, if you both change, and in different directions, then things start to fall apart. I've seen it happen a good many times. It could have happened to Dorothy and me. Who knows?'

'But when a couple get married, isn't it for better or worse? Isn't that a wedding vow? So isn't it a wife's duty, more even than a man's, to honour him, to support him, morally — to go in the same direction as him — and so avoid such difficulties?'

'Perhaps . . . in principle. But in practice it sometimes requires the virtues of a saint for one person to put up with another, however much in love they might have been in the beginning.'

'Losing the child must have been a double blow.'

'Dorothy suspected the child had died because she hadn't felt it move for a couple of weeks. Then the doctor confirmed it. It was that that caused the problem, really. The actual birth was traumatic for her . . . just too much.' He shook his head as the memory of it all overwhelmed him. 'I don't understand all the technicalities of what went wrong . . . We wanted that child . . . She suffered too much . . . She died the next day.'

Henzey watched his eyes well up with tears for a second then looked away, filling both their cups again to divert her own attention. Will smiled and thanked her.

She said, 'But it must have been dreadful for you, Will. I can't imagine that much suffering – that much heartbreak.'

'It *was* fairly trying.'

'And what about now? Do you have a lady friend now?'

'No romantic attachments . . . To be honest, Henzey, I haven't found the need. If something happens to change it, then so be it – I keep an open mind. But the fear of it all happening again has been a restraining influence. It's tempered any thoughts I've had of women. The prospect of going through it all again rather puts me off. I couldn't stand to lose anybody else. I could never go through that again. Never . . . I tend to blame myself for Dorothy's death.'

'But you shouldn't, Will. Childbirth is the most natural thing on earth, even if it does go wrong occasionally.'

'But, you see, it was at my insistence that we decided to start a family. Look at it this way – if we'd never met, if we'd never married, she'd be alive today.'

'You can't be sure of that, Will. In any case Dorothy also wanted the child, so you can hardly blame yourself.'

Will finished his second cup of tea and put the cup down. 'Nonetheless, I do.'

'You're like my mother,' she said, sounding benignly exasperated. 'When I was just a little girl, my father decided that he should do his bit for king and country and went off to fight in the war. Naturally, she didn't want him to go but she says she didn't really make enough of a fuss to stop him. For more than three years she didn't catch sight of him, till an army lorry turned up outside our house and two soldiers brought him back home, wounded. I can see it all now, as clear as if it were yesterday. I watched as they lifted him out of the truck on a stretcher and when they took him off again to get him upstairs. I couldn't remember him. I'd forgotten what he looked like and everything.

He'd been fighting in the front line at Arras, in France. For years he suffered, till finally he gave up the will to live and died. Now, my mother, bless her heart, blames herself for it. She always reckons that, if she'd been stronger and stood up to my dad, she could've prevented him going to war. Whose fault do *you* think it was, Will?'

'It was the fault of neither. Your father's conscience told him to go and fight. Your mother at that time couldn't see into the future, could she? She didn't have the benefit of hindsight, so her resolve to prevent him going wouldn't have been as strong. And maybe your father wouldn't have listened anyway.'

'But it wasn't my father's fault either, was it?'

'Certainly not.'

'So in the same way, it's not your fault that you lost your wife and baby in childbirth. Nor is it hers. The same arguments apply. Don't you see?'

Will laughed. 'You argue well, Henzey. You should be in politics.'

'I must get it from my dad. He should have been a politician. I think he would have been, if he'd been well when the war ended.'

He looked at his wrist-watch. 'D'you have time for more tea, or must you go?'

'I don't have to go yet.' It was certain she had missed the train she'd thought to take, but she was enjoying the company of this man so much that she was quite prepared to take the next. In any case, she did not have to rush back. 'Actually, I'm getting hungry now so, if you're not pressed for time either, I'll stay and eat . . . If you think I'm not being too cheeky suggesting it.'

'Not at all.'

He called over the waitress and, while she weaved through the tables and chairs to get to them, Henzey said she would like a ham and tomato sandwich. Will ordered the same for himself, too, an egg custard each and another pot of tea.

Afterwards, Will insisted on walking with Henzey to Hockley station, then waiting with her till her train came.

'If you were just a child during the war, you can't be more than eighteen or nineteen now,' he fished as they took a seat on the platform.

She smiled. 'I'm eighteen. Nineteen next March.'

'And brothers and sisters at home, I imagine?'

'Yes, and all younger than me.' She told him about them briefly as the platform filled up with people.

Will said, 'I expect it's been difficult for your mother to cope, with four children to look after all these years.'

'Thankfully she's not a widow anymore. She remarried last May. She has another baby now. A boy. They christened him Richard. Oh, he's beautiful.'

'And do you get on with your stepfather?'

'Stepfather?' She let out a little laugh. 'It's strange, but I never ever think of him as that. Yes, we all get on with him really well. He's more like a real father to us and we treat him as if he is. Oh, you should see our house sometimes, it's Bedlam.' She gave another little chuckle. 'There's Richard squawking, Alice complaining that she can't get in the bathroom to get ready to go out because Herbert's there and won't hurry. Maxi's usually agonising over her music – she wants to be a professional cellist, by the way – most unladylike. My mom's usually fretting over something, or threatening Alice to be in at a respectable time and Jesse, if he's not tending the horses or cleaning churns out, he's trying to balance his books.'

'And you? Drawing, perhaps?'

'Not always. I do whatever takes my fancy. I draw, I read. Sometimes I listen to the wireless, sometimes I go out, roller skating, dancing occasionally.' The weather was still warm for late September and, as she sat, Henzey unbuttoned her coat. 'And you, Will? What do you do?'

'Much the same as you, by the sound of it, except that sometimes I go out at night and play darts. On Saturday I might go to a football match – to the Hawthorns when West Brom are either at home, or playing at Wolves or Villa – or Brum. There are social functions and club activities at the works. Sometimes I go to them if I feel like company. I enjoy singing in the choir on a Sunday, as well. I take life much as it comes these days.'

She flicked her hair from her face as the wind ruffled it. 'What about your folks? Do you see them much?'

'My mother and father live at Great Bridge now.'

They heard the rumblings of a train in the distance. Henzey turned to look, bracing herself for the awesome noise that would accompany it into the station.

'Oh, I have a sister and a brother. Sophie is eight years older than me, and there's Samuel, about ten years older. We've always got on well. I see Sophie quite often. She married well and has two pretty daughters, almost grown-up.'

Their conversation was adjourned. The locomotive whistled, its clanking and squealing increasing in volume till they could no longer talk without having to shout. It hissed and roared like a steel dragon, and Henzey put her hands to her ears.

When she was satisfied she could be heard again she shouted: 'Thanks, Will, for the tea and the sandwich, and for escorting me here. I've really enjoyed talking to you.'

'You're welcome, Henzey. I've enjoyed it, too.'

'Perhaps I'll see you at the works one of the days.'

'I hope so.'

'I'll bring your picture back when the exhibition's finished.'

The door to the compartment was already open. She stepped up to it, then turned, waved and gave him the most devastating smile.

Chapter Twelve

Will Parish walked home to his end-of-terrace house in Daisy Road, Ladywood, with feelings inside him the likes of which he had not experienced for years. Young Henzey Kite had impressed him with her logic, her honesty and her thoughtfulness more than any other woman he had ever met. And that, he admitted, included his late wife Dorothy. Such mature and charming qualities in a girl so young was astonishing. To add to all her virtues, it had been many a long year since he had met a girl so beautiful – and she had spent two whole hours with him, willingly, while they drank tea and ate sandwiches and talked. She had turned his head when he thought it was beyond turning. She had succeeded in getting under his skin and he rather liked the feeling.

But what vibrant young girl of eighteen, with the looks of a fairy-tale princess, would be interested in him? He was a widower, now into his thirties – old in her eyes. It was ridiculous to even contemplate such a liaison. Besides, he'd confessed that he did not feel the need for a mate. He could kick himself now, though, for having said it, especially since it was no longer true.

Till today, Will Parish had had little use or belief in the abstractions of storybook romance, especially with a fairy-tale princess. He was more pragmatic than that. Till today, it would have taken a gigantic effort to lead him anywhere near the brink of a relationship with a woman, and those women, since Dorothy, who had set their caps at him had suffered only long and fruitless waits. Not that he disliked women. On the contrary, he adored them and, if they were genteel, well turned out, intelligent, beautiful, affable and smelled fresh, he adored them the more. But few women measured up to his standards. At work he was surrounded by girls. All around him were women of all shapes and sizes, of all ages, of all colourings and complexities, from the striking to the dowdy. Yet few appealed. Only this Henzey Kite had ever really stirred his interest since Dorothy died.

The very word 'romance' had been relegated to the appendix of his vocabulary, and his innate selectivity had ensured celibacy. That is not to say that he was incapable of love or romance. He had loved Dorothy with all his heart and soul and they'd had their romantic moments; moments that now existed only in his memory. The kind of love Dorothy gave was undramatic and unsentimental. She discovered early on in their relationship that tears, highly charged emotions and gushing affection cut no ice with him. Nonetheless, she melted his heart with a love that set its premium on quality and not quantity. That was what he favoured; and that was why he'd had no other real love affairs since she died. Nobody could match her in his eyes — till today.

Will engaged the heartbreak of his wife's death by immersing himself in work and staying away from people socially. He had no desire to lose himself in other women; other women's vices only enhanced Dorothy's virtues and hence prolonged the grief. For him it was the easiest thing in the world to be chaste and he was aware that it would take an extraordinary woman to turn him from his chastity. He could live with celibacy as easily as he could contend with any other self-imposed discipline. If fate decreed that the rest of his life he remain single, he believed he could accept it with neither regret nor undue emotion — till today.

Now, at last, he felt his slumbering emotions stirring within him, growing as remorselessly as the buds on the trees in springtime. It was sudden and unexpected, but he was quick to recognise it. Perhaps it was time to think in terms of a love affair, but he would only be interested in a love affair with this one particular girl. Nobody else. If only there were a remote chance that she could be the slightest bit interested in him. But what was her response when he asked if she had a young man now? She wanted nobody. She was still smarting from her last love affair. She'd said so. Clearly, she meant it.

He was home at last, hardly remembering the walk back. He would have time to get to the Hawthorns before the kick-off if he hurried, but football suddenly had no more appeal that day. It all seemed too trivial. He closed the front door behind him and sat on the settee in front of the empty fireplace, looking at the cast-iron fire basket. There had been no fire in this room since Dorothy died. He recalled how they'd had this new fire grate installed. It was one of the more modern ones with a panel of decorated, ceramic tiles on each side of the low cast-iron fire opening.

On the mantelpiece was a clock, which he religiously wound up every day; their wedding photograph was in a frame at one end and a photo of Dorothy posing alone at the other. Between the clock in the middle and the two end pictures, stood two bronze Art Nouveau statuettes of nubile water nymphs, each on a plinth, each semi-nude, standing seductively in reflective pose – fodder for the gods Zeus or Pan; old-fashioned now, but they were a wedding gift. The whole arrangement was how Dorothy had set it out. Oh, he dusted it all and polished it every week, but never could he, nor would he, alter its arrangement; that would be sacrilege. It was the same throughout the whole house. Although this house was his home, it was still a shrine to her.

Beyond the front room in which he sat, there was a comfortable living-room. Beyond that was a scullery with a gas cooker, a gas boiler, a sink with cold running water, a mangle and a galvanised bath hanging from the wall by a nail. Will never used the mangle, however. All his laundry he wrapped in a sheet and handed it to Mrs Fothergill next door, who would, in turn, hand it with her own dirty washing to the Co-operative Laundry man on a Monday morning. It would come back on a Wednesday, clean and fresh, with his collars and cuffs beautifully starched. The boiler he would use, of course, whenever he needed to fill the bath.

He sat down and pondered the frailty and tenuousness of human life. It seemed strange that an inanimate object like that clock on the mantelpiece, its face marked out and painted by a craftsman, its case carefully carved, its mechanism cleverly engineered to precise tolerances, could exist in the same state from day to day, from year to year, when the woman he had loved so dearly had expired in her endeavour to fulfil the vows taken at their marriage; marriage that first and foremost was ordained for the procreation of children. Life, love, could be so cruel.

But what to do about this Henzey Kite? Perhaps nothing, yet. She was still smarting from a love affair. She wanted nobody. It was inopportune to be thinking about her in such terms. If he began paying attention to her yet he was just as likely to scare her off. Besides, how did you go about asking a girl out these days? Things had changed so much in ten years.

Henzey's exhibition came and went, and from it she received enquiries for more and more portraits. Florrie Shuker told her she was a fool to do any more without charging for them and Henzey agreed that the extra money would come in handy. So every new enquirer was told that there would be a charge of four shillings and sixpence per portrait. It rather succeeded in sorting the genuine out from those with the something-for-nothing mentality. Those who were prepared to pay had good value, but the others all said they would let her know, and invariably didn't.

She took Will Parish's portrait back to him herself during the first dinner break after the exhibition had finished. A creature of habit, he was as usual eating his sandwiches and reading the *Daily Mail*. When he saw her at his office door, which was always kept open, he smiled with genuine delight, folded his paper up and put his sandwiches in the top drawer of his desk.

'Henzey, come in and pull up a chair.'

'I just came to bring your picture back and to thank you for letting me borrow it.' She sat on the edge of the chair facing his desk, her hands primly in her lap.

'How did it go?'

'Oh, fine, thank you . . . But, look, I won't stop and interrupt your dinner.' She made to get up again but he held his hand up emphatically.

'No, don't rush off. The sandwiches can wait. I'd much rather talk to you.' He was tempted to say he'd thought about her a great deal – that she had been on his mind constantly in fact, but he thought better of it.

They chatted for a few minutes longer, about her exhibition and the general reaction to it, until Henzey insisted on going so that Will could finish his dinner. When she had gone he opened up his newspaper again and began reading. He digested not a word. His thoughts were on Henzey Kite. What a poor conversationalist she must think he was, having had nothing interesting to say that might keep her there. She seemed keen to leave him. So keen that any chance he might have had the other Saturday must surely be gone now. Damn! Strange how the accord they'd enjoyed then seemed to exist no longer.

Henzey, though, had not considered Will an admirer; merely a new friend. Even if she sussed his interest, her yet fragile spirit was not ready for the risks it might incur. Getting involved was one thing, but the prospect of her poor heart breaking and aching again as a result, was another. She had learned her lesson. Yet she liked Will. He was always well turned out; always looked fresh and clean as if he'd just been returned from the laundry.

That was how she liked men. She found him easy to talk to; he was agreeable company and she felt she could broach any subject with him, no matter how delicate, or indelicate.

As the weeks and months passed, he became a true friend and, each time they parted, she looked forward to the next time they would meet. But at no time since that Saturday morning had he asked her to accompany him to the Copper Kettle, nor anywhere else for that matter. They frequently ran into each other – always by chance, never contrived – coming in or going out of work and passing in corridors, especially at break times. Always they had a pleasant word to exchange and always made time to talk about themselves, about each other, about their respective families, to confide little secrets or discuss any problems they had. Thus they became close. And there was that certain indefinable something about Will's smile that was always so appealing. At no time did she think of him as being twelve years older than herself; not that it would have mattered anyway.

Henzey's nineteenth birthday arrived. It fell on a Saturday, that March 1931 and, that morning, she received a card in the post from Will Parish. It was the first inkling she'd had of his true feelings towards her. The verse inside it, in his own handwriting, read:

> My heart hides timidly behind my dreams,
> Eloquence evading,
> Like exquisite flowers I stop to pick,
> Which at my touch start fading.
> Yet flowery words, howe'er refined
> Cannot do justice to thee,
> Nor yet to what I feel inside,
> Persistently, constantly, truly.

It was signed, 'With all my Love, Will'.

The message touched her, triggering off new lines of thought. Could it really be that he was in love with her? And if so, did he really lack the ability or the courage to tell her to her face as his poem suggested? He had never given her any indication of such feelings when they were together. If he had, she was too blind to see. So how should she behave with him now? After all this time of being friends, should she now avoid him or act as if she had never received this card? Neither would be fair. She could not ignore him; she had far too much respect for him. Maybe she should broach the subject and then they could discuss it rationally. After all, she really could discuss anything with him. But, no. That would be too systematic and would inhibit any romance.

Her mind ran on . . .

If he asked her to go out one evening she certainly would not refuse. On the contrary, she would be glad of the opportunity. Scarcely did she go out at night nowadays, especially in the week. In any case, Will was most presentable. She would be proud to be seen on his arm, a tall, good-looking, well-dressed man of thirty with intriguingly soulful, brown eyes and the sort of lips any girl would relish kissing.

But not yet. She needed time to contemplate and understand this. It was all so sudden.

Just before noon, a bouquet of red roses arrived. They bore no note but she guessed who had sent them.

These days, thoughts of Billy Witts failed to set her heart thumping. Thank God she was over him now, though there were still odd nights when she wished he was lying by her side. But now, after nearly fifteen months, the starving hunger for him had abated and she was more or less acclimatised to celibacy. Perhaps too acclimatised. Oh, what the hell! Perhaps it was time to give her battered emotions an airing again, if only to see if she was still capable of that warmth, that passion, that ecstasy she had known with Billy? At least now she felt some ability, some willingness, to give love.

But for a while she went out of her way to avoid Will Parish, even though she realised it was ungracious in the extreme. Over the last few months she had become familiar with his movements. When she visited the ladies' toilet on her floor during her mid-morning break, she would invariably bump into Will on his way to some meeting or other. So she visited the ladies' at the end of her break, rather than at the beginning, thereby eluding him. When it was time to go home, she got lost in the surging crowd leaving the factory, rather than linger around the production line for a few minutes till the crowds had dispersed. Thus she reduced the risk of seeing him. But all she was doing was postponing the inevitable. Sooner or later they were bound to meet and she guessed that, by now, he would be thinking it mighty impolite that he had not seen her since he sent that birthday card.

She managed to avoid Will till 24th April, a Friday. Not only had her conscience got the better of her, but he had been occupying her thoughts far more than normal. That birthday card and its message had percolated through the defensive wall she had erected around herself. He had expressed his feelings so intriguingly, with no gushing admissions of love. The words were typical of him; they had an attractive, yet melancholy ring; a poignancy tinged with hope, understated, relying only on her understanding of the message. It was irresistible now. Having expressed those feelings so subtly, the perceived knowledge that he was in love with her was having a positive, cumulative effect. She could ignore it no longer. Just one thing was troubling her: although they shared many intimate secrets, never once had she intimated that she was not a virgin. He might already have guessed as much, but would he still want her when he knew for certain? To some men it meant everything.

Will, on the other hand, hoped that Henzey would weigh up his poetic words, mull them over and eventually come to some sort of a decision. That it would be in her own time he was also aware. The fact that he had not caught sight of her for nearly a month came as no great surprise, though he was somewhat disappointed. Had he wished, he could easily have intercepted her somewhere, but it would have been to no avail. She would come to him one way or the other, without pressure, when she was good and ready.

And he could wait.

So finally, at dinnertime, with butterflies in her stomach, Henzey visited him in his department. Just to say hello. He was where she expected to find him, in his office, but this time he wasn't reading a newspaper, he was reading a lengthy office memorandum. His door was open, of course, and she tapped on it gently, since he did not see her approach.

'Good Lord,' he exclaimed when he saw her and his face lit up. 'I thought you'd left the country. You been away ill or something?'

She smiled demurely and he returned the smile with a typical, unwitting scratching of his head. This time there was no sadness in his eyes but she thought she detected him colour up slightly. It moved her to blush too. They were like old friends who had been away so long that they felt almost like strangers again; strangers, too, because there was this new unspoken and unconfirmed intrigue, which transmuted mere rapport into something far more substantial, yet far more fragile. Whether it came to fruition or even failed to take root, she could not tell yet. Either way, they were on the brink of a new kind of relationship.

Still smiling that fabulous smile which made her blue, blue eyes sparkle like fine-cut sapphires, she answered quietly: 'Will, I haven't seen you for so long. I thought it was time I came to say hello.'

He laughed self-consciously. 'And not before time. I thought you'd forgotten me. Sit down, for goodness' sake.' He put down the memorandum he was reading while she sat down, her back elegantly erect, her head set beautifully. 'So how've you been? You look well. In fact you look smashing. But then you always do.'

'Thanks, Will. I'm fine. Never felt better.'

He made a mental note of that. Maybe it was a euphemism; her way of saying she was no longer smarting over her lost love. But still he kept the initial conversation to generalities; safe ground, while they fenced conversationally to draw each other out.

'And how's everyone at home? Richard well?'

'Oh, he's lovely. He's a bit of a handful these days, walking and getting into everything. Nothing's sacred anymore. Mom has to tie all the cupboard doors and sideboard doors together so he can't get at anything. He's a proper little monkey.' She laughed nervously. 'He's been a bit off the hooks the last week or so, though. A bit feverish and a runny nose.'

'And Alice?'

'Oh, I'm still worried about her. You remember I told you about what she gets up to with Jack? She still sees him, but she's not so hostile to me now.'

He nodded sagely. 'Good . . . And Maxine?'

'Still dedicated to her music.'

'And how's Herbert?'

'He's courting now. Did I tell you that before? I've met her. She seems a nice girl, quiet, very plain, the same age as himself. I don't think she suits him really. He met her on his milk round. Her mother's one of his customers . . . So how are your family, Will? Are they well?'

'Oh, Mother's not so good on her legs these days. Father's still managing to do a bit in his allotment, getting it ready for his vegetables and his chrysanths.'

'I see you aren't reading your newspaper today.' She was aware that she was forcing conversation. 'I thought you liked your paper.'

He picked up the memorandum and held it in front of him. 'No, I was reading this. It's an outline of some new American-style wages incentive scheme they want to introduce. I'm surprised you haven't heard about it.'

'Well if we all get more money out of it so much the better. Are you in favour of it, Will?'

'From what I can gather, it will do us all a bit of good. It's supposed to work well in America.'

'I don't think their Prohibition would work here, though, do you? Not that I drink, but Jesse likes his pint. So does Herbert now.'

Will smiled, and their was a lull in the conversation. Both were instantly aware of it, but it was Henzey who broke it. She saw it as her chance to get straight to the point.

'I . . . er . . . I never had the chance to thank you for the birthday card and the flowers you sent me.' She stared self-consciously at her fingernails on her lap. Then she looked up again, more boldly. Their eyes met and held. 'To be honest, Will, after I received them I kept out of your way . . . ' Her eyes went to her lap again. 'Not because I wasn't happy to get them, I was . . . and not because I didn't want to see you either, because I did . . . But what you wrote was . . . was sort of unexpected . . . This is difficult . . . It's just that . . . I needed time to think . . . to sort out my own feelings. You know how I've been these last fifteen months.'

'I know exactly.' His voice was thin with anticipation. 'That's why I didn't do it sooner. I expect it all came as a bit of a shock.'

'Well, it's not every day that someone as close as you've been, lets me know he's . . . in love with me. And since we are such close friends, you deserve . . . well, you deserve some consideration as to my own feelings about it . . . I'm not explaining myself very well, am I?'

'I hope you're trying to say, Henzey, that you've sorted out your own emotions.' His voice began to tremble and he hoped she hadn't noticed.

She nodded, still staring into her lap. 'I think I have.'

'And?' He swallowed hard. The next few seconds could realise his dream.

She looked up and smiled. '*My heart hides timidly behind my dreams, eloquence evading . . .* Shall I go on?'

He nodded. 'Please. If you can remember it.'

'Oh, I can remember it all right. Every word. I'll never forget it . . . *My heart hides timidly behind my dreams, eloquence evading. Like beautiful flowers I stop to pick, which at my touch start fading. Yet flowery words, howe'er refined cannot do justice to thee, nor yet to what I feel inside . . .*' Her voice became strained with emotion, '*persistently . . . constantly . . . truly.*' Again she looked at her lap, but the buttons on her overall seemed to grow misty as tears filled her eyes. She looked up at him. 'The poem says it all for me as well.' She bit her bottom lip to stem her weeping.

'Henzey,' he breathed, yearning to hold her.

'Oh, Will.' Tears streamed down her face.

'Oh, Henzey. I never . . . You've been on my mind, you know, for such a long time now . . . I . . . For a long time I've wanted you to . . . to become a part of me and my life, and I've wanted to be a part of your world, your life.'

She took her handkerchief from the pocket of her overall and wiped her eyes. 'Stop it,' she said, a laugh bursting through her tears. 'You're making me all happy.'

'I want to be with you . . . always. I want to experience the world with you, talk with you, listen to you. I want to protect you from the world and all its pains, but I also want to share its joys and pleasures with you . . . I wish I could find the words to say more.'

'You make it sound so beautiful.'

'I just crave for the privilege of knowing you better – knowing every single beat of your heart. I want to enjoy every kiss you're able to give . . . Sorry. Am I going too fast?'

She cast her eyes down once more. 'No, no, Will. You're not going too fast . . . but before you . . . There's just one thing . . .'

'What?'

She looked into his eyes earnestly. 'Billy and me, we . . . I'm not a virgin, Will. I think it's only fair you should know.'

'Well, neither am I,' he said with a little laugh of relief. For a second he feared she was about to introduce some insurmountable impediment. 'But I'd assumed you weren't . . . after a love affair like yours. Do you think it matters?'

'It matters to lots of men, they say. I just wanted to tell you before we begin anything.'

'Henzey, it's already begun. And the fact that you're not a virgin is neither here nor there. It doesn't alter the way I feel. It can't alter the way I feel.'

Her hand went across his desk and he covered it with his own. 'Please try not to make me unhappy, Will,' she breathed. 'I don't ever want to be unhappy again.'

'Nor shall you be. Oh, I just want to take you up in my arms right now.'

Henzey began to laugh through her tears and he laughed too. 'You daren't,' she said. 'You know you daren't. Not here.'

In the goldfish bowl of an office in which they sat, such an action, in full view of everyone in the department, would have caused a minor scandal and possibly put their jobs in jeopardy. They both knew it, of course, and it provoked their laughter.

'Best save it for when we're alone,' she said.

'And when do you suppose that might be?'

One of her shrugs. 'I'm not doing anything tomorrow night.'

'Oh, dear God,' he sighed, frustrated, 'wouldn't you just know it! Tomorrow I'm going to Wembley. It's the Cup Final. West Brom are playing Brum. There's scores going from Lucas's. It'll be a riot. God knows what time I'll be back. Tell you what – I'll sell my ticket.'

'No, Will, I wouldn't hear of it. You must go to the Cup Final if you've got a ticket. It's your team that's playing. I'll still be here when you get back. We've waited this long, another day won't make any difference. Anyway, now we seem to have got ourselves sorted out another day waiting will make our next meeting all the sweeter.'

'I don't know if I want to wait any longer, Henzey. I want to be with you. I don't think I can wait now I know how you feel.'

'Oh, yes you can. Go and enjoy the Cup Final, and I hope Albion win for you.'

'Well, if they do it's going to be some double celebration, I can tell you.'

Henzey and Will met after they finished work that day. They walked hand in hand to the station in Icknield Street. The late April afternoon was cool and the sky was burdened with grey clouds, but occasionally the low sun would sneak through for a few minutes to cast long shadows and a yellow brilliance that was dazzling. The platform was crowded. They sat on a bench and talked, oblivious to anyone else. When the train steamed in Henzey said she didn't want to leave him yet so they sat and waited till the next one came in, forty minutes later. As its carriages clanked to a halt, they stood and she held her face up to him, poised for a kiss. He lingered when he felt the lush softness of her mouth, and it became a full, probing, hungry kiss. As their arms went about each other some wag gave them a wolf-whistle, reminding them to break off, just in time for Henzey to get on the train.

They had arranged to meet on Sunday afternoon.

Chapter Thirteen

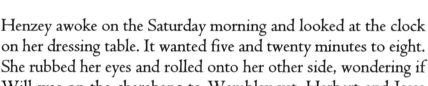

Henzey awoke on the Saturday morning and looked at the clock on her dressing table. It wanted five and twenty minutes to eight. She rubbed her eyes and rolled onto her other side, wondering if Will was on the charabanc to Wembley yet. Herbert and Jesse would be up and working by now. Already they would have collected the milk churns from the railway station and be doling out fresh milk into the jugs of early risers. She heard Richard coughing; still he had a running nose and a high temperature.

At once Henzey's mind was filled with Will Parish and their new-found love. She pondered how, over the last month, his poem had awakened feelings she had always subconsciously harboured. It had been like a potent caress, triggering love. She likened herself to the fairy-tale princess awakened with a kiss by the handsome prince after sleeping for a hundred years. That was how long it seemed she had been in the wilderness over that rogue Billy Witts. But now, at last, Will's poem had freed her of all that. It was wonderful to wake up so.

A bedroom door opened and closed, interrupting her thoughts, then the bathroom door. The lavatory seat squeaked as it was lowered. A pause. It was flushed. Over the sound of the cistern refilling, she heard somebody retching. The lavatory was flushed again. Whoever it was had eaten something to upset them. Luckily, she had not been affected herself.

Her thoughts drifted back to Will. Ever since she'd received that card, inducing her to avoid him, she had been lured somehow into thinking about him a great deal more, drawn inescapably like a honeybee to a blossom. It would not have done to just blithely turn him down then, nor even to blindly accept what he was offering without first searching her own heart. So she had diligently searched her heart and found her true emotions. Now she was sure. Not only did she love him as a friend, but she was also in love with him, the man, the widower, twelve years older than herself.

Once more, she heard the sound of retching. While the toilet flushed again she got out of bed. She put on her dressing-gown and slippers, ran her fingers through her hair and opened her bedroom door. The aroma of bacon and eggs lingered temptingly from the breakfast Jesse had cooked earlier for himself and Herbert. The bathroom door opened and Alice emerged looking deathly white.

'Are you all right?' Henzey asked.

'I am now. The smell of bacon and eggs made me sick. I think I'll go back to bed for another ten minutes.'

Henzey visited the bathroom herself and afterwards went downstairs. Maxine was already sitting at the table, her nose in a book.

'You're up already, our Maxi.'

'There's nothing quite so annoying as somebody stating the obvious,' Maxine replied, feigning disdain.

Henzey laughed. 'All right, clever clogs. What I should have said was, what brings you up so early?'

'Oh, Alice woke me, moaning about feeling sick again. She's like it every morning lately. It must be awful to keep having these bilious attacks.'

'Bilious attacks?'

'She's been getting them for the last two or three weeks. Surely if she went to see the doctor he could give her something? She won't have any breakfast or anything. You wouldn't know that, though, Henzey, since you have to leave home so early for work.'

'Had your breakfast yet, Maxi?'

'Not yet. I don't really know what I fancy.'

'Toast? Bacon and egg? Porridge?'

'I think I'll have some porridge.'

'I'll have some with you. I'll make it if you'll make some fresh tea.'

Maxine considered it a fair deal and they went into the kitchen together. Eventually, Henzey ladled dollops of thick porridge into two bowls, one of which she handed to Maxine.

'Oh, ta. Pass me the treacle as well, will you?'

Alice, dressed ready for work, appeared at the door looking pale and drawn still. She pulled a face and said, 'Oh, you'm not having treacle on your porridge again, Maxine? Yuk!'

Henzey took the tin of Lyle's Golden Syrup from the cupboard above her and handed it to Maxine. Maxine took it, along with her breakfast, to the sitting-room, leaving Henzey and Alice together.

'I take it you don't want any breakfast, our Alice.'

'I'll do without.' There was still a coolness between them.

'Are you sure you're all right?'

Henzey sprinkled a teaspoon of sugar over her own bowl of porridge.

'Course I am. Have yer made enough tea for me as well?'

'There's a pot full.'

Alice reached for a cup.

'Look, Alice, I know you're not keen on me poking my nose in, but if there's something wrong and I can help, you only have to say. I am your sister, after all.'

'What could be wrong?'

Henzey took a spoon out of the cutlery drawer. 'I'm not sure. But if I was being sick every morning after doing what you seem to do every night, I'd be worried.'

Alice shrugged.

There was another pause while Henzey began eating her breakfast, standing casually against the kitchen cabinet. 'Have you told Jack?'

Alice turned away.

Henzey knew she'd struck a chord. 'Have you told Jack?' she asked again.

Alice shook her head. She was looking into her teacup, her back towards Henzey.

'Then don't you think you should?' Henzey put her breakfast down on the small kitchen table.

Alice turned towards her. A tear trembled on her dark lashes. Henzey thought how pathetic and lost her sister looked. Her petiteness made her seem frail and vulnerable, while her prettiness was marred by the anxiety in her face. Still only sixteen years old and sexually experienced; but not sufficiently so to have insisted that Jack took the requisite precautions to have prevented this. He should have had more thought, but carelessness was typical of him. Alice rushed into Henzey's arms. As Henzey held her tight Alice broke down, heaving, sobbing. Henzey stroked her hair and uttered soothing words, but it only seemed to make her worse. For some minutes she wept.

Then she heaved a great sigh of self-pity. 'What should I do, Henzey? I never thought it would 'appen to me.'

Henzey answered quietly, consolingly. 'Well, first thing, I should have thought, would be to tell Jack. You've *got* to tell him, Alice . . . Does he love you?'

Alice nodded.

'Then, you'll have to start thinking about getting married, provided he'll marry you. You'll have to go and see the doctor to get it confirmed. Then you'll have to tell Mom and Jesse.'

'Tell Mom and Jesse what?' It was their mother standing at the kitchen door in her dressing-gown.

Henzey looked at Alice with an expression that suggested she should tell the truth and get it over with. They let go of each other and Alice looked at the floor, trying to hide her tears from

Lizzie. But Lizzie had picked up the signals as if they had been broadcast over the wireless.

Lizzie looked first at Alice, apprehensively, then at Henzey. 'What's the matter?'

'You might as well say now,' Henzey advised.

'I think I'm pregnant, Mom . . . I think I'm pregnant.' Alice broke down again, and Henzey felt profoundly sorry for her. Once more she put her arms around her to comfort her.

Lizzie's face was a portrait of anxiety. 'How many times have you missed?'

'Twice.'

'And what does *he* say about it?'

'He don't know yet,' Alice sobbed.

'Well, I reckon you'd best tell him, and quick. Have you had it confirmed?'

Alice shook her head.

'Then you'd better get to Donald Clark's.'

'Will he be able to get rid of it for me?'

'Get rid of it? It's a fine time to talk about getting rid of it, our Alice. It should never have got there in the first place at your age. You've made your bed, you can damn-well lie in it, same as everybody else. If he'll marry you there'll be no need for thinking about getting rid of it. You should've thought about all this before you let him have his way.'

Lizzie was angry with Alice for being so stupid, but she recalled the time, not so long ago, when she herself was caught out with Richard. She was ashamed and angry with herself then but, most of all, she needed the support of the people she loved. She was lucky: she got support immediately. But she remembered her desolation over Henzey's resentment. There was nothing to suppose Alice would feel any different. But being so young she would need even more support.

'You don't have to make it sound so dirty, Mom,' Alice said defiantly. 'I love Jack. With all my heart an' soul I love him. I did it out of love for him. I ain't ashamed o' that, neither. I'm just worried what'll 'appen. I'm worried about what you all think.'

'Oh, our Alice,' Lizzie said, tears welling up in her own eyes. She held her arms out and Alice left Henzey's embrace in favour of her mother's. 'You're no more than a child yourself. God, as if one daughter isn't enough to worry about, I'm blessed with three. I'll be grey before I'm much older.' Then, she spoke more quietly. 'Listen. You tell that Jack Harper about it as soon as you can. When we know how he feels, we'll know better what we've got to do. Are you supposed to see him tonight?'

'Yes. He wants to marry me, Mom. I know that already. He's said as much.'

'Then let's hope he'll still want to marry you now you're carrying his child. It tends to put a different slant on things. If he does, all you need worry about is where you're going to live.'

Maxine appeared at the door. She said, 'I thought I heard a fuss. What's up?'

When Alice had finally left for work, Lizzie, Henzey and Maxine stood in the kitchen talking, wondering what Jesse and Herbert were likely to say about Alice and her predicament. Henzey had become vacant, not really listening to what the other two were saying. She was again in her own private world of new love.

Out of the blue, she said, 'I wonder if the Cup Final's on the wireless this afternoon.'

Lizzie looked at Maxine incredulously. 'How the hell you can think about the Cup Final when there's our Alice to worry about beats me.'

'Since when have you been interested in football?' Maxine asked.

'Since yesterday.' Henzey turned towards the kitchen table. 'I might as well throw this porridge away now. It's as cold as charity.'

'How come you're so interested in the Cup Final all of a sudden?'

Henzey placed the bowl of porridge on the draining board. 'Will's gone to see it with a crowd from work.'

Lizzie and Maxine looked at each other again. 'Oh? Who's Will, then?' Lizzie enquired, still reeling from Alice's confession and perceiving further cause for concern.

'A fellow from Lucas's. I'm seeing him tomorrow afternoon.'

'Is he the one who sent you the flowers? I thought there was something in the wind. Was that him you did a picture of a while ago?'

Henzey nodded. This was not the best moment to have chosen to talk about Will.

'I thought he was married.'

'He's a widower. Lost his wife nearly six years ago.'

'A widower? Well, I hope you know what you're doing, our Henzey.'

Henzey looked challengingly into her mother's eyes. 'Didn't Jesse know what he was doing when he married a widow?'

Lizzie conceded that Henzey had made a relevant point. 'All right, all right. But he's a lot older than you, isn't he?'

'He's thirty-one next month. All right, so he's twelve years older than me. I've always said the women of this family like their men more mature.'

'Yes, and our men will be our damned downfall from what I can see of it.' They remained quiet for a while. Lizzie filled the enamel bowl with hot water from the geyser to start the washing-up. She sighed pensively. 'I don't really think any of us intend to bring trouble. But when you fall in love it's so hard to deny yourself the pleasure that loving can bring. I don't think many women can, although they mean to . . . and they generally pretend they can. So it's even more important that you're careful . . . Are you listening? I mean, look at our Alice. Ooh, I could brain her, I really could. As if she'd got no more sense. It wouldn't be so bad but she's had no life. She'll be just seventeen and a mother at that.'

'Well, at least Jack Harper's in work, Mom,' Henzey remarked. 'The best thing they could do would be to get married and try and rent a house somewhere. She'll be able to work for a long time yet. I daresay they'll be happy enough.'

They all heard Richard coughing upstairs, and Lizzie went up.

Dresses were tending to get longer but Henzey was doing her best to resist the dictates of fashion, still preferring to wear her skirts and dresses short. She had slim, shapely legs and was not averse to showing them; her neatly turned ankles drew many a second glance. But it was becoming increasingly difficult to find new clothes that were not appreciably longer. True, she thought, the higher waistline — the bust nobody had to flatten anymore — the longer skirt and the more complex cut produced a shape more natural, more feminine and infinitely more sensual than the boyish look of previous years. But she would be sorry to see the demise of the short skirt. So it was with mixed feelings that, on Saturday afternoon while the Cup Final was being played, she bought a new, sky-blue, day dress in rayon for tomorrow. The hem was a mere twelve inches above the ground, but the skirt was cut on the bias, which gave some moulding from her waist to her feminine hips and her prettily protruding bottom.

She wore it when she met Will on Sunday afternoon, well teamed with short jacket, matching shoes and gloves and flesh-coloured silk stockings. She looked and felt good.

The weather was fair with a light breeze. White clouds scudded briskly across a sunshine sky. They had arranged to meet at three o'clock at the tram stop at the railway station. Will was already waiting when she arrived. He took both her hands, then keeping her at arms' length for a moment, looked her up and down.

He smiled. 'Oh, very elegant. Brings out the colour of your eyes. Nice change from your overall.'

'Thank you. And look at you. Grey flannels and navy-blue blazer — you look very smart yourself.'

'Thank *you*. Well, the weather's good. Shall we walk round the castle grounds?'

'If you like.'

Hand in hand they strolled up Castle Hill to the entrance close to where the statue of the Earl of Dudley stood. Will told Henzey of his trip to Wembley and how pleased he was that Albion had won the cup. They'd celebrated the victory with some enthusiasm and hadn't arrived home till past two o'clock that morning.

'And did you go to church this morning?'

'Yes,' he replied, 'and I told them I wouldn't be there tonight.'

'So will the other tenors be able to manage without you?'

'I doubt it,' he jested, 'but I won't be there to worry about it.'

'How come you're not religious, going to church that often?'

He gave a little grunt of a laugh. 'I go to sing, Henzey. I love singing with other people. There's nothing quite like it.'

'But you said your family *were* religious. You said they're Methodists.'

'They are. But their fanaticism drove me from it. My father always used to be spouting from the Bible. I think he knew it by heart.'

'But if they were Methodists, how come you sing in a Church of England choir?'

'Rebellion, I reckon — against Methodist fundamentalism.'

They reached the entrance to the castle grounds and went in. The steep, winding pathways were shaded by tall trees swaying gracefully in the breeze, their green foliage well forward for April due to a spell of fine weather. They took a route which meandered to and fro across the side of the hill. It would eventually lead them over a wide ditch that was once the moat, and into the castle courtyard.

'There's some trouble at home,' Henzey said.

'Oh?'

The sun shining through the new foliage of the elm trees cast a mobile, dappled shadow across her lovely face. Will watched, fascinated, as it seemed to caress her skin.

'Our Alice is pregnant.'

'Oh, no. Poor kid.'

'Oh, I do feel sorry for her, Will, but she was warned. I've told you before how I came across them once, didn't I?' Henzey explained how Alice had confessed and how her mother had reacted. 'She told Jack last night and he's told her he wants to marry her, so they're going to as soon as they can. This morning she was sick again, but she seemed much happier. Relieved that it's out in the open, I expect.'

'In many ways she's lucky,' Will commented. 'Not everybody relishes the thought of *having* to get married, but if she's going to . . . Well, there's a good many who wish they were in a similar position, I daresay.'

They stopped while Will watched the rooks squawking and flapping between their nests, high in the elms. Henzey was glad of the brief rest.

'Well, I'm blowed,' he said. 'Haven't seen a red squirrel for years. There. See? Bet there's a few more round here.'

'Oh, isn't he lovely? Just look at him. Will you catch him for me, Will, so's I can take him home?'

He laughed. 'Yes, course. Just hang on while I shin up this tree.'

They started walking again.

Henzey said, 'There are two things I'm really daft about – animals and babies.'

'Well, there'll soon be another baby in the family to drool over when Alice has hers.' He looked into her eyes for her response.

'How do you feel about children now, Will?' she asked, turning to look at him. 'If you were ever to get married again, I mean. You know? After what happened to Dorothy.'

He took a moment to formulate his answer. He felt he should choose his words with care. 'I'd be loath to put any woman's life at risk again, Henzey. I'm certainly not against having a family in the generally accepted sense. But, frankly, I think I'd be scared to death to knowingly start one. The spectre of what can happen – what's already happened to me – still haunts me. Graveyards are full of women who died having babies.'

The path turned sharply and steeply, almost in the opposite direction.

Their eyes met again and Henzey squeezed his hand. 'I think I can understand how you feel. But not every woman dies giving birth, do they? My own mother had all us children and who's to say she won't have more? Like shelling peas, she says it is.' She laughed. 'Actually, I've heard her put it a sight more earthily than that. But most women accept the risk, such as it is.'

'Maybe they do, but I doubt if *I'd* be prepared to take that risk again. If it happened that my wife became pregnant, by accident say, that would be different, I suppose. But I'd be on tenterhooks till it was all safely over.'

'So would most men with any care in their hearts, I should think.' She was reminded of Billy Witts putting Nellie Dewsbury in the family way. Had such a caring thought crossed his mind? 'But if you were ever to get that far, would that be a sticking point between you and your new wife?' She laughed, half-teasing, half-serious, hoping it would not sound presumptuous.

He smiled. 'Who knows?'

'Whoever she might be, she'd have to convince you somehow that you were taking a very negative point of view. If I ever get married I'd certainly want children, though I admit, not necessarily straight away. I suppose it would depend how old I was. You must admit, Will, that if everyone took your view the whole human race would be extinct in no time.'

'And who's to say that would be a bad thing?'

They were climbing higher. Through the trees, they could see the red-brick tower of St Edmund's church way below and, on the ridge beyond, the smoke-blackened granite spire of St Thomas's, or Top Church as it was known locally, dominating the far end of the town and the horizon. They stopped to look at the view. When they continued walking she linked her arm through his as if it were the most natural thing in the world.

'Besides, your mother lived through childbirth,' Henzey said, persisting with the topic.

'Presumably. Actually, I don't know that for certain.'

Henzey looked at him, puzzled. 'What do you mean?'

'I don't know if I ever knew my real mother. Nor my real father. Didn't I tell you? I was a foster child. I thought I'd told you.'

'No, you never said. I'd have remembered that.'

'I could have sworn I'd told you . . . Well, I have no idea who my real parents were. They might be still alive for all I know. I don't know, I never asked about them.'

'And you were never told?'

'Not that I can remember.'

'Aren't you interested in finding out?'

'I've thought about them, Henzey. But when I was a lad in my early teens, I remember thinking that they must have thought little or nothing of me to have deserted me, or given me away. Either way, it amounts to the same thing. So, in my youthful arrogance, I thought, why should I concern myself with them? So I didn't . . . Maybe I was illegitimate, Henzey.'

'Don't, Will.'

'Would that bother you?'

She squeezed his arm. 'No, it wouldn't. But it doesn't have to be so. It's just as likely your parents were married. Maybe your father was a soldier and got killed in the Boer War or something. If so, maybe your mother couldn't cope. Maybe she died, even – I've heard of such things. It might be any one of a thousand reasons why you were fostered. You mustn't judge them too harshly if you don't know.'

'But there's another reason I never bothered to ask about them . . . I was loved anyway, secure in the Parish family. I always felt that, if I asked my foster parents anything about my real parents, they would interpret that as dissatisfaction. I know how sensitive they've always been and it would've grieved me to upset them, because I've always loved them dearly.'

'I'm sure they would've understood.'

'Maybe they would, but I was never prepared to take the risk. Even now, I couldn't bring myself to ask them.'

'But you had a happy childhood?'

'I had a very happy childhood. And that's the point.'

They arrived at the stone bridge over the dry moat and strolled under the four-centred, Tudor arch of the barbican, through the triple Gateway of the gatehouse. All was in ruins, but the pale, limestone walls were glowing bright in the sunshine.

'Mom said I was to take you home for tea,' Henzey remarked.

'That's nice of her.'

'She wants to inspect you. I didn't promise, though. I said I'd suggest it to you. Richard's got whooping cough, you see, poor little thing. I didn't really think you'd want your first visit to our house to be memorable because of him coughing all the while, bless his heart. It's terrible for him, but I know how upsetting it can be for everybody else.'

'Oh, I don't mind that, Henzey. The hardship is Richard's unfortunately, not mine. I'd love to meet your family. I've been looking forward to it. I think I should anyway. Otherwise how can they make up their mind about me? I expect your mother wants to see the sort of man her best daughter's starting to associate with.'

'Well, what with this trouble with Alice and everything, she's concerned about our well-being and our morality – or our lack of it.' She gave a little laugh. 'I'm not certain which way she sees it now. She's always worried about us girls. It'd set her mind at rest to know I'm in good hands.'

He laughed. 'Is that how you see yourself, then? In good hands?'

'I trust you, Will. I don't think you'd hurt me like that rat I used to go with.'

Chapter Fourteen

1931 hosted deepening gloom. The number of people unemployed in Britain stood at more than two and a half million and the world seemed to be going mad again. In Germany, mobs, supporters of the increasingly influential Nazi party, were attacking Jewish traders and their property and, in Italy, Mussolini and his Fascisti banned all Catholic youth organisations and all secret societies.

Oblivious to the rest of the world and its idiosyncrasies, John Cephas Harper, twenty-three, and Alice Kite, sixteen years old and with child, were married and witnessed the same before God on Whit Sunday, 25th May. They spent their wedding night at the dairy house where they were to continue to dwell, occupying Henzey's cherished bedroom. Henzey gave it up reluctantly to share with Maxine.

In July, the most drastic reductions in state expenditure in Britain's illustrious history were proposed, with recommended salary cuts for teachers, the armed forces and the police, all to help achieve economies. The German mark collapsed and their banks shut their doors in an effort to halt a run on funds. In August, Ramsay MacDonald's Labour government fell, while the country suffered its worst ever financial crisis. A new cabinet, comprised of Labour, Tory and Liberal ministers, assumed responsibility for running the show. In September the King decided to take a pay cut of some fifty thousand pounds a year, but twelve thousand Royal Navy ratings mutinied at Invergordon over their pay cuts. Come October, and another general election, the National Government, as it was by this time known, remained in power after a landslide victory that routed Labour.

During this time, Henzey Kite and Will Parish developed their courtship, becoming increasingly caught up in each other. From the outset, this liaison was serious. Three times a week Henzey honed her cookery skills, preparing a meal for them both at Will's house after work. She had her own key in case he worked late and he gave her *carte blanche* to make any changes she wished, that would make his home more comfortable. Many of the things Dorothy had established, she altered, and many of her own ideas she introduced. Will's life had changed, so his surroundings had also to change to reflect his new situation.

Back in Cromwell Street, Henzey found it a little embarrassing at first having Jack Harper, one of her old sweethearts, living in the same house, now married to her younger sister. Thankfully she was not at home so much, since she spent so much time with Will, but when she returned at night he was often sitting downstairs alone, reading the paper or listening to the wireless.

She returned home one night after the family had, with the exception of Jack, retired to bed. As she hung her hat and coat on the stand in the hall, she could see a light shining through from the sitting-room and went to see who was still up, hoping it might be her mother.

'Henzey!' Jack greeted from one of the armchairs in front of the greying embers of the fire. 'Watcha. Fancy a drop o' beer?' He was nursing a glass in both hands and, on the floor at the side of the chair, stood a half-empty bottle.

'No thanks,' she replied from the doorway. 'I'll put some milk on to boil for a cup of cocoa to take to bed with me.'

'Why don't yer stop and talk a bit? We could 'ave a chat, like. Like we used to in the old days when we was courtin'.'

'Don't you think it's time you were upstairs?' she suggested evenly. 'How long since Alice went up?' She turned to go.

He shrugged. 'I dunno. Half an hour. An hour, maybe. Anyway, Alice is no fun now she's got a big belly.'

'I don't imagine it's much fun for Alice either, being eight months pregnant. You should give her more support, Jack. You could start by going to bed and giving her a cuddle at any rate.'

'A cuddle?' he scoffed. 'What use is a flippin' cuddle? Is that all you've 'ad tonight with that Will Parish? A cuddle?'

'What's it got to do with you?' Henzey turned and walked out of the sitting-room, and into the kitchen, irritated both by his innuendo and his immaturity. She poured milk into a pan and put it on the gas, then reached for the tin of cocoa from the cupboard behind her and spooned some into a mug. After a couple of minutes watching the pan of milk she sensed that somebody was watching her. Jack was leaning against the door jamb, looking her up and down with a confident leer. In his hand was his replenished glass.

'Yer can make me a cup, if yer like, Henzey.'

'I'll put some more milk into the pan for you, Jack,' she answered calmly, 'but you can make your own cocoa. I'm not waiting on you.'

As she reached for the jug of milk she felt Jack's hands on her waist and his breath hot on the back of her neck. At once she twisted and dodged out of his reach, deeply disappointed that he should attempt such familiarity.

'Yer never did that in the old days,' he said, smirking. 'Yer never did that before when I used to put me arm round yer. In fact yer used to like me to.' She turned to her milk again without answering. His leer turned into an open grin, lightening his expression. 'D'yer remember how we used to kiss in the entry afore I went 'ome, Henzey? Yer was a smashin' kisser, yer know. I still miss kissin' yer.'

'Fancy,' she replied, feigning a surprised smile.

'What about that time we was kissin' in the entry an' the chimney set afire? D'yer remember that?'

'No, it's funny, I don't . . .' She did, but she had no intention of admitting it to him. The milk came to the boil and she lifted it from the heat, filled her mug and gave it a stir. 'There's enough milk there for another mug of cocoa. Don't forget to turn the light out when you've finished. Good night.'

What had she ever seen in him? She was sixteen when she met Jack Harper. At first she was taken with him, but she soon discovered that, despite her tender years, she could have him dangling on a string. Jack was no challenge, even then, so she just as soon lost interest in him. Even in those days she realised he had always been a little devious, though never dangerously so; it never mattered particularly, since she was always at least one step ahead of him. Now, marriage had bestowed on him a confidence he'd lacked before. His bright, alert eyes seemed to regard Henzey lately with a disarming candour that seemed to say that she was just the kind of woman he would choose as a mistress. Under normal circumstances she would not have resented it; she might even have found it amusing; but since the fool had been married to her own sister she could see how pathetic he was.

On 25th November, Alice gave birth to a baby boy, seven pound four ounces, at the dairy house. Her labour was not prolonged, and both she and the child were well. The proud father went to announce his good fortune to his own family and returned the worse for drink. He was made to sleep on the settee in the front room. Jack favoured the name Gary for his son, after Gary Cooper, but Alice and the rest of the family preferred Edward, after the Prince of Wales. They settled on the latter.

'What's Jack doing?' Lizzie asked Alice one Sunday morning after Christmas. 'Is he ever going to get up and come down for his breakfast? I want to get this lot cleared away.'

'I expect he's havin' a swill,' Alice replied, guiding her nipple back into Edward's hungry mouth after he'd momentarily lost it. She was sitting in an armchair, still in her night-gown, the top buttons open so she could feed the child.

'Then let's hope he cleans the wash basin out. I'm sick of going in there after him and finding a ring of scum all round it.'

'Why don't you tell him?' Alice suggested indifferently.

'I think it's up to you to tell him,' her mother said, stacking crockery on the table to take into the kitchen. 'It's not just the wash basin, either. When he has a pee, he never pulls the chain after him. God knows how he's been brought up.'

'Well, he's not used to usin' a lavatory where you have to pull the chain,' Alice defended. 'At their house they've got an earth closet up the yard.' Her eyes met Lizzie's. 'He just forgets, I suppose.'

'Well, remind him, our Alice. Tell him that other folk would like to find the bathroom in the same condition he finds it in. I've got enough to do without going round cleaning and tidying up after *him*. And another thing . . .' Lizzie saw this as an ideal opportunity to remedy Jack's other faults that had been annoying her, 'get him to hang his jacket up instead of leaving it lying about. Just look . . . Over there . . . He always leaves it draped over the back of that chair. And when everybody's gone to bed he invariably helps himself to a bottle of Jesse's beer out of the verandah and drinks it – never offers any money for it – then he has the cheek to leave his dirty glass and the empty bottle in the sitting-room for me to clear up next morning. Well, I'm not having it, Alice. I'm not having it and it's up to you to tell him.'

'Why does everybody have to keep goin' on all the time?' Alice replied huffily. 'Don't do this. Don't do that. Do this. Do that. Tell Jack this. Tell Jack that. Blimey, I'm sick of it.' In her peevishness the child lost her nipple once more. He wailed again. 'Oh, Edward,' she sighed in exasperation and got up, fastening the buttons of her night-gown with her free hand. 'That's it. You'll 'ave to wait.'

'Finish feeding the child,' Lizzie advised evenly. 'He's still hungry.'

'You feed him. I've had enough. Besides, I've got to get Jack downstairs for his breakfast. *You* said so.'

'Well, if he doesn't come down soon, he'll get no breakfast.'

Edward continued to clamour at being so rudely deprived of his own breakfast, but, as Alice moved to hand the baby to Lizzie, Henzey intercepted and took the child.

'I wish I could feed him,' she said holding him close as Alice stormed out of the room. 'Poor little mite. You know, Mom, I dread to think what might happen to this child if those two were left to their own devices. How could anybody be so indifferent to a poor, helpless baby?'

'It's a certain fact she needs a few lessons,' Lizzie replied. 'A certain fact.'

'I could never be like that if the child was mine. He needs a bit of love as well . . . See? He's stopped crying now he can feel he's being loved.' Henzey continued rocking Edward gently in her arms, cooing and smiling as he gazed into her eyes. She wiped away his tears and marvelled at the beautiful clarity of his infant eyes and the softness of his skin. 'If I ever get married I'd want half a dozen like him.'

'Yes,' Lizzie said knowingly, 'but wait till you are married, eh?'

Henzey chuckled. 'Oh, I know. It runs in the family getting pregnant before you're married, doesn't it?'

'Cheeky madam!'

Throughout 1932, things showed little sign of improvement.

'I don't know how you stand it, Henzey,' Will said one evening just before Christmas, when Jack and Alice had cropped up in conversation.

'I can't stand it,' she replied. 'They've been told they've got to find somewhere else to live. It's Jesse's house, after all, and he wants a quiet life. He shouldn't have to put up with all that hassle from Jack and Alice.'

'Maxine told me she can't even practise her cello nowadays without being interrupted,' Will said.

'I know. It's true. And Herbert won't take Sally back there when he knows they're in – which happens to be most of the time.'

'Well, I'm not that keen on seeing them either if you want the truth, Henzey. I'd just as soon not go when they're there.'

'I know,' she answered pensively. 'You've no idea how much I appreciate being able to come here with you. I love the peace and quiet here.'

'Well, you know the answer.'

She looked at him and smiled. 'Do I?'

'Yes . . .'

'Oh? So what is the answer, then?'

'Marry me.'

She laughed. 'Oh, be serious. I'm not going to marry you just to get away from Alice and Jack. In no time now they'll find somewhere to live and they'll be gone.'

Will looked somewhat hurt. 'Henzey, I am being serious. I've never been more serious in my life. I want to marry you, not just to save you from their nuisance, but because I love you. I want us to be together – all the time. You're right, this place is a haven for us but it's you that's made it so. Don't you see? When you're not here, it's never quite the same. It's almost as if the house itself reacts to you. You've made it a home, Henzey – our home. It misses you when you're not here, the same as I miss you. I want you here, in it, with me. What do you say? Shall we get married?'

His words touched her. She leaned over to him and their lips met. Her hand gently stroked the back of his head, then she broke off the kiss and looked directly into his eyes for a few intense seconds, their faces only inches apart. Love was unmistakable in her eyes.

'You haven't answered my question,' he persisted. 'Kissing me won't sidetrack me.'

'Tell it me all again.'

He laughed. 'Just say you'll marry me.'

She smiled radiantly. 'Oh, Will. Yes, I'll marry you. How soon? Tomorrow? Saturday? Next week? Next month?'

'I've been looking at the calendar . . .'

'Oh, so you were sure of my answer?'

'Optimistic. It pays to be prepared. And I always like to be organised.'

'How soon can we start a family?'

'Well, not straight away . . .'

She looked dejected.

'. . . But soon.'

She smiled.

'I thought it'd be best if we waited till you were twenty-one for the wedding,' he continued. 'Don't you think? Then we won't have to seek anybody's permission. Your birthday falls on a Tuesday. The Sunday after that's the second of April. Let's do it then.'

She squeezed his knee. 'I see it as a good omen that you didn't suggest the day before.'

'The day before? The day before is the first.'

'That's what I mean. April Fools' day.'

Both families were informed of the forthcoming marriage, and the banns were duly published at St John's, Kates Hill, and at St John's, Ladywood. It was a very intense business choosing a wedding dress but, with the help and advice of Lizzie and Florrie Shuker, Henzey chose one. She and Will had to content themselves with waiting a further week for their wedding, however, till 9th April. Only immediate families were to be invited, plus a few close friends, and there was to be a party at the dairy house afterwards.

Ever since their first outing, that sunny April afternoon nearly two years ago in the castle grounds, Henzey had known she would marry Will Parish. There was much to do: Will wanted to make improvements to his home, one of which was converting the smallest bedroom into a bathroom; he intended to redecorate the entire house; they agreed to buy new furniture, especially a new bed. Although it was the same house that Dorothy had lived in, all these introductions would render it a different home and thus help eliminate any memories of her. Not that Henzey resented her being remembered; far from it, but she wanted to stamp her own identity on it, since she was to be the mistress of it. So they worked hard getting it ready for the big day.

And before they knew it, April arrived . . .

'Dearly beloved, we are gathered together here in the sight of God, and in the face of this congregation, to join together this man and this woman in holy matrimony . . .' The Reverend John Mainwaring thoroughly enjoyed officiating at a rattling good solemnisation of matrimony. As he delivered the rich phrases he loved and knew so well, he peered over the rim of his half-moon spectacles, taking stock of the congregation. He observed significantly more people on the bride's side than on the bridegroom's. *'. . . and is not by any to be enterprised, nor taken in hand, unadvisedly, lightly, or wantonly, to satisfy men's carnal lusts and appetites . . .'* Henzey's eyelids dropped, lest the vicar wondered whether any of this carnal lust business applied to her. *'First it was ordained for the procreation of children . . .'* Henzey looked up at Will. Through her veil he saw the plea in her soft blue eyes. He was aware how much she wanted children. He smiled back non-committally. *'. . . Second, it was ordained for a remedy against sin, and to avoid fornication; that such persons as have not the gift of continency might marry . . .'*

Will had been tempted to turn and watch his bride walk up the aisle on Jesse's arm, but had resisted. Just in time he remembered he'd done exactly that when he married Dorothy. It was supposed to bring bad luck and look what had happened to her. So this time he waited till his bride glided to his side at the steps of the chancel, then caught his first glimpse of her and the first whiff of her familiar perfume.

Now, every few seconds she would turn to look at him and he could see her eyes, bright, happy, smiling through the white veil, which was crowned with a chaplet of orange blossom. She had refused to tell him beforehand what her dress was like, but now he could see for himself. It was a long, sheathed, satin gown overlaid with lace, with a trailing, white, satin train and long, tight, lace sleeves. The bodice was lace yoked with a high neck at the front, but cut low at the back. In her hand she carried a bouquet of freesias. She stood beside him, elegant, statuesque, her beautiful figure enhanced in this dress that fitted perfectly. *'Thirdly it was ordained for the mutual society, help and comfort that the one ought to have of the other, both in prosperity and adversity . . .'* He pondered how fortunate he was to have won the love of this girl, whom he had found irresistible from the start; this girl, who was breathtakingly beautiful today. But it was not just her looks, it was her whole self, her demeanour, her integrity, her gentle wit. Above all, it was the love she gave him in return; warm, unselfish. If he ever lost her, life would surely not be worth living. If ever he had the gross misfortune to lose her as well to childbirth . . .

'. . . Therefore, if any man can shew any just cause why they may not be lawfully joined together, let him now speak, or else hereafter forever hold his peace.'

Yes, he might well have to resist pressure to start a family. It was not a consideration yet. With any luck it would be a couple of years before the topic was really ripe for discussion. In any case, was there any point in bringing children into this uncertain world, tainted as it was with the threat of Nazism and Communism? *'I require and charge you both as ye will answer at the dreadful day of judgement . . .'* They could surround themselves with creature comforts instead.

'. . . William John, wilt thou have this woman to thy wedded wife, to live together after God's ordinance in the holy estate of matrimony . . .' Certainly,

what Henzey was about to save in rail fares from Dudley to Hockley on the Great Western line would be tantamount to a significant wage rise. Four and a penny a week they wouldn't have to find. '. . . *and forsaking all other, keep thee only unto her, so long as ye both shall live?*'

'I will.'

'*Henzey, wilt thou have this man to thy wedded husband . . .*' Nervous now, trembling a little. Funny how it gets you like that in the end. Catch Will's eye, smile reassurance, clear throat ready for the response. Will smiling in anticipation. There's that funny melancholy look in his eyes again. '. . . *Wilt thou obey him and serve him, love, honour and keep him . . .*' What's going through his mind right now? Oh, to be able to hold him tight this very minute, just to love him. '. . . *and forsaking all other, keep thee only unto him, so long as ye both shall live.*'

'I will.' *Oh, I will.*

Will wondered, too, what was going through her mind. Often he could tell. She looked up at him and gave him one of her devastating smiles. Now she just looked happy . . . and perhaps a little overcome.

'*Who giveth this woman to be married to this man?*'

Out of the corner of his eye, Will saw Jesse shuffle proudly forward.

The Reverend Mainwaring went on: 'Repeat after me . . . *I William John, take thee, Henzey . . .*'

'I, William John, take thee, Henzey.'

'*. . . To my wedded wife . . .*'

Henzey watched Will's lips as he made his vows. She could not help recalling the first time she had kissed those smooth, manly lips on Hockley station; how, when she was drawing his portrait before that, she had imagined how they might feel on hers. If only she had known then that she would marry this man. But at that time she could never have guessed it, still smarting from Billy Witts . . . *Him* . . . She was so glad all that was behind her. But it's funny how people fall in love; even the most unlikely pairs make couples. If she scoured the whole world she could not have wished for a more honest, principled and intelligent man than Will. Fate had played a hand. Fate had sent her to Lucas's to work, exploiting her talent as an artist, contriving their meeting. Thank God for that talent. Thank God for Lucas's. Thank God for Will.

'. . . *And thereto I plight thee my troth.*'

While Henzey had been plighting her troth, promising to love, cherish and to obey, Samuel, the man Will looked upon as his elder brother, discharged part of his duties as best man and handed over the wedding ring. John Mainwaring took it, placed it on his open *Book of Common Prayer*, and blessed it. He looked at Will. Will took the ring.

Almost there now. He was trembling a little, too, as he took her left hand and she sensed it in the way he touched her. She spread out her slender fingers and felt his ring slide down her third finger, stalling momentarily at the knuckle, then seating comfortably in its rightful place. She watched, capturing it all in her memory. Never would she forget this moment. Again she looked up at Will, misty through the tears she was trying to suppress.

'Will, repeat after me. *With this ring I thee wed.*'

He held her gaze. 'With this ring I thee wed.'

'. . . *With my body I thee worship . . .*'

'With my body I thee worship.'

'. . . *And with all my worldly goods I thee endow.*'

'And with all my worldly goods I thee endow.'

'*In the name of the Father . . .*'

She knelt down, a married woman.

A married woman. It was scarcely believable. Her family was his, his family was hers.

'*Oh, Eternal God, Creator and Preserver of all mankind, Giver of all spiritual grace, the Author of everlasting life; send thy blessing upon these thy servants, this man and this woman . . .*' Samuel, his brother, must be about forty-three or forty-four; old enough to be her father, and about the same age as her mother. His face reflected that life had been hard, that they'd been poor when they were children. '. . . *whereof this Ring given and received is a token and pledge . . .*' His mother and father bore testimony to that. Old Mr and Mrs Parish were not well off now, and their clothes had that impoverished look about them still, though they were spotlessly clean. Good to know that people who were so poor could devote so much of their life to God and bring up their children in the fear and nurture of God, rather than blame Him for their misfortunes. Yet since they were so poor, maybe God was all they had. '. . . *through Jesus Christ our Lord. Amen.*'

Mr Mainwaring joined their right hands together. '*Those whom God hath joined together, let no man put asunder . . .*' He looked over his glasses again and addressed the congregation, continuing his oratory with a self-satisfied smile, until: '. . . *I pronounce that they be man and wife together. In the name of the father, and of the Son, and of the Holy Ghost. Amen.*'

Bride and groom looked at each other once more. Her right hand searched for his left hand at her side and found it. It was like being in a dream. Mr Mainwaring sportingly invited Will to kiss the bride, so Maxine stepped forward to carefully pull back Henzey's veil. He kissed her and Henzey blushed, then smiled self-consciously. There were more prayers, a psalm, a hymn and more prayers still before they were asked to follow the vicar into the vestry to sign the register.

It was when they walked down the aisle arm in arm that Henzey noticed how many uninvited guests had actually taken the trouble to come to the ceremony to see her married off. There was a party from George Mason's, including Clara Maitland, and about a dozen girls from the Headlamp Department at Lucas's, as well as neighbours and old school friends, all anxious to endow her and Will with confetti, rice, and their best wishes, between having photographs taken outside in the bright, but cool April sunshine.

Afterwards, the formalities over, the invited assembled at the

MICHAEL TAYLOR

dairy house for the party. Fortunately, the house was of an adequate size to accommodate all the guests. Trestle tables were brought in so that everybody could sit down to the hot dinner prepared by Hilda Bottlebrush, who always put on a good spread. After the toasts and the speeches, the two families got to know each other.

Joe, Lizzie's brother, as ever on such occasions as this, played the pianola, encouraging everyone to sing, which May, Joe's wife, led. When they'd sung enough, Maxine herself installed a roll in the pianola and pedalled like mad to keep the music going with a few choice marches.

From the settee in the sitting-room, where he sat with his arm around the shy and thick-ankled Sally, Herbert Kite's eyes hungrily followed the slender, youthful body of Elizabeth Knight, one of Will's nieces, as she glided from room to room in her peach bridesmaid's dress. Will, aware of Jack Harper's weakness for the fairer sex, observed him lusting over Ruth Knight, her sister, who was another bridesmaid. Jack stood with a pint glass of beer in his hand and watched her every move, choosing not to hear anything anyone said to him. Everybody believed him to be in a drunken stupor, but Alice's eyes were monitoring him.

When Ruth Knight rebuffed Jack Harper, he set his sights on her younger sister, for he always reckoned to have more success with younger girls. Alice's eyes only left him for a second but, in that instant, he slipped his leash and found Elizabeth alone in the scullery conscientiously stacking dirty crockery. But Herbert saw him and jealously intervened, coldly suggesting that he return to Alice. Caught out, Jack returned to Alice's side and gave her a guilty smile. Meanwhile, Herbert plucked up the courage to ask Elizabeth if he could take her out some time and, glory be, she accepted.

During the late afternoon, after Henzey had changed her outfit, there was additional sustenance in the form of sandwiches and cakes, with cups of tea or Camp coffee for those who wanted it. The party went on into the evening, by which time Henzey and Will had thanked everybody for coming and for the lovely wedding gifts.

At about ten o'clock the bride and groom decided it was time to take their leave and retire to their home in Daisy Road, Ladywood. Rex, their brother-in-law, who owned a motor car, offered to drive them over, save taking the tram, and they willingly accepted. Amidst all the goodbyes and good wishes, Henzey, though undoubtedly happier than she had ever been before in her life, felt a pang of sorrow that she was leaving the tender mercies of her mother after all these years.

Lizzie felt it, too.

It was the end of an era.

Chapter Fifteen

Even before marriage, Henzey had grown into Will's life and into his house. There was no going back for either of them now, not that they wanted to. Marriage brought a new way of life; more convenient than the old. He was considerate and she respected him. He talked to her about anything and everything; the latest news, fashion, the price of potatoes, religion, work and holidays. He encouraged her to do more drawing and painting, which she'd had little time for while they were courting. Will was a serious man, sometimes intense, but he was almost always pleasant, and she amused him with that quick, gentle wit of hers. They were comfortable with each other and there was a trust between them that she had never felt before she met him.

As if to conspire with their happiness, the summer seemed sunny and warm every day. It was simply that they ignored the rainy days. Even on what few wet evenings there were, Henzey perversely insisted that they go for a walk around Rotton Park Reservoir, just to be under a gamp with Will and hear the rain beating down on it. It was romantic, especially when you were married, and she was determined that marriage should not betoken the end of romance.

Will, too, could not recall being happier. His long, lonely years when he'd grieved for Dorothy now seemed light-years away. He looked back and was thankful that he'd not taken up with any other woman during that time, for to have done so would have robbed himself of the opportunity of happiness with this vision. He was on a different plane of existence these days. This young woman lying by his side in the bed they shared, was his by her own free choice. Those soft blue eyes, that addictive skin and that lush, dark hair were the key that unlocked his desire and his love for her. They were so close in those early months, almost one person; as a married couple certainly one entity; yet they were separate beings, irrevocably different, apart from the obvious differences of gender. And for all that, there were times already when he thought he knew what she was thinking, what she was feeling, by the outward signs and expressions she revealed.

It would be an unmitigated tragedy to lose her as well as Dorothy to childbirth.

Henzey, too, was learning how to read Will; the way he might react in a given situation. Her mother had always told her, 'You have to live with them and lie with them before you really get to know them.' And the more she knew and understood him, the more profound was her love.

In a ridiculously short time, it seemed there had never been anything in life except each other. Marriage decreed that they need never meet at work unless one had a message for the other; unlike when they were courting and they arranged to meet as often as they could. It also ordained that Will could go out alone a couple of nights a week for a pint or two of beer and to play darts at the Reservoir public house, but she didn't mind that. His absence gave her chance to catch up with housework, or baking cakes and pies.

On Sunday mornings, when Will was singing in the choir at church and Henzey was getting herself ready or doing her chores, she could look out of her kitchen window and watch men fishing in the reservoir, mallards dipping their heads into the water, seagulls screeching overhead and riding the breeze, moorhens cruising close to the bank. If someone had told her four years earlier, when she was a regular patron of the Tower Ballroom, that she would marry and live just round the corner from it, she would never have believed them. She felt it was a lovely place to live and the longer she lived there the more she appreciated it. She could not have been happier. There was just one trouble-some thought that kept recurring, the only shadow in her life of sunshine – how long would it be before she became pregnant? For Will seemed to be avoiding the subject.

'Another bottle o' beer, Will?' Ned Bingham said, turning round in his seat as best he could to talk to Will Parish. Ned was proffering a bottle of beer in one hand, a bottle opener poised at the ready in the other. His wife, Phoebe, was at his side, tucking into her personal supper, a cheese and pickle sandwich.

'Oh, cheers,' Will said.

Ned prised off the cap and handed him the bottle. As he put it to his mouth the coach swayed and lurched, making it difficult to drink without catching his teeth on it.

"Ow 'bout you, Henzey?' Ned said. 'Bottle o' beer? You young 'uns am supposed to be able to drink.'

'I wouldn't mind a shandy, Ned.'

'A shandy?' he exclaimed, in a show of mock irritation. ''Er wants a bloody shandy. That means a perishin' glass, don' it?' Ned was in charge of the drinks on this outing, a job he now regretted volunteering for, since tending to others' wishes meant getting more drink down his best trousers than down his throat.

'Oh, stop your moanin' an' gi' the wench a shandy,' Phoebe jibed.

A crate of beer for the adults and one of lemonade for the children sat in the stairwell of the coach, refreshment for them all. Ned, severely impeded by his fat belly, reached down for one of the glasses lying wrapped in cloths in a cardboard box beside the crates. He grabbed one, half filled it with lemonade, and struggled to top it up with beer. But it was frothing over him as the coach bumped on erratically.

'Oh, bugger it!' he muttered, waiting for the froth to subside a little.

Phoebe croaked with laughter at her husband's frustration. 'Why, yo'll stink loike Davenport's brewery boi the toime yer've finished. Y'only took on this job 'cause yer thought as yo'd get yer hands on more beer. Sairves yer right, yer drunken ol' bugger.' She turned round to Henzey. 'Sairves him right, don' it, Henzey?'

Henzey smiled at Phoebe and looked at the glass Ned was filling. 'That's enough, Ned,' she said. 'That'll do for me. I don't want you to look as if you've just waded out of Rotton Park Reservoir, on my account.'

Phoebe's ample flesh seemed to roll as she wobbled with laughter. 'What? Nothin' would get him that close to water.'

Henzey took the glass that Ned passed to her. 'Oh, that's not fair, Phoebe. He was paddling in the sea at Rhyl with me and some of the kids. Weren't you, Ned?' She took a sip of her drink and her nose went into the froth with the bumping of the coach. She wiped it off with the back of her hand.

'Course I was, an' if I'd had one o' them bathin' costumes I'd have gone for a swim, an' all.'

'Yer wouldn't want to see 'im in a bathin' costume, young Henzey, I can tell ya.'

All the way back, there had been shrieks of laughter and hints that severe boisterousness might break out at any moment. Some children were standing, some sitting, others darting nimbly between seats, and one pair wrestling. All were noisy. Suddenly, from half the thirty or so eight- and nine-year-olds occupying the rest of the coach, a chorus of 'Show me the Way to go Home' soared over the din and the laboured droning of the engine. The other half, giggling, started singing 'Pack up your Troubles in your Old Kit Bag', in fierce competition.

'God, you'd think as this lot'd be tired out by now, wun't ya?' Phoebe shouted, trying to be heard.

Will Parish had suggested organising this trip to Rhyl for the younger choirboys and deprived children of the Osler Street School, where Dorothy Parish used to teach. The choir had duly raised a kitty by holding fund-raising events, and this was the big day. Canon Gittins from St John's, and two teachers from the school, were also there to help supervise the children. Now, on the road back, somewhere in Shropshire between Whitchurch and Newport, nobody minded their rowdiness for they were happy. For the first time in their lives they had seen and smelled the sea, built sandcastles on the beach and tasted ice cream. And to top it all, they'd had a gloriously warm and sunny day.

Phoebe had finished her supper and was trying to read a newspaper she'd bought in Rhyl. She turned round to Henzey. 'With all this trouble goin' on in the wairld it makes yer wonder if it's wairth bringin' kids into it, don' it?'

'Why, what do you mean, Phoebe?'

'I've just bin readin' how this sod Hitler's had hundreds shot in Germany, p'raps thousands even, it says here. Some even his own supporters, an' all. Cor! He's an evil sod, that Hitler.'

'I know. It's a worry. Did you see those pictures in the paper of the Italian football team giving that Fascist salute when they'd won some football match or other? The crowd looked as if they were going mad.'

'That was the World Cup Final, Henzey,' Will said. 'Italy beat Czechoslovakia. We weren't even invited to take part . . .'

'Good job, an' all,' Phoebe remarked. 'We want nothin' to do with the likes o' them.'

Ned leaned across the aisle of the coach to Canon Gittins. 'Another beer, Canon?'

The Canon declined.

'. . . But you're right, it is a worry,' Will went on. 'Remember last April, how the Austrians made Dollfuss a Fascist dictator?'

'But what is Fascism, Will?' Henzey asked. 'What does it mean?'

Canon Gittins heard her question and leaned towards her.

'It's a philosophy that advocates government by an extreme right dictatorship, Mrs Parish. Sadly, it holds belligerent nationalism as one of its ideologies.'

Ned turned round to Henzey. He said, 'It ain't so much worryin' as frightenin', I reckon. If you'm again' 'em they just bump you off. They point a gun at you and, bang, you're flippin' dead, mate! He's an evil swine, that Hitler, an' no doubt. I'd love to meet him in our entry one dark night if I was carryin' three foot o' lead pipin'. Did yer know as he's ordered all folk sufferin' from any physical deformity to be sterilised?'

'Cor! You'd be done straight away with that big fat belly o' your'n, then, Ned,' Phoebe said, making Henzey chuckle. 'Mind yer, it must be terrible for all them poor Jews. Knockin' 'em about scandalous, they am, them brown-shirts. Even women and babs. An' Jesus was a Jew, wan't 'e?'

Canon Gittins nodded his head sagely. 'It's tragic that the Nazis continue to blame the Jews for Jesus's death two thousand years after the event. It's ridiculous. Significant, too, that Hitler's quit the League of Nations. He'll do just as he likes – internationally.' He shook his head. 'Could be very dangerous.'

'And look at that Oswald Mosely,' Henzey said. 'He's another, isn't he, except he's English? . . . Oh, I don't want to think about it.'

'Well, somebody has to think about it, my love,' Will said. 'Fortunately, it seems the government has finally realised that Germany's a potential threat yet again – and just for a change they're talking of spending money to boost the armed forces. But I wonder if they've left it too late.'

'Nobody wants war again,' Canon Gittins said, 'but we must be ready to defend ourselves if it comes. The Germans have no reason to fight us now, but we all abhor what they're doing in their own country. Just think what they'd do to us if they could invade us – or any other country for that matter. We must have a deterrent.'

'True,' Will said. 'And in any case, increased spending on

arms will help to get more people back to work. Thankfully, the numbers unemployed are on the decline already, if we're to believe the figures they publish.'

'Do you have plenty of work on at Lucas's now, Will?'

'Oh, yes, Canon. Plenty. We're taking on more people again.'

'Well, that's certainly good news. And shall you continue to work, Mrs Parish?'

'Oh, I reckon I shall be there forever.' She smiled, and looked at Will, who was taking a swig from his bottle of beer.

'Be at work forever?' Phoebe exclaimed over the din. 'I don't know about work, young Henzey. It's time yer started a family. How long yer bin married now?'

'Two years last April.'

'There y'are then.'

Will laughed aloud. 'Make your mind up, Phoebe. Two minutes ago you were wondering whether it's worth bringing kids into the world.'

'Yes, I know I said that, Will. But all the same, you still have to have kids, don't yer? If yer dint have kids the human race would perish, wun't it? Then where would we be?'

'Well, I'm inclined to agree with your first comment, Phoebe,' Will said and took another slurp from his bottle of beer. 'I think there's too much trouble afoot to think about having children. Besides, in another year or so, at the rate we're going, Henzey and me should be able to buy a new, modern house in some leafy suburb. Semi-detached.'

'We already live in a semi-detached, Will.'

'No, it's the end house of a terrace, Henzey.'

'So it's semi-detached.'

'Henzey, it's not quite the same thing. We've already discussed this.'

'Yes, we've discussed it, Will,' Henzey said, 'but, as I recall, we reached no decision.'

'Forgive us washing our dirty linen in public, Phoebe,' he said, sounding irritated by Henzey's disregard.

Phoebe glanced apprehensively at Canon Gittins.

'You see, Phoebe, I'd rather have a baby,' Henzey explained. 'I'm quite content to stay where we are in Daisy Road and start a family. I don't see any sense in moving. Doing that would only delay starting a family anyway. Besides, it's not every house in Birmingham that overlooks a lake.'

'Reservoir,' Will interrupted.

'Lake . . . It's nice there, Phoebe. It's peaceful and it's tranquil. We've got nice neighbours. It's an ideal place to raise a family.'

'Quite right, young Henzey,' Phoebe concurred, glancing at the clergyman again, then looking intently at Will. 'Yer see, Will? Your wife wants a bab. It's on'y natural as a young married woman should want a bab. Most natural thing in the world, a bab. Don't you agree, Vicar?'

Later, in their bedroom, Henzey and Will discussed the day, recounting some of the amusing things that had happened. They agreed that the trip had been worthwhile. Will felt an affinity for those kids who had nothing. Because their families were so poor they never did anything that might give them even a hint that the world was vastly bigger than Birmingham.

'There, but for the grace of God, go I,' he said philosophically, pulling his shirt out of the waistband of his trousers. 'Years ago, I mean.'

Henzey was sitting at her dressing table wearing just her knickers, applying Pond's cleansing cream to her face. 'Perhaps we should do it again next year. To see the joy on the faces of those kids was worth the effort of fixing it all up, don't you think?'

He smiled and unfastened his trousers, allowing them to fall around his legs. He kicked them off deftly and picked them up by the turn-ups. 'Henzey . . . I know we haven't really talked about it for a long time, till this evening on the coach. . .' He paused, turning to grab a hanger.

'Talked about what?'

'Oh . . . kids . . . You know . . . Starting a family and all that . . .'

She stopped what she was doing and looked at him. 'And whose fault's that? You never seem to want to talk about it. Whenever I mention anything, that might suggest to you that I want to talk about it, you change the subject or clam up altogether.'

'What I was going to say is this,' he went on, ignoring her complaint, 'have you considered us fostering a child? When we're ready, that is?'

'No,' she answered decisively, and returned to her cleansing, deeply hurt.

He hung his trousers in his wardrobe, then took off his socks. After a minute he said, 'It would be an answer, you know . . . to both our . . . problems.'

'Problems? What problems? I haven't got any problems. I just want my own child, not some ready-made one that's had the misfortune to be born to the wrong mother.'

'But you know *my* problem . . . my phobia.'

'Oh, I understand your fears about me having to go through childbirth, Will, but I don't accept them any longer. I can't. You'll have to get over it, for your own peace of mind. It's not only totally irrational but it's not fair either. I want children, Will, regardless of your phobia. Most women want children, but I want children of my own first and foremost.' She paused for a few seconds, returning momentarily to her face-cleansing. 'Oh, Will, I don't mean to be unkind or sound uncharitable, but I'm a healthy girl. I'm well capable of bearing children. There's no history of death during childbirth on either side of my family. And you've already proved that you can father a child. Why should we saddle ourselves with somebody else's mistake?'

'Perhaps I shouldn't have mentioned it,' he said, feeling peeved. 'It was just a thought. I was adopted as a child, remember. I thought it might be appropriate for us to help some other poor little devil.'

She stood up and walked over to him, sorry that she had upset him. He was standing naked now. She put her arms around his waist and felt his lean, supple body, hard against the more yielding firmness of her own skin. He took her in his arms and his caressing hands explored her silken shoulders, savouring her skin while she lay her head on his chest. His hands followed the contours of her body down to her slender waist, taking in the small of her back, then down, down, under the waistband of her knickers to the firm flesh of her bottom. He felt a stirring within him at the feel of her warm, smooth buttocks beneath his fingers. With a tentative smile she looked up at him and his lips came down on hers. As she pressed her breasts gently against his chest, she felt him harden against her belly.

'We could make love without a French letter for once,' she suggested, hopefully. 'It's safe enough, this time of the month.'

'A French letter should be used at every conceivable opportunity.' He sounded very serious.

She looked up and, seeing humour in his eyes, smiled. 'Oh, very funny. Now you're mocking me.'

'Course I'm not. There's still a risk.'

'Hardly at all. Even so — don't you think knowing there's a risk might make it all the more exciting?'

'Oh, I see. Is it not exciting enough for you now?'

She kissed him again and they slumped backwards onto the bed. As he teased a nipple with his tongue, his fingers savoured the silkiness of her skin . . .

But he felt under pressure. He felt under pressure to make love without protection. He wanted her more than anything in the world; yearned to feel himself sliding inside her; longed to enjoy her eager response. But he loved her far too much to risk losing her. Losing her was unthinkable. So, unspeaking, he broke off their embrace to reach for a condom from the drawer in his bedside table.

Henzey sighed. Yet again she grieved, silently submissive, for her only hope was that this condom would be defective.

Chapter Sixteen

The company Neville Worthington owned and ran was establishing itself at last as a manufacturer of reliable, light commercial vehicles. During the twenties, they had designed and put into production a three-wheeled van, powered by a small twin-cylinder air-cooled engine. The revenue it generated funded the development of another, bigger van which, thankfully, was making greater profits. The family firm was founded in 1851, the year of the Great Exhibition, as The Worthington Steam Engine Company. So entrenched were they in steam in those days that even a bride was sought from a steam family for Neville's father when the time came for him to marry; Neville's mother, Magdalen, was a descendant of the famous Matthew Boulton who, in 1762, opened the exemplary Soho Works near Hockley Brook where James Watt developed the newly invented steam engine for commercial use. The Black Country had been a lucrative catchment area for the Worthingtons' engines, used in collieries for pumping away water, for providing traction for the cages that took men down to their work levels and brought them back up at the end of their shifts. They were used to generate the raw motive power for batteries of forging hammers, to blow blast furnaces and to turn the lathes, grinders and drilling machines from which all sorts of precision pieces were contrived. But that was all in the past. Collieries now were closing down at an alarming rate, had been for years and, in the enterprises that still thrived, electricity was relentlessly replacing steam.

With their engineering expertise in reciprocating engines, it seemed a logical progression to opt for manufacture of internal combustion engines, thus exploiting the engineering facilities they already enjoyed in their iron foundry, their fabrication and machine shops. Neville had, wisely, he believed, avoided the more capricious motor-car market with its airy-fairy whims and fashions; and the number of firms making motor cars that had gone out of business in the last ten years seemed to substantiate his judgement. Commercial vehicles were more down to earth, more basic – not unlike himself – and enjoyed a more stable market.

Worthington Commercials had recently won a government contract to develop and manufacture two types of vehicles for the armed forces. Both were general purpose vehicles for carrying personnel and goods, one, little larger than a motor car, the other more akin to a lorry. This had been spurred by the growing threat to peace and stability from the excesses of the Nazi party in Germany and the political demands they were making on their neighbours. Germany was defiantly flouting the limitations set on the size of its armed forces by the Treaty of Versailles; and subsequent condemnation by the League of Nations only succeeded in precipitating Hitler into a tantrum. Britain must be ready to face any threat. New aircraft, bombers and fighters were on the drawing board; new battleships; new tanks. It was obvious that new types of vehicles would also be needed to service these with men and supplies.

Neville insisted on undertaking most of the important aspects of business himself, even down to negotiating with suppliers on details of design, of pricing and scheduling of deliveries. There was not so much as one nut or bolt, on any vehicle that his factory produced, that he had not been intimately involved with at some point in its evolution, though he employed many people to whom he might entrust such responsibilities. It was this meticulous care and a reluctance to delegate that took him to Lucas's Great King Street factory for the first time in May 1935. There were many people to see. He had to discuss the design and specification of starting, ignition and lighting equipment, their costs and lead times, from placing orders to receiving finished goods.

Will Parish was sitting in his office poring over some drawings just sent to him from the Drawing Office. A memorandum accompanied them, suggesting he study them prior to imminent negotiations with the customer. One was for a starter motor, one a dynamo, another for a distributor, a couple for lighting, and others besides.

It was going to be another unseasonably warm day for early May. He could feel it already. Close; humid; uncomfortable. He loosened his tie and undid the collar-stud at his throat, looking again at the design for the starter motor. This was his forte; electric motors. His hand went to his chin and he looked at the drawing thoughtfully. The armature looked familiar – a Lucas design – as were the bearings and the brushes; but the housing he hadn't seen before. He shifted it out of the way and perused another sheet containing details of the dynamo. Again, the various component parts he was acquainted with; but this, too, was a new housing. There must be casting drawings here. He thumbed through the sheaf.

Will chanced to look up. Two men were approaching. One of them, Jack Heggety, a design engineer from the drawing office, he knew. The other, a taller, bearded man, he had not seen before. He pored over the drawings again; a knock at his open door.

'Morning, Will,' Jack Heggety greeted. 'I've brought along Neville Worthington to meet you. Mr Worthington . . . Will Parish . . '

Will looked at Neville Worthington and smiled affably. 'Nice to meet you, Mr Worthington.' They shook hands.

'Will, you should have received a sheaf of drawings by now. . .'

'These, you mean, Jack? They arrived on my desk a few minutes ago.'

'Mr Worthington would like to go over a few things with you, Will. Discuss the suitability of the windings, materials, and so forth, since you're the chap who'll have to see they're right.'

Will looked out of the window and beckoned Sidney Joel, one of his team, to join the discussion. 'Sidney has a good eye for this sort of thing. I've hardly had a chance yet to see what's what, but my initial impression is that they're heavy-duty applications. Some sort of commercial vehicle?'

Neville studied Will's eyes. 'A bit more than that actually. They're for two new general purpose vehicles for the armed forces. Part of the rearmament programme the government's at last seen fit to implement. We've won a contract to develop and to manufacture. Prototypes, at any rate.'

Sidney Joel tapped on the door and hovered. Will called him in, introduced him and explained what they knew so far about this new project.

Neville added, 'Reliability and durability are the things I'm most concerned with, Will . . . do you mind if I call you Will?' Will said he didn't mind. 'Good. Call me Neville. Could we just flip through the drawings so I can get your initial reaction, do you think?'

Will spread the drawings about and the other three stood looking at them pensively, waiting for his comments. 'Well, here, on this starter motor, the electrics will be fine. They're tried and tested. But if we have to think in terms of war – shell damage, shocks from explosions and such, then I think you'd be better advised to design in greater impact resistance in the casing. Same on the dynamo.'

'Make them thicker, you mean?' Neville asked.

'Well, yes. There'll be a penalty in increased weight, but I would've thought *that* hardly an impediment in a vehicle of this type. The point is, the thicker the section, the higher grade material we could get them cast in. And because a higher grade would have greater tensile strength, we would get a two-fold advantage.'

'All of which eats up time, Will. Actually, my own foundry could cast these. We have to have a prototype vehicle for the Ministry in little more than six months, and we have many other suppliers and components to worry about.'

'Well, we can soon knock up some new drawings, Neville,' Jack assured. 'That's not a problem. But what about development, Will? How long do you need on all this?'

Will regarded Neville. 'This is a special application and there are many things to consider. In the light of what we've been saying maybe we should consider uprating the electrics. That means that Jack and his design team will have to reconsider bearings and lubrication, wiring, insulation material and so on. In this department, Neville, we analyse system behaviour. To do that we usually have to resort to experimental methods and they take time, too.'

'Are we talking about a virtual redesign?'

'Certainly some modifications,' Jack Heggety remarked.

Neville rubbed his chin thoughtfully. 'Look, chaps. These trucks are going to get the absolute dickens of a bashing if ever there's a war. I'd like to think they're not going to fail because we didn't take account of that.'

'We can get onto uprating straight away, Neville. But it's only fair to warn you that there's going to be a lot of overtime worked in this department to get everything ready if it's needed that soon. That's going to cost money . . .'

'It's top priority,' Neville stressed. 'Never mind overtime. I'm not certain mere overtime's enough. Can you not organise a two- or three-shift system in this department to speed things up even more?'

Will and Jack looked at each other, and the latter, feeling the heat, wiped his brow with the back of his hand.

'That's not a decision we can make here, Neville,' Will answered.

'Then let's talk to the Board. I was assured of their full co-operation.'

'If they promised it you'll get it.'

Later that day Neville Worthington drove to his home, Wessex House, situated on Hagley Road in Edgbaston amidst other large, prestigious houses belonging to the industrial upper classes and professional folk. As he travelled from his office in Wash-wood Health he pondered his meeting earlier in the day at Lucas Electrical. The manager of the Product Development Department was bothering him.

'You seem distant, Neville,' Eunice, his wife remarked over the dinner table. 'Has it been such a harrowing day?'

'It's been a damned warm one,' Neville replied. He pushed his plate out of the way and ran his forefinger around the inside of his stiff collar to emphasise his statement. 'I can't ever remember a May being so warm. It's more like July.'

'Is that why you are so pensive?'

'Pensive? No, sorry. I didn't realise I seemed pensive. Actually, I was pondering a chap I met today, that's all. Can't even remember his name right now. It's just that I thought I knew him from somewhere. I was trying to place him.'

'Masonic lodge, maybe?'

Neville shook his head. 'No. I recall his handshake.'

'The golf club, perhaps? Some function that you've attended.'

'Mmm . . . Maybe some golf club or other. Maybe he was at my school . . . maybe he was in the Boy Scouts . . . Oxford, even. Oh, but all that was years ago. Frustrating, really,' he mused. 'Maybe we have played golf together at some time. I was so sure I knew him from somewhere . . . Not that it matters.'

*　　*　　*

Earlier that same evening, Henzey and Will Parish were strolling around Rotton Park Reservoir arm in arm. The heat of the day had thankfully subsided and now there was a pleasant, faint breeze bringing welcome freshness to the air, gently stirring the trees. The sky was cloudless and the low sun, ahead of them, was yellowing in preparation for a colourful bedtime. A duck and a drake led a flotilla of fluffy offspring sedately away from the bank where they walked. They stopped to watch, amused and impressed.

'They remind me of when I was a little lad,' Will said. 'Mother took me to Great Bridge market once. I was seven or eight at the time, I reckon. It was getting late and the traders were packing up ready to go home. We came to a stall where a chap was selling day-old chicks. He looked down at me and said in broad Black Country, "I've got just six left, young mon. Gi' me a tanner an' yo' can 'ave 'em. Otherwise I'll put me foot on the little buggers an' squash 'em. I want to goo 'um." Well, I looked at the chicks. They were all yellow and fluffy and I couldn't bear the thought of them coming to such a sticky end, so I looked pleadingly up at Mother. Anyway she took pity on me and gave the man sixpence. As he handed me the box with them in she said, 'I expect they'll all be dead by mornin'.' Anyway, we got them home, and I put a pair of Mother's old flannel drawers in the box with them to keep them warm, and gave them some warm milk. I sat up with them till God knows what time, thinking how terrible if that man had trodden on the poor creatures.'

'And did you rear them?' Henzey asked.

'Just one. Four died and the cat got the fifth. The one that survived, we called her Lady Astor. Our Sophie called her Foul Fowl. For some reason the hen disliked her. Every time the poor girl came home — she'd be about eighteen then, I suppose — the thing would fly at her. We had to leave a broom at the top of the entry so she could shoo Lady Astor away with it. Poor Sophie was terrified.'

'What happened to it?'

'What, the broom?'

She laughed. 'Of course the broom. You don't think I'm interested in the chicken?'

He laughed too, at her well-meant sarcasm. 'Well, we weren't very well off, Henzey. We had to eat it.'

'We're still talking about the broom?'

'Of course the broom,' he mimicked. 'You don't think we'd eat a chicken for Christmas dinner do you?'

When they had stopped laughing, she said, 'Fancy eating Lady Astor. I hope you didn't enjoy her.'

'Sophie relished what *she* had.'

The ducks had swum towards the centre of the lake so Will and Henzey walked on. A clamour of magpies, looking for trouble, flapped threateningly around a pair of fat wood-pigeons. Will looked at Henzey. The low, yellowing sun lent a golden, tanned look to her face and neck, but her eyes still radiated a rich blueness. He thought how beautiful she looked. Fleetingly, their eyes met and she caught something of what he was thinking from his expression.

She turned her look away from him and tried to divert him. 'It's lovely now, isn't it? A lovely time for a stroll.'

'Perfect.' He kicked a stone from the path and it plopped into the water. 'We should make the most of it.' There seemed to be something ominous in the way he said it.

'Oh? Why do you say that?'

'Well, for this summer anyway. There's a bit of a panic on at work. Some new stuff for the Ministry of Defence. It's all got to be tested, durability trials run. When all that's finished, modifications are sure to be needed. That'll mean more testing. Some shift work's on the cards. You don't mind, do you?'

'For better, for worse . . . When's it due to start?'

'A couple of weeks, I reckon. There's nothing we can do till we've got some hardware to test. It's all top priority stuff. Army vehicles. It seems the government's re-arming at last.

Worthington Commercials have won the contract to develop and manufacture them. They're only in Washwood Heath.'

'Worthington Commercials? That name rings a bell. Don't they make little three-wheel vans? I could have sworn I'd seen one recently.'

'They do. Fancy you noticing a thing like that.'

'Well, it's not so surprising is it, since I work in the motor industry?' she said, feigning arrogance. 'It's a professional interest I take.'

He laughed. She never failed to amuse him with her own self-mockery. 'How could I ever forget? Every time we see a Morris Oxford or a Wolseley nowadays, you point to the headlamps, jump up and down and say, 'Look! One of mine! One of mine!'

'Well, I can't help it. I get so involved in my work. You should be pleased I'm such a conscientious worker. I contribute a lot to road safety, you know. Had you thought about that?' She stuck her tongue out to him playfully and they walked on a few yards further, Will still laughing.

'Anyway, me and Neville Worthington, the chap who owns the company, were discussing the designs,' he said at last.

'Neville Worthington?'

'Yes, the chap who owns this Worthington Commercials firm . . . Strange . . . He looked ever so familiar. I swear I've met him before but I can't think where.'

'Yes, his name does sound familiar.'

They walked on a while without speaking. It suddenly registered with Henzey that she had met Neville Worthington; he was the intriguing man who, years ago, had said some outrageous things to her that made her laugh when she should really have been appalled.

By now they were at the opposite side of the reservoir to their home. Henzey said, 'It's just come back to me, Will. I know why that Neville Worthington's name is familiar. I met him once . . . years ago . . . with Billy Witts. We all had dinner together one night at that posh hotel on Colmore Row. He seemed such a nice chap . . . I remember, I liked him. I felt a bit sorry for him, actually. I don't think he got on too well with his wife . . . Actually, I think he fancied me, you know . . . Has he still got that too awful beard?'

'Yes, he's got a big bushy beard . . . Fancied you, did he?'

'I think he did . . . Oh, I remember what he said . . . He said he was disenchanted with married life.' She reminded herself of the other thing he'd said; that he was looking for a lover, though she didn't mention that to Will. She wondered if Neville had ever found one.

Alice Harper was sitting in the parlour of the tiny terraced house that she and Jack now rented in Nith Place at Shaver's End, on the elevated west side of Dudley. The house, a modest two-up-one-down affair, was not unlike the one the Kites had occupied in Cromwell Street when she was a child, except that it was smaller, and the brewhouse and the privy were shared by three other houses on the yard. They had moved out of the dairy house six months after Henzey and Will were married.

While she sat, Alice mended a pair of trousers for Edward, more hand-me-downs from Richard, her little half-brother. She contemplated Jack's whereabouts that night, for he had taken to going out most nights on the secondhand motorcycle he'd bought some weeks earlier. She looked at the clock sitting on the mantelpiece over the blackleaded grate. It said ten past eleven. Edward had been in bed three hours and was sleeping soundly in the tiny back bedroom. She sighed, put down her mending and got up. There was no sense in waiting up any longer for Jack and, in any case, he was no company when he was home. So she lit the oil lamp to light her way across the back yard to the privy, before she retired to bed.

She did what she had to do hurriedly, for she thought she saw a rat scuffle under the privy door in the shadows, and there were plenty of rats about. She grabbed the oil lamp from its hook and opened the door, glad to be outside in the fresh air again, when she heard the heavy throb of Jack's AJS motorcycle. The din, as he rode it through the entry and into the yard, created Bedlam. The overspill from the headlight fanned out in rays into the inky sky, throwing the brewhouse and its leaning chimney, which were between her and him, into stark silhouette.

As she turned the corner by the brewhouse, she saw Jack dismount and lean the machine against the wall of the house. The glow of the oil lamp coming towards him drew his attention, but he did not acknowledge Alice. He thrust open the back door and went in. Edward was crying.

'Go and shut 'im up,' Jack demanded.

Alice followed him in and closed the door behind her. 'It's your row what's woke him, the poor little soul,' she said indignantly. 'Why can't you turn the engine off in the street and shove your damned motorbike quietly up the entry, like any normal person would?'

"Cause I'd rather ride it up, that's why. It's too 'eavy to push.'

'I suppose you've gone an' woke all the neighbours as well, an' you know old Mister Anslow's poorly.'

He doffed his jacket and, when he'd hung it on the hook at the back of the door, he took himself into the parlour and sat down on the secondhand couch they'd been given. 'Bring me a bottle o' beer in, and mek me a sandwich . . . An' look sharp about it.'

'Get your own beer, Jack, and cut your own sandwich if you'm that 'ungry,' Alice replied haughtily. 'I'm goin' up to settle Edward, then I'm goin' to bed.'

He stood up again and leered. 'I suppose you won't cut me a sandwich 'cause there's no soddin' bread and nothin' to put on it anyway, bar a scrapin' o' drippin'.'

'There's not even a scrapin' o' drippin', Jack,' she answered acidly, her hand on the stairs door latch. 'And you know why? 'Cause it's been three weeks since I had any housekeepin' money, that's why. How d'you expect us to live if you don't turn any money up, eh? D'you think I'm a flippin' magician?'

'Witch, more like.'

'Well, even if I am a witch, there's still Edward to think of. You surely don't begrudge him eatin' every now an' again, do yer, and havin' some decent clothes once in a while?'

'He gets Richard's leave-offs. You know he does.'

Alice was struggling to keep her temper under control. 'Yes, Jack, I know he does. And a good thing, too. If we relied on you we'd be in Queer Street, an' no two ways. That stupid motorbike gets more spent on it than we do.'

'You could always find a job yourself. But you won't, will yer? 'Cause you'm a bone idle little slut, that's why.'

'Oh, talk sense. How can I get a job with a three-year-old child to look after?'

'Send 'im to your mother's.'

'And that's about all you care, Jack Harper. I'm going to bed.'

'Well sod off then.'

Alice sighed as she climbed the narrow stairs. Who would have believed, after those heady nights of upright sexual abandon against the privy door of the dairy house when she was sixteen, that things could possibly have turned out like this? Lately, she couldn't stand Jack even to touch her; not that he showed any inclination to do so anyway, these days. Yet she was aware, more than anyone else, that he was a physically attractive man to anyone who didn't know him well. She was also aware, more than anyone else, that Jack's attractiveness was only skin deep.

Yet Alice was still a very pretty girl. Her figure was as trim as when she was sixteen, no doubt because she had been so young when she had her baby, and she always took care to look her best, despite the constraints of an empty purse. She was twenty, and womanhood and motherhood had had a beneficial effect, especially on her looks and her bearing. Heads swivelled whenever she walked through the town.

But the following morning, when Jack had gone to work,

Alice went to move his jacket. In the light that was streaming in through the scullery window, a long, wavy blonde hair shone against the navy material of the coat. Alice picked it off and saw that, stretched out, it was about twelve inches long. She sniffed the coat and swore she could detect the fading fragrance of an unfamiliar perfume. Then she slid her hand into each of the pockets. The search yielded nothing unusual until, from the last pocket, she pulled out a packet with an unfamiliar design. It was a packet, however, that she knew must have contained three French letters. Yet only one remained.

Chapter Seventeen

With no money left to buy food for herself and her child, Alice squashed everything that she owned into two large shopping bags and a basket, and left the little house in Nith Place that had been home. Edward trailed behind her, unaware of the abrupt change taking place in his life.

'How's this?' Lizzie asked when she saw Alice open the door.

'I've left him,' Alice replied.

'It took you long enough.'

Alice told her mother everything, about the lack of housekeeping, about his contempt for Edward, about his going out every night, about the other woman, or women.

'Then you'd best stay here, our Alice. At least till you sort yourself out.'

'What d'you think Jesse'll say, Mom?'

'Oh, Jesse won't mind, you know that, but so sure as that husband of yours shows his face here he'll get turned away with a boot up his backside. So you'd better be sure this is what you want. I don't want him sweet-talking you back to Nith Place if you're not happy there.'

'I've made me mind up, Mom. He don't love me, an' I don't love him. Oh, Edward loves him all right, but he don't understand what's a-goin' on, does he? Look at him. You have to feel sorry for the poor little soul, but in a week or two he won't know no different.'

Lizzie shook her head. 'I always thought it'd be Henzey who'd bring trouble. She's always been the flighty one. I never dreamed it'd be you, Alice. Still – let's hope things take a turn for the better. You'll be twenty-one soon. There's plenty time for you to meet somebody else. Some nice chap, who'll look after you properly.'

'Oh, Mom. Who's gunna want somebody like me with a three-year-old kid tied to me apron strings? Besides, when do I ever get the chance to go out an' meet anybody?'

'Well, that's hardly likely to be a problem now, is it, living here? We hardly ever go out, me and Jesse. And while we're here, Edward'll be all right. You're still young and you're a nice-looking girl, Alice. Enjoy yourself while you can. There's still plenty of your old friends about, still single. Some of them might be at the street party on Monday. Have you forgotten it's the King's Silver Jubilee?'

'It never crossed me mind, what with all this trouble,' Alice replied. 'Well, it's somethin' to look forward to. I'll have to sort me out a decent frock.'

'There's just one thing, our Alice . . .'

'Oh, I can guess, Mom. I can guess just what you'm goin' to say – don't get pregnant again. Don't worry. That's somethin' as I'll never do unless I get married again, and that won't be in a rush, I can tell you.'

Lizzie smiled. 'Come on, let's sort you out a bedroom. You might as well have Maxine's room while she's lodging in Brum. Edward can sleep with Richard.'

'Oh, he'll love that.'

Having been married more than four years and mistress of her own household, she regarded the return to the good offices of her mother as a retrograde social step. It was a compromise, a temporary inconvenience. After a week there was no sign of it being easy to settle. Lizzie was the dominant female and Alice was finding that fact hard to accept. Alice herself had grown accustomed to the role in her own household. 'Our Alice, you shouldn't let this child play in the dirt like that,' Lizzie would counsel. 'He might pick up a germ or something.' And Alice would reply indignantly that he hadn't picked up a germ yet and, in any case, the child enjoyed clawing at the soil and digging with Jesse's trowel.

Her twenty-first birthday fell on the third Friday in June 1935, and they put on a fine spread. The family was due to arrive when they each finished work. At half past five Herbert went to fetch Elizabeth on his new motorbike. They had been courting steadily for over two years now, and Jesse suspected they might be announcing their engagement soon. Alice had written to Maxine, who was now a professional cellist with the Birmingham Hippodrome's pit orchestra and she, too, was expected with Stephen Hemming, her young man.

The family gathering went off smoothly, till the one uninvited guest, whom they all suspected might turn up, actually arrived. Jack Harper knocked on the verandah door at a few minutes after half past eight when they were eating. There was a quick discussion as to who should answer his knock, till Alice said it was really her business.

'I need to talk to yer, Alice,' Jack said.

She had opened the door halfway and was standing leaning against it and the door jamb so he could not enter. 'I'm here, standin' in front of you. Talk. But hurry up. I'm in the middle of my tea.'

'I want to know when yo'm comin' back, like?'

'I ain't goin' back, Jack. I ain't never goin' back. There's no joy in bein' taken for granted. There's no joy in starvin' an' seein' your own child go hungry just because your husband's too mean to give you any housekeepin'. There's no joy either in knowin' as he's off with other women when he could be at home doin' things with his son. No, I'm never goin' back. It might not be perfect here but at least they love me an' Edward. An' I know as they'll look after us both.'

He fidgeted, moving his weight from one foot to the other.

'I've been thinkin' about you an the little un a lot, Alice. I miss ya. I miss ya both. I'll change. I know I've been a swine, like, but I'll mek it up to ya. Just come back, an' you'll see.'

'I don't need to go back to see, Jack. I can see enough from here. No thanks. Once bitten . . .'

''Ere. I've bought yer a present for your birthday.' He took a small box out of his pocket and offered it to her. 'Ain't yer gonn' ask me in for a drink, like?'

'Jack, I don't want your present. You never bought me anythin' before except trouble. Don't be such a damned hypocrite as to try an' give me anythin' now. An' no, I'm not invitin' you in for a drink. You might get a thick ear if Jesse or our Herbert cops hold of you, and that's the best you could hope for. I should go now while the goin's good.'

He shrugged and left. It was his token attempt at reconciliation. He had done his bit to satisfy the appeals of his shamed family, but he could report back that it was to no avail. He would tell them that he had pleaded with the girl from the bottom of his heart to return home, pleaded for his second chance to be a good father to the son he loved dearly. He would tell them also that her family was not even prepared to welcome him in. The Harpers would soon turn against the Kites after that.

Alice was angry that he had not even enquired about Edward. He had not even congratulated her on her birthday. Oh, she had got the measure of him all right. She was certainly better off without him.

It had been an uncomfortable journey, so hot that Neville Worthington drove all the way to Wessex House with the two front windows open just to make it bearable. He drew his new Swallow SSI Saloon to a halt on the sweeping drive in front of the house and got out.

He entered the house and threw his hat on the hat-stand. 'Eunice!'

'I'm in the drawing-room.'

'Are you doing anything vitally important right now?'

'Nothing. Why? What's the matter?'

In the drawing-room he flopped into one of the soft arm-chairs. 'I want to tell you something.'

He loosened his tie and stroked his thick, brown beard thoughtfully; this growth that made him look so much older than his thirty-five years. Will Parish was thirty-five, too, he had discovered today, but he didn't look this old. Eunice was right. Who, having any respect for their appearance these days, wore a beard, apart from the King and George Bernard Shaw?

'What is it you want to tell me?' She shuffled uncomfortably on her chair and sat in elegant anticipation.

Unable to sit still, he got up again and walked over to the French window. In the vain hope of catching a waft of cooler air, he thrust open further the other casement and stared out into the back garden, a riot of lupins and foxgloves.

'As you know, in the last couple of weeks I've been visiting the Lucas works at Great King Street,' he began. 'That chap I've been dealing with – the one I told you about – you know – the one I thought I knew from somewhere – he's called Will Parish. Pleasant chap. Good engineer. Jolly-well knows his stuff.'

'Go on.' Eunice could sense there was much more to come.

'It's just that I have this feeling about him, Eunice . . . I think he might fit in rather well at Worthington Commercials, if he could be tempted.'

'As an engineer?'

'Well . . . Sort of.'

'So? Why are you telling me this? Head-hunting is your domain.'

'Well, first, I'd like to invite him and his wife over to dinner one evening. To see what you think. To sound him out.'

'Have you met his wife?'

He shook his head. 'No. It's not his wife I'm interested in.'

'But be wary. You know what some of these people are like, Neville.'

'It's of no consequence what she's like, I tell you. It's him I want. He would be an asset – truly.'

'Yes, all right,' Eunice agreed. 'I'm certain we could fix an evening to look over the . . . the Parishes, did you say? . . . Might I suggest a Tuesday or a Thursday evening?'

'Oh, no. Not midweek. It must be a Friday or a Saturday.'

'Goodness me. This Will Parish must really have potential. Well, this coming weekend is out, of course, but the following week . . .'

'Good. Good. Then I'll see what I can arrange.'

Neville lingered at Eunice's side, half wanting to leave to take his shower, half wanting to say more. Eunice sensed it.

'Is there something else, Neville?'

'Yes, there is actually, Eunice,' he confessed. 'You'll probably think me a fool, though.'

'No more than usual.'

'This Will Parish . . . You see, he's been bothering me quite a bit.'

'You said so after you'd first met him.'

'Yes, I thought he seemed vaguely familiar, but I just couldn't place him.'

'But now you have?'

'I think so.'

'Ah! Somebody from your early youth, I'll wager?'

He nodded, thoughtful. 'He goes way, way back. Way back to the very beginning, Eunice. I racked my brains trying to place him. I went through everything. My school days, Bible class, clubs, Masons, ex-employees, dinners, meetings . . . Then it dawned on me and I cursed myself for being so blind. I saw it in his eyes first but didn't recognise it – the Worthington look . . . Eunice, I'm certain he's my long lost twin brother. As certain as I'm standing here.'

'You mean . . . ?'

He nodded. Then silence.

Eunice sighed. This moment, she had always known, would come. She did not fear it. In a way she welcomed it. But she foresaw the possibility of Neville becoming over-emotional about it, of him being taken advantage of because of it.

'You seem sceptical,' Neville remarked, disappointed.

'Then if I do, it's because I'd have thought you might have recognised him at once, without having to struggle to place him? If he's your twin brother the odds are that he's very much like you.'

He gave a little laugh. 'Of course, and nobody could argue with your logic, Eunice.'

'So how certain are you?'

'I'm just certain. It's a gut feeling, but it's much more than that. I've had to ask myself first whether I would know what my twin brother looks like when I've quite forgotten what I look like myself? My face has been hidden behind this beard for years, as you so frequently tell me. But not only has it been hidden from the world and from you, my dear, it's also been hidden from myself. I suppose you haven't accounted for that. Even I have forgotten what I look like without my beard. So it's no wonder, is it, that Will wasn't immediately identifiable? It's no wonder I only saw the resemblance in his eyes.'

'Yes, well . . . Maybe so.'

'There's no *maybe* about it, Eunice. It *is* so.'

Eunice's face brightened. 'Dare we hope, then, that you are about to shave it off at last and present him, and the rest of us, with the bare-faced evidence?'

He turned from the window to face her in her chair. 'Not yet. I've given this some thought. If he has no knowledge of a twin, it might come as a hell of a shock to find out. I think we must first establish whether he knows anything of his real parentage. That's why I wanted to invite him to dinner. To talk to him. I'd like to get close to him. I want to make him feel comfortable with us before I present him with it.'

'And that's also the reason you want him to come and work for the firm, eh?'

'If he is my long lost brother it's only right that he should be a part of the firm. He should be an integral part of it at that. A seat on the board where he belongs at the very least. I should say he's certainly capable enough. He could be Director of Engineering. I owe him something, you see that surely? I want to share with him what I've got. My father gave him nothing.'

'He could take some of the load off you, perhaps, yes. Well, Neville, I expect you must feel quite excited.'

'Oh, I'm not sure that *excited* is quite the word. Apprehensive, more like. It's rather a shock to the old system, you know. I've always had the feeling he's been out there, somewhere, but I've never known with any certainty that I would ever get to meet him. Now that I have, I'm really rather nervous about it.'

'I can imagine, dear. But it'll be jolly interesting getting his story, don't you think? Do you think he has any idea?'

'Good God, no. I don't think he has the vaguest notion.'

They heard a commotion in the hall and a child's voice. 'Mommy, Mommy! We're home.'

'Daddy and I are in the drawing-room, darling,' Eunice called.

A fair-haired little girl, the image of Eunice, blustered in and tripped on the tassels of the carpet as she entered, but steadied herself by catching the brass door knob. She laughed.

'Oops!'

'Oops!' Eunice echoed. 'Goodness, you must be more careful, Kitty. You'll hurt yourself.'

'Better take more water with it, next time,' Neville jested.

The little girl ran toward him and, as he caught her, he lifted her into the air, squeezed her, then let her gently down to the floor again.

'Do it again, Daddy,' she asked beseechingly.

'I daren't, Kitty,' he replied. 'You're getting much too big for that sort of thing now. Just consider my poor back. Have you had a jolly time?'

'Yes, we had a very jolly time. We've been to the park. Nanny bought me an ice cream.'

'Pity you didn't bring some back for Mommy and Daddy, too,' Neville said. 'I bet Mommy would love an ice cream.'

'Oh, Daddy! It would have melted by now. Silly!'

'Here's an interesting piece of news, my love,' Will said, looking up from his *Evening Mail.*

It was the first Friday in July. He had commenced his shift working to get the Worthington Commercials project moving but, this particular week and next, he was working the day shift. They had just returned home together from work. Will was sitting on the settee in the living-room while Henzey was putting away some eggs and some cheese they had just bought from Woodward's.

She left the kitchen and stood beside him. 'What news?'

'Here.' He pointed to the article on the third page, and she sat beside him to read it. It reported that the Ministry of Transport had announced yesterday that dipping car headlights would become compulsory. 'That's going to keep your department busy, Henzey. We've been working on them for years.'

'Mmm, fancy that!' She shifted to the other end of the settee and sat facing him, putting her stockinged feet up, legs out-stretched. She continued reading the paper. When she'd glanced through it, she said, 'Are you hungry yet?'

'Yes, I'm hungry.'

'All right, I'll get tea ready.'

'Talking of tea . . . has just reminded me,' he said. 'Neville Worthington has been in to see me today. We had a meeting about some bits and pieces we're working on. He's invited us to his home for dinner next Saturday evening.'

'To dinner? Oh, my God! Did you mention that I'd met him before?'

'No, of course not. I never even mentioned you.'

There was a pause. 'Do we have to go?'

'Well, I think it would be a bit ungracious not to, especially as I've already accepted.'

'You've already accepted? Ah well. With any luck he won't recognise me after all this time.'

'He's sure to recognise you, Henzey, not that it matters . . . God, it's still so damned hot, isn't it?'

'I know . . . All this sunshine. Have you thought any more about a holiday for us, Will?'

'It's going to be awkward if I have to work through the shut-down. In fact it'll be nigh impossible.'

'But you'll get two weeks off later. I'll take two weeks without pay.'

'You're likely to have that supervisor's job by then, Henzey. They won't take kindly to that.'

'Oh, I don't care. Life's too short . . . It might all be a waste of time anyway . . . if I get pregnant.'

'Here we go again! Henzey, don't talk again of getting pregnant,' he said huffily.

'Oh, and why not?' she asked, at once resentful.

'Because I'm bored with it. You know why.' He got up from the settee.

'That's a silly attitude, Will. And a damned selfish one, if you really want the truth. I want a baby, you know I do. I want a baby more than anything.'

He didn't answer. He didn't need to. She knew well enough how he felt about it.

Chapter Eighteen

The car that Neville Worthington had arranged collected Henzey and Will from Daisy Road promptly at seven, and delivered them up the sweeping gravel drive to the heavy front door of Wessex House at five past. Wessex House looked impressive with its ornate twisting chimneys. Clematis and variegated ivy flourished symbiotically against the mock Tudor frontage, while a fine show of summer flowers adorned the flowerbeds set amid the well-manicured lawns of the front garden.

Henzey wore a slender, full-length evening dress in black satin, expensive, and bought especially for the occasion. It complemented her abundant, dark hair. But the vivid blue of her eyes and her bright red lips assumed a striking contrast and Will was quick to comment on it. Her hair was cut shorter these days and was very fashionable.

Neville himself met them at the front door.

'Will. So nice to see you.' He offered his hand.

'Quite a place you have here, Neville,' Will replied affably. 'Beautiful garden . . . This is Henzey, my wife. Henzey . . . Neville Worthington.'

Neville studied her for no more than a second, but his soulful eyes manifested an expression that lay somewhere between shock and disbelief. As quickly as he could he mustered his wits. 'Mrs

Parish! How nice to meet you.' He could barely hide an element of recognition in his voice, but *noblesse* prevented him blurting out that they had met before. Gently she shook his outstretched hand and he resisted the temptation to take hers to his lips and kiss the back of it, as any gallant might have done years ago. Overawed, he merely squeezed it, released it, and said, 'Welcome. Please come in.'

Henzey had wondered what his reaction might be at seeing her again. She sensed that he was reluctant to acknowledge in front of Will that they had been in each other's company before, and she wished to release him from such a trivial dilemma. 'We've met before, I think,' she admitted at once, smiling beautifully.

He stood to one side, allowing his guests to enter, Henzey first. 'Of course we have. How could I forget? But it was some years ago . . . I say, Will, your wife and I have already met.'

Will laughed. 'Yes, she told me, Neville. Small world, isn't it?'

'And you never let on, you old scoundrel. I must say she's just as beautiful as ever she was. No, I lie . . . she's even more beautiful if that's possible. Marriage evidently suits you, Mrs Parish . . . Hell! That sounds so formal. Do you mind terribly if I call you Henzey?'

'Of course not. And I'll call you Neville,' she answered impishly. At once she felt at ease with him.

'Good gracious, I'm absolutely staggered, you know. Taken the wind right out of me sails, you have . . . Why didn't you warn me, Will? I imagine Eunice will recognise you, too, Henzey, even after so long.'

'How is Eunice? I'm not so sure I'd recognise her.'

'She's in the garden sipping sherry. Come through, both of you. As it's such a beautiful evening we thought you'd enjoy an aperitif outside before dinner. We've had such a wonderful summer, so far.'

They were ushered through the plush drawing-room with its

oil-painted portraits and landscapes hanging on the walls, through a French window and down a wooden ramp to a sheltered, paved patio surrounded by flowers. A table and three chairs were set out and a drinks trolley. Eunice had her back towards them as they stepped onto the patio, but she turned her head as soon as she heard voices.

Henzey then saw, to her amazement, that Eunice was in a wheelchair.

'Will, meet Eunice . . . Eunice, Will and Henzey Parish.'

They shook hands and greeted each other warmly.

Eunice regarded Henzey uncertainly for a few seconds, then said, 'We've met before . . . Dinner . . . The Grand Hotel on Colmore Row. 1929. Just before the Wall Street Crash.'

Henzey laughed self-consciously, surprised that Eunice remembered the time and place so accurately. 'That's right, it was.' She was at a loss to know whether to acknowledge Eunice's incapacity, and yet she felt she could hardly ignore it.

'But you weren't with Will then, I remember.'

'No, I didn't know Will then. I was with my young man at the time – Billy Witts . . . It's all right, we can mention him.' She laughed again with mild embarrassment and glanced at Will. 'Will knows all about him.'

'Of course, Billy Witts. Whatever happened to him, I wonder?' Eunice said.

'Oh, he married somebody else and started a family.'

'So I believe,' Neville remarked. 'The Crash all but bankrupted him, we heard, eh, Eunice? But he's a big noise in a foundry business now, I understand. Still – enough of him, eh? Look. Please sit down. Make yourselves at home.'

Henzey smoothed her black satin dress against her bottom and thighs as she sat down, facing Eunice. Neville noticed how the dress accentuated every curve of her body.

'Forgive me,' he stammered, reluctantly dragging his eyes away from his guest. 'I, er . . . I haven't asked you yet what you'd like to drink.'

He'd been in Henzey's company less than five minutes and already he felt himself trembling. That same potent desire he'd known six years earlier was already stirring inexorably within him once more. She'd barely aged, except that after six long years and marriage, she had evolved into much more of a woman; a much more sophisticated woman; an even more desirable woman. With a sensation in his chest that felt as if he'd downed a jug full of ice-cold water, he took the extra glasses that were standing in the middle of the table and poured dry sherry which he handed to his guests. Conversation dwindled meanwhile to how pleasant the weather had been lately, what a fine show of lupins and foxgloves there was this year, and look how the lawn was yellowing despite frequent watering by the gardener.

Henzey sipped her drink and her eyes met Eunice's.

'How long have you and Will been married, Henzey?'

'Just over two years, Mrs Worthington. We married in April thirty-three. Just after my twenty-first birthday.'

'Oh, please call me Eunice. I'd like to think of us as friends, even after all this time. I must confess I somehow did not expect Will to arrive with such a young wife. I mean no offence, Will, but Neville had led me to expect a man of about thirty-five.'

'That is my age, Eunice. Henzey's my second wife, though. I lost my first.'

'Oh, I say. How jolly clumsy of me. Do forgive me. Of course, I had no idea.'

'Well, of course you didn't,' Will agreed. 'My first wife died some years ago. You weren't to know.'

'That's awful. How did she die? Do you mind talking about it?'

'Not at all. She died in childbirth. It would have been our first child.'

'But how utterly tragic. Did you lose the child as well?'

Will nodded.

'That must have knocked you for six, old man,' Neville commented.

Will tasted his sherry and put his glass on the table. 'Oh, at the time, yes. And for a long time afterwards, I can tell you. I'd more or less resigned myself to being a widower for the rest of my days. Till I met Henzey . . .'

'So how did you two meet?' Eunice wanted to know.

Will and Henzey explained together, each filling in snippets that the other failed to impart. Eunice and Neville listened with interest. By the time they'd finished their story, Eunice received a signal to say that dinner was ready.

'I didn't realise you were such a celebrated artist, Henzey,' Neville said, seizing the opportunity to flatter her again. 'Perhaps I should commission you to do portraits of Eunice and myself.'

Henzey smiled. 'I'd be glad to, if only I could find the time. Being a housewife and working for a living keeps me ever so busy.'

'Oh, I can well imagine,' Eunice said. 'It surprises me that they don't apply a marriage bar at Lucas's, you know. Do many married women work there nowadays?'

'Quite a few,' Henzey replied. 'If you work well, they look after you. Nobody suggested I should give up my job when I got married. In fact, I'm being made up to supervisor soon.'

Neville said, 'Well, congratulations. I'm certain you deserve it, too. But times are changing, don't you think? I see no good reason for firms nowadays to bar married women, like some do, especially now the economy seems to be picking up at long last. Hell, we've had over five years of Depression now. It's enough for anybody . . .'

Eunice intervened. She had no wish for her guests to be bored by one of Neville's dissertations on the state of the economy. 'Well, I hope you're all hungry. Cook's done us rather proud this evening.'

'I can smell it,' Will said. 'It smells wonderful.'

'Then shall we go in?'

Neville went to the back of Eunice's wheelchair and wheeled her up the ramp that gave easy access to the French window,

MICHAEL TAYLOR

leaving their glasses on the table outside for the maid to clear away. Neville settled her in front of the table before gallantly seating Henzey opposite her.

The dining-room was spacious, oak panelled, with another gallery of oil paintings hanging on the walls. An elaborate crystal chandelier that had been converted to electricity hung ethereally over the table. The table was not large, but it was immaculately laid with silver cutlery and fine-cut crystal glassware. Another maid hovered, ready to serve.

The first course was smoked salmon, served with a dry white wine that Neville informed them was a Sancerre. Conversation remained light; about the wine, about some of the pictures in the room, and the house. While they waited for their main course they discussed graver issues: the apprehension they all felt about Germany's increasing naval power and the implications, following the resignation of Ramsay MacDonald, of Stanley Baldwin once more becoming Prime Minister of the all-party National Government.

A main course of roast duck followed and it was the first time Henzey had tasted duck, although she didn't wish to let it be known. She privately decided that it was delicious and thoroughly enjoyed it, while Neville and Will led the conversation.

'Tell us about yourself, Will,' Neville said after sipping the fine 1929 Beaune he'd chosen from his cellar, to accompany the main course.

'Oh, there's not much to tell,' Will answered modestly. 'You know about my first wife's death and my meeting Henzey.'

'Then tell us about your early life, your childhood, your upbringing.'

'I was brought up in very modest circumstances, Neville. My mother and father were very religious . . . and very strict with it. We were quite poor, I recall, but that was unimportant to us at the time. We all seemed to manage well enough. My father was a hammer driver in a forge making hand tools and, as long as he owed nobody money, he was content. He never drank, nor swore

either. I can't say I'm religious, though. It didn't rub off on me.'
He smiled and resumed eating.

'Do you have any brothers or sisters, Will?' Eunice asked.

'Mmm,' he nodded, and swallowed. 'A sister, Sophie, and a
brother called Samuel. Both quite a bit older than me. I think
Sophie was ten when I arrived, and Sam was twelve.'

'That seems quite a gap,' Neville commented.

'I suppose it would be normally,' Henzey said. 'Tell them,
Will, that Sophie and Sam are not your real brother and sister.'

Neville and Eunice glanced at each other.

Will sipped his wine, then placed his glass back on the table.
'Yes, that's true. I was a fostered child, you see.'

'I say,' Neville exclaimed, with another brief but triumphal
glance at Eunice. 'And do you know who your real parents were?'

'Not really. I like to imagine they were a married couple and
that they both died – but who knows? I once toyed with the idea
of trying to find out but, when I thought about it more deeply, I
decided against it. I imagined that if I asked any questions it
would upset my foster parents, and I wouldn't have done that for
the world. They loved me dearly and I loved them. They gave me
their name, they sacrificed their own worldly comforts so that I
could have a decent education. They gave me everything I had.
Why appear to be discontent by digging for information about
my real mother and father?'

'And are your foster parents still alive?' It was Eunice who
enquired.

'Oh, yes. They're not so active in their religious fervour these
days but they're both still very much alive.'

'And you see them regularly?'

'Of course. They're not neglected. Far from it. We visit them
often . . .' Will made a show of looking around him. 'I imagine
that my upbringing was drastically different from yours, Neville,
if this house is anything to go by?'

Ironically, it would have been a perfect cue to ease Will into
the certain knowledge that he was Neville's own long lost twin

brother. It was the reason he had been invited to dinner. It was the one thing that had consumed Neville lately. To be reunited with his brother after so many years, after so long wondering who and where he was, had been a latent priority. And now, finally, they had met.

But Neville had not reckoned on his brother's wife being Henzey Kite. Seeing her again, being close to her, close enough to touch her, to smell her perfume, had rekindled that ardent desire for her which had tormented him before. He could not help it. In 1929 he had fallen in love with her at first sight, and would have been prepared to give up everything just to be with her. Nothing would have held him back. Not even Eunice's wealth. Things had changed since, however. Nowadays he called the tune. By virtue of her incapacity Eunice was totally reliant on him now.

Neville had believed he would never see Henzey again, although visions of her with that cad Billy Witts plagued him intolerably for more than a year afterwards. She was gone, lost forever, and thoughts of her diminished with the years. Yet, unbelievably, here she was some six years later, sitting opposite him at his own table, smiling radiantly at him, waiting for him to tell his life story; but accompanied by her husband who, damn it, was the twin brother he'd longed to know. She was the most beautiful, most desirable creature he'd ever had the good fortune to meet and he wanted her more now than he did in 1929. She might be married. She might have been caught. It did not mean she had been secured.

Neville's desire created a huge dilemma, though. How could he now offer Will Parish all that he'd so graciously planned, when his most basic instinct was to take his wife? Given half a chance he knew he would steal her from him, sleep with her, make love to her with the utmost conviction, without sparing so much as a thought for Will. He would be prepared to make a cuckold of his own brother. How could he have been prepared to give him so much with one hand and now, suddenly, contrive to rob him of so much more with the other? To do so would make him the biggest hypocrite who ever drew breath.

Best to offer Will nothing. Best to even forget him.

He glanced at Henzey again. Her bright, blue eyes were still sparkling at him with anticipation over her crystal goblet.

'We're still waiting,' she said familiarly and sipped her wine.

'Yes, we're still waiting,' Eunice confirmed. 'Tell our guests about how you were similarly dropped into the bosom of the Worthington household.'

Damn Eunice!

He shot her a glare. She'd practically given it all way. Deliberately, no doubt, for she would have guessed already about the turmoil building up inside him. Already she would have recognised his rejuvenated longing for this girl. Already she would have realised the struggle that was raging between his noblest and his basest instincts, for she knew him well. He took some wine to stall giving an answer and called the maid to pour more for his guests. He needed a few more seconds to think. If he must reveal this aspect of his life which he would now prefer to keep quiet, then he would give away as little as possible. Certainly, he no longer wished it known that he had a twin brother. Not now.

The maid finished pouring the wine and left them. The other three around the table were all looking at him, waiting for him to speak. At last, he did.

'Surprisingly, like you, Will, my mother was not who she seemed to be, though my father was. I'll explain . . . It appears that my father was partial to seducing the more attractive maids of the household, and some who were not, I daresay . . .'

'A common enough pastime among the gentry,' Will remarked, smiling.

'Indeed, but one that had a direct bearing on me, Will. My real mother, you see, was one such maid . . . That makes me illegitimate, if you hadn't already worked it out. She died, apparently, when I was still very small, and the head of a modest family who had befriended her returned me here, apparently with the intention of challenging my father to accept responsibility for me. It so transpires, however, that my over-sexed father had died by this time in the Boer War, leaving a young, childless and very attractive widow, who was happy to accept me and bring me up as her own.' He sipped his wine again. 'So you see, Will, our beginnings were not so different. That I was reared in wealth doesn't necessarily mean I've lived a more fulfilled life, that I've been more fortunate than yourself.' He glanced at Henzey, a knowing glance, and she believed she perceived his meaning, remembering what he had insinuated years ago about his flawed marriage. 'Some things cannot be measured in monetary value.'

'But tell them about the twin,' Eunice urged.

Neville sighed, and could have murdered his invalid wife there and then. 'Yes,' he reluctantly confessed, 'it seems I had a twin brother. But goodness only knows what happened to him.' His eyes met Eunice's with an expression that defied her to gainsay it.

'You've no idea who he was?' Henzey asked.

'Pos—' But Eunice was immediately cut off by Neville nudging her sharply under the table.

'No idea at all, Henzey. No idea at all.'

'It's a great shame,' Eunice commented, going along with Neville's change of tack; but grudgingly, because she was certain she could perceive Henzey as the cause of it. 'It's a great shame because whoever he turned out to be, I'm certain that Neville would be more than willing to share with him the Worthington family's good fortune in some way or other.' She looked first at Neville, then at Will and recognised the resemblance in their eyes that had so far eluded Henzey.

Henzey laid her knife and fork on her dinner plate and leaned back in her seat. 'You know, I've heard your story before, Neville,' she said with resignation. 'A friend of mine I used to work with told me the story years ago. A maid — her mother's friend actually — worked at some well-to-do house in Birmingham, and she was put in the family way by the owner's son. She had twins, but she died two years later from consumption. Somebody took one of the babies and looked after him, but they couldn't afford to keep the other as well. They were very poor, you see. So my friend's grandfather took this other baby to this well-to-do house so that the real father could take the responsibility of looking after it. I bet it's you she was talking about, Neville. I bet any money it's you . . . Fancy that.'

'Whose grandfather?' Eunice asked, trying to assimilate the story. 'Whose grandfather delivered the child to this house you mention?'

'My friend's grandfather,' she answered excitedly. 'It was my friend's mother who was a friend of . . . d'you know, I nearly had her name then . . . the girl who had the twins.'

Neville could have provided Henzey with his real mother's name but thought better of it. It could provide confirmation of the truth of the story at some later date.

'That's uncannily interesting,' he said. 'And more than a coincidence, it seems to me, Henzey. Where did this maid who had the twins go to live when she left this well-to-do house, as you call it?'

'Oh, somewhere in Dudley, I think.'

'And it was your friend's mother who knew her?'

'Yes.'

'Is she still alive – your friend's mother?'

'Oh, yes.'

Neville's nobler instincts were emerging again. Often he had wondered about his real mother. He knew very little about her and was anxious to know more. 'Could you put me in touch with her, d'you think?'

'Clara . . . that's my friend . . . works in George Mason's in Dudley Market Place. She has Wednesday afternoons off. I could telephone her from work for you, if you like, and she could probably take you to her mother's one Wednesday afternoon.'

'Oh, I'd like to do that, Henzey, if you could arrange it. I'd love to talk to her. The old lady, whoever she is, must have some information about my mother. Perhaps even a photograph.'

'She might know something about your twin brother, as well.'

'Yes, yes, of course. My twin brother. Who knows what information she might have stored in her memories.'

'I'll see what I can arrange, Neville.'

'I'd appreciate it very much.'

There was a lull in the conversation while everybody finished their course. As the plates were cleared away, the topic changed and Eunice began asking Henzey about her own family. Henzey held their attention until pudding was served, during which time Neville and Will became engrossed in their own discussion about their mutual project at Lucas's.

Eventually coffee was served, followed by brandies, and the four decided to go out into the garden once again before darkness robbed the sun of its reddening glow. Eunice was keen to show Henzey the flowers and shrubs she conscientiously tended herself from her wheelchair throughout the summer. She asked Henzey to take over pushing her across the lawn towards the flowerbeds while they split away from Will and Neville. A paper aeroplane floated past Henzey, prompting her to look up, and a cheeky boyish face grinned down at her from an upstairs window.

Henzey picked it up. 'Oh, is this yours?' she called pleasantly.

The boy nodded.

'Frederic!' his mother chided. 'We have guests.' Then to Henzey: 'One's son.' And back to Frederic: 'Please don't litter the garden, dear.'

'May we come down and fetch it?' the child asked.

'We? . . . If you're very quick . . . and if you avoid trying to find an excuse to linger.'

The boy was gone from the window and half a minute later presented himself in his pyjamas in the garden, together with his younger sister.

'I'm Frederic,' he said confidently to Henzey and held his hand out.

'Yes, I know,' she said with a smile as she shook it. 'And I'm Henzey. Pleased to meet you.'

'And this is Kitty.'

'Well, hello, Kitty.' The child shook Henzey's hand like her brother had. 'How nice to meet you.' Henzey turned to Eunice. 'She has such lovely golden hair, Eunice.'

Eunice nodded and smiled.

Frederic said, 'I didn't mean to scare you with the plane. Sorry.'

'It didn't scare me, Frederic,' Henzey replied.

'Take it at once and go back to your room, please,' Eunice instructed. 'Both of you.' So Henzey handed him his paper plane and the children withdrew. 'Sorry about that.'

'Oh, he's a lovely boy,' Henzey commented. 'Very well mannered. Very obedient. My brother would've given forty words for one at that age.'

'He is a delightful child,' Eunice agreed.

'And Kitty,' Henzey said. 'She's absolutely gorgeous. I could munch her.'

'*Munch* her?'

'Squeeze her – hug her. She's such a beautiful child.'

'You must visit us again, Henzey, when she's up and about. Get to know her better.'

'Yes, that would be nice. Does she have a nanny?' Henzey enquired.

'Oh, yes, she has a nanny. Though she fends for herself very well. I imagine you and Will are contemplating starting a family, Henzey?'

'Oh, if a child came along I wouldn't mind.' She sighed heavily, causing Eunice to glance up at her.

Eunice thought she detected despondency in her companion's expression. 'Oh, the truth now, Henzey.'

'All right, Eunice, it's more than that. I've reached the stage now when I'd dearly love a child. I really would. We've been married over two years now, but Will's dead set against the idea. Understandable, I suppose, after what he went through when his first wife died. But I'm working on him, not that it's likely to do me any good.'

'You must not allow wanting a child to become an obsession, you know. It'd be a big mistake. It could make you very miserable. It could make you very unhappy.'

'Oh, I try not to let it . . . But it's hard, Eunice. Very hard. In every other way Will's a good husband. He's loving, and . . .'

'Be more relaxed about it. I'm sure he'll come round to your way of thinking eventually. It'll be worth the wait.'

Henzey smiled, grateful for Eunice's concern. 'And you, Eunice? Are you and Neville likely to have more children, do you think?'

'Oh, very unlikely, I should say, especially in view of my incapacity. No, ours is more a marriage of convenience. Not that it was intended that way, you understand, but that's the way it's turned out ultimately . . . But you don't want to hear about our problems.'

They ambled on, through an arbour covered in clematis and wisteria. They stopped to admire it before Eunice said she'd like to sit for a while at the ornamental fish pond. Once there, Henzey sat facing her on a low wall that surrounded it. She turned her head and gazed absently into the water.

'Do you mind if I ask you something, Eunice?' she said after a few moments' silence.

'What, my dear? Ask what you will.'

'Last time I saw you – in 1929 – I don't remember you being in a wheelchair. I just wondered . . . well, I just wondered what's the matter with you, that's all . . . Nobody's mentioned it and it seems so impolite of me to carry on with you as if it wasn't there, when I've already been pushing you along.'

'Oh, thank you for your directness, Henzey. It's no great

secret, so I apologise for not mentioning it. I just assumed you knew. I just assumed that Neville had forewarned Will.'

'Not to my knowledge.'

'I have what the doctors refer to as Cruveilhier's atrophy, or sclerosis. It's a muscular disease that gets progressively worse. It developed rather rapidly in me, I'm afraid. I've been wheelchair bound for almost two years now. But you are right. I was not in it when first we met. I was a healthy woman then. Very fit, as I thought.'

'I am sorry, Eunice.'

'Thank you. I'm learning to live with it.'

'But will it get worse?'

'It's expected to, certainly.'

'Much worse?'

'Oh, much worse. I try not to think about it.'

'I am sorry.'

A pause.

'Such a coincidence that both Will and Neville were adopted, don't you think?' Eunice said, changing the conversation. 'And at such an early age.'

'Oh, and that bit about the twin brother, Eunice. It's an amazing coincidence – that story my friend Clara told me. One of them must be Neville. Shame the other one's still a mystery, though, isn't it?'

'Quite,' Eunice lied, but without conviction. 'But I have a very strong suspicion he might still turn up.'

Chapter Nineteen

There were some exquisite counter-point harmonies to enrich the melodic passages in the choir's anthem, 'How Lovely is Thy Dwelling Place' from Brahms's Requiem. The trebles soared almost to the limit of their range, their crystal-clear ring echoing hauntingly round the ornate, vaulted roof of St John's church in Ladywood. Tenor voices, like sterling silver, blended heroically with the smooth ivory of the altos and the dark, rich bronze of the basses. It was, along with the organ, an inspirational melding of sounds.

Canon Gittins then preached a fine sermon from the elaborately carved pulpit, taking as his text a passage from Romans: '*I had not known sin, but by the law: for I had not known lust, except the law had said, Thou shalt not covet.*'

Neville Worthington, immaculately dressed in a dark grey suit, white shirt and a conservatively patterned tie, listened intently at the back of the church. At appropriate times he nodded, seemingly concurring with the wisdom of the preached word.

Canon Gittins was noted for his sermons of reasonable length, more direct than rambling, and it was not long before he mumbled his blessing and stepped down. The congregation shuffled, took their *Hymns Ancient and Modern* and turned to 'Ye Holy Angles Bright', ready to present another stirring rendition.

When the service finished the choir trooped out in slow procession to the vestry where Canon Gittins thanked them for their vocal endeavours. The boys, as ever, were in a rush to remove their cassocks and surplices and tumble boisterously out into the cool Ladywood evening in their Sunday-best jackets. The men, however, were content to take their time and discuss their performance of the anthem, in turn with yesterday's cricket scores or the state of the beer at dinnertime in the Hyde Arms.

Lately, Henzey did not accompany Will to church on a Sunday evening, and this evening was no exception. In the days when she did, she was happy to join him and the other choristers afterwards for a drink, usually in the Hyde Arms, but sometimes in the Belle Vue on Icknield Port Road. Will did not intend joining his fellow choristers for a drink tonight, but would make his leisurely way home in due course. There was no rush. He chatted first with Ned and Phoebe Bingham, then with Arthur Price, a fine alto. After a while they strolled round to the front of the church and went their separate ways.

Neville Worthington was standing uncertainly just inside the grounds of the church. When he saw Will, he approached him.

'Excuse me, young man,' he said, with a twinkle in his eye, 'are you a regular worshipper here?'

'Neville!' Will exclaimed. 'Were you in church? I didn't see you.'

'Well, I try not to be too conspicuous,' he said. 'Splendid anthem. Thoroughly enjoyed it.'

'Good. Actually, we enjoy singing that one.'

'You have a splendid choir, Will. I'm very impressed.'

'Nice of you to say so . . . I take it you're alone?'

They stood facing each other, smiling like old friends.

'Oh, yes. Eunice was never one for going to church. Doesn't mean we shouldn't send the children though, eh?'

'I'm sure they'd benefit.'

'Doesn't Henzey come to church with you, Will?'

'Oh, occasionally. When it's a religious festival. She came last week actually. It was the Sunday School Anniversary last week. She likes to see the children all done up in their new Sunday best.' He smiled.

'Then I'm sorry to have missed her this evening. I rather hoped I'd see her after what she told us last night.'

'Thanks again for last night, Neville. We had a smashing time. Henzey really enjoyed herself.'

'I tell you, Will, it was such a shock seeing her again . . . After all those years. I couldn't believe it when I beheld her standing at my front door.'

'She thought maybe you wouldn't recognise her, you know.'

Neville laughed. 'Little fear of that. You never forget a face like that, Will. You're a damn lucky chap, you know.'

Will thought of Eunice languishing in her wheelchair. 'You don't need to remind me. Henzey's one in a million . . . Look, I was going straight home but, if you fancy a drink, I'll stand you a pint in the Belle Vue.'

'No, I'd rather not if you don't mind, old man. I'll give you a lift home though, gladly.'

'Fine. Thanks.'

'Car's here.' Neville pointed to his black Swallow SSI thirty yards away. 'Save your legs, eh?'

They walked towards it and Will waved to two fellow choristers who were crossing the road, before opening the door and sitting in the front passenger seat.

Neville fired the engine. 'You'll have to direct me, Will.'

'Straight on till I tell you to turn right . . . Chauffeur's day off today?'

'Part time, old man.' Neville peered into his rearview mirror and they sped off up Monument Road. 'I send for him when I need him. Bit of an extravagance, really. Too costly to employ all the time.'

'He seemed to have found us easily enough last night.'

Neville was spouting the virtues of his chauffeur when Will

signalled him to turn right. Their conversation ceased while Neville concentrated on negotiating the tight corners and narrow roads of Ladywood. In no time they were outside the Parishes' end-of-terrace house in Daisy Road.

'If you're keen to talk to Henzey, Neville, come in and see her now. She'll like that. You're welcome to a cup of tea, or even something stronger if you like.'

Neville, of course, had hoped he would be offered the chance to be close to Henzey, to breathe the same air that she breathed. She was his sole reason for coming out tonight. 'Thanks, I will. I'm anxious to see this friend's mother she mentioned.'

They got out of the car. The usual group of young boys were playing cricket, their wickets chalked on the front of one of the houses at the opposite end of the street.

'That takes me back,' Will commented, closing the car door. He allowed Neville to go first up the path to the side door. 'It's a great way to learn the game.'

'You know, I always envied the kids who played cricket in the streets,' Neville said. 'I was never allowed. Only ever played it on the school field.'

Will opened the door and invited Neville to enter. A wireless was playing softly in the living-room. 'Yoo-hoo, Henzey! A visitor for you,' he called. 'Come through, Neville.'

Henzey opened the living-room door, wondering who Will had brought home with him. She was wearing a light, flowery, summer dress that fitted beautifully, sleeveless, with a low neckline. When she saw Neville she gave a little gasp, but smiled and said what a pleasant surprise it was to see him again so soon.

'I've been to church.'

'Why? Do you need to be saved?' she asked flippantly.

He laughed. 'Oh, most certainly, but only from myself. That's not why I went, though.'

'Oh?'

'Frankly, I hoped I might see you, Henzey. Your husband

kindly invited me in when I gave him a lift back. So I've accomplished my mission after all.'

'It was the least he could do, after you looked after us so well last night. We had a lovely time. Come and sit down.'

'I wanted to see you about your friend Clara's mother, actually.'

'I thought so,' she said with a smile.

'Look, I'll put the kettle on,' Will suggested, 'unless Neville wants something stronger. D'you fancy a scotch or a beer, Neville?'

'Tea will be fine, thanks.' Neville made himself comfortable on the settee. 'Lovely day we've had again, Henzey. We've been so lucky with the weather this summer. I can't remember it being so gorgeous.'

'I know, it's beautiful.' She sat down in an armchair while Will disappeared into the kitchen.

'You've been sunbathing, too. I see the sun's caught your face . . .' Neville's eyes wandered inexorably to the unblemished skin of her neck and her chest, glowing from exposure to the sun, and down to the sensuous curves that formed her silky cleavage. He swallowed hard. '. . . and the soft skin of your bosom, look.'

Without thinking, she pulled the low neckline away from herself to better see where the sun had caressed her.

'Oh, I sat out this afternoon for a while in a new bathing costume I bought. Will was talking about a holiday at the seaside.'

'I bet your legs have caught it as well, then.'

Henzey hitched her skirt well above her knees to inspect her thighs, then realised she had unwittingly given Neville a peep show.

'You should rub some oil or something into your skin, Henzey . . . Or get somebody to do it for you . . .'

Their eyes met; she smiled and the saucy flicker in his eyes ensured she caught his innuendo. She blushed, taken aback that she found his spicy impropriety so stimulating. Why, she wondered, did Neville have such a wickedly invigorating influence on her? She avoided his eyes then, for it was obvious what he was thinking. She ought to have been scandalised by his intimations, but she was not. Rather she was flattered. Years ago she'd been excited by this same directness. Her inner response to it, she realised, had not altered radically with the change in her situation. She had not grown out of it.

'I . . . I've been watching the birds over the reservoir while Will's been out,' she remarked lightly, trying to change the subject. 'The young ducks and moorhens are practically full grown now . . . And I saw a heron earlier.'

'A heron, eh? After the fish, I expect.'

'It looked as if it had a rat in its beak. I suppose they'll eat anything.'

'Yes, I daresay . . . So tell me – when are you taking this holiday?'

'The holiday? Oh, we would have gone the main holiday weeks – to Eastbourne probably. But since Will has to work while everybody else is away – getting your work ready, Neville – we've had to postpone it.'

He detected a mild chiding in her tone. 'Sorry about that. Sorry if Worthington's has mucked up your plans. It'll be worth the wait, though.'

''Tis to be hoped. Will needs a break. He's been working ever so hard.'

'He has, Henzey. I know he has. So how long do you hope to be away?'

'We'd planned on two weeks.'

'Two weeks, eh? Wish I could come with you. Look, I own a cottage at a little place on the south coast near Bognor Regis . . . Middleton-on-Sea. You're welcome to use it for a couple of weeks if you'd like.'

'Gracious, Neville! That's good of you. You don't have to . . . offer it, I mean.'

'Not at all. There's a boat there, too, you could use.'

'A boat? Oh, wait till Will knows. Is it nice? The cottage . . . Is it a nice cottage?'

'Not bad at all. Quite modern really. All mod cons. I rather like it down there. Don't get down there as often as I'd wish, so maybe the garden's a bit overgrown – although I do pay a man to keep it half decent. It overlooks the sea directly.'

'Oh, it sounds lovely. Thanks. Thanks ever so much. Can we let you know . . . I mean . . . if . . . when we're likely to want it?'

'It's there whenever you want. It won't interfere with me or my family. Not this side of October anyway.'

'You must let us know how much you charge.'

'Oh, piffle! I don't want money for it.'

'Oh, you must. You must, Neville.'

'Nonsense.'

'Then I'll do a portrait of you.'

'Hey, now I might hold you to that. Just arrange for me to meet that woman you believe knew my mother. That would be payment enough.'

She looked at him earnestly. 'I'll do that anyway.'

'But we didn't make any final arrangements. That's why I'm here. Sorry if I seem persistent. It means a lot to me.'

The kettle whistled in the scullery and crockery chinked as Will prepared the tea.

'You don't have to apologise, Neville, I imagine it means such a lot to you. I'll telephone her from work tomorrow. I'll get Will to let you know as soon as it's arranged.'

'Why not phone me yourself? Here. Here's my number at the office.' He felt in the top pocket of his jacket and fished out a business card, which he handed to her.

Will put his head round the door. 'Anybody fancy a sandwich or anything for supper? I'm feeling a bit peckish myself. I can do it while the tea's steeping.'

'Oh, yes, Neville. We've got some cheese, or some lovely

roast pork and stuffing from the joint we had at dinnertime,' Henzey offered. 'Or even some boiled ham.'

'I say, I rather fancy roast pork if it's no trouble. And stuffing, of course.'

'Pork and stuffing then,' Henzey said, rising from the armchair. 'I'll do it, Will.'

'Sit where you are, my flower,' Will insisted. 'It's no trouble. I'm quite capable of cutting a few sandwiches.'

Henzey sat down again. 'Will, Neville says he's got a cottage at the seaside we can borrow for our holidays. Where did you say it is, Neville?'

'Middleton-on-Sea. Near Bognor Regis. On the south coast.'

'It sounds lovely. And there's a boat.'

'Borrow, did you say? I wouldn't hear of it, Neville. You'd have to let us pay.'

'I wouldn't allow you to pay, old man. You'd be my invited guests. Use it at your leisure.'

'That's very decent of you, Neville.'

'Neville says if I arrange for him to meet Clara Maitland and her mother, that'll be payment enough.'

'Then the very least you could do, Henzey, would be to offer to take Neville to meet Clara. You know where she lives. It would save him the time and trouble of trying to find it himself.'

'You mean this week?' she queried, uncertainly.

'Why not? I'm working afternoons – two till ten. It would fit in quite nicely.'

Henzey retired to bed earlier than Will that night. She had to be up at the normal time for work, whereas he did not. As she lay in bed she pondered Neville Worthington's directness and smiled to herself. She could not take offence at any of his comments. It was quite a novelty that he so evidently fancied her. Quite a lark, really. Something vanity allowed her to enjoy. Perhaps she should play up to him more – flirt with him – play him at his own game? After all, meeting him all those years ago she felt she already knew him well enough; well enough to realise they still had a sort of tacit understanding and could say almost anything to each other; certainly enough to tease him a bit. It was strange how she felt this accord, this rapport. It didn't matter about his appearance, his old-fashioned beard. She liked him for himself, for his saucy company. But there was something about his eyes which was appealing: sensitive; so eloquent; and so hauntingly familiar as well, as if she'd known him all her life.

It was remarkable that he and Eunice seemed so taken with them both. Neville evidently got on well with Will, else they would never have been invited to the Worthingtons' home in the first place. Such a notable coincidence that she had met them both before. Eunice was a charming person, too; such grace and presence for a woman crippled with a muscular disease. Tragic, really. And yet, somehow, she was something of a liberal in her points of view. The result of a fine education, no doubt. She could learn a lot from Eunice. Pity too, about their marriage, even though they seemed to carry if off so well. Obviously friends still, if lovers no more. A well-matched couple in an unconventional way.

And they were all truly firm friends now – the four of them; even to the extent of Neville offering the free loan of his cottage at the seaside. She and Will must, of course, invite them to dinner at Daisy Road. Neville, certainly, would never look down his nose at their home, however modest, and neither did she believe Eunice would. They were lovely, refined people. Gracious. Born to wealth; not like the Billy Wittses of this world, who had made money fast but still lacked the grace and culture that people born to it possessed.

She would help Neville all she could to find out about his real mother. It was fortunate that she could be of help; such a fortunate coincidence that she, of all people, had been told the story of that poor maid who'd had twins by Neville's father; amazing that Neville was actually one of those poor twins.

Already she was looking forward to telephoning Clara; to hearing her cries of disbelief when she explained how she actually knew one of those twins.

Alice Harper walked between the market stalls in Dudley on Monday morning with a renewed interest in life. New crockery and curtains she did not need, but children's clothes Edward certainly did. Hand-me-downs from Richard came in very useful and saved her a lot of money, but it would be nice, just once, to be able to buy the child something new; something he could call his own. This week she could not afford it, but next week she might. As she browsed at every stall she thought what a change it would be to be able to buy everything she and Edward needed without having to stop and reckon up whether she could afford it. Soon, she hoped it would be like that. Lizzie and Jesse had been more than generous; they gave her money, they fed the two of them, provided a roof over their heads. Alice was grateful for it but she was concerned that she was becoming a burden.

Emotionally, Jack Harper was no longer a part of her. But the independence she had found in marriage still lingered; and that independence from her family she had relished. Now she had all but lost it by returning to the dairy house. Her mother and Jesse didn't regard her as a child anymore and she had free rein to do as she wished, within reason, but they always had to be considered now. And that she found limiting. So the three of them had discussed the fors and against of her finding a job. On balance, a job seemed the ideal answer. It would get Alice out of the house during the day, provide her with some independent means, and Lizzie would be happy to look after Edward, if only to make sure he was brought up properly.

Just a couple of days later a job was advertised in the *Dudley Herald* for a female clerk to perform general duties at the offices of a firm of Solicitors and Commissioners for Oaths. Alice had experience of using a typewriter, filing, fetching, carrying and making tea at Bean Cars; this experience was sure to stand her in good stead. So she applied. By return of post she received an invitation to attend for an interview.

It seemed to go well. Her interviewer, a young, good-looking solicitor of about twenty-seven, called Charles Wells, seemed desperately at odds with his drab surroundings. It was evident that he was more interested in Alice for her looks than for her likely qualifications. She perceived this and took advantage, teasing him with bright, flirting eyes when he asked her questions and laughing readily at the little jokes he made while trying to impress her. When she disclosed that although she was married she and her husband were living apart, and she might feasibly be seeking a divorce in the foreseeable future, his eyes lit up. Two minutes later, he offered her the job. She would soon pick up all there was to know, he assured her, working under his close supervision. The situation appealed, especially him, so she accepted and agreed to commence her duties the following Monday.

Now, as she wandered through the open market, she felt that at last her life might be about to change for the better. She'd be earning money again . . . at least.

'I've got some bostin' news for yer, Henzey,' Florrie Shuker said, above the hubbub of the Headlamp Department. She nonchalantly fitted a connector to one of the headlamps she had picked up from the conveyor that slid between the workbench she shared with Henzey and the girls who worked opposite. 'Me an' Oliver am gettin' married at Christmas.'

Henzey looked up from what she was doing, and smiled. 'Oh, Florrie! At last. I was beginning to think he'd never ask you.'

'He din't ask me, Henzey. I asked him. Otherwise, I could've waited till doomsday. I'm gettin' no younger, yer know, an' I'd like to think as I could have me share o' babbies afore I'm too old.'

'But you're only twenty-three, Florrie. You're hardly on the shelf yet. You've got years ahead of you. Anyway, how did it come about as you asked him?'

Florrie finished the headlamp she'd been working on and picked up another from the conveyor. 'Oh, we went out dancin' Saturday night, and I think I had a gin an' orange too many. Well, as we was walkin' back we got talkin' – it was a lovely night – and he happened to mention as he wouldn't like to go through life without fatherin' any children. So I said, "Well what about it then?" I think he took me wrong, 'cause he tried to get me into somebody's entry – playful, like, yer know? But I said, "Gerroff," I said. "If you want that you'll have to marry me first." An' straight out the blue, he said, "All right, I'll marry yer, Florrie," he said. "When?" I said. "Soon as yer like," he said. So we decided on Christmas.' She smiled contentedly. 'We'm fixin' up to see the vicar some time this week.'

'Florrie, I think that's lovely. I'm ever so pleased for you. Wait till I tell Will.'

'Well, you'll both be invited. How is Will anyway? How's he takin' to workin' shifts?'

'Not very well, but at least it won't be for long, thank goodness.'

Florrie smiled, a knowing look on her face. 'That Neville Worthington's got a lot to answer for, takin' your husband off yer nights. I bet it's knocking your sex life about scandalous, eh?' She gave Henzey a nudge. 'You'll never get in the family way.'

'Don't remind me,' Henzey sighed. 'It's bad enough as it is, him insisting on using a French letter every time, without losing the chances to try.'

'Don't worry. One of 'em might bost. You could even put holes in 'em yourself.' She winked at Henzey. 'Have yer thought about that? He wouldn't know, would he? But there's plenty time. Like you just said, there's plenty years ahead for that . . . for both of us. Stop your frettin', Henzey.'

Henzey sighed again. 'Oh, I hope you're right, Florrie. But

I'm sick of waiting now. Sick of Will's perpetual excuse that he's scared in case anything happens to me. What if something happened to him and I didn't have his child?'

They fell silent for a few minutes, each pondering the weight of their conversation, till Florrie spoke again.

'What did Clara say when you telephoned her?'

'She couldn't believe it. I think she's more excited about it than I am. She says to take Neville over to her house on Wednesday afternoon and she'll take us to meet her mother.'

'You takin' the afternoon off then?'

'Looks like it, but keep it to yourself. I'll have to pretend to be ill on the morning and ask to go home.'

'You old skiver, Henzey. So what did Neville say when you phoned him?'

'He sounded excited as well. We've arranged for him to pick me up from home at half past two.'

'Pick you up? From home? Henzey, you'll get talked about vile, havin' half a day off and bein' picked up by a strange man. What'll Will say?'

'Oh, Will suggested it in the first place. He'll be at work till ten anyway, so it won't affect him.'

'I dai' mean that, Henzey. But I know Oliver wun't like it if I went off with a bloke I 'ardly knowed, no matter what the excuse.'

'Well, it's not as if I'm going to do anything wrong, is it?'

'I should hope not.'

'Anyway, Will trusts me, Florrie. He knows he can trust me.'

'If I was Will I think I'd be worried sick about yer, gallivantin' off with wealthy Brummagem businessmen while I was hard at work.'

Henzey laughed dismissively. 'Gallivanting? It's hardly gallivanting.'

'Will might be able to trust you, but can he trust that Neville Worthington? From what yer've told me he sounds a right old lag.'

'Oh, it's just a lark with Neville Worthington. I'll come to no harm with him, Florrie. You haven't seen him. I don't fancy him anyway. He's too eccentric. He's just nice to be with.'

'Huh! There you am, yer see. Nice to be with. That's how it all starts, Henzey. *And* he's got plenty money. Just mind what you'm up to.'

'Oh, Florrie, you are funny.' Henzey put her workpiece down on the conveyor, reached for another, and turned to Florrie, laughing. 'Neville Worthington means nothing to me. Neither does his money. And, besides, do you think I'd do anything to hurt Will after what he's already been through? Do you think I'd do anything to make things even more awkward for poor Eunice?'

Florrie shook her head, looking guilty for thinking it; as though she should know better. 'No, course not,' she conceded. 'I know you wouldn't.'

Chapter Twenty

Henzey's and Will's paths coincided at home that Wednesday dinnertime. It was the 17th July and the weather was still set fair, auguring well for the works' holidays. She arrived home from work early in order to keep her appointment with Neville Worthington. While she had a few spare minutes she ran upstairs to gather the dirty washing that she hadn't had time to collect earlier. As she got it ready for Mrs Fothergill next door to hand to the laundry man, she saw Will was ready to leave to commence his shift.

He collected his sandwiches and thermos of tea from the scullery table. 'Shall you be back before me, d'you think?' he asked.

'I would have thought so. Hours before. We're only going to Clara's mother's. I'll be back well before teatime.'

'But you don't know how long these things are likely to take . . . once folk start reminiscing . . . If they're anything like my mother.'

She kissed him on the lips. 'I'll be back, and I'll have a meal ready.'

He gave her a hug. 'See you later. Have an interesting afternoon. You can tell me all about it tonight. Bye.'

He went into the hall and Henzey heard him pick up his keys.

'Will!'

'What, sweetheart?'

She went to him as he stood by the front door. 'Do you mind my meeting Neville this afternoon?'

He uttered a little laugh of surprise. 'No, why should I?'

'It was just something Florrie Shuker said . . .'

'Oh, what? What did she say?'

She shrugged. 'That her Oliver wouldn't like it if she went out for an afternoon with another man.'

Will laughed again. 'Well, that's up to him. Maybe he doesn't trust Florrie . . . I trust you.'

'But do you trust Neville?'

He gave a puzzled frown. 'If I trust you I don't even have to consider Neville, do I? But I have noticed the way he looks at you.'

She laughed dismissively. 'Oh, I know. I've got a feeling he fancies me.'

'And I know you could handle him if you had to. I'm not concerned, Henzey, but I'm happy you mentioned it. Look, I'd better go else I'll be late. See you later.'

They kissed again briefly and he left. Henzey made a sandwich for herself and boiled the kettle for some tea, then went upstairs to get ready. By the time she'd finished it was half past two. Just as she reached the bottom of the stairs she heard a car outside, then a knock at the door. It was Neville.

'Hello. You're very punctual,' she greeted affably.

'Time's precious, Henzey. Too precious to be spent waiting.'

They walked down the path to his Swallow. Its gleaming paintwork and glistening chrome seemed incongruous with the modest terraces of Daisy Road. There was no chauffeur today, Henzey noticed. Before he opened the door for her to get in, she peered at the headlamps and patted the one closest to her. Neville watched and smiled.

'That headlamp crafted by your own fair hand, eh?'

It was hot in the car and she laughed as she made herself comfortable. 'Could've been.'

He got in, started the engine and they pulled away. 'What time's Clara expecting us?'

'Oh, about three.'

'Plenty of time, then. We'll go along the new road, eh? Oldbury can be a bit of a bottleneck, especially if we get stuck behind a tram. So how are you today, Henzey?'

'Fine, thanks. Lord, it's so hot in here.'

'Wind the window down if you want. And how's Will?'

'Fine.'

They turned right into Monument Road, then Hagley Road. As they motored past Wessex House, Henzey peered out to see if she could see Eunice to wave to. A gardener in a collarless shirt and twisted braces was hoeing the soil around the bottom of a group of cypress trees.

'How many people do you have working for you at your house?' she asked.

'Well, there's George the gardener on Mondays, Wednesdays and Fridays. Lilian, and Iris, the maids, and Miss Newby, the nanny, are full time. And Alec, the chauffeur, just occasionally. Used to have a butler up until eight years ago, but Eunice said he was a shameful luxury when so many folk were on the breadline.'

'So she added to the breadline by putting him on it. That was clever.'

Neville laughed. 'Sharp, aren't you? As a matter of fact, I found him a job at the factory. I couldn't see the poor chap suffer. He'd been with the family for years. Good old stick, he was.'

'You're not a bad sort yourself if you found him other work.'

He seemed to swell with pride that she'd complimented him and smiled to himself. 'It was the least I could do. I'm not so sure Eunice would have been so beneficent though.'

'I like Eunice,' Henzey declared, 'but I get the feeling she's sort of . . . not . . . not comfortable with wealth.'

He laughed again and turned to look at her. 'She'd be damned uncomfortable without it. I suppose when you've got money it's not important. Money only becomes important when you have none. She doesn't know what it's like to live without money. So her politics are definitely inclined towards the left. She believes that everyone is, or should be, equal . . . But, she tends to look down her nose at anybody not her equal. Which just goes to show she's a hypocrite . . . But that's typical of human nature . . . and typifies the flaw in socialism, too.'

'How?'

'Well . . . by not taking into account human nature. Not taking into account folks' hypocrisy and greed. Or the inevitable belief that we're better than our neighbour in some way. Who *doesn't* look down their nose at somebody? We're all guilty of it. We all think sometimes we're entitled to, or deserving of something more than our neighbour, by virtue of something or other.'

'Such as?'

'Such as thinking we're cleverer, harder working, more intelligent, more talented at some sport for instance, or more adept at playing some musical instrument. Anything. And some people *are* better at some things than others, so we're not all equal, are we? Don't you think a doctor, who's studied his profession for years in order to qualify, warrants more money, more respect and greater privileges in society than say somebody who . . . who fastens broom heads to broomsticks, for example? A job that requires little or no training?'

'But they both provide a service to people.'

'They do indeed, Henzey, but the point is, are their services of equal value to that community? I would have thought the doctor's infinitely more so.'

She grinned impishly, intent on winding him up. 'Well, I suppose it depends whether you have somebody ill in the family, or whether you are desperate to find a broom.'

He laughed. 'You'll get on well with Eunice, if that's how you

argue . . . Years ago Eunice would've championed the suffra-
gettes' cause, had she been old enough.'

'So how old is she?'

'Thirty-three. Two years younger than me.'

'Hmm. She doesn't look it, for all her being stuck in a
wheelchair. She's a lovely-looking woman . . . I bet you fell head
over heels for her when you first met. Before she . . .'

'Yes, I did rather . . . But that's another story.'

'So you're only the same age as Will? Fancy. And I thought
you were older.'

'*She* always says I look older than my years. She reckons it's
the beard.'

'So why don't you shave it off? I bet you're really quite nice-
looking underneath all those thick, black whiskers,' she said
archly. 'That's all anybody can see. You've got nice, expressive
eyes, though. I've always thought you've got nice eyes. Will's got
nice eyes, too.'

Her candour amused him and he chuckled, despite the
comparison with Will. Evidently, she still had not connected
them. 'Oh? You notice such things?'

'It's the artist in me. I can't help it. I notice everybody's
features. As if everybody is a potential subject.'

'So, if I shaved off the beard you might fancy me?'

'I didn't say that.'

'I know you didn't. I'm just testing the water.'

She smiled to her herself. 'In any case your hair's too long,'
she ventured playfully.

He didn't answer and she wondered whether she had
offended him by her well-meant honesty. She wanted to apologise, but didn't see how she could plausibly gainsay something
she firmly believed. They drove on in silence for a while, through
Bearwood, towards Quinton and the start of the fast new road
that took you as far as Wolverhampton.

She needn't have worried, however. How could he argue with
what he knew to be the truth? He'd been told it often enough.

Resolutely he stepped on the throttle pedal and the powerful car surged forward, the wind noise from the open windows increasing with the speed. Henzey wound up the window on her side to lessen the howl and the draught, leaving just a slot at the top. He turned his head and smiled reassuringly at her, taking in her slender figure beside him; the flawless, lightly tanned skin of her arms; how her light, summer skirt tormentingly outlined the contours of her thighs as she sat. She looked so clean and fresh and he longed to touch her, to hold her to him, to feel her firm, young woman's body against his own. He yearned to sniff her hair, her creamy skin, to experience her sweet gentle breath on his face. He'd been looking forward so much to being alone with her, dreaming of what might come of it, ever since she'd first mentioned Clara Maitland and her mother. God bless Clara Maitland. And the added bonus was that Henzey was here with the blessings of both Will and Eunice.

He drove expertly; fast. The speed was exhilarating but Henzey felt safe. She was enjoying herself, her well-being increasing with her growing awareness of his partiality for her. Yet she had no notion of the raging intensity of it. She had no idea at all how fiercely the flame within him was burning. How could she? He could hardly declare it now she was a married woman. Nor would she have expected him to anyway, him being a friend and colleague of her husband. Thus, she felt no pressure; just contentment.

They left the wide, arrow-straight road at Burnt Tree and headed towards Dudley town. The limestone keep of the old castle, bathed in sunshine, came into view high on their right. As they crossed the railway bridge at the station, a cloud of dense white steam from a passing locomotive in the cutting beneath it engulfed the hoardings that advertised Palethorpe's Sausage, Barber's Teas and Sunlight Soap, only to disperse in the heat of the sunny afternoon. The Station Hotel reminded Henzey of Billy Witts and their first tryst on her seventeenth birthday. It seemed a lifetime ago. She smiled to herself and wound her window down again. What would Billy make of it if he could see her now in Neville Worthington's lovely new Swallow?

'It it far now?' Neville enquired.

'Just a couple of minutes.' They drove through the Market Place, deserted since today was early closing. She peered between the empty market trestles and the red and white awnings that rippled in the warm breeze, to take a look at George Mason's store. Life had changed so much since she worked there as a young girl. They passed Top Church on their left, and Henzey caught the rich, savoury smell emanating from Julia Hanson's Brewery opposite, evoking more memories. 'That smell always makes me feel hungry,' she commented. 'It reminds me of potatoes cooking.'

Then the pungent aroma of a pickled onion factory filled the air.

'I suppose that smell reminds you of cheese sandwiches, eh?' Neville suggested.

'No, the pickled herrings my mother used to cook for our suppers sometimes.'

'I've never had pickled herrings.'

'You don't know what you've missed. Honestly.'

'As each day passes I realise it the more.'

'Turn left here, Neville . . . now right. Here we are, Brettell Street . . . A bit further . . . Pull up here, on the right.'

Neville stopped the car and they got out. Clara was peering through the nets of her front-room window, awaiting their arrival. She waved, then opened the door to them.

'I can't believe you're one of those little twins, Mr Worthington,' Clara said when she and Henzey had brought each other reasonably up to date with gossip. 'My mother can't wait to meet you.'

'I can't wait to meet your mother, Mrs Maitland.'

'It was just on the off chance that I happened to tell Henzey the story, years ago. Now, would you like a cup of tea here, or would you rather wait till we get to mother's? It's not far.'

'I'm keen to meet your mother,' Neville said. 'We'll wait, if it's all the same to you, Mrs Maitland.'

'Oh, call me Clara. Let's not be so formal.'

So they agreed to call each other by their Christian names. They filed out and climbed into Neville's car.

'Ooh, I say, this is a lovely motor car,' Clara said, settling herself in as if for a long ride.

Henzey nodded and smiled. Two minutes later they clambered out again outside a row of crumbling, old, terraced houses in a road called Angel Street; houses not unlike the one the Kites lived in before they moved to the dairy house. They walked through an entry that led onto an open dirt yard with a brewhouse, overlooked by a squalid factory with rusty cast-iron window frames and dozens of broken panes. They turned left to see an open door, which Clara entered.

'Yoo-hoo! Mother?'

A voice answered.

Clara, smiling, beckoned Henzey and Neville forward, having held back politely until they knew Clara's mother was aware of their presence. Now they followed her into the small scullery, Henzey first, then Neville. It was so much like their old house in Cromwell Street with its black-leaded grate, its gales holding a black enamelled kettle that sighed over the coals. There was a similar chenille fringe hanging from the mantelshelf, a crucifix upon it, the mirror over it; an old, black, marble clock with gold painted pillars flanking the face, an elaborately decorated, japanned tea caddy and a pin-cushion. The bottom stair jutted out into the room and, adjacent to the stairs door stood the cellar door. It was home from home. Only the furniture was different — big and dark and robust, filling the room with its overbearing Victorian bulk. Hanging from a picture rail on the back wall, next to a huge dresser, was a faded old sepia-toned photograph of a man, which Neville scrutinised with interest after they had all been introduced.

'That was my father, Theophilus Newton, God rest his soul,'

Mrs Round, Clara's mother, informed him. 'A good man, he was.'

'Is there any water in the kettle, Mother?' Clara enquired.

'Ar, I filled it just afore yo' come. It's hot a'ready. It wo' tek long to come to the boil.'

'I'll put some tea in the pot then.'

But Mrs Round pointed out that it was all done, ready. Cups and saucers were already laid on a tray on the sideboard with milk and sugar, and fruit cake on a glass cake stand that was adorned with a spotless white lace doily. 'I like to be organised,' she said, almost apologetically.

Neville smiled at her. 'An admirable virtue, Mrs Round.'

'Well, years agoo I was in service, an' I still like to observe the niceties. Specially when I get a bit o' company. Sit yer down each.'

Charlotte Round was about sixty, Henzey imagined. She had a homely plumpness, and her eyes were bright. Her hair was grey and swept back into a bun, and you could see the hairpins sticking out of it. Her spectacles were rimless and her teeth were her own, except that a front one was missing from the top row. Gold earrings bobbed from her pierced ears. She wore a plain, navy frock and a clean pinafore, that still showed the creases from when she had ironed it.

'I ai' clapped eyes on yo', young Henzey, since yo' worked at George Mason's. How long's that bin?'

'Must be five years, Mrs Round.'

'Well, whatever they'm a-doin' to yer, my wench, yo'm lookin' well on it. So is this your 'usband?'

Henzey laughed and glanced at Neville. 'No, Neville's not my husband. He's a friend of my husband, though.'

'But you'm one of the twins, Clara tells me.'

'I believe so,' Neville replied. 'At any rate my circumstances seem to match those of one of the twins your daughter told Henzey about. If we can establish that I am one of them, I'm keen to find out whatever I can about my mother.'

'Well, fust of all,' Mrs Round said, shuffling in anticipation, 'do yer know the name o' your mother, just to mek sure as yo' ai' tryin' to kid me?'

'Bessie Hipkiss,' he answered without hesitation.

'Bessie Hipkiss!' Henzey exclaimed. 'That's the name I was trying to think of on Saturday night. Do you remember, Neville? So you knew it all the time and didn't say. You crafty old devil.'

'She was a maid in service at Wessex House, our family home,' he went on. 'My grandfather employed her before he died. All I know is that she and my father had a brief but er . . . active love affair before he announced his engagement to the woman he subsequently married, Magdalen Boulton-Hart, as she was then. Magdalen brought me up.'

Charlotte Round pressed her hands together in grateful thanks and looked up at the whitewashed ceiling, as if searching for sight of her Maker. She said, 'Well, well, well! So you'm the one me father took back to that big house he told us about. Except as your father was already dead by then, wasn't he? I looked after yer meself for weeks after Bessie died, yer know. Me and Mr Round was quite prepared to foster yer, but me father –' she nodded at the photograph – 'insisted that your real father should be forced to face his own responsibilities. It was a risk he took when he took yer back. But it paid off, lookin' at yer now in your fine suit o' clothes.'

'Tell me about my mother, please, Mrs Round. What happened to her when she left Wessex House?'

'She din't leave of her own free will, Neville, she was kicked out. She would've bin an embarrassment to 'em, wun't she, if she'd stayed? So she come directly to look for me father. I answered the door to her and I can remember it as if it was yesterday. It was bitter cold – proper brass monkey weather – windy and snowin'. New Year's Day, it was, nineteen hundred.'

'But why should she seek your father, Mrs Round? I don't understand that at all. What was so special about him, as far as she was concerned?'

'She was three or four months gone by this time and had got nowhere to live and nobody to turn to. Not a soul. By this time, yer see, her own mother an' father was both dead and buried. My own father and mother had always bin close friends of Bessie's mother and father, through the Methodist church, yer see. Strong Methodists, they was, all of 'em. They all 'elp one another out, if need be, Methodists. Bessie's mother was Welsh, yer know and, 'course, a lot o' Welsh folk am Methodists.'

'So how was your father able to help her?'

'Bessie was anxious as they shouldn't put her in the work'ouse. They would've done in them days, yer know — not married and carryin' a child. God, it was looked on worse than murder. She was determined to work an' support her child when it arrived. But she needed a roof over her head. Not that she was askin' me father to take her in. Oh, no, she wanted her independence, she made that plain. She wanted to be beholden to nobody and be a burden on nobody, God bless her. Me father owned a few old properties, as it happened, and he had an 'ouse vacant in Flood Street. It was in a vile state, though, filthy dirty. He let it to her rent free. Anyway, I took her to see it, an' I could see as she was disappointed with it, 'cause it was in such a terrible state. Condemned, it was, to tell you the truth, but there was nothin' else. Anyway, she took it an' made the most of it, an' got a job at the Midland Café in the Market Place till it was her time. She scrimped and saved and bought a few bits and pieces, and me and Mr Round gi'd her some bits an' bobs o' furniture of our own as we could spare.'

The kettle started to boil and Clara got up to make the tea. While it steeped, she sat down again to listen to the story.

'Everybody was so kind, it seems,' Neville was saying. 'If only my own father could have contributed in some way instead of booting her out, she might be alive today.'

'Well, that's as maybe, my son. Summat as we'll never know. But she tried hard, did Bessie. The biggest shock of all, though, was givin' birth to twins. Can you imagine bein' in the family way with no husband, an' no money, knowin' you'm gunn'ave a child, then havin' two?'

'She must have wondered what she'd done to deserve double punishment,' Neville said.

'Well, she accepted it quick enough. She was a worker, was Bessie. A lovely wench. After you was born she managed to get a bit of parish relief but, what little it was, soon went on food and coal and clothes for yo' babbies. I helped as much as I could – I did, honest – but Mr Round was out o' work at the time. More often than not Bessie went without food herself so's you two had summat in your bellies. But it was all too much for her and she suffered unmerciful. Bit by bit, she got worse. Pitiful, it was, to see her fadin'. Me father paid for the doctor to come, but he said she was consumptive. By the time you and your brother was two years old, she died – in my arms. I'll never forget it.'

Charlotte took a handkerchief from the pocket of her pinafore and wiped a tear that was seeping from her left eye. They all remained quiet for a few moments while she relived that time with Bessie.

'So did you and your husband look after both us babies when our mother died, Mrs Round?' Neville asked.

'For a time. But me father knew somebody at the chapel, who was only too glad to foster a child. The trouble was, they was poor themselves and they could only afford to take one of you. It was such a damn shame to split you up but, honestly, dear old father saw no other way round it. I bet you'd like to know what happened to your brother, wouldn't you, Neville?'

'Oh, I certainly would.' It suddenly occurred to him that he might be wrong about Will Parish. He hoped he was. It would make his conscience so much easier where Henzey was concerned. 'I most certainly would.'

'Well, I'm sorry, my son, but after all these years I can't even remember the name o' the family what took him. I've got a feelin' they moved out o' Dudley, round about nineteen-twelve. Before the war at any rate. I lost track of 'em altogether.'

'You never know, Mrs Round. He might well show up.'

'Oh, I dearly hope he does,' Charlotte said. 'I've had the pleasure of seein' you again after all these years. I should dearly love to see th'other one. I can remember Bessie called him William, after Mr Gladstone. She called you Joseph, you know – after Joseph Chamberlain. She admired Joseph Chamberlain. I think she met him a time or two – at your house.'

Neville shook his head in disbelief. 'It's staggering to think that, if she'd lived, I'd be Joe Hipkiss and leading an altogether different life. I can't begin to imagine it.'

'So how come they called you Neville?' Henzey asked.

'After Joseph Chamberlain's son, Neville,' he answered. 'Astonishing, isn't it, that the Chamberlain family should influence my real mother and my foster mother to that extent?'

Clara got up, stirred the tea steeping in the pot and began to pour. She placed a cup and saucer in front of everyone, offered them milk and sugar, then a piece of her home-baked cake. Talk of the twins was adjourned while they refreshed themselves, but was resumed afterwards. It was at about half past four that Henzey, concerned about preparing Will's meal, suggested they should perhaps be leaving.

'Well, yo'n gi'd me no end to think about, Neville, seein' yer again after all these years,' Charlotte said. 'It's bin such a pleasure to know yer again, lookin' so well and so prosperous. Your mother would've bin ever so proud o' yer, believe me. Any road, I hope as you'll come and see me again, when Mr Round's about next time. He'd love to see yer.'

'That, I fully intend to do,' Neville promised.

'Well, you know where we live now. There's no excuse to stop away.'

'And may I say, Mrs Round – on my own behalf, and on behalf of my lost twin brother as well – thanks for everything you did for our poor mother, and for us. We shall be forever in your debt.'

Charlotte waved away talk of thanks. 'Anybody would've

done the same, my son. We was no different to anybody else. Me and Mr Round just happened to be there.'

'Joe Hipkiss!' Henzey exclaimed, in gentle mockery. 'I don't think that name suits you at all. I do prefer Neville Worthington. It's much grander. You could stick a 'Sir' in front of Neville Worthington — Sir Neville Worthington. It wouldn't have the same ring stuck in front of Joe Hipkiss.'

·   Neville was driving them back home along Oakham Road, directed by Henzey, towards the Birmingham New Road via the back way.

'What's in a name, Henzey? I'd have still been the same me. The same sad, old face, the same flesh and blood, the same suffering heart.'

Henzey thought he sounded morbid, sorry for himself, considering the fascinating afternoon he'd had. She glanced across at him challengingly. 'But you'd be leading a totally different way of life. You'd be a totally different person.'

'Do you think so?'

'It stands to reason, Neville. You'd be living like the rest of us in some terraced house, I daresay, working in some factory or as a clerk somewhere. Hardly the splendour you do enjoy. You'd probably have six or seven kids screaming round you and a wife that looked as if she had, old before her time, nagging you to death.'

'Instead of the housebound cripple I'm now married to, you mean? Henzey, my dear, I might as well be common or garden Joe Hipkiss. Chances are I'd be a jolly sight happier.'

After watching his eyes alight all afternoon in Charlotte's company, Henzey was concerned about his melancholy now and his unkind comments about Eunice, which she found unfair. She sighed. 'Oh, Neville. After what you've learnt today I thought you'd be ever so happy. What's eating at you?'

At once he swerved into a drive on the left and, with a gasp,

Henzey lurched to her right in her seat. She knew it to be the driveway to the Dudley Golf Club, overhung with trees. Before they reached the clubhouse, he pulled up in the shade of a huge oak tree and killed the engine.

'What's wrong? You frightened me to death.'

'Sorry about that, Henzey. Look I want to tell you about *me*. *All* about me. Things I've wanted to tell you for ages. This seems as good a place and as convenient a time as any. I'm in the mood and at least I've got you all to myself.'

'Just so long as I'm back home in time to get Will's meal ready.'

'I expect you will be.' His voice was tinged with cynicism. 'First, let me tell you about Eunice.'

Henzey wound the window down and leaned her arm out, relishing the coolness of the shade beneath the oak tree. Her clothes were sticking to her body in the humidity. The leaves above them stirred as if agitated and she looked up to see a squirrel bounding energetically from one branch to another, being harangued by two magpies. She watched them for a few seconds, diverted from Neville's intensity.

'Henzey, I want to tell you about Eunice.'

'I'm listening.'

He paused, and sighed. 'I met her one Christmas when I was at university – one Christmas when I didn't go home. It was at a party I was invited to, given by some of my friends. I was strongly attracted to her the moment I saw her and I got somebody to introduce us. Well, we talked and we seemed to get on very well. In fact, we talked for ages. We neither seemed to notice anyone else there. Anyway, she agreed to meet me again, and I took her to an organ recital at my college. Afterwards, we went for a drink at a pub in Oxford. We had so much to say to each other we hardly had time to draw breath. I soon realised we had fallen deeply in love.

'That summer we managed to sneak away to France together for a holiday. My mother thought I was going camping with some of my chums, and her folks believed she was going to stay with a friend she had in Hereford. Even in those days I was blessed with a motor car, so we motored to the Loire in France, taking our time, staying overnight in small hotels . . . as Mr and Mrs Worthington . . . The memory of those wonderful nights of endless lovemaking torments me now, Henzey. I believed then that Eunice and I were meant for each other. That we were each other's destiny.

'When we returned home, things went on apace. For two years we couldn't bear to be apart. So we married soon after I graduated and we moved into Wessex House with my mother and all her staff. It was always taken for granted that I should assume the running of the family business, which I did. Anyway, before long my son was born. Things couldn't have been better. Eunice and I were happy, we lived extremely well and Frederic was a healthy, beautiful baby.'

Henzey saw the squirrel run down the trunk of the tree and sit for a few moments on the grass, its tail erect, before it darted up another tree, indifferent to the magpies. But her mind was not on the squirrel anymore, nor the magpies. It was concentrated on Neville, Eunice, their nights of love and the birth of their child. Eunice was lucky. Eunice had had her children already.

'But then things started to go wrong,' Neville went on. 'Worthington Commercials started losing money – badly.'

'Oh? Why was that?'

'We'd developed a new, streamlined, electric tram. It cost us a fortune. In fact it cost so much that we were in the red at the bank for thousands, with little prospect of revenue from sales of the vehicle recovering it. In fact there were no takers at all. Public transport operators said it couldn't carry enough passengers for such a high investment, you see. So we had to set our sights lower. We concentrated on a modest little three-wheeled van I'd been toying with, in the hope that it would save us. Meanwhile, while I'd been working my fingers to the bone, burning the midnight oil at the factory, Eunice had found a stimulating diversion . . .'

'Oh? What?'

'You mean who . . . The disavowed son of a wealthy landowner; a certain Harris Channon, who was five years younger than Eunice and who used to pay her the most outrageous compliments. He turned her head and . . . well . . . they became lovers. You can imagine, Henzey, that I was utterly distraught.'

'Oh, but that's terrible, Neville. I knew you were . . . that something was amiss with your marriage first time I met you, but I had no idea what.'

'Oh, I loved my wife, Henzey — I loved her with all my heart. But with that to face, as well as the business going to the wall, I was at my wits' end. I pleaded with Eunice not to leave me, that it was a frivolous affair she'd embarked on and that it would pass. But months later there was no sign of it waning. In fact, it seemed to me to be intensifying and she began demanding whole weekends away with him. Of course, I refused to allow it and threatened to expose her behaviour to her family if she so much as mentioned it again. By this time, the banks had all but foreclosed on us. I'd already sold my car — a Rolls Royce — Wessex House would have to be sold too, as would everything else I owned, to pay off debts.

'Then Eunice came up with a proposition. She would throw in her fortune — a not inconsiderable sum I might say, which had been held in trust pending her twenty-fifth birthday — not her marriage, significantly. Her father, before he died, didn't altogether approve of his only daughter being married to the illegitimate son of a long forgotten industrialist. So, provided I would allow her to conduct her affair freely with young Harris Channon and, at the same time, make her a director in the business, I could use the money — all of it. Frankly, Henzey, it was the answer to all my prayers and I accepted without hesitation. It meant that Eunice would still be my wife, remaining at Wessex House. I would still have her and Frederic with me and the house and the business would be saved. Of course, I didn't relish the idea of her wild nights of passion with damned Harris Channon. It made me sick to contemplate it. But I had no choice. Her money saved us from ruin and I was glad of that. Better I had it than him. And I knew it would be just a matter of time before she was back with me in spirit.'

'I really had no idea, Neville. Good gracious . . . When did all this happen? Before the Wall Street Crash?'

'Oh, yes. Long before the Crash.'

'So what happened to this Harris Channon?'

'She continued to see him for some little while afterwards. But, when he realised that her money was gone, propping up Worthington Commercials, he seemed to lose interest rapidly. And by the time Eunice realised it was only her money he'd been interested in, I had lost interest in Eunice as well. If she'd wanted to go then, she could have done, as far as I was concerned. But of course she couldn't. She had nowhere to go and no money left to go with. She was reliant on me. Ironic, isn't it?'

'But then Kitty came along. Had you not counted on having another child?'

'Kitty was a shock to both of us, I can tell you. A hell of a shock.'

'But she's beautiful. You must love her to bits.'

'Naturally.'

'And Eunice's illness? When did she become ill?'

'She'd shown symptoms while she was carrying Kitty, although we were blind to them. But when she began to lose the use of her legs after it all, the doctor diagnosed her problem as Cruveilhier's atrophy . . . multiple sclerosis.'

'She won't get better, either, will she?'

He shook his head ruefully. 'No, she won't get better. So you see, Henzey, Eunice and I are somehow stuck with each other.'

'For better, for worse.'

He smiled sadly. 'For richer, for poorer. In sickness and in health.'

'And how long have you felt like this about her? Indifferent, I mean.'

'I felt it already when you and I first met, Henzey. Six years ago now.'

'Before she fell ill. I remember you saying you were disenchanted with marriage, but not with love. Something like that, at any rate.'

'Oh, that's the absolute truth. And when first I set eyes on you, it brought it right home to me. You see, Henzey, I fell in love with you the moment I saw you. Desperately in love. I've been in love with you ever since.'

'Oh, Neville!' Strangely, she felt shock and disappointment. She wanted to curl up into a ball and put her hands over her ears so she could hear no more such words. She was a married woman after all. And his own wife depended on him for her very existence, despite what she'd done to hurt him. 'Neville, you should have the grace not to say such things,' she said in admonishment.

'But you must have known it, Henzey. I didn't try to hide it. I didn't even try to hide it from Eunice.'

'I only saw you that once. I just thought that you wanted to . . . oh, you know . . . you know what men are like.' She cast her eyes down. 'You said some very outlandish things to me. I certainly wouldn't have called it love. Lust, maybe . . .'

'Well, I hope I didn't offend you.'

She laughed now, tossing her head back. 'No, you didn't offend me. I thought it was funny.'

'Good.' He smiled at her, his eyes brighter, striving to push back the dulling veil of bad memories. 'I wanted to invite you and that Billy Witts over to dinner, just so I could see you again . . . but time and events prevented it. Then, next thing I knew, the Wall Street Crash had hit us and you and him were no longer an entity. After that I resigned myself to having lost you forever. I had no idea how to find you. I certainly couldn't ask *him*.'

'And how did you know that Billy and me were no longer an *entity*, as you put it?'

'Oh, I heard. I forget how, but I heard it somewhere.'

'So it must have been a shock to see me with Will?'

'Shock? My God, you'll never know just how much of a shock. But I hadn't forgotten you, Henzey. Often I thought about you, wondering where you were, what you were doing.'

'And, all the time, I've been living only half a mile from you, as the crow flies.'

'I know. So near and yet so far, I think the expression is.'

Boldly he slid his left arm across the back of her seat and touched her neck. Henzey recoiled slightly at his touch but looked into his eyes. She felt desperately sorry for him and the emotional torment he had endured with Eunice, before and since her illness. His expression of insecurity now was hardly surprising in the circumstances. He was uncertain of himself at this very moment, uncertain how she would react, and she could sense it. For him to make this small move of touching her neck had taken some courage, especially since he must know that he would receive only a rebuttal.

'I think it's time we went, Neville, don't you?' she said, without haughtiness. There was even a trace of humility in her voice.

'Not until I know you understand how I feel.'

'But Neville, it can do you no good, can it? I'm married to Will. I love him. I love him dearly. Nothing can alter that.'

'But he won't give you a child, will he?'

There was a pause while she collected her thoughts.

His comment stunned her. It was grossly unfair. It was unfair on her, and on Will.

'That's our business,' she replied coldly.

'I only know what Eunice told me. You were talking to her about it, I understand. She said how desperate you are for a child.'

'Then if you know that much, you must also know about Will's phobia. But I *will* have my child, Neville. All in good time.

I can understand Will's fears after losing his first wife in childbirth. Can't you? He'll get over it. I'll help him get over it.'

'I'm sorry,' he said, but impatiently. 'I shouldn't have said that. I accept all that you say. But the fact remains, Henzey – I am hopelessly, helplessly in love with you.'

'Neville!' Mild exasperation.

'I know, I know. The woman I have come to hold dearer than even life itself is happily married to the very man I have come to admire most. How do you think that sits with me, Henzey?'

She shrugged. 'Not comfortably, I imagine.'

He sighed. 'Not comfortably is a bit of an understatement, I can assure you. But your being married to him doesn't alter the way I feel. I can't help the way I feel.'

'Neville, I'm so sorry. I . . .'

'I haven't slept properly since I saw you again. You're constantly on my mind. I want you to understand that.'

She shook her head slowly. 'Neville, I don't know what to say . . . I'm flattered. Of course I'm flattered. But that's all. I can never give you back what you say you feel for me. Never.'

'You know, Henzey, when I'm lying in bed at night I try to imagine you by my side. I try to imagine your kisses, the feel of your skin next to mine, the smoothness of your thighs as I part them with mine . . .'

'Neville!'

'I shock you, Henzey. Good.'

'Well, I'm hardly used to that kind of talk.'

'I want you . . . Badly . . . I can't help it.'

'Will you take me home now, please?'

'Only if you're sure you understand how I feel.'

'Oh, I understand perfectly now.'

'I don't think you do, Henzey. I don't think you'll ever understand. But you must understand that I am not the happiest of men . . .'

She turned to look at him. His eyes were full and watery,

about to weep, which moved her to tears herself. She turned away, biting her lip, trying desperately to stem the flow.

He said, 'I'll take you home.' His voice was ragged with emotion.

Chapter Twenty-One

Henzey filled her kettle with water and placed it on the gas. She desperately needed a cup of strong tea and an hour or so of quiet contemplation to try and come to terms with Neville's unsettling confession of love. Oh, she'd known all along that he fancied her, but she had no inkling at all that his emotions ran so dangerously deep; emotions that were so unnerving. His lust, captive within his own mind, his admiring glances, she could cope with easily as long as she was protected by Will's or Eunice's presence; then she could even flirt with him, playfully egg him on. But this was deadly serious now. It required some contemplation, some assimilation and even consideration as to whether or not she should confide it all to Will.

Neville and she had said little more to each other as they drove back to Ladywood, both trying to come to terms with this new state of affairs that would forever alter any future dealings they might have. As she alighted from his Swallow his parting words were: 'Sorry, Henzey. It's how I feel . . . You've no idea . . . I had to let you know.' And she'd smiled, a smile that to him seemed to suggest she felt sorry for him. Then she was gone.

The kettle began to whistle, interrupting her thoughts as she stood, propping herself against the sink, gazing absently through the window across the reservoir. Above the trees, on the opposite side, she could just discern the twisted chimneys of Wessex

House and knew that Neville would be there already, pondering above all their encounter, not the visit to Charlotte and Clara. Pensively, she reached for the tea caddy and loaded two spoonfuls of tea leaves into the brown, ceramic teapot. Why did Neville have to complicate *her* life? She was happy, she was content – well, not quite content yet – but almost content. She would be utterly content when she had a child – even when she knew she was carrying a child. So why did another man have to encroach on that contentment, hoping to claim a share of it? Although she did not want to be romantically involved with Neville – indeed she could not, even if she wanted to – his revelation was disturbing. It would not be nearly so bad if she disliked him; she could simply turn away and ignore his overtures. But she did like him. She enjoyed his company. He amused her, stimulated her with his directness and sometimes even shocked her. Oh yes, he'd shocked her now; to the source of her very soul.

She drenched the leaves in the pot with the boiling water and set it on the stove to steep, knowing it would be impossible to turn her back on him. He was a friend and had to be treated thus. Of course she had been as honest with him as he with her, and told him in forthright terms that she could never requite his love. She could not have put it more plainly. But, being the kind of person she was, she could disregard neither his devotion nor the anguish he must be suffering because of it. There was nothing worse than to be in love with someone who belonged to, or loved, or preferred to be with somebody else, as she knew from her own bitter experience. Imagining the object of your desire lying in bed with another was absolute hell. She knew it from her own anguish over Billy Witts and Nellie Dewsbury. It would be no different for Neville.

It crossed her mind whether Neville's obsession for her might have a detrimental effect on Will's position at work. If Neville wished to be vindictive, as a customer of Lucas Electrical, might he have any influence with the hierarchy and begin a whispering campaign to unsettle their confidence in him and thus render his job less secure? But as she reached for a cup and saucer, she dismissed that notion. If she had read Neville correctly he was in as much turmoil over the betrayal of his new friendship with Will as he was with his yearning for herself. After all, it was Will whose company had been sought for dinner at Wessex House, not hers; they were not aware she still existed. To be thus invited, he must have been well liked and well respected.

Damn it, this had all happened so quickly. She'd hardly had time to draw breath.

And what about that offer to lend them the cottage by the sea? It would hardly be fitting to accept now. Hopefully Will would not mention it again and, if he did, she would simply say that she had changed her mind about going; that she did not wish to be beholden to Neville. If she could avoid Neville, that would ensure that he didn't mention it either.

No. On no account must Will know the truth. The two men had to liaise through work. There must be no animosity, no mistrust. Will must be allowed to get on with his work as though nothing had happened; with no outside influences discolouring his relationship with Neville.

With a heavy sigh, she tipped some milk into her cup and, lifting the teapot, gave it a swirl before pouring. Then she took her drink into the sitting-room and flopped disconsolately onto the settee. She sipped her tea. How could she possibly be at ease knowing she was responsible for making another person un-happy? Knowing that another man was in love with her, a man she actually liked and admired, was a heavy burden. Even heavier because she could do nothing to alleviate Neville's longing. Guilt began to permeate her conscience.

Heavy hearted, she rested her head on the back of the settee. 'Neville! Oh, Neville,' she sighed in frustration. 'You damn, great fool!'

But before she could muster any further thoughts she was

asleep and her cup of tea was going cold. For she found that sleep afforded a wonderful respite from reality.

Having dropped Henzey at Daisy Street at a few minutes before five o' clock, Neville drove home to Wessex House. His feelings were mixed as he parked his car on the sweeping drive. At least Henzey now knew something of his obsessive ardour, but he was afraid that he had alienated her with his confession. In a panic, he offered a prayer to the Almighty that she would not see fit to report it all to Will. He decided that in case she did, it would be preferable to delegate any meeting with Will Parish and his department from now on. That way he would not come into direct contact with Will again which would, at a stroke, eliminate any possibility of embarrassment. He could no longer face Will when he was so obsessed with his wife. But, conversely, he was not displeased that he had almost certainly committed Will Parish, however unwittingly, to some weeks of shift work. He had ensured Henzey had some nights alone in her bed . . . God in heaven! – alone in her bed. His imagination was at once fired with disturbing images of her lying naked in the sultry night, her smooth skin moist with perspiration. Suddenly his throat was dry again.

He slipped out of the car and ambled to the front door of the house. He undid the lock and, as he opened it, Roger, his young red setter, bounded across the hall and began jumping up at him, panting from the heat but energetic nonetheless.

'Get down, Roger,' he snorted impatiently, giving the dog a token pat on the head.

'Oh, so you're back,' Eunice called. 'We've eaten already. At six o'clock, Frederic and Kitty were starving so we decided not to wait any longer. Yours is in the oven. I wouldn't be surprised if it's ruined.'

'If it's ruined it's ruined,' he answered edgily. 'Perhaps Lilian would be so kind as to prepare something else in that event. I'll eat in half an hour or so. I'm going upstairs to shower first.'

He leapt up the stairs, taking off the jacket to his three-piece suit as he went. He loosened his tie and, as he walked into his bedroom, he unfastened his collar-studs, placing them in a delicate china bowl on his chest of drawers. He undid his cuff-links and laid them in the same bowl. Stripped to his Aertex underpants, he walked into the luxurious bathroom which was *en suite* with his bedroom.

He looked at himself in the mirror over the wash basin and fingered his features experimentally, pulling his lower eyelids down. '*You've got nice, expressive eyes. I've always thought you've got nice eyes. Will's got nice eyes, too.*' He opened his mouth and examined his teeth. He had a good set of teeth, quite even, quite white. Will Parish also had a good set of teeth, he'd noticed. Oh, damn Will Parish.

He tugged at his beard; his disguise that rendered him so old-fashioned. '*So why don't you shave it off? I bet you're really quite nice-looking underneath all those thick black whiskers. That's all anybody can see.*'

'Damn it, I will,' he muttered to himself.

In the top drawer of his tallboy was a pair of nail scissors in a manicure set. He fetched them and resolutely started snipping off great clumps of whiskers, cutting as close to the skin as possible without nicking it. When he had removed as much as he could he stood back to assess the overall effect. It was awful. He reminded himself of one of those poor, scruffy kids with headlice he saw in Nechells, who had their hair shaved off or cut in steps. There was a safety razor and an old stick of shaving soap in his bathroom cabinet, together with a shaving brush; Eunice had bought them years ago as a broad hint that he should remove it then. He took them and placed them on the wash basin. He found a crumpled paper bag from the rubbish can in his bedroom and, when he'd opened it up, he scooped all the hair out of the sink into the bag. Then he ran the hot water till it was steaming and held the shaving brush under it. This was a routine Neville was not used to, but he quickly induced the wetted shaving stick to yield a dense, white lather on his brush. He painted it over the tatty remains of the beard and moustache that had thrived on his face for seventeen – or was it eighteen – years?

It was a distinctly unusual sight, the lower part of his face covered in a thick layer of shaving soap, but a sight he would have to get used to. He held the safety razor under the scalding tap for a few seconds to make it hot, then tentatively scraped it down his right cheek. He braced himself in anticipation of the discomfort he imagined it would bring. But, not too bad, actually. This razor must be keener than he expected. Inch by inch he scraped away all remnants of his beard and moustache, concentrating at every stroke to avoid cutting himself. By now the bathroom was hot and steamy from the constant running of piping hot water into the wash basin, and the mirror was misting up with condensation, despite the summer heat.

When the last bit of shaving soap had been scraped away, taking with it the last strands of his beloved beard, he rinsed out the wash basin and filled it with lukewarm water. This, he swilled over his face, washing away all traces of shaving soap. With a towel he dabbed it dry. His fingers glided sensually over his newly exposed skin. It felt almost as smooth as a baby's bottom, though it was hot and sore from the unaccustomed friction of a razor blade. He peered into the mirror but it was all steamed up. The towel would clear it. He wiped the mirror and looked at himself intently, seeing himself like this for the first time since early manhood.

He might as well have been looking straight at Will Parish.

Henzey awoke with a start. In the grey, failing light she peered at the clock and discerned, to her horror, that it was half past nine. Will would be home soon and she hadn't prepared his meal. As she got up from the chair to rush to the kitchen she knocked over the cup of cold tea that had been standing on the arm of the chair and she cursed herself. The cup rolled under the table but, thankfully, did not break; the tea soaked into the rug. Uttering another string of words her mother had not taught her, she picked up the cup and saucer, then dashed out to fetch the floor cloth to mop up the mess. Delays she did not need.

But in no time she had the situation under control. She lit the gas oven, found the lamb chops she had bought on her way home from work, peeled the potatoes and shelled the peas. While they were cooking she ran upstairs to change.

Downstairs again, Neville Worthington was still preying on her mind with his irreconcilable unhappiness. How despicably cruel Eunice had been to dispossess him of his contentment when she knew so well how much he loved her. And yet, despite the fact that she had been so grossly unfaithful, despite the fact that he was no longer in love with her, Eunice was still in his tender care. He had not forsaken her. Evidently he still considered her a friend; they still shared the same house, the same bedroom for all she knew. Evidently, they still discussed things with civility. But civility, even in the bedroom, did not constitute deep, abiding affection, and was no substitute for it. How the poor, poor man must have suffered; and him so kind and so considerate.

She was mulling over, and confirming to herself her own inability to offer Neville any comfort, when she heard the door at the side of the house unlatch and Will call, 'It's only me.'

She opened the oven door and the thick, meaty aroma of lamb roasting to perfection filled her nostrils. Will stood at the kitchen door. She turned to him and smiled, then placed the meat tin on the draining board.

'By God that smells good, love,' he said. 'I'm ravenous.'

'You nearly didn't get it,' she answered, stooping to lift the plates that she'd put in the oven to warm. 'I fell asleep. I didn't wake up till half nine. I shan't be able to sleep when it's bedtime.'

'No matter. I'm not tired either. I didn't get up till late myself. We'll just have a late night. Tell you what, I think I'll open that bottle of wine. I just fancy a drink, don't you?'

She placed the lamb chops onto the plates and reached over for the potatoes, to drain the water into another saucepan ready to make gravy. 'Ooh, yes, now you mention it. A glass of wine might help me sleep as well. Would you stir the gravy for me first, while I drain the peas?'

'All right.'

'How was work?'

He adjusted the flame under the pan while he stirred. 'Busy, same as ever. And one of the girls in the office has announced she's getting married in September.'

'Oh, who?'

'Dilys Moy. I don't know whether you know her. She's a typist.'

'Course I know Dilys. I knew she was courting. I didn't realise it was that serious. Fancy.' Henzey doled out the potatoes, then the peas. 'I'll open that bottle of wine while we wait for the gravy to come to the boil. Turn it up a bit, Will, else the rest of it'll be cold by the time you've finished.'

From the pantry she fetched a bottle of burgundy they'd been given ages ago. When she'd retrieved the bottle opener from the drawer and reached for two wine glasses, she drew the cork and poured. She took a slurp from one and savoured it as it assailed the back of her throat. She had not realised just how thirsty she was, and took another long swig.

'Gravy's done,' Will announced.

'Just pour it over the dinners.' She took the bottle and the glasses to the table. Within a few seconds she was back. 'Damn. I even forgot to lay the table. I'm so disorganised.' She fished in another drawer for the table cloth, then the cutlery drawer for knives and forks.

As she finished laying the table, Will entered, carrying their plates. He set them down, sat opposite her, took a drink from his glass and picked up his knife and fork.

'You've forgotten, haven't you?' she said.

'Forgotten what?'

'My visit to Dudley with Neville.'

'Blimey, yes. Gone clean out of my head . . . Sorry . . . How did it go?'

'Oh, fine.' She avoided his eyes and gave a half shrug, hurt that she was evidently so far from his thoughts. 'Are you sure you're interested?'

'Of course I'm interested.'

'Well, there's no doubt that Neville's one of those twins. He even knew the name of his real mother. Bessie Hipkiss. D'you remember, I couldn't think of it at their house?'

He nodded, sawing at a piece of meat.

'He knew it all along. We had the full story from Charlotte Round.'

As they ate she related the poignant tale of Bessie Hipkiss and how Charlotte had looked after Neville and his twin brother as babies. She commented on how the house re-minded her of the house she'd lived in as a child in Cromwell Street.

'So what time did you get home?'

'About six.' Henzey pushed her plate away, finished off the wine in her glass and refilled it.

'You didn't have to fend off Neville, then?' He smiled.

She drank before formulating her answer, feeling her colour come up.

'Fend him off? Course not.'

'Well, I should hope not. I've got him marked down as an honourable man.'

A pause. Henzey took another drink of wine.

'I feel sorry for Neville, you know, Will. I feel ever so sorry for him.'

'Oh?'

'He told me all about Eunice . . . their marriage and all that. He's not happy, you know. He's very unhappy. Eunice used to have a lover – somebody called Harris Channon . . . She wanted to run off with him, from what I can gather.'

'Blimey. But she didn't, obviously.'

Nerves and an unwarranted guilty conscience prompted Henzey to take another drink, because the glass partially hid her reddening face. Before long she had emptied it again. She refilled both glasses.

'Steady on,' Will said. 'You'll be drunk as a lord. Tell me about Neville and Eunice.'

She told him as much as she knew about Eunice's indiscretions; how Worthington Commercials had all but had to close down and how Eunice's money had saved the firm, but subsequently ruined her affair with Harris Channon. She told him how Neville's devotion to his wife had since waned, leaving him empty, grossly unhappy and unfulfilled. And then, to top it all, how Eunice had fallen victim to that appalling muscular disease.

'Oh, Will, I'm so sad,' she said, looking into his eyes now.

'For him?'

'Yes, for him.'

'Is that why you're drinking so much? I've never seen you drink so much.'

'It's not that, I'm thirsty. I haven't had a drink since leaving Mrs Round's.'

'Then have some water.' He shoved his plate away and, with his elbows on the table, cupped his chin in his hands, watching her. 'He's had an effect on you, hasn't he? He's moved you, I mean.'

She nodded guiltily.

'You shouldn't let him get to you, Henzey, my love,' he advised gently. 'Neville Worthington's problems are his own, and probably of his own making if only we knew the truth of it. If Eunice saw fit to have an affair with somebody else it was probably because of some failing in him.'

'Really? Then beware that some failing in you doesn't drive me away, Will,' she said, hardly aware of the wounding barbs in her words.

'What failing in particular? I must have plenty.'

'You know what failing.'

He winced. He knew exactly what she meant. But he had not considered that his unwillingness to put her through the pains of childbirth was a failing; even less, that such a failing might drive her away.

Then she saw Will's hurt expression and realised what she had said. Immediately she regretted it. It was the wine. She was not used to it; how it loosened your tongue. 'Oh, I'm sorry, Will, my love. I shouldn't have said . . .'

'It would be interesting to hear Eunice's version of events,' he replied, immediately recovering.

She sighed. 'Oh, but if you could have heard him today . . . you'd know he was being sincere.' She sipped her wine again and put the glass down wistfully. 'I do wish there was something I could do. Something to make him a bit happier . . . If I could just laugh with him a bit, talk to him, go for drives with him from time to time . . .'

'And you reckon he'd be satisfied with that?' Will sounded cynical.

'Oh, maybe not . . . He'd have to be, though . . . In any case . . . Maybe it's not such a good idea.' She shrugged and drank again. 'But I don't have to see him any more now I've taken him to Charlotte's, do I? He can find his own way in future.'

'So what about that offer he made to lend us his holiday house on the coast? You seemed so keen. Are we to forget that now?'

'We don't want to be beholden to him, Will.'

'So is that what I tell him next time I see him?'

'Say nothing. Maybe he'll just forget all about it.'

'Oh, I doubt that now, Henzey. I doubt it very much.'

Eunice found Neville's new hairless face something of an unveiling. She had never seen him before without a beard. Now she saw how handsome he really was. While he ate that evening she sat with him and watched him, fascinated. His eyes looked different in the context of his new countenance. His cheekbones were high, that she knew, but the sallowness of his cheeks had never been evident before. Nor his chin; it was proud, patrician, masculine. His mouth, too, was good on this fresh face.

'You know, Neville, I believe I much prefer you without a beard,' she commented, 'even though you are the image of Will Parish – a perfect match. There's certainly no separating you two.'

He looked up from his dinner, still chewing a piece of beef, showing no emotion. 'Coming from you, my dear, that's indeed a compliment. Perhaps I should have done it years ago.'

'I have suggested it countless times,' she said self-righteously. 'Now, if you'll be advised by me, first thing tomorrow morning go into town, find a decent barber and jolly-well get your hair cut. It's simply too, too awful, Neville. It makes you look so . . . so awfully Bohemian.'

'Yes, I'll do it. I fully intend to.'

'But, it'll be obvious both to Will and Henzey who your long lost twin brother really is. So what shall you do then? Shall you implement your original plan to lure him away from Lucas's and offer him a seat on the board? Or is it your intention to try and lure Henzey away instead?'

Chapter Twenty-Two

It was just after nine o'clock one warm Tuesday evening in early July that Neville Worthington, wearing a black two-piece suit and a trilby hat, in half a mind to call on Henzey on some as yet undecided pretext, had been hovering around Daisy Road. One consideration above all others, however, was holding him back: she might not welcome him. She might even take exception to his calling if she thought he was unheroically trying to force his attentions on her while Will was still at work. And of course, if she saw him now, now that he was clean-shaven and sporting a new haircut like Will's, she would know at once that her husband was his missing twin brother and there would be no prospect at all of any romantic liaison. And deep in his heart that was what he wanted more than anything else in the world – a romantic liaison.

His mouth was bone dry at the prospect of seeing her, of being so close that he could actually touch her, actually smell her beautiful sweet self. Just to see her fabulous smile and feast his eyes on her would brighten his tormented, heart-aching day. But at the prospect of both a certain rebuff and ultimately making himself look a bigger fool, he decided that it was not a good time. He could always use the cottage by the sea as his excuse, but even that would seem too contrived right now. He would devise some better reason at a more appropriate time.

He was utterly obsessed, and this obsession, he knew, had already made him look a fool in Henzey's eyes. God knows how he would appear to Will if he ever discovered how he felt. It did not bear thinking about. Thus he convinced himself to reconsider what he was doing. Instead of all these pie-in-the-sky dreams of being Henzey's lover, might it not be better to do the noble thing after all, and see through his original intention of acknowledging Will, welcoming him into his family and ultimately offering him a seat on the board of Worthington Commercials? He turned away from Daisy Road with the intention of walking back home in the still warm dusk, content that this was the right thing to do, that this action would also ease his troubled conscience.

But it was going to be extremely difficult to simply shut Henzey from his mind, and he wondered if he could ever be that self-willed. He only had to think of her skin, her lips, her body, her smile, her voice, and his mind was in a whirl. And even under these nobler arrangements he envisaged, she would be around him frequently. It would take, therefore, a massive amount of self-control, which he knew he did not possess.

He was so thirsty. His racy thoughts had rendered his mouth dry, prompting him to do something he would never normally have done: enter a public house. The one he entered was the Reservoir. Just a quick pint of shandy would help slake his thirst before he returned home.

A door on one side of the passage was marked 'Public Bar', the one on the other side, 'Smoke Room'. He went into the latter where three other men were sitting round a table playing three-card brag. Both rooms were serviced by the same servery.

'I'll have a pint of shandy, please, landlord,' he said with an unwitting superiority to the man who was evidently the licensee.

'Shandy?' he queried.

Neville nodded.

The man pulled at the beer pump. 'Gorra thairst on or summat? There's sod all wrong with the bitter.'

Neville mopped his brow with his handkerchief. 'Thirsty. It's so close, this weather. Uncomfortably close.'

The landlord held the glass up to ascertain that it was approximately half filled with beer, then flipped the top off a bottle of lemonade. 'Close? If it gets any closer it'll be bleedin' touchin'.' Froth was oozing over the top of the glass and Neville waited, anxious to feel its cool bite at the back of his throat. 'E'y'am, mate.'

Neville handed him a shilling and put the change in the blind box while the landlord went to serve in the bar. As he quaffed his drink with relish he heard the landlord say, 'Will's in the smoke room, Sidney.' At once Neville froze. He had failed to spot that Will Parish was one of the three other men in the room. He turned around slowly to look. They were engrossed in their cards. But none of them was Will Parish. One smiled familiarly and said, 'Warm enough for yer, mate?' Suddenly the door opened and the man he recognised as Sidney Joel, whom he had been introduced to at Lucas's, was standing before him.

'Will,' he greeted. 'What yer doin' in 'ere? I thought yer was at wairk tonight. Come on in the bar. I'll gi' yer a gaime o' darts. Three hundred an' one up, eh?'

Neville was tempted to turn round again to see which of the three men Sidney was talking to, till he realised it was himself. God above! Were they so much alike that even Sidney Joel could mistake him for Will? Neville decided to play along with it. It could be an interesting adventure.

He picked up his drink from the counter and followed Sidney into the other room. The smell of stale beer and smoke permeated the place.

'Bloimey, where yer bin, Will? After another job? Yer look as if yer've jus' fell out o' the Fifty Shillin' Tailor's winda.'

'No, I just thought it would be a nice change to come out in a suit,' he said experimentally.

'An' no need to sound so bleedin' lah-di-dah, neither,' Sidney said. 'You'm with us now, not them toffs at Lucas's.'

Neville realised his more refined cadences did not sound like Will Parish. Will spoke with a local accent; not marked, but certainly enough to make the difference noticeable. He must try and emulate Will's speech for this to work.

'Got yer darts wi' yer, Will?'

'Sorry, Sidney. Never thought to bring 'em.'

'Never mind, use mine. Middle for diddle, eh?'

Neville was confused. He had never played darts in a public bar before. What the rules or rituals were he had no idea. What the hell was 'middle for diddle'? 'You go first, Sidney.'

Sidney shrugged and threw one dart at the bull's-eye. It landed in the small ring around it. Then he handed a dart to Neville.

Presuming the idea was to get a dart in the centre Neville threw it. It wobbled on its trajectory, missed the board, and landed in the felt that surrounded it.

'Yer never could throw with these darts,' Sidney crowed. 'Looks like I'll skin yer. Go on. Mugs away.' He handed him the set.

What the hell happens now? Is there some pattern or sequence of numbers you have to follow, or do you throw the darts anywhere in the board? No. Aim for that section with the number one. It's logical to start at one and proceed till you get to twenty. Steady. Concentrate. Neville threw the dart.

'Oh, bostin' shot, Will. Double top fairst try. You'm away already.'

Neville felt like asking what he was supposed to do next after his first lucky throw. He was wet with sweat, and trembling slightly. What was he doing in this charade anyway? He stood, ready to throw his next dart. It missed the board again. He cursed under his breath, but at least it was a safe thing to do. The last dart; he aimed and threw. In the board it went, but outside the scoring area, just below the nineteen.

'Forty,' said Sidney, more to himself than to Neville. Neville leaned against the bar while Sidney strode over to the board to pick two darts from it and one off the floor. "Kin' 'ell, Will. Do I 'ave to fetch me own darts back an' all?' he complained. 'An' ain't ya gonna chalk up ya score?'

'Sorry, Sidney. I was miles away.' He walked over to the board and grabbed a piece of chalk. 'What did I score? I've forgotten.'

Sidney shook his head slowly and grinned. 'Come on, Will, lad. Pull yerself tergetha. Yer scored forty, din't ya?'

'Right. Forty.' He wrote forty on the board.

'From three hundred an' one, yer great twerp. Jesus. I reckon that young missis o' yourn's killin' ya, Will,' he chuckled. 'But wharra way to goo, eh?'

Neville smiled in acknowledgement of the truth of Sidney's last comment. *If only*, he thought. *If only*. He took another draft from his shandy and emptied the glass. Sidney was throwing his darts now, interspersed with damns and blasts. Neville heard him say, 'Double five,' then he chalked up his score.

'What do you want to drink, Sidney?' he asked. 'I'm about to re-order.'

'Re-order? Christ, 'ark at him, Arthur. Re-order! It's funny what wearin' a suit does to your ord'n'ry langwidge, in't it? I'll have a pint o' the usual if ya mean you'm gerrin' 'em in.'

'A pint for Sidney and a pint of shandy for me,' Neville said to the landlord.

'Shandy?' Sidney queried. 'You flippin' well hate the sight o' shandy. Wha's wrong with the bitter?'

'I wondered what was up with him when he come in the smoke an' asked for a pint o' shandy,' the landlord remarked.

'He's in a funny mood, Arthur,' Sid said. 'It's that Henzey.'

'Well, if her's too much for ya, ya can alw'ys send her round here, Will,' Arthur guffawed.

Neville smiled, uncertain what his reaction should be to such outrageous familiarity. Banter it was, and coarse, but presumably Will would be inclined to take it in good part.

'It's time he babbied her,' Sid said. 'Everybody's sayin' as he's got no lead in his pencil.'

Neville smiled inadequately and, as they all laughed, another man walked in.

'Evenin' George,' Arthur said. 'Will's in the chair. Usual?'

'Goo on, then.'

Neville was glad when he had finished his second pint and his game of darts, in which he made some serious errors. He decided he should leave, so he made his excuses. It had not been a successful experiment at all.

'What about the next match, Will?' Sidney enquired. 'D'ya still wanna play after tonight's performance?'

'Oh, of course. I'll be all right. I've had things on my mind tonight, that's all. Do me a favour, though, Sidney, will you?'

'O' course.'

'Don't remind me of this night. Ever. I mean it. Especially not in front of Henzey.'

'Oh, o' course not, old shoe. Not a word. I know as ya wun't want nobody else to know 'ow bad ya played.'

At half past nine on the evening of the tenth of July, a Wednesday, Henzey handed Will his pack of sandwiches and a flask of tea and kissed him good night as he left for his shift. It felt little different to the times when he went out to play darts on a normal Wednesday night, except that tonight she would lie in bed alone and remain there till about half past six next morning. But she did not mind.

She settled down to read both the morning's and the evening's papers, with the wireless on quietly in the background for company. The heat of the day was subsiding and the sky, pregnant with dark clouds, threatened a storm. She had finished her chores: the bed was made, the washing-up was done, the remaining ironing was done. The windows needed cleaning inside but they could wait till tomorrow. It was time to relax.

But the newspapers told of nothing that interested her: all was doom and gloom. Henzey walked to the kitchen and put some milk in a pan to make herself a mug of Ovaltine, which she took upstairs to drink while she was getting ready for bed. First she went into the back bedroom to gaze through the window over the reservoir. The swollen red sun had dipped below the line of trees on the opposite side, leaving a ribbon of magenta and cyan between them and the black clouds that hung like heavy bags, dominating the rest of the sky. A few lights twinkled and the open window admitted the far-off hum of an occasional motor vehicle as it sped up Hagley Road beyond the trees – past Wessex House. The cluster on the near bank beyond their tiny back garden began to rustle as if stirred by some warm wind, and she realised that it was rain she could hear falling on the leaves. A flash of lightning, followed by a distant rumble of thunder, confirmed the change in the weather.

She was about to go into her own bedroom when she heard a knock at the door. Still holding her mug of Ovaltine, she picked her way downstairs in the darkness. Before going to see who it was, she went into the kitchen and found the matches, struck one and lit the gaslight in the sitting-room. The clock said quarter past ten . . . Whoever it was knocked on the door again. It must be Mrs Fothergill wanting to borrow a cup of sugar or a few teaspoons of tea. Henzey took her key, unlocked the door and opened it gingerly. It was dark outside but there was enough light for her to discern that it was Will.

'What are you doing back here?'

'Hello, my love. I didn't startle you did I? I realised I'd forgotten to take my key, so I decided to come back for it now to save having to wake you early in the morning.'

'Hurry up inside. You'll get soaked standing there. You should've taken your raincoat.'

He stepped inside the hallway, looking at her in the half light, and followed her into the kitchen.

'Make yourself a drink while I have a look for them,' she suggested.

'No, I'd better get back as quick as I can.'

In the sitting-room she looked in the fruit bowl where Will usually kept his keys; on the mantelpiece and in the sideboard; even in the coal-scuttle. They were not there. There was no sign of them.

She turned to him. 'I can't see them anywhere. Maybe you put them in your desk after all, without realising it.'

'I bet that's what I've done – put them in my desk without thinking.'

'It's unlike you, Will. You ought to be more careful. Look at the time you've wasted because of your carelessness.'

He laughed dismissively. 'I know. You can smack my backside if you want.' He gazed at her.

'Take the spare key just in case.' She felt in one of the drawers and fished out a key on a leather fob which she handed to him.

'Thanks . . . I'd best be getting back to work before Sidney misses me.'

They moved to the hallway.

'I thought Sidney was on the afternoon shift. That's what you said.'

'Oh, so I did. I forgot.'

'Will, you're getting forgetful in your old age,' she teased.

'Yes, a moment of senility. Pressure of work.'

She stopped and looked at him for a few seconds. How tense he seemed. She reached for his raincoat. 'Here, take this, else you'll get soaked.'

'I don't need it, Henzey.'

'But it's pouring.'

He took it reluctantly and while he put it on he saw a puzzled expression on her face.

'Will, I could have sworn you went out in your blue shirt tonight.'

'Er . . . No, my love. I had the white one on. Must have been a trick of the light . . . See you in the morning.'

She reached out to him, and he wrapped her enthusiastically

in his arms. It was so good to feel her body against him. He held on to her tightly, as if she might float up to the ceiling if he didn't and thought his heart would burst through his chest as he bent his head to feel those succulent red lips on his, so soft, so yielding.

'I love you so much, Henzey,' he breathed. 'But I must go.'

Neville Worthington pulled up the collar of Will Parish's raincoat, the rain lashing him mercilessly as he ambled in a daze down Reservoir Road on his way home. After his adventure in the Reservoir public house he could scarcely believe how easy it had been to pass himself off yet again as Will Parish; but this time, significantly, he had fooled even Henzey. He had deftly side-stepped the issue of the colour of his shirt, blaming the light. She had even given him a spare door key; an unexpected bonus. But could he be so bold as to use it? Did he possess the brass-bound nerve to let himself into the house in Daisy Road and pass himself off yet again? In the middle of the night, say, when she was lying in bed alone, with Will safely working the night shift? He shrank from the idea. No, that would be taking things too far. He'd got away with tonight's little raid, a raid he had been driven to by sheer despair, just so he could cast his eyes on her again; and even that had drained him of every ounce of courage he possessed. To believe he could pull it off again would be really pushing his luck. What if Will actually returned home while he was there? Murder might be committed.

Thunder cracked overhead and rivers of lightning split the sky in a dozen places. The butterflies, formed by the rain hitting the street, seemed to freeze with each flash of lightning. Rain was running through Neville's hair, tracking down his neck, off the end of his nose and under his chin; but he did not mind. His world-weary blood was surging through his veins with renewed vigour at what he had achieved this night. If only he could muster the gall to use this key, which Henzey had so innocently handed him.

He pondered her with a deep and abiding love in his heart as he stepped nonchalantly through swirling puddles and gutters running swift and wide with water. The streets were deserted. Only somebody obsessed with a woman would consider venturing out on such a night. He must be mad. Not even a dog, crazed with the scent of a bitch on heat, would go to this trouble; yet he had; and the object of his desire was certainly not on heat for him.

If he carried on with this longing, with these lunatic ideas of entering her home pretending to be her husband, nothing but disaster lay ahead. That, he knew. It was rational to think that way. But he could hardly be rational. He was in no fit state to be rational. He was overwhelmed, overwrought, beguiled, infatuated, plagued, utterly bewitched and totally preoccupied.

Next morning when Henzey awoke, Will was at the foot of the bed in his underpants. His suit was already hanging in the wardrobe and his shirt and socks were in the dirty washing basket. He sensed her peering at him. Smiling, he pointed towards the bedside table at a cup of tea he had brought upstairs for her, and brightly wished her good morning.

'You'd got your key then, love?' she asked sleepily.

'My key? Of course I'd got my key,' he replied with a puzzled frown.

'Did you get wet?'

'No.'

'Oh, you caught the tram, then?'

He smiled. 'Yes. Just as I walked by the stop one came, so I hopped on. Lucky, that. Saved my legs at least.' He stretched and yawned, then pulled the bedclothes back. 'I'll get into bed with you, love. Give us a cuddle, eh? Give your poor husband, who's been out at work all night, a nice cuddle.'

'Let's have a sip of tea first.' As he slipped into bed beside her she raised herself up, ran her fingers through her hair and turned to adjust her pillow. 'Did you get a newspaper?'

'Yes, it's downstairs.'

She sipped the hot tea. 'Why didn't you bring it up? Oh, fetch it for me, please, Will, there's an angel.'

He smiled. 'After . . .'

She could tell by the dreamlike look in his eyes what was on his mind, but she did not feel that way inclined this morning. Only if it was going to be worth it. Only if he would relax his irrational, selfish attitude and indulge her in her fondest wish. 'After what?' she asked, seeing it as an opportunity to re-open the discussion and, perhaps, even force his hand.

'After we've made love.' He put his hand to her belly and slid it tentatively up to her breasts, cupping one, then kneading it gently.

She sipped her tea and shrugged, unmoved. 'What's the point?'

'The point is, I love you . . . And I want you.'

She saw the mulish look around his soft mouth, but stayed silent, her saucer in one hand, her cup held to her mouth with the other.

'Don't you want me, Henzey?' he said when he realised he was eliciting no response.

She shrugged again coolly. The whole tedious routine, if the last few months were anything to go by, would take no more than a minute or two. Perhaps she should submit once more. But no. Why should she? Merely submitting to this fleeting lust would not help her cause. It would not help her cause at all. She hardened her resolve.

'I don't see any point,' she said decisively and, placing the cup and saucer on her bedside table, she slid her legs out of bed.

'Oh, Henzey,' he sighed, crossly, like a little boy deprived of a toy. 'What's the matter? Why don't you want to? It's never that time of the month again already?'

'No, it's not that time of the month, Will. But when you decide to make love to me without wearing those awful rubber things you persist in calling Johnnies, then I might change my mind. Until then, no more sex. Until you agree to oblige me and start seriously trying for a family we're having no more sex.'

He looked at her in disbelief. 'Hey, that's not fair.'

She turned and looked into his eyes. 'No? Just think how much more pleasurable it might be, Will. Just imagine how much nicer it would feel without that smelly piece of rubber between us. For me as well as for yourself.' She made sure he caught a tantalising glimpse of her naked body before reaching for her dressing-gown to cover herself up.

At the mere sight, at the mere promise of her smooth, unblemished, young skin, that he knew was warm and firm and accommodating, his desire stirred.

'This is blackmail, Henzey.'

'I know.'

He sighed, like a punctured bladder of wind. 'Well, it won't work. You'll give in before I do.'

'Do you really think so? We'll see.'

Never before had she refused him. And she refused him now but with deep regret, knowing it would mark a turning point in their relationship. She loved Will and she would be the happiest woman on God's earth if only he would just say, 'Yes, it's time we started a family.' That's all it would take. But this conflict of emotions was tearing her apart, levering her away from him. Every time they spoke about it he refused her. And every time they made love, with ever-diminishing ardour these days on her part, she would afterwards seek clues as to whether the French letter had burst and left a drop or two of his semen inside her. And every month, when she saw the first signs of her bleeding, she would weep silently and tell herself *perhaps next time*. How desperately she wanted his child.

She stood by the bedroom door and turned to him, her hand on the edge. 'All I want is our baby, Will.' Tears welled up in her eyes and she allowed one to trickle down her cheek unchecked. 'Are you blind? Can't you see my heart is breaking for want of a child? Can't you see what this is doing to *us*? Unless you give me your support, I swear, Will, it'll ruin our marriage.'

A narrow shaft of pink sunlight penetrated the room, expanding as the sun's early morning haste drove it higher into the summer sky. It did not warm her and she shivered. The tick of the clock seemed loud and intrusive as she stood waiting for him to formulate his response.

'Then that would break my heart,' he said at last, and his voice was strained. 'You know I couldn't stand to lose you. And because I couldn't stand it, you know that's the reason I don't want you to have a baby. If you're not pregnant, then you can't die giving birth, don't you see that? I lost Dorothy because of it. I refuse to put you to the same risk.'

She sighed heavily and wiped her tears with the back of her hand. 'Is that your last word?'

His face was a mask of confusion. 'You don't know what I went through before, Henzey. You don't know how I felt, how I blamed myself, how I wanted to die . . . You know my fears for you. I can't help it.'

'That's all I hear, Will – your fears, your fears. God, it's like a damned echo that repeats my every waking second, like some . . . some hideous howling in a nightmare I can't escape from, no matter how much I struggle. Oh, Will, I really don't think you realise what you're doing to us, do you? How can I make you see? How can I, when all the time you acknowledge only your own fears and desires? For God's sake, seek some advice. Go and see the doctor. See if he can put your fears to rest.'

He looked into her eyes earnestly. 'I don't need to see a doctor, Henzey. You're the one who needs to see a doctor.' His voice was low, even, and, worst of all, rational. 'This child thing of yours is becoming an obsession. A damned obsession. I think you're going mad. You're getting irrational, illogical, over-emotional. You need to calm down and take stock of things before it drives you completely mad. But for this obsession of yours, Henzey, we have a fine marriage.'

'You think so? We *had* a fine marriage, Will. But not anymore.'

With tears in her eyes she turned her back on him and went to the bathroom. When she returned ten minutes later he was lying in bed, his eyes closed; to all intents and purposes he seemed to be sleeping. She shed her dressing-gown and dressed herself, as quietly as she could lest she wake him. But he was not asleep. He opened his eyes and watched her. She did not know he was watching her. He saw her eyes, red from crying and, for once, he felt a bitter pang of remorse at his own obstinacy. He saw that his inflexibility was making her grossly unhappy. The last thing in the world he wanted was to make her unhappy. Maybe he should rethink his position. Maybe he, too, was being obsessive; yes, even to the point of ruining their marriage.

He saw her delve into the wicker washing basket to retrieve the dirty laundry to take downstairs. He watched her pick up and scrutinise with a frown the blue shirt he'd worn for work the night before, unaware of the significance she placed on it.

But why should he know?

On Tuesday of the following week, the sixteenth, Henzey returned home from work to find her meal ready for her. When on night shift Will slept during the day, but started to get up in plenty of time to prepare their evening meal. It was the only redeeming feature of this unsettling shift work, she thought. Will enjoyed cooking from time to time and was indeed an adept cook; his years looking after himself as a widower had ensured that. That night he had prepared grilled pork chops with carrots, kidney beans, potatoes and gravy; it smelled delicious as she walked into the house.

Will was trying hard to get back into her good books. His attitude to their starting a family was softening, but he had made no mention of it yet. Sooner or later he would have to acquiesce if they were to maintain their love and affinity, he realised. But it must not appear to be a major capitulation. He had been threatened with celibacy. His masculine pride did not easily tolerate the prospect of such severe intimidation without some show of defiance. So he would tell her, or show her, in his own way, in his own time.

He led her to the table in the sitting-room and brought in their food like a waiter, making a great show of it, which made her laugh. They began to eat.

'Did you sleep well today?' she enquired.

'Oh, on and off. I can't get used to this change in routine, though. I doubt if I ever would. It just doesn't seem right sleeping through the day. I can't seem to settle.'

A bluebottle entered by the open door and was exploring the room with great vigour. It swooped low and Will took a swipe at it, but missed it by a mile before it flew out.

'No, this shift working doesn't suit me at all,' he continued, picking his knife up again. 'My heart goes out to the poor devils who have to do it all the time. Hopefully we shall complete Neville Worthington's work in a month or so.'

'Oh, let's hope so. Have you seen much of him lately?'

'Nothing. One of his minions has been liaising with us.'

'I hope he's all right. I was concerned about him after the last time I saw him.'

'Oh, he'll be all right. We all have a cross to bear, Henzey. Eunice is his, but he married her for better or worse. I wish you'd concern yourself with things nearer home. I haven't felt well at all today. I expect it's the change in routine. It can affect people like that, you know. And you're very offish as well. That doesn't help.'

'I am concerned for you, Will. All this shift working. Maybe you shouldn't go to work tonight. I can run down to the works and tell them you won't be in. There's no sense in working yourself to a standstill.'

'Oh, I'll be all right.' He envisaged lying beside her, frustrated at not being allowed to touch her. 'I have to go, otherwise this work will drag on and on.'

'I don't want you to be ill.'

'It's nothing,' he assured her, shaking his head. 'Just a stomach-ache. A bit of wind. Maybe I shouldn't have eaten this.'

But they finished their meal in silence, although he helped her with the washing up. Afterwards they sat together, Will reading the newspapers, Henzey reading a novel, till it was time for Will to leave for work.

Henzey went to bed early with her book but, by eleven o' clock, her concentration was diminishing. It was time for sleep. She doused the light, fluffed up her pillow and settled down, naked because of the heat, under just one sheet. She wondered if Will was feeling better, what it was he'd eaten during the day to give him stomach pains. He said he'd slept most of the day, but she'd noticed that half the pork pie she'd bought the day before was gone. Perhaps it was that. In this heat nothing stayed fresh for long.

Within minutes she drifted off to sleep. It seemed she had been asleep for hours when a tentative knocking at the front door woke her. At once she sat up in bed, wondering if it had been a trick of her imagination. It was not. She heard it again. It must be Will returned home. But why hadn't he used his key? She jumped quickly out of bed, threw on her dressing-gown and made her way downstairs in the darkness . . . Of course . . . She had forgotten to remove the key from the lock, so he couldn't get his key in from outside. She unlocked the door and opened it. He was standing there sheepishly.

'Oh, Will. Do you still feel poorly?'

'Were you in bed?'

'I was asleep. What time is it?'

'Just after half past eleven.'

'I must have only just dropped off . . . How do you feel now?'

'I feel fine.'

He shuffled into the hallway and she sensed he was as taut as a cheese wire.

'What's wrong?'

Henzey had not tied her dressing-gown in her rush to answer the door and it gaped open, exposing her nakedness in the shadowy darkness.

He went hot and a lump came to his throat. 'Nothing. Nothing's wrong.' On impulse he thrust his hands inside her dressing-gown and held her around the waist but, true to her threat, she pushed him away.

'So what brings you back home?'

'I needed to get away for a while. I . . . I wanted to be with you . . . You can't get any peace down there, there's just too much going on.'

'Do you want a drink or something? I'll make you one before I go back to bed.'

'No, it's all right,' he answered. 'I want to come upstairs and lie with you.'

She shrugged her indifference and turned to go upstairs. Maybe his enforced celibacy was already having the effect she wanted. Maybe he was relenting at last. Dare she hope that he had come round to her way of thinking?

In the darkness of the bedroom he could just discern her removing her dressing-grown and saw her body, a stimulating, erotic silhouette against the weakly back-lit curtains. Fumbling, impatient, he took off his own clothes and left them in a heap on the floor before slipping into bed beside her. It was warm; her warmth. He snuggled up to her, uncertain at first, then slid his leg over her smooth thighs and ran his eager fingers over her breasts, which were rising and falling almost imperceptibly beneath his hands as she breathed.

'I've been thinking,' he whispered.

'Thinking what?' Her heart pounded with anticipation. Had he changed his stance?

'That maybe it's time we tried for a baby after all.'

'Oh, Will . . . Oh, Will.' He saw the glistening of tears welling up in her eyes. 'You really mean it?'

'Yes.'

'Oh, Will, thank you. Thank you.'

He shoved the sheet away with his feet. Her skin seemed to shimmer. The contours of her body were enhanced, dimly highlighted by the scant glow from the curtained window. He strained his eyes to better appreciate the sight. The sweet smell of her soft skin aroused him further and, as his right hand ventured lower than her belly, she turned her face to him and kissed him. He could just discern the smile in her heartbreakingly beautiful eyes. He breathed her name and, hungry for her lips, he pressed his open mouth on hers. She turned submissively towards him in grateful response and her arm came about him. He wanted her so much that he thought she must be able to hear the pounding of his heart. His hands wandered all over her body, savouring the silkiness of her skin and the firmness of her flesh, teasing her, but teasing himself also. They rolled about the bed, first one way, then another, their passion increasing inexorably. He allowed her to take the initiative. As he lay beneath her, her easy weight a delight, she guided herself gently onto him like a butterfly settling on a blossom.

After they had made love a second time, Henzey whispered: 'Why can't you leave your shift every night, Will? It's almost like having a clandestine affair you creeping here in the middle of the night. Especially when you're like *this*. What a change in you.'

'It's nice to maintain some romance in marriage,' he said.

'I can't remember you ever being so passionate.'

'You'll never know how much I wanted you.'

'I could tell how much. It's never been like that before. You seemed different tonight. I thought you seemed more . . . more committed, somehow.'

'Give me another half-hour and I'll be committed again.'

'Lord above!' She chuckled now. 'Look, I've no wish to set a further limit on your conjugal rights, but can I go to sleep now?'

He laughed, the tension he'd arrived with gone. 'I'd better get dressed and go, before I fall asleep here.'

She stretched like a contented cat and sighed, then huddled under the bedclothes. 'When you get back you'll most likely find you've had the sack for not being on the job.'

'Or for being on it,' he wisecracked.

'I can see you're feeling better now,' she said sleepily.

'Believe me, I haven't felt this good for years.'

'Good night, then, my darling. See you in the morning. Try not to wake me when you come in.'

Chapter Twenty-Three

Assembling headlights for motor cars had become second nature to Henzey. It did not demand excessive concentration and, when she was not chatting to one of her friends sitting on each side of her as she worked, she tended to get lost in her dreams, drifting to heaven knows where. And lost in thoughts, reliving situations and moments, the time flew inordinately fast. So it was, the morning after her heady encounter with Will.

She had never known such ardour. Even Billy Witts had never elicited responses in her like she'd given last night. Her own wildly passionate caresses reminded her of how she used to join so enthusiastically with *him* during those warm summer nights in the grass at Enville Common. With hindsight, it always seemed that she was more ready, anxious even, to make love than *he* ever was. Not so last night, however, with Will. She smiled as she relived it. As she privately blessed every wonderful moment, she experienced again the same feelings of happiness. He had certainly been hiding his light under a bushel.

So far this morning she'd had no opportunity to sidle up to her husband and whisper how magical last night had been, for Will evidently had to work later than the end of his shift. There'd been no opportunity to thank him for his dramatic change of heart that would put new, much needed zest into their marriage. Nor had he returned home by the time she left for work.

But one little peculiarity was marring total contentment: the incident over the blue shirt. It was unaccountably odd. If Will knew he had put on a blue shirt that night of the storm, why was he wearing a white one when he popped back home later? Why had he said it was a trick of the light when she'd mentioned it? It was strange. It was very strange. Neither had she seen his raincoat since; not that that was significant; he could have left it at work, of course.

Florrie Shuker nudged her, rousing her from her daydreams. 'Ain't yer gun 'ave a break, Henzey,' she said reaching into her basket for her Thermos flask and an apple. 'The flippin' track's stopped. It's half past ten.'

Henzey peered with some surprise at the clock on the far wall of the shop. 'So it is.'

'You've bin miles away this mornin', Henzey. You've hardly spoke since yer sat down. Everythin' all right?'

She smiled dreamily, put down her workpiece and reached into her own basket which was at her feet. 'Yes, I was deep in thought,' she agreed. '. . . Nice thoughts.' She smiled again, signifying to Florrie that she did not wish to share them at this precise moment.

But she recalled with a start that earlier last evening Will had been complaining of pains in his stomach. His sterling performance in the middle of the night had cleared it completely from her mind. 'Perhaps I should go and see if Will's still here, Florrie. He hadn't come home when I left for work, and last night he was complaining of stomach pains. I think I ought to pop over to his department, just to make certain everything's all right. I'll drink my tea when I come back.'

'See yer in a bit, then.'

'No, Will ain't here now, bab,' Sidney Joel confirmed when she reached Product Development. 'He left about ten to nine this mornin'. They've had a right night of it, by all accounts. Everythin's gone wrong. Nothin' wairkin' right. It maikes yer wonder if it's all wairth it, all the effort everybody's bin puttin' in.'

'Did he seem all right, Sidney? Did you see him when you came in?'

Sidney guffawed. 'He looked a bit rough, to tell yer the truth, Henzey. I ain't surprised, mind, if he spent as much time on the lavatory as he said he did. Said he'd had rotten guts ache all night. Said he'd been on the lavatory half the night.'

She smiled to herself. That, of course, would be his excuse for being away so long; his excuse for sneaking away from his shift to be with her. It was a valid one as well, since he had been suffering earlier.

'Yes,' she confirmed. 'He did have stomach-ache before he left home. I hope he's all right.'

Sidney drew her aside, as if others might be listening, although nobody was. 'Has he bin all right lately?'

'What do you mean, Sidney?'

He shrugged and tightened his lips. 'I was wonderin' if all this work was gettin' to him, that's all.'

'Why? What makes you say that?'

'I hesitate to say anythin' really – you know me – but the other Tuesday night he come into the Reservoir pub . . .'

'The other Tuesday?'

'Ar. But I couldn't fathom him out. We all said the same after . . .' He looked about him to make sure nobody was within earshot.

'What do you mean? . . . Go on, Sidney, you can tell me.'

'Well, first off he went in the smoke. He never goos in the smoke, bab. He always uses the bar. Then he was drinkin' shandy. He can't abide shandy, you know he can't – he's a pale ale man. An' I was that surprised to see him in his best suit, an' all, all done up like a dog's dinner . . . An' talkin' posh – real hoity-toity. I told him straight – "Cut the posh talk," I said. "You ain't with the lah-di-dah set from Lucas's now," I said. It was almost as if he was pretendin' to be somebody else.'

'Fancy,' Henzey replied, puzzled. 'You're sure it was a Tuesday?'

'I know it was a Tuesday all right. I'd got a darts match the next night . . . An' that's summat else, an' all. He played darts like a proper nincompoop, though he asked me never to mention it to yer.'

'At the match, you mean?'

'No, he was at work the night o' the match, I expect. I mean at the Reservoir – that Tuesday. It was as if he'd never picked up a set o' darts in his life before. I couldn't believe it. I looked at him gone out.'

'Fancy,' she repeated, her thoughts drifting, confused, alarmed.

'I was that concerned, bab. I thought you ought to know. But for God's sake don't tell him I told yer.'

'Thanks, Sidney, I won't tell him. I'm glad you told me, though. To tell you the truth, he hasn't been quite himself lately. He's had a lot on his mind – one way and another.'

She returned to her own department, bewildered, her earlier euphoria gone. She sat at her place on the line and poured the tea from her flask, not knowing what to make of what she had been told. Florrie enquired if everything was all right and Henzey replied that she did not know. Break time was ending and she finished her drink quickly. As the track started moving again she picked up a piece of work and became engrossed in her thoughts once more.

So nobody had missed Will last night when he returned home, yet he must have been gone two or three hours at least. Even they must have realised he wouldn't be in the lavatory that long. But this talk about him visiting the Reservoir public house the other Tuesday could not be right. He had not been out on a Tuesday night for months, except to go to work, and even then it would have been getting towards closing time. Sidney had been adamant, though. Yes, Will had been different lately. But that could be for any number of reasons; the pressure she herself had been putting on him to start a family; shift working and its inherent change in routine.

But that shirt was still niggling her. Why would he lie about it? She had seen without doubt that he had gone out in his blue shirt that night, and the same blue shirt was in the dirty laundry now. But he was definitely wearing a white one when he came back for his keys. If he had changed it, that meant he must have another shirt at work. But he couldn't have. All his shirts were accounted for. It was almost as if he had been another person that night, as Sidney had suggested.

Florrie nudged her again. 'By the way, Henzey, I forgot to tell yer – Molly Parkes wants yer to draw a portrait of her husband for his birthday present.'

'Molly Parkes? Oh, right. I'll go and see her later.'

'I'd rather yo' than me, though,' Florrie chuckled. 'Have yer sid him? My God, he's an ugly sod. I wun't like to meet him comin' up our entry of a dark night. He meks Boris Karloff look like Ronald Colman.'

Henzey laughed. 'I'd have to do it from a photo anyway, Florrie. I wouldn't have time to go to their house or anything.'

'Yo' ain't done no pictures for a while, have yer?' she said conversationally.

'I suppose not. Hardly any since I've been married. It's having the time.'

'Yo'll be gettin' rusty.'

'I daresay I'm rusty already.'

'Well, with Will workin' nights it'll gi' yer the chance to do some more, wo' it? Was he still in his department?'

'No, he left about ten to nine, Sidney Joel said.'

'An' how was he?

Henzey grinned impishly. 'He'd been on the lavatory half the night.'

'Poor soul. Oliver had a bout o' that a wik or two agoo . . .'

While Florrie soliloquised on the extraordinary bowel movements of her fiancé, Henzey drifted off again into her current preoccupation. Because of Molly Parkes' wish for her to draw Mr Parkes, she was reminded of the drawing she'd done of Will from a photograph; the drawing that had brought them together. She could recall the first attempt that she felt was not quite right; the drawing that failed to capture his openness. It was finished, but she had not been satisfied with it. She remembered each pencil stroke she made in building up the eyes of the second one, and relived their construction as they seemed to speak to her from the textured drawing paper. There was no other feature in her mind's eye; only Will's eyes, searching, uncannily revealing the suffering he'd endured at the loss of his wife and child. Just the eyes; sad, soulful; but at the same time conveying a burning inner fire, strangely subdued yet bursting to come to the surface.

And then, for no reason that she could comprehend, she knew she was also seeing Neville Worthington's eyes. The same sad, soulful statement over the virtual loss of his wife but, in his case, through her infidelity rather than her death and, more latterly, through her muscular disease. And there was that same suppressed passion, anticipating release, like a hare expecting to be sprung from a trap. They were so similar they could be brothers.

They could be brothers!

That realisation jolted her violently.

Of course they could be brothers. Will had been adopted, as had Neville at about the same age. He did not know who his real parents were. He could feasibly be Neville's missing twin, they were so alike. Of course! Why had she not considered the possibility before when all the time the evidence had been quite literally staring her in the face? But she had to check somehow. How could she possibly prove this new perception without yet alerting him?

She thought she saw a way.

'Florrie, I'm going.' She put down the headlight she was assembling and reached for her basket as she got up from her chair. 'I've got to go, Florrie. Tell the supervisor for me that something urgent's cropped up.'

'What is it, Henzey?' Florrie queried with genuine alarm. 'Is there summat I can do?'

Henzey touched Florrie's arm in gratitude. 'Thanks for the offer, but there's something I've got to sort out. I'll see you tomorrow.'

Henzey reached the dairy house about an hour later. Lizzie was in the kitchen preparing vegetables. When she saw Henzey she dried her hands on a towel and greeted her with a kiss.

'I was just thinking about you, our Henzey. But I didn't expect to see you. How come you're here?'

'I didn't expect to see you either,' Henzey replied, panting and hot from her run from the station. 'But I had to come. Where are all my drawings, Mom?'

'In your old bedroom, just where you left them. Why, what's the matter?'

She darted out of the kitchen and ran upstairs. The bedroom that used to be hers had changed. Now Alice slept here, occasionally sharing her bed with Elizabeth, Herbert's fiancée, when she stayed. Now it was littered with Alice's things, arranged in Alice's way. Henzey opened the wardrobe door and stooped down, parting the dense curtain of dresses and coats. A random pile of Alice's shoes greeted her but, underneath them all, she could see a brown, paper parcel which she knew contained most of the drawings she'd ever done, bundled with pencils, pens and a set of watercolours. Purposefully she flung the shoes to one side and grabbed the parcel.

It was shrouded in dust which she blew away. She sat on the bed, put the parcel at her side and, when she'd opened it, began flipping through the pages of the several sketchbooks. It was a trip into her past and she lingered over those drawings and paintings that meant most to her. There were those early ones of her father, showing enormous promise; some pictures of her first boyfriends; of Herbert; of Alice; of Jack Harper. Another sketchbook: drawings of Jesse in his wedding suit; of her mother; of Maxine. In another book were watercolours, some of Cromwell

Street, some of Peel Street and the Tin Mission where she used to attend Sunday school, of the Sixcore and its overhanging trees, of St John's church and its pretty lychgate, of the ruined limestone castle that dominated the town. There were views across the fields from Hill Street where her father's allotment used to be, drawings of the old sandstone church in Kinver where she and Billy Witts had sheltered from the rain. Each reminded her of something dear to her. But where was the drawing she was seeking?

She opened another pad. Portraits, countless portraits of Billy Witts and his artful eyes. Her first real love. She lingered over him, recalling the good times they'd had, remembering with a shudder how he'd broken her heart. How was he now, she wondered? Was he happy? Did he ever think of her? Did he ever wish he'd married her instead of that snooty Nellie Dewsbury? That she still felt resentment towards Nellie Dewsbury came as a surprise. More of a surprise, however, was that she felt at liberty to allow herself to wallow in memories of Billy Witts. She hadn't dared afford herself this freedom before. But as she perused these drawings of him and thought about him, memories of the heartbreak came streaming back.

What is it about men like him that make them what they are, she pondered? Why do they lead you to believe they are so ardently in love with you when all the time they are so callous and so ruthless? Why can't they be like women? Women are steadfast, loyal, sentimental, gentle creatures – well, some of them . . . Men are only interested in one thing. Always they are headed for the bottom line. Whatever they sincerely tell you, whatever they earnestly promise, their prime motivation is to get into your underwear. However they go about it, whether by wining you and dining you, by turning your head with sweet words of love, by astounding wit, or by expensive gifts, the aim is always the same: seduction; to get between your legs. And once they've been there, they know you are hooked; because that's how us women are; because they know a woman feels this illogical commitment to a man when he's well and truly had her. Maybe women should be more like men after all; maybe they should kiss and run; maybe they should run a mile in the opposite direction, as fast as they can go.

She thumbed through another book. Faces from Lucas's. She flipped each page over carefully and saw girls from her department, one or two from goodness knows where because she'd since forgotten . . . At last, she found it: the drawing of Will Parish. The first she'd done of him from those photographs the girls in his department had given her. It was the drawing she didn't think she'd got quite right. She looked at it intently. It was good enough for what she had in mind. The second one, the perfect one, was in its frame of course, hanging over the fireplace in their front room in Daisy Road, a keepsake of the time they met. She could hardly use that for her purpose without prompting Will to ask seriously unwelcome questions.

Her heart was beating fast and she felt hot. What she was about to do was likely to confirm something, one way or the other, she was certain, but the implications she dare not contemplate yet. One step at a time; it might still prove nothing. She took the softest pencil and, clutching it tightly, her hand hovered over the drawing for a few seconds for want of the courage to make any mark. She urged herself on. Do it, go on, do it.

She drew a fluid line in a shallow arc from the top of his right cheek to well below his chin. Then another, and another. The same on the other side of his face, from the upper cheek to under his chin. Then she began filling it with more lines, wavy, from top to bottom; then heavy shading. She looked at the whole and her heart was hammering inside her breast. Before long she had drawn a thick, bushy beard on him, just like Neville Worthington's. Now the moustache to flow into the beard.

All this facial hair emphasised the forehead, the cheekbones, but particularly the eyes. Just a finishing touch now: thicken the hair, draw some sprouting from the back of his neck and over his collar.

There.

It *was* him, as she had feared. It was the face of Neville Worthington.

There could be no doubt. There could be no doubt at all. Will was Neville Worthington's missing twin brother. They were a match. This drawing proved it beyond doubt.

She sighed profoundly, put the drawing and the pencil down and ran her hands through her hair, deep in thought. She had made this connection, but what did it mean? What could it mean? Consider carefully now. Could it mean that Neville knew all along that Will was his brother? Had he recognised Will as his brother when he met him at work? He could have done so as soon as he saw him. Will would have found it virtually impossible to do the same, not knowing the existence of a twin; and especially if Neville's features were hidden behind a beard.

It struck her then, that just as she had added a beard to this drawing, so Neville could just as easily shave his off. Maybe he had done so already. If so, it could well have been Neville Worthington that Sidney Joel had seen in the Reservoir public house. Which in turn could mean that Neville might have been impersonating Will, rather than Will pretending to be somebody else, as Sidney had suggested.

At this possibility she felt her temperature rise and her heart pound. How many other times might he have impersonated Will? Could it possibly have been Neville who came to the house that night, claiming to have lost his key? No. Of course not. She would have seen some difference in their likeness, even though the light was poor. Neville could not fool her. She knew her own husband well enough to spot even the most subtle differences; and there must be *some* differences. No two people were that much alike. In any case they spoke quite differently.

But what if . . . ? What if they were so alike that even she could not tell the difference? What if it *had* been Neville?

Impossible.

. . . The shirt!

The shirt *was* different; Will had worn a blue one all the time, not a white one. The dirty laundry in the linen basket bore testimony to that.

In horror, she buried her head in her hands, and the altered drawing slid to the floor. If it had been Neville – if he had actually fooled even her with an impersonation of Will that night – it might just as feasibly have been Neville that visited her last night while Will was at work. It might just as feasibly have been Neville that made love to her last night with more passion and commitment than she had ever known . . . from Will. If that were so . . . and if she were pregnant as a result . . .

She did not know how long her mother had been standing at her side. She scarcely had the courage to think about what had almost certainly happened, and the possible consequences. All she could think of was an urgent, compulsive need to be home. She wanted to be alone in her bedroom with the door locked, the sheets and blankets over her head, hidden from the world. She wanted to cry; she wanted to die.

'Whatever's the matter, our Henzey? You look as if you've seen a ghost.'

A shaft of sunlight, diffused by the net curtains at the window, illuminated the oilcloth on the floor and warmed Henzey's ankles. It was like a trigger to get a grip on herself. Quickly she collected all her loose drawings and shuffled them together into a pile, then re-wrapped them in the brown paper.

'Oh, it's nothing, Mom,' she answered, sorry for the need to lie. 'I just wanted to have a look at these drawings of Will.'

'Oh. Are you doing another one of him then?'

'No,' she said. The drawing left on the floor was facing up for Lizzie to see. 'I wanted to see what he'd look like with a beard . . . I, er . . . and I wanted to check on how I'd done something.'

'Why don't you take them with you? Alice could do with the extra space in her wardrobe.'

'I'd rather leave them here, if that's all right. I'll take my pencils and paints, though. I daresay I'll find them useful.'

Henzey took the tram back to Ladywood. It seemed the simplest way. She did not know the times of the afternoon trains and, besides, she was too preoccupied with her thoughts to make sense of any timetables. As the tram rumbled and clanked through Tividale, Oldbury and Smethwick, she was unaware of her changing surroundings. All she could think about was that Will had to be Neville's twin brother. Now she had considered it, they not only had the same eyes, they had the same nose, the same forehead. Physically they were identical, too; the same height exactly, the same colouring. A matching pair. Both had come from humble beginnings. Will had been the one fostered by the poor Methodist family Clara had told her about. Even that connection had eluded her before.

Yet, troubling her much more than that was the certainty that Neville had violated her. He had stolen enjoyment of her body when she had not the vaguest notion that it was him. He had made a cuckold of Will, his own flesh and blood, and he had turned her into an adulteress when she had no intention ever of deceiving her husband. An odd shiver ran down her spine. She had been used and abused by Neville Worthington to satisfy his own lust; a lust she had been aware of all along; a lust she could never have taken seriously till he confessed it the other day.

But the worst of his misdeeds was that he had hidden beneath Will's identity. That hurt more than anything. It was unforgivable. It was the behaviour of an inveterate cheat and it made her very angry. She could not really credit it. It was too outlandish to contemplate.

She needed desperately to talk to Will. When she arrived home and spoke to him she would get to know for sure. But she must give nothing away. He must have no inkling of what she believed had happened. She must coax out of him whether he did return home for three hours last night, or whether he was detained at Lucas's by a stomach upset. That was the pin on which it all hinged. When she knew for absolute certain, she could ponder what to do next.

She stepped off the tram at the bottom of Osler Street into bright, summer afternoon sun and walked the half-mile or so to Daisy Road, wondering how to approach Will. Should she at least suggest that he might be Neville's long lost twin? Oh, it was such an awful dilemma! The safest way, she was certain, was to suggest no such thing. She would only say anything at all if she had to. In fact, she would only say anything at all if she found eventually that, God forbid, she was pregnant from the encounter. The thought brought a paradoxical smile to her lips. Never had she contemplated, in her former state of mind, that she would ever have to hope and pray that she was not pregnant. Never could she have contemplated such wicked irony.

She opened the front door and walked in, her head swimming from all the possibilities and probabilities. She could smell food and realised she had eaten nothing all day. The clock on the mantelpiece said ten to three and, as she hung her shoulder bag over the back of a chair, she heard Will descending the stairs.

'Blimey, you're back early,' he said. 'Given you the sack, have they?'

She turned to face him, looking into his eyes, stupidly trying to see if there was anything she'd missed when she did that drawing of him long ago. She thought he looked pale and out of sorts. 'You're up already. I didn't know if you'd still be in bed.'

'I've been up ages. Had to go to the lavatory again. After last night I thought I was over it. I've had my trousers up and down more than a whore's drawers these last few hours.'

She smiled, but felt her heartbeat quicken at what his words implied. 'How are you, Will? When you didn't come home this morning I went to see if you were still at work. Sidney said you left about ten to nine. He said you'd been suffering in the night.'

He smiled, shaking his head. 'God knows what it was I had to eat, but I was on and off the lavatory most of the time after I went from here. I don't know how I managed to get back home this morning without an embarrassing accident. Shall I make you a cup of tea?'

'It's all right, I'll do it.'

He followed her into the kitchen where she filled the kettle from the tap. Her back towards him, he put his hands to her waist and gave her a gentle squeeze.

'How come you're home early, Henzey? Have you got it as well?'

She was thankful for an excuse. 'I wouldn't be surprised.' Guiltily, she manoeuvred herself away from him and lit the gas. 'I felt some pains in my stomach, so I thought I'd best get back.'

'Have a nip of whisky. That might help. It helps kill the germs that cause it.'

She reached two cups and saucers from the cupboard and laid them out. 'What time did it start then, Will? Your trips to the privy, I mean?'

'God knows. What time did I leave here?'

She shrugged, hedging, not knowing which time to give. 'I don't know.' She did not know whether he meant quarter to ten at night, or five past two in the morning. And if it had been Neville who had called, who had trapped her into becoming an adulteress, how could she possibly suggest it had been five past two? If it were five past two, and it had been Neville, she would not want Will to know.

There was a knock at the door. Will went to answer it. Henzey sighed heavily in frustration when she heard him greet Mrs Fothergill from next door and ask her in. They joined Henzey in the kitchen.

'I've on'y come to borra a cup o' sugar, Henzey,' Mrs Fothergill explained apologetically. 'On'y I've run out, an' I ain't goin' to the shops till tomorra.'

'That's all right, Mrs Fothergill. We've got plenty sugar.' She reached into a cupboard and drew out a blue bag.

'Well, while you're here, Mrs Fothergill, you might as well have a cup of tea,' Will suggested. 'We've just put the kettle on.'

'Ooh, luvely.' The cup she'd brought for the sugar she placed on the table.

Henzey sighed again. She could have done without this interruption. But at least she now had the truth; or half the truth at least. 'Take the whole bag, Mrs Fothergill. Just get me a bag to replace it when you go to the shops.'

'Bless yer, Henzey.'

Henzey, still deep in thought, still preoccupied, reached for another cup and saucer which she placed next to the others. After this interruption, it would seem strange to Will if she kept probing about his activities last night. She would have to be satisfied with the information she had already gleaned. And that information suggested that he had not returned home last night. How could he have done? He had been ill; certainly too ill to rush back home; certainly too ill to make love like that.

So it must have been Neville.

At this final realisation her heart was pounding and she thought her knees would buckle as she felt her colour rise with shame and guilt. She daren't look into Will's eyes any more lest he read the outrageous secret she now held locked behind hers.

Then she was filled with horror. What if Mrs Fothergill had witnessed Neville's coming and going in the night? What if she mentioned it now?

'You'm on nights this week, ain't yer, Will?'

'Yes, unfortunately, Mrs Fothergill. But I'm not going tonight. Last night I had a stomach upset. My guts are still unsettled. So I'm going to stay at home tonight.'

'Funny yer should say that. My guts have bin anyhow this last day or two. There must be summat goin' round. There's always summat goin' round . . .'

*   *   *

345

They were not late going to bed. Henzey lay awake in her cotton night-gown, recalling that unspeakable love session last night. Will snuggled down and she sat in his lap in the bed, his arm around her affectionately. In horror she leapt out of bed. If Neville came now, while Will was at home, he would think she'd been having a clandestine affair with him the whole time he was away at work. There would be hell to pay. So she went to the front door and checked that it was locked and bolted.

Chapter Twenty-Four

The summer was rolling on, nights were drawing in, and life went on. Miners dug their coal, foundries cast their iron, forges hammered their steel, and women pottered across cobbled streets to do their shopping. Despite the bleak prospect of war, cricketers stroked red leather balls across white boundaries and spectators duly applauded; Sunday schools held their anniversary processions with pride through canyons of red brick; horses raced, athletes jumped hurdles and threw javelins into the eternal blue sky.

Will's two-week stint of night shifts ended, to be followed by two weeks of days when life reverted temporarily back to normal. During this time Henzey's anger, which had been directed principally at Neville Worthington, was shifting and becoming focused on Will. He had given her not the slightest inkling that he was prepared, after all, to father her child. Oh, he was hot for her all right. Most nights he tried to have his way, but she was not submitting. She was not submitting till he told her outright that he was now intent on fathering her child. So, those nights he wanted to make love she shoved him away, turned her back, and made him endure the celibacy she'd threatened. His stubbornness, that was testing their marriage, remained. It saddened her to acknowledge that he was prepared to see her unhappy. How could he be so heartless? How could he be so self-centered? How could he deliberately forego his marriage vows? How could he spit in the face of convention and defy the institution of marriage, which was intended for the procreation of children?

Henzey was growing more disconsolate. The happiness she had known when she was first married had evaporated and she knew not where it had gone. It did not gladden her that the very thing which would make her happy would render her husband unhappy and frightened. Their differences seemed irreconcilable and she seemed doomed to accept it. Only time and old age would mend the widening rift that was keeping them spiritually apart. She could have been the happiest girl in the world if only Will had tried to accommodate her, but apparently, he saw fit not to. It would take only one kind word from him to mend things; just one word; but that word was not forthcoming. However, they continued to be civil to each other. They did not fall out, as jealous lovers or children might; but the atmosphere at home was no more than . . . civil.

She would have given anything to return to the former days of warmth and richness; to that love and companionship, in however small a degree, which had been lacking these last weeks. But she had marked out her pitch and it seemed she was the sole participant in her game. This last couple of weeks she had lain beside him in bed at night without even speaking, hurt, deeply resentful that she should be blessed with a husband so unfeeling. And while she lay in the darkness, feeling unloved, unwanted and dreadfully alone, she could not help recalling that momentous night nearly three weeks ago when Neville had invaded her bed and her body. She could not help recalling that it was the most glorious night of love she had ever known. She could admit it to herself now, but she would never have the nerve to tell anyone else. It was a secret she held locked in her heart; a secret that must remain in her heart forever, unspoken.

On the first Monday evening of Will's new stint of night-shift working, Henzey went to bed early with a book. Outside the sun still shone, yet low in the evening sky. She would be able to read for some time without the aid of a light. So she undressed, attended to her toiletries and settled herself in bed to enjoy the idiosyncratic romance that had blossomed between Jane Eyre and Mr Rochester. But she had toiled hard that day, the light was fading and her eyes soon began to close as she scanned the pages; her subconscious mind began to invent another story line . . . She was asleep.

She had been asleep for over three hours when she was awakened. Her book fell to the floor with a thud and she gasped, disorientated and irritated by the intrusion of a cold body beside her in the darkness.

'Oh, Will!' she croaked, ruffled at being woken up. 'What time is it?'

'Just after midnight.'

'Why aren't you at work? . . . Oh, get off. You're freezing cold.'

For a couple of minutes she lay without moving, her back towards him, her senses gradually shedding the intoxication of deep sleep. She looked to the window and saw that she had not closed the curtains. A curved sliver of pale yellow, which was a new moon, was steering its way through a thousand tiny stars, affording feeble illumination to fall into the room.

Then she froze with apprehension.

What if Will was still at work? What if it was *not* Will lying by her side, warming now, gently nuzzling up to her, his breath hot on the back of her neck, his gentle hand shifting up to her breast? She continued to lie, unmoving, unresponsive to these sensuous caresses. But the spittle in her mouth thickened as if a raging thirst had suddenly struck her. Her heartbeat quickened and it hammered good and hard inside her. It must be Neville.

She had never expected a repeat. Never, she believed, would he have the nerve to take such a risk again. He must be mad. He must be stark, staring mad. Of course, she had wondered how she might respond a second time to such a visit, having the advantage of knowing, this time, that it was not Will; knowing for certain that it had to be Neville. And she had wondered how on earth she would be able to resist the promise of another night of ardent love. She feared that indeed she would be unable to resist. Such love and tenderness was devastatingly enticing, and her fears were becoming more justified with every second that passed. His toe-curling kisses on the back of her neck, his sensuous stroking where it had most impact, were irresistible and she yearned to respond.

Without uttering a word she turned towards him and at once felt his lips on hers, hungry, searching, probing. Her breathing quickened as she held him in her arms, feeling his hard, compelling body against her own yielding flesh. His arousal made her shiver with wordless anticipation, for she knew he would satisfy her like never before; she knew too, above all else, that he wanted to give her what Will would not: a child. Thus she felt her guilt evaporate into the night till she felt no guilt at all. She was being driven by Nature. The warm heat of stimulation was surging through her body and all self-control was ebbing away fast. She was ready. She wanted him inside her. Her hand slid down the smooth ridge of his back and clenched his buttocks. Her mouth opened wide under his and he rolled upon her like a wave breaking, then lowered his head to kiss her breast.

'Henzey,' he said softly, as if savouring a delicious cocktail of her name and her body, and pushed up her night-gown to kiss her warm belly. Then he shifted downwards and lapped her between her legs till she cried out, helpless and astounded with pleasure. 'Henzey,' he whispered again, so tenderly, as if hers was the only name in the world worth repeating, and licked her while she clenched his hair and squirmed and moaned with little sighs of pleasure. When he entered her at last, his piercing sweetness elicited a gasp from her at the pleasure of it and at the madness as well of this unanticipated night.

'Henzey, I love you so much,' he breathed as they rested afterwards.

She did not answer. She had not spoken the whole time. She did not want to say anything. She desired no conversation. To converse might prompt her to admit what she knew: that he was not Will; that she had submitted to a man other than the man to whom she'd made her wedding vows. So she lay there silent, entirely sated, yet silently weeping, a thousand unanswered questions whirling through her head. How could she ever assimilate in her mind what was happening? How could she ever believe that this was happening at all? It was all impossible. She could hardly throw her arms around Neville right now, and say, 'Neville, I know it's you, and I love you for it.' She could hardly acknowledge Neville at all, let alone utter a confession of love. She certainly did not love him. She still loved Will, despite his stupid foibles. But how could she stop what was happening? Indeed, did she want to stop it?

'You're very quiet,' he whispered and touched her cheek. 'Turn towards me so I can hold you.'

She shifted towards him biddably, and raised her head so that he could put his arm around her shoulders.

He hugged her with a great fund of affection. 'There. That's better.'

Tears quivered in her eyes at this little show of tenderness; tenderness that had been missing from her life for too long. She felt the urge to cry out and sniffed, in an attempt to stem it. With her head against his chest she heard his breathing quicken as his desire for her rose again. But he felt her tears falling moist upon his chest and he lowered his head and kissed her eyes, to taste her tears, to blot them up.

'What is it, my love? What's hurting you?'

'Nothing, Will,' she said softly, trying hard to sound unemotional, glad of the cover of darkness that was hiding her shame for deliberately trying to bluff him by using the wrong name. 'I just hope all this is going to be worth it.'

He uttered a quiet little laugh and raised himself up on his elbow. 'That you'll get pregnant, you mean?'

He felt her nod and he kissed her again on the lips. As he pressed himself to her, the feel of her smooth yielding skin against his, aroused him once more. 'I'm doing my best, my love,' he sighed. 'I'm doing my absolute damnedest.'

She caught her breath as he slid into her once again.

The first Friday in September was not the finest day the long summer had presented. It had started dull and, by eleven, a fine drizzle had commenced which, though soft on your face, drenched your clothes in no time at all. It looked as though it had set in for the rest of the day. The once-mooted trip to Neville Worthington's cottage by the sea had been long forgotten, since Will had had no further contact with him and Neville had sent no messages. However, the weather was still warm, and Will, tired of being pent up in his office and anxious to get out, suggested that he take the day off. Henzey had no objection to being taken shopping in the city. Besides, she wanted to buy a decent table cloth, and they could do with a new coal scuttle since the one they already possessed looked as if it had been kicked round Pat Collins's fair, she said.

So, shortly after mid-day, they walked to the tram stop in Ladywood Road and travelled to the city centre, to streets that were ravines of Victorian architecture, ornate, Gothic. The red bricks had lent a warmth and resplendence when clean but, in Birmingham's smoke-laden atmosphere, their beauty had lain for decades beneath a shroud of grime. The one brilliant exception that stood out, even on this grey day, was the Hall of Memory, white and glistening like a solitary, pristine tooth in a mouthful of decaying molars.

As the tram rumbled past it at the bottom of Broad Street, Will remarked: 'You know, Henzey, I'm not one really for travelling on trams or buses. I'm all for buying a car to get about

— something decent. What do you think?' It had been on his mind for some weeks; a diversion that might take her mind off motherhood; another device by which he could minimise this preoccupation that was making her so unpredictable and irrational, so hard to live with.

'A car? Yes, a car would be lovely, but they cost money. They cost money to run, too. I don't know how much petrol costs but I'm sure it's expensive. Can we afford it?'

'Yes, we can afford it. We're not short of a shilling or two. Just think of the freedom it would give us. Freedom to go out when we wanted, and not having to waste time waiting around for buses and trams. We could tour. There are some lovely places to visit. We live in a country that's noted for its landscapes, but you won't see much of them stuck in Brum.'

The idea did not lack appeal, but she thought about the holiday they'd intended having. 'You were supposed to be taking me away to the seaside, if you recall,' she said.

'I'd forgotten all about that.'

'Ah, well. It'll have to be forgotten anyway if we buy a car.'

'Oh, I don't know. There's nothing to stop us doing both. We could use a car to travel to wherever we want to go.'

It had occurred to Henzey that she might be pregnant already. Every time she thought about it, it sent a surge of joy through her, followed by a shudder of shame and guilt and foreboding of the undoubted traumas ahead if Will ever discovered the truth. How would she be able to tell him? If and when that time came, should she confess everything and end up in the certainty of divorce? She would be ruined, a fallen woman, with a child he laid no claim to.

'What if I happened to be pregnant?' she said experimentally. 'We wouldn't be able to afford a car then. I'd have to give up working. We'd have to think of the baby.'

'Do you think you might be pregnant?'

She shrugged. 'How do you know one of your precious

French letters didn't burst? How do you know I haven't sabotaged them?'

He glanced around him self-consciously. 'Shhh! People might hear!'

She swivelled her head to check. There was nobody within earshot. In any case, the rumble and clatter of the tram prevented anyone else hearing them and Henzey realised it.

'You wouldn't have done that, would you?' he asked, laughing. 'Have you ever sabotaged any?'

'I might have — driven by desperation.'

'I can't believe you ever would.'

'I might have.'

'You're kidding me, Henzey.'

'And what if I'm not? It wouldn't be the end of the world. At least I'd be happy. It's as if you don't want me to be happy.'

'How can you say that? Of course I want you to be happy. You *know* I want you to be happy.'

'Then why won't you let me be?'

'You have to give it time, Henzey.'

'How much time, Will?'

'God, I give up,' he said in a huff. 'This preoccupation of yours is doing things to your mind — sending you funny.'

Henzey saw that bringing up the subject yet again ended in another petty argument. So, they fell into silence once more, another long, cold silence; and her resentment of him increased by another degree.

Considering they were twins there was a world of difference between Will and Neville. If only Will were as warm and as giving of himself as Neville. What a pity that his shift working was behind them now. What a pity that Neville could no longer slip into her bed at night as he had done so many times. Her earnest desire for a child had driven her, no less intensely than he had been driven to her bed, to steal an hour or two of comfort. They had taken advantage of each other, her and Neville. But now it had all come to an end. Yet never once had she let him know that she was aware of his real identity. During all of those energetic love sessions she had always called him 'Will', even in the heat of passion. It had taken some doing, but she had managed it, and she was glad she did.

'Look, we can get off here,' Henzey suddenly remarked. She stood up and held on to a hanging strap. 'There's this nice restaurant in New Street. Let's have some dinner there since we're so well off.'

After their meal they wandered down New Street, through the market by the Bullring, then made their way back to Corporation Street and into Henzey's favourite store, Lewis's. She would have made a beeline for the baby department to drool over little white bootees, little mittens, little smocked dresses, but that would have been too provocative and might have prompted another argument. So, she avoided it, venturing no further than haberdashery to buy a new pair of gloves. In the household linen department she bought her table cloth, and the hardware department yielded up a brass coal scuttle that appealed.

By the time they stepped off the tram in Ladywood Road on their way home the rain had stopped.

'Let's just call at the greengrocer's in Monument Road, Will,' she said, struggling with shopping bags and parcels. 'I really fancy some plums.'

'Okay. And I want to buy a paper.'

They crossed over Monument Road and Henzey bought her plums. In Reservoir Road Will bought his paper and tried unsuccessfully to read it while they walked back to Daisy Road. As they opened the door to the house, they saw a letter lying on the floor. Henzey put down her shopping and picked it up. It was addressed to Mr and Mrs W. Parish.

'This must have come in the second post,' she said, prising it open with her thumb. She took it from the envelope, unfolded it and read it aloud: ' *"Dear friends, Henzey and Will, Neville and I would relish the pleasure of your company for dinner next Saturday at Wessex House, seven thirty for eight. It is the occasion of my birthday and I cannot think of two people I would rather enjoy it with. I do hope you will be able to come. If transport is a problem we could always send Alec with the car. Do let me know as soon as you can. A note in the post would of course suffice. With fondest regards, Eunice."* '

'That's very nice of her,' Will remarked. 'How considerate of her to think of us. Of course, we'll go. We'd better write, thanking her. Will you do it, Henzey?'

'Must I?'

'Well, I shan't have time. Besides, we don't want to disappoint them, do we? That would be very discourteous.'

'All right,' she agreed reluctantly.

But Henzey did not want to go. She really did not want to go. How on earth could she face Neville?

That same evening Alice Harper was sitting outside the dairy house in the Austin Seven of Charles Wells. They had been out together for the first time to the cinema to see Fred Astaire and Ginger Rogers in *The Gay Divorcee*. The title, coincidentally, seemed very appropriate to Alice. She and Charles had been getting along very well working together, and she liked him. He was manifestly interested in her, of course, and had been since her interview. After weeks of suggesting that they go out together one evening, she had finally yielded. Charles was single, it turned out, though he had been on the point of getting engaged to a girl some two years earlier, who had thankfully changed her mind. Alice found him amusing and somewhat irreverent, not a bit how she thought a solicitor ought to be. He still lived with his parents in the village of Kingswinford, about five miles west of Dudley. The car was his own, paid for out of his own earnings. It transpired that he was the nephew of Harold Golightly, one of the original partners in the firm. Charles was nothing like John Harper. At least this man appeared to have some scruples. He was intelligent, steady and responsible, despite his ability and desire to make her laugh and forget all her worries. Yes, she liked Charles Wells.

During the weeks that Alice had been working with Charles, he had got to know all about her. She had been honest about herself and he had listened with keen interest, not in the least deterred by what he heard. Rather, he seemed somewhat stimulated. He would help her all he could, when she was ready, to get a divorce from Jack on the grounds of his adultery. It would cost very little, he assured her. They both, therefore, had a vested interest in that project: hers financial; his emotional. He told her, frankly, that she had been foolish and rash to get pregnant so young and, whilst she agreed with him in principle, she argued that had she not done so she would be without the young son she idolised. Charles hoped that he would be able to meet Edward soon.

But Alice was not going to fall into the trap of giving herself as easily as she had with Jack. This time, for a change, she wanted to be wooed graciously, not ravished in lust every time they met, for lust's sake. Charles could get to know her a bit at a time. Of course, the idea was that they would end up as lovers eventually, but she wanted him to feel that lovemaking was a prized achievement; an achievement gained in admiration, through a steadily growing affection and mutual respect. She wanted to allay any suspicion that she was a woman of easy virtue. Although Charles might have sussed that she had once been, he would discover soon enough that she was no longer.

And it had begun promisingly. Before she got out of the car to go home he asked her if he might be allowed to kiss her, and she offered only her cheek. All the same, she wondered what it would be like making love with him.

The following Tuesday, Neville Worthington returned from the factory. His day had not been memorable; the usual minor crises of production, the eminently forgettable whinging from the one or two of his work force who were noted for it anyway. He called to Eunice, who was in the drawing-room, and told her he was going upstairs to change. As he climbed the stairs he was already unfastening his neck tie. When he entered their bedroom he threw the tie on his bed and began fumbling with his collar stud. He spotted a letter lying loosely folded on Eunice's bedside table. With idle curiosity, he crossed the bedroom and stood hovering over it. He picked it up, flipped it open, and saw Henzey's name signed at the bottom.

At once he ceased trying to undo his collar stud and peered at the letter intently. It read:

> *Dear Eunice,*
>
> *Thank you for your kind note. It was quite a surprise to hear from you, but Will and I are happy to accept your kind invitation to dinner next Saturday. We are looking forward to it already. It has been ages since we last saw you. We hope you are both keeping well.*
>
> *Best regards,*
>
> *Henzey Parish*
>
> *P.S. Please don't trouble about sending your car. We shall walk, and no doubt the exercise will do us both good.*

Neville read it again with disbelief. It was the first he knew of it. Why had Eunice not told him she'd invited the Parishes? What was she up to? As soon as they saw him without his beard it would be evident who his long lost brother was. That was not what he wanted. That was not how he'd intended to break his cover.

He read it again and contemplated Henzey. He was desperately in love with her, but he knew that, barring Eunice's premature demise and something tragic befalling Will, she could never belong to him. For that reason Neville was unhappy and his discontent had been growing as the bitter realisation engulfed him, pitching him into the depths of depression. But what could he do? He had brought this despair on himself. If only he'd had the courage to be open at the outset, to have declared his real identity, he would be in no worse a position. But he lacked courage, and his timidity had resolved nothing for his aching heart; it had achieved nothing.

Neville re-read the letter. It would be wonderful to see Henzey again. He longed to see her once more, however painful it might be. But not under these circumstances. Not with Will present. Not with Eunice observing his every move. But why had Eunice invited them? What were her reasons?

Clutching the letter he went downstairs to confront her.

'Eunice, I see you have received a letter from Henzey Parish.' He waved it before her. 'She and Will accept *your* kind invitation to dinner on Saturday evening.'

'I know. Excellent news, isn't it?'

'Why did you not tell me you were inviting them?'

Eunice placed the book she was reading on her lap and twisted herself round in her wheelchair to face him. 'Because you have procrastinated long enough, Neville. You have a twin brother – your own flesh and blood – who was lost and is now found, and from the outset it was you who wished to offer him a seat on the board of Worthington's and the opportunity to share what wealth you enjoy. You wished to share with him some of what you've had all your life. *Your* sentiments, Neville, not mine particularly. At least, not then. But I have come to the opinion also, that he is able and worthy of such consideration. This coming evening will give us the opportunity to put that wish into practice.'

'But I've changed my mind, Eunice. I no longer wish to acknowledge him as my brother. He doesn't know anyway, so there's no harm done.'

'But *I* know, Neville. *I* know he's your brother. And they'll only have to see you now without that dreadful beard of yours and they'll know too. Face it – when they see you, the game is up.'

'What *game?*' he said scornfully.

'Oh, you know what game. The game that keeps you yearning for your brother's wife. The game that I believe has driven you to impersonate him, in your attempt, no doubt, to fool her. Have you wilfully tried to delude her, Neville? For that's the only way you could have her, I suspect. I most certainly doubt whether you would declare yourself to be Neville Worthington.'

He got up and walked over to the window so that she could not see his face. 'You do speak arrant nonsense at times, Eunice. Do credit me with a bit more sense.'

'But I don't, Neville. I can't. I know you too well, my love. I've seen you preoccupied, distant, and I know where your thoughts have been. Not with me; not with Frederic; and certainly not with Kitty. I know you are in love with Will's wife and I don't doubt the sincerity of it . . . Neither do I blame you, if I'm honest with myself.' She shrugged her shoulders.

'I see,' he said, and there was resentment in his tone. 'So what you're really doing by inviting them here for this grand revelation, is protecting your own skin. By letting them see who I am and enticing them into the family, you believe you will eliminate the possibility of any future liaison between me and her?'

'Liaison, no. Elopement, yes . . .' Eunice sighed profoundly. 'I feel very vulnerable, Neville. You would, too, in the same position.'

'Eunice, you've had your affairs, during which time I was excluded from your bed and your thoughts. I have remained celibate for years and have not enjoyed it, but you certainly didn't seem to care. Now if I seek to find feminine comfort elsewhere please don't deny me the pleasure. I am hardly likely to abandon you, after all. I'm hardly likely to leave you. I could never leave you. You know that.'

'Except in spirit.'

'As you left me. So, if you do not agree to cancel this senseless evening, I shall certainly embarrass you by being absent. I've told you I no longer wish to acknowledge Will Parish. Now you are aware of my reasons.' His voice trailed off.

'Do as you see fit, Neville. I was aware of your reasons before. But remember this – whether you are present or not – I shall tell them both the truth. I shall tell them that Will *is* your long lost brother and what you intended for him from the outset. I shall, in my capacity as a director of the company, offer him the position of Director of Engineering – your idea – at a salary that will be impossible to refuse . . . plus shares in the company which will not have to be paid for for ten years. In other words, Neville, you will have to work with him side by side, in your own company.'

'You wouldn't do that, Eunice. I forbid you to do it.'

'If you try in any way to prevent me, I shall go further. I shall take Will aside and tell him that you seriously covet his wife . . . yes, I shall even tell him that I strongly suspect you've been impersonating him. Unless you comply with your own original proposal.'

'That would make working with Will impossible. That plan is self-defeating, Eunice. Don't you see that?'

'I do see. The scandal and the recriminations would make it impossible for all of us. It would render futile all we've striven for over the years. That's why I'm sure you'll see sense and forget Henzey. Will is going to be far more important to you in the long run. He is the one who will make Worthington Commercials the force to be reckoned with in quality commercial vehicles over the next few years. On the other hand, over the next few years Henzey Parish's looks will fade. What then? Dump her like garbage and find someone younger to replace her? Get your priorities right, Neville. For God's sake, *grow up!* For God's sake, *think* where the money is.'

Neville sighed. Eunice was right. Her logic made sense. All could be ruined if he did not abide by her wishes. There would be a scandal of immeasurable proportions that could ruin them all if the truth got out. But it was going to be difficult to abandon his dream of Henzey. He still wanted her passionately.

Chapter Twenty-Five

Magdalen Worthington, née Boulton-Hart, was fifty-seven. As a beautiful twenty-two-year-old heiress she had married Oswald Worthington, the father of Neville and of Will Parish, in 1900, in a ceremony described by many as Birmingham's wedding of the decade. It was attended by many dignitaries, notable among them Joseph Chamberlain, who had supped frequently at the family's table over many years. Fourteen months later, however, Magdalen was a heartbroken widow, her husband a needless victim of the Boer War.

By the time Oswald had departed England's shores with his regiment, Magdalen was carrying their first child, and its arrival would have sustained her until Oswald returned. But the trauma of learning of his death in a field hospital on his way to relieving Mafeking, caused her to miscarry. Magdalen was utterly devastated. Her husband was dead and with him had departed the prospect of any children. So when a man, calling himself Theo Newton, presented himself at the front door of Wessex House in 1902, accompanied by a two-year-old child that he was claiming to be Oswald's, it was with curiosity and a quickening pulse that she agreed to see him.

Now, with the same degree of curiosity, she was waiting to meet the other twin who had eluded her then. If only she could have been blessed with the opportunity to mother both. To have been mother to Neville had been ordained by heaven, since she had regarded him as the child she herself had lost in the heartbreak of grief. Accepting him had neutralised that grief, provided an alternative, living focal point.

Magdalen now lived in another part of Wessex House, separate and self-contained, away from Neville and his family. She was not remote, however. They had contact most days, but this living arrangement meant that neither party could intrude on, or unduly influence the other. It seemed to suit everybody, including her grandchildren, who spent time with her every day. And Magdalen liked to entertain her own friends sometimes, without inflicting them on the others.

And so, having taken a last look at herself in the cheval glass in her bedroom, and satisfied that she looked her usual immaculate self, she stepped downstairs unhurriedly to the drawing-room, to await the arrival of Neville's and Eunice's special guests.

Prompt at half past seven, Lilian, the maid, answered the front door bell. She led Henzey and Will Parish into the drawing-room where Eunice and Magdalen were sitting. Magdalen stood up as they entered. The guests greeted Eunice with warmth and she offered her cheek. Then she introduced them to Magdalen, who smiled serenely and shook their hands in turn.

'I am so happy to meet you,' Magdalen said sincerely to Will, letting her hand linger in his for a second or two while she studied him. She turned to Eunice. 'You are right, my dear. The resemblance is astonishing. There can be no mistake.'

Will looked at Henzey, puzzled, and she returned his smile blandly.

Eunice said, 'Please do sit down and I'll ask Lilian to pour you drinks. Are you both well? Henzey, you look radiant.'

'Thank you. We're both well.'

'It seems so long since last we met. Such a pity. But we've asked you to join us this evening for a very special reason.'

'Yes,' Will said. 'And many happy returns.'

At the prompt Henzey fished in her handbag and pulled out an envelope. 'I almost forgot . . . A birthday card for you, Eunice.' She handed it over. 'Many happy returns of the day. But we had no idea what to give you. So in the end I bought this.' She delved again into her bag and brought out a small parcel, neatly wrapped in silver paper.

'That's very kind of you, Henzey, but really there was no need.' She opened the card, read it, smiled and thanked them again, then opened the gift. It was a ceramic model of a house, exquisitely made, similar in style to Wessex House. 'Oh, that's too delightful. Thank you again. I shall treasure it.' Eunice handed the card and gift to Lilian, who placed the card with others and positioned the model house on the mantelpiece, before proceeding to offer Henzey and Will sherry. 'Thank you, Lilian,' Eunice said when she had finished, and Lilian departed.

'Where's Neville?' Henzey asked casually. It seemed to her odd that he should not be present. And she was strangely keen to see him in the full light of day; to discern just how much like Will he really was.

'He's joining us in a few minutes. First, however, I have to explain the other reason you were invited. It's not just a birthday celebration, you see. We hope it will be much more than that.'

'Oh?' Will uttered, with curiosity.

'It concerns you both, of course, but you in particular, Will. It will also explain Magdalen's presence. Now breathe deeply, you two, and brace yourselves. This may come as quite a surprise, I fear.' Henzey held her breath, fearfully certain of what was coming next. 'You see, we know who Neville's missing twin brother is.'

About to break before her was confirmation of what she had privately known for weeks; that Neville Worthington was Will's twin brother and had been her erstwhile secret lover. But she must not let it show. She had to appear as surprised and as bewildered at the imminent revelation as Will was sure to be. She had to, for the sake of her marriage. She had made this visit unwillingly. When the invitation to dinner was received, she shuddered at the prospect of the outcome. She'd tried to press Will into declining, but he was adamant that they attend.

'But that's unbelievable,' she said, surprised at the ease with which she could carry it off. 'What a turn-up for the books. So, who is he? Do we know him?'

'Actually, he's right here, in this very room.'

Will glanced round to see if someone else had entered the room unseen, causing Eunice to chuckle.

'No, it's no one outside these four walls, I'm happy to say. It's you, Will. You are the missing twin.'

If Henzey had been of a weak constitution and was going to faint, it would have been then. But she maintained her composure and, with no sign of the emotion within her, she sat confidently, elegant, her back erect, her head poised beautifully.

Will glanced at her with doubt written all over his face, but she avoided his eyes. He looked at Magdalen for confirmation, then at Eunice. 'But . . . But how can that be? How can you be so sure, when I don't even know myself who my real mother and father were?'

'But we know, Will,' Magdalen said self-assuredly.

'I don't see how you possibly can.'

'Be in no doubt that Bessie Hipkiss, whom you have doubtless heard mentioned, was your mother, too, Will. Oswald Worthington, my dear late husband, was indeed your father.'

Eunice said, 'Please just try to accept it for the moment, Will. In the meantime, Neville and I have agreed to put before you a proposition which we dearly hope will be acceptable to you . . . To both Henzey and yourself.'

'A proposition?'

'Broadly, Worthington Commercials wish to offer you, Will, a directorship and a substantial quantity of shares in the company. The particular situation we envisage is Director of Engineering, with responsibility for engineering development, reliability and quality of the products we manufacture. A seat on the Board would give you the opportunity of sharing decisions and accountability with the other board members, who are Neville, Magdalen, John Worthington who is your uncle on your father's side, and myself. John, unfortunately cannot be with us tonight. It means that the company would benefit in turn from your input and experience. You would have a say in formulating and reformulating the policies of the firm, implementing them, and deciding on future projects and direction. We have in mind a salary of twelve hundred pounds a year to begin with . . .'

'It sounds just up my street, Eunice,' Will said, 'but twelve hundred? That's a fortune.'

'It's also a job with that sort of responsibility, Will . . . Relieving Neville of that particular burden. He has seen your work. He is aware of your capabilities. He recognises that you are right for the job and right for Worthington Commercials – and not just because you're his brother. We are all most anxious that you accept.'

Will looked at Henzey, perplexed. 'This is all beyond me,' he said. 'It's all happened so fast, I'm utterly confused . . . totally unprepared.'

'But you'll accept.'

'Of course, on the face of it I'm inclined to accept. It's an incredible offer . . . and I thank you most heartily for bestowing this sort of . . . of beneficence upon me. It really was the last thing . . .'

'Both Neville and I have been keen for you to share something of his good fortune,' Eunice explained, 'ever since we were aware of your real identity. For years, he has firmly believed his twin brother would reappear and he's looked forward to that day eagerly. Very eagerly, in fact. It has been one of his deepest regrets that you were not with him to share his life, his education, his play, his hobbies and interests – and more latterly, the family business. He sees this as a way of helping redress the balance. Both Magdalen and I are in complete agreement with him.'

'It really is a most generous offer,' Will said.

'An offer based equally on your merits. Not just on nepotism.'

'I'm literally dumbfounded. I don't know what to say.' He turned to Henzey again for help. 'Did you know anything of this?'

Henzey shook her head. 'Nothing.'

This offer was as much of a surprise to her as to her husband. Naturally she could see the benefits and she believed that Will should accept, if only to better himself. Her thoughts were not for herself, only for him. It might mean more job satisfaction, greater interest, greater involvement, and greater incentive to do a fine job.

'Lucas's will miss you, Will,' she added. 'You've been a good and loyal servant to them. But they're big and they'll survive without you. In any case, I imagine you'd still be dealing with them from time to time. I doubt if you'd lose contact.'

'Of course, of course . . .' She had put it into proper perspective. 'Yes, I accept, Eunice. I'm very happy to accept Worthington Commercials' very generous offer.' He laughed at his own confusion, induced by both his incredulity and his unexpected good fortune. 'In a minute or two I shall wake up and realise it was all a dream.'

'It's no dream, Will.' It was Neville who spoke.

He stood in the doorway from the hall, smiling expectantly.

Henzey looked at him with astonishment. Although she'd lain with him, it had always been in darkness or low light. She'd had no opportunity to study him closely in his clean-shaven guise. The eccentric she'd known before, with the long hair and thick beard, had gone. Instead, she saw the image of Will. The smile, the nose, the chin, and most of all those soulful tortoiseshell eyes. The eyes were the spitting image of Will's, exactly as her drawing had depicted. She asked herself again why she had never spotted the similarity before. Why had she failed to consider Will's fostering, and hence his candidature for Neville's twin?

'You've shaved your beard off,' she said with deliberate inadequacy, aware of a tremble in her voice.

'And had my hair cut.'

'I . . . I must say, it suits you better. Was that when you realised Will was your brother? When you shaved your beard off and saw the likeness?'

'No, no, it was before then,' he replied awkwardly. 'It was a gradual realisation. First one thing, then another.'

'Did you know when we visited Clara Maitland and her mother?'

'Yes, I was aware of it then.'

'And yet you never let on.' She uttered the words lightly for the audience, but his confessions of love for her, while they sat sweltering in his car on the drive of the golf club, flooded back.

Neville knew he was being secretly reprimanded and made no further reply. Instead he turned to Will who was now standing, fidgeting like an old maid, uncertain what to do, uncertain how to greet his new-found brother. Neville held out his hand, and Will took it, smiling, his eyes filling with emotion as he recognised his own likeness in Neville. Now, for him too, it was proof enough.

'Welcome home, Will,' Neville said, gripping his shoulder fraternally with his left hand. 'Welcome to the family, old boy. I'm sorry to spring it on you so unexpectedly, but I'm so glad I can acknowledge you as my brother at last.'

Will said, 'I'm flabbergasted, you know. When did . . ?'

Neville dismissed the question with a wave of his hand. 'It's time to celebrate.'

Two bottles of champagne were standing on the sideboard in a silver cooler. Neville took one, wiped it with the white cloth lying next to it and undid the wire around the cork. He prised the cork out with his thumbs. It popped and, at once, he turned to the five crystal-glass flutes waiting to be filled. Hardly losing a drop as it bubbled energetically out of the bottle, he deftly began to pour.

He turned round, carrying the tray with the glasses of champagne before him. He handed one first to Henzey and she peered into his eyes intensely. He caught her glance and raised his eyebrows for an instant to privately declare his admiration. His eyes sparkled impishly and, as they told again of his desire for her, she felt a gush of hot blood through her veins. Always there had been something about him that attracted; something beyond the unfashionable beard and long hair. Now here he stood in all his glory, physically the image of Will; but conversely, the image of what Will might be if he had Neville's presence and expensive grooming.

He handed out the rest of the glasses and proposed a toast to Will; to a prosperous future with Worthington Commercials.

When they sat down for dinner in the dining-room, Magdalen led much of the conversation, telling them her side of the story. 'You know, Will,' she said with a sincere smile, placing her knife and fork together on her plate, 'I prayed that you would come to me. I wanted you under my wing so badly, for my own, as much as for Neville's benefit. Of course, I would never have robbed your foster parents of you as long as they wanted and loved you, but I prayed something would happen to make you available to me. But it was not to be. And I never had the presence of mind to ask Mr Newton his address so that I could contact him and find out where you were. Yet here you are now, thirty-three years later, found at last, under circumstances I never could have imagined. But no longer a child, of course.'

'It's going to take me some time to get used to it,' Will responded. He'd been picking at his poached haddock half-heartedly, barely interested in food. 'It's quite a shock to the old system to know who you really are, when you've never really known; when you've never really sought to know.'

'So shall you tell your foster parents about this?' Eunice enquired.

He hesitated. 'Not for the time being. I'm certain it would unsettle them, although they would be proud enough once they'd got used to the idea. I think I'll leave it a while. I don't think we'll tell anybody till it's all cut and dried. Neither my folks, nor Henzey's.'

'I have a letter here,' Magdalen said. She leant down to reach her handbag and fished out a folded piece of paper. 'It's a note from Bessie to your father, Will. I'd very much like to read it out . . . *"Dearest Ossie,"* it says *"I realise it's awkward for you to see me today because of your special guest,"* meaning me, since I was staying at the house, *"but there is something I have to tell you what won't keep any longer."* Her grammar was not perfect, Will, but I think we may easily forgive her that. *'I'm pregnant, and you are the father of the child, a fact I'm certain you'll witness as the truth. I understand the difficulty this puts you in, Ossie, but I'm not unreasonable and I won't make a fuss. I'm prepared to leave quietly if you can see your way clear to making some provision for me and your child. I would much rather have told you face to face, but you said not to bother you today and I am in the depths of despair, and have to let you know now. This is the only way I know how. I want you to know I regret nothing, and that I love you truly. Your ever faithful servant and friend, Bessie Hipkiss.'*

There was a silence that lasted some five or six seconds, but seemed much longer. Magdalen broke it by saying: 'Can you imagine how she felt? She wrote this on New Year's Day, in the year nineteen hundred. The day after your father announced his engagement to me. She must have been heartbroken, poor girl.'

'If only she'd known what fate awaited her,' Henzey commented.

'But Ossie made no provision for her. I found this letter when Ossie had gone away to South Africa. Naturally, at the time, I was astounded and very, very upset. But when I was faced with the prospect of either turning Neville away or accepting him into our home, I recalled this letter. It helped me to decide that taking him was the right thing to do anyway.'

'May I see it, please?' Will asked.

Magdalen handed it to him. He fingered it with care, in the knowledge that his own mother had handled it years ago, and he read it slowly before passing it to Henzey.

Eunice said, 'I imagine it will take some time for all this to sink in. But be happy, Will. It's the start of a wonderful new life for you and Henzey. A whole new way of life. I'm certain you'll both be extremely happy in it.'

Will smiled. 'Oh, we shall, Eunice. Once I've got used to my new identity.'

Conversation continued affably, with talk about the policies and politics of Worthington Commercials taking up more of the conversation. Neville shifted his eyes from Henzey and spoke purposefully about how they should be planning a new range of vehicles and making contingency plans in case of war. He told how the resurging economic growth of Germany was winning the industrialists over to Hitler's politics.

'Oh, please, let's have no more war,' Magdalen entreated. 'Leave Herr Hitler to his own devices. He'll not bother us.'

'He's ever likely to seek us out as allies,' Neville said. 'Trouble is, we can't condone what he's doing to the poor Jews, can we? Anyone as ruthless as that will have to be reckoned with. God knows what purgatory they'll have to face next.'

For a time, talk reverted to the motor trade, and Malcolm Campbell's smashing the world speed record in his Bluebird car at over 300 miles per hour.

'A veritable achievement,' Neville said. 'It can only do the British motor trade a power of good.'

Henzey was thankful when dinner broke up. Neville had been sitting at the head of the table and she was seated on his left, opposite Will. All through dinner she had sensed Neville's eyes on her and she had felt self-conscious because of it, certain that Eunice must be aware of her guilty secret.

The weather that day had been fine and warm for September, and Eunice suggested they take a stroll through the garden in the dusk. They could take coffee and brandy later. Nobody was inclined to refuse and, when her wheelchair was manoeuvred through the French window and onto the patio, Will came forward to claim the privilege of pushing her in whichever direction she deemed worthy of attention. Magdalen attached herself to Will in turn, taking his arm proprietorily as they strolled.

So, Henzey found herself being partnered by Neville once again. They said nothing for the first minute or two, only smiled tentatively at each other, listening instead to Eunice, Will, and Magdalen as they stopped to admire this or that rose.

Then he said, 'I'm delighted Will has agreed to join us. You are too, presumably?'

'It's knocked him for six suddenly being faced with you as his twin brother, though. It has me, as well,' she lied. 'You'll never know how much. But I suppose we'll get used to it.'

'But are you pleased?'

She lowered her voice. 'Yes, of course I'm pleased. But I can't believe that, while you were confessing your love and devotion for me, you knew all along that my husband was your brother.'

To her great surprise, his hand reached for hers and he squeezed it tenderly. She made no attempt to take it back and reproach him for it, but remembered its loving caresses over her naked body in those hot, perspiring nights of July and August.

'That was what hurt most,' he said. 'I told you . . . I couldn't help how I felt about you.'

'Hopefully, your feelings have changed by now.'

'My feelings are stronger now.'

'Oh, Neville!'

'Oh, don't worry, Henzey, I'll try and keep them under control. Trouble is, my love for you is not something that's going to suddenly vanish. I should be a fickle fellow if it did.'

'But you are a fickle fellow,' she said, whispering acidly, turning away and freeing herself of his hand. 'Fickle to your brother.' She stopped to finger a plant and to put more distance between them and the others, for she was afraid they might overhear.

'Maybe not so fickle after all. It's just possible I've done him an enormous favour, don't you think?'

'I don't doubt you have, with your generous offer. At least I hope so, for his sake. But how you can look him in the eye beats me.'

'Oh, don't chastise me, Henzey. What about our own little secret?'

The others had moved on, through the arbour, and Henzey could just about hear their buzz of indistinct conversation.

'Secret? What little secret do you mean?' Her voice was low, but her temperature was rising, for she was certain that he was about to confess his partnering her in bed. How should she react to that? Why indeed should she have to? Why could he not allow her to pretend that it had been Will?

He began to whisper. 'Have you lost or mislaid something over the last few weeks?'

She frowned, side-tracked, mystified as to what he meant. 'Nothing that I can think of.'

'Are you sure?'

'Yes, Neville, I'm sure,' she said, almost certain of herself for once.

He felt in his jacket pocket and dangled a key with a leather fob in front of her. 'Then what about this?'

'It's a key.'

'I know it's a key. It's your key, actually. It's your spare key.'

She blushed vivid red. It *was* her key, and she could not deny it. She had all but forgotten that she had handed it to him; that with it she had handed over her virtue.

'You gave it to me. That night when it poured with rain. Remember? You also gave me Will's raincoat.'

She sighed, hopelessly disappointed at the inevitable. Obviously he was about to point out to her what she had been aware of almost from the beginning. It was pointless now to pretend that she had not known. 'So what are you driving at, Neville?' she asked resignedly. 'What are you trying to prove?'

'I think you know already.'

He regarded her steadily, as if waiting for her response, but she merely shrugged, at a loss to know what to say. Images of the two of them making love with energetic passion flickered through her mind like a Hollywood film show, and the way he looked into her eyes it was as if he could peer straight into her mind and share the images too.

'I love you more than life itself, Henzey,' he said tenderly. 'I would rather die than face life without you. I have such wonderful dreams of us being together, a vision of us both tending lovingly to a child. *Our* child, Henzey. The fruit of *our* love . . . But maybe it's not to be. We can never belong . . . I suppose I have to accept that.'

Henzey looked down to the ground, biting her top lip. Neville certainly knew her Achilles' heel and how to exploit it. It would be useless to deny anything to him now. It would be pointless. But she had her pride. She still wished to cling to her pretence.

'Neville, I've told nobody else and I think it's only proper that you should be the first to know . . . that I'm pregnant now. I hope you'll be happy for me, but you have to understand that it's Will's child I'm carrying . . .'

She tore away from him hurriedly, tears stinging her eyes, hoping she could stem them by the time she caught up with the others, not looking back at him, not waiting for him.

Chapter Twenty-Six

Henzey could not sleep that night. Under normal circumstances the fuss and palaver with Will would, in itself, have been enough to keep her awake. She might not sleep for nights yet, thinking about everything that had happened to her over the last few weeks.

Will, she knew, was asleep. His stilted breathing told her so. He had celebrated well his incredible good fortune, not only with champagne, then wine, but also with brandy, so he was entitled to sleep.

When they arrived home, driven back by Neville, they barely spoke. She was preoccupied with her own thoughts and Will was too overcome by what he had learned that night about his own origins for much talk. They would talk tomorrow. There was plenty to discuss.

She lay a while longer, unable to forget that she had been loved hard and ardently those steamy nights and that she had relished it. Those midnight incursions into her bed, seeking her softest, most secret places, had brought her the utmost pleasure and satisfaction. Neville had left her more physically contented than she had ever been in her life: drained; exhausted; exalted; ecstatic. The pretence in her own mind then, that at last she might get pregnant, had added extra warmth and enthusiasm to this lovemaking.

She stared at the dim slit of night light that parted the curtains and slipped out of bed. In the darkness she found her dressing-gown, put it on and crept down the stairs. There was a bottle of whisky in the cupboard in the kitchen. She reached for a glass and poured herself an ample measure, unusual for her, then walked outside into the back yard. As she sipped the whisky she saw how the stars lent an eerie sheen to the reservoir, and an owl screeched as it wafted windlessly over the tree tops. The September night was chilly but it did not bother her. She shivered only at the enormity of what she had done so secretly, and at her guilty conscience.

She had been unfaithful to Will. Whichever way you looked at it she had been unfaithful. It was a heavy cross to bear. Will had always been so kind and considerate, except in the one vital need she had, that had been driving them apart. He had provided a decent standard of living, had given her his love, his name, his home, his confidence and his trust; and she had betrayed that trust with another man. If only she could live with this burden of guilt and put it behind her there was the promise of an even better life to come.

But in her heart of hearts she knew that her yearning for her own child, and Will's lack of co-operation, had been destroying her, urging her irrevocably to respond ever more thankfully to Neville's outlandish visits. She had been preoccupied for months, and her preoccupation had been eating away corrosively at her former contentment. It was not that her love for Will was waning; it was not, she was certain it was not; but she'd been growing impatient and frustrated with him. She had been desperate for a child, and a desperate woman will go to any lengths.

She huddled inside her dressing-gown for warmth and took a gulp of the neat whisky. It stung her throat and she gasped as it trickled hotly down, for she was not used to it. She looked out over the reservoir again, smooth, unrippled by any breeze. It was quiet. No trees stirred, no creature cried. The city slept. The only sound was that of her own breathing.

So what of the future? For she was certainly pregnant. Pregnant, but with Neville's child. It had been nearly eight weeks since her last monthly bleeding. Only Neville had made love to her in all that time, and he had held nothing back. She was already craving for plums, buying them at every turn. That in itself was a sure sign. So what should she do?

The whisky seemed to be making her light-headed already but she took another gulp. At least it might help her sleep afterwards. However, infiltrating her profound feelings of guilt, and perhaps abetted by the alcohol, was a sort of subdued excitement that irrespective of who was the father, she was at last carrying the child she'd longed for. It was overriding her self-condemnation. She knew, though, that she had to see this deceit through and carry it off successfully, for she intended to have the baby.

She took her last sip of whisky, draining the glass, and shivered again. Then she turned and went inside. Upstairs, in their room, she slid into bed beside Will and he stirred.

'Are you awake?' she asked in a whisper.

'I am now,' he muttered irritably. 'What's the matter?'

'I can't sleep, what with the excitement of everything. I've been downstairs.'

He slid his hand over the cool skin of her shoulders and down her arm. 'You're freezing. Cuddle up and let me warm you.'

As she submitted to his warmth this once, he found her lips and parted them with his own.

'You taste of whisky.'

'I had a drop when I was downstairs. I thought it would help me sleep. You don't *have* to kiss me.'

He sensed her tenseness as his hands caressed her body. 'Are you all right?'

'Yes, course I am.'

Encouraged, he kissed her again.

She didn't really feel like making love with him, especially since he had not yet redeemed himself. But it had been so long she felt she ought not to deny him; and it might be over in no time anyway. So she closed her eyes and thought about those nights when Neville had loved her. As Will caressed her she could not help but imagine it was Neville and found that her appetite was whetted. She responded more willingly too, in the awareness that, for once, because she had caught him unawares, Will was not using a French letter.

He rolled easily onto her and she surrendered to the familiar rocking of his body, raising her hips to let him in more deeply. But it was turning out to be half-hearted on her part. She was unable to maintain the fantasy that it was Neville. She thought she sensed, for the very first time, Will's reserve, his inhibition, his anxiety lest he allow his seed to enter her. Anyway, that's how it seemed, and it was a perception that she resented bitterly. So when she sensed that he was ready to climax, she held him there vengefully, pulling him hard into her before he could withdraw. He groaned in ecstasy, his face in the pillow, and apologised for it being over so quickly.

They lay a while longer, talking quietly, skimming the surface of what had befallen Will, until he fell asleep again. Cocooned in his arms, she stared again at the ceiling and could just make out the shape of the gaslight hanging over the bed. She heaved a profound, shuddering sigh of disillusionment, but stroked Will's forehead as he drifted into sleep. She wished she still loved him with all her heart; she wished she was still as much in love with him now as she was before; but when they had made love this time, it was not like it had been during those highly sexual nocturnal sorties. It was not like it had been with Neville.

And comparison was inevitable.

At breakfast, Will was bubbling, but Henzey seemed subdued, he thought.

'Did you sleep all right after?' he asked as she put a plate of bacon, eggs and tomatoes before him.

'Eventually,' she replied.

'You look tired.'

'I *am* tired, Will.' She placed her own breakfast on the table and sat down.

'It still hasn't struck me what happened last night.'

'Nor me,' she said, concealing the bitter irony in what she felt.

'You don't seem altogether pleased this morning. I thought you'd be overjoyed.'

She was shaking pepper over her breakfast. 'Oh, I am, I am. It just hasn't sunk in yet.'

'No second thoughts?'

'No, course not.'

'I half expected to wake up this morning to find I'd been dreaming. But it's no dream, Henzey . . . Tell me it isn't a dream. Four weeks from tomorrow I shall be a director of Worthington Commercials . . . the family firm!'

When she'd finished chewing, she said, 'It'll mean a whole new way of life – for both of us, Will. Completely different. You realise that, don't you?'

'And what a change. Just think of what we'll be able to do with all that extra money. Right away we'll have that car we talked about . . . Something with a bit of class. I think I fancy a two and a half litre Swallow SSI – like Neville's. A different colour from Neville's car, of course. A nice maroon one, eh? Otherwise folks won't be able to tell us apart.' He gave a chuckle. 'I was amazed when I saw him without his beard. Weren't you?'

'You're both very much alike. *Very* much alike. Anybody could be forgiven for mixing you up.'

'I'll hand in my notice tomorrow . . . By the way, we're borrowing Neville's seaside cottage for two weeks. I forgot to tell you last night.'

'When?'

'From the twentieth.'

'I wish you'd said sooner.'

'It doesn't make any difference. You'll have to tell them at work that you want your two weeks' holiday. They still owe me two weeks as well. I'll take it as part of my notice. Then it's a whole new career, Henzey. Eunice says that Neville will show me round the works before that, though . . . I can't believe this has all happened to me . . . to us.'

She dipped a piece of bacon into her egg yolk without enthusiasm. 'Amazing, when you consider you've never been bothered about finding out who your real parents were.'

'I know . . . Oh, isn't it strange how things happen? Who'd have believed it? Who'd have thought it possible?'

When she'd swallowed the food she said, 'You're lucky in another way, Will – you get on well with Neville. Fortunate that, isn't it?'

'Well, I suppose, if I hadn't, this would never have happened.'

Henzey shoved her plate away. She had no appetite for bacon and eggs. Instead she went to the pantry and brought out a brown paper bag containing some plums she'd bought the previous day. She wiped one on her apron and bit into it.

'I've got a craving for plums,' she said, in half a mind to explain why. 'Had you noticed?'

'God! How can you eat plums when there's bacon and eggs and tomatoes on the table?' He reached over and spiked the bacon that remained on her plate with his own fork. 'I'll finish yours as well, then.'

But both her courage and the opportunity evaporated in that instant. She would tell him some other time; when she could prepare properly what she wanted to say; when it was more timely. There seemed little point in spoiling what, for him, was going to be a wonderful day.

'So how are we getting to this seaside cottage of Neville's?' she enquired.

'By train, I expect. How else?'

'Neville not offered to take us?'

'Well, I wouldn't expect it, love. He has enough to do.'

'Yes, I expect he has.' She bit into another plum voraciously. 'Will . . . I . . . I might take Wednesday afternoon off from work.'

'Oh?'

'I think I ought to visit Clara Maitland. She'll be beside herself to learn that you're the missing twin. I bet she won't believe it. I bet she won't believe how I failed to spot the similarity between you and Neville.'

'His face was hidden by his beard, Henzey. You could be forgiven.'

She could be forgiven! If only. If only she *could* be forgiven for carrying Neville's child she might even be tempted to confess it now. But that would take a lot more courage than she could muster right now; immeasurably more. It was impossible to tell him. Will was on the threshold of a dream. His hard work and engineering endeavours were about to pay off beyond his wildest imaginings. He was about to embark on a career that would change and better their lives inestimably. He had been offered the place that was rightfully his as a member of one of the most respected families in the city. She could hardly rob him of such glory. Besides, he needed her; more than ever now. In his eyes she was as much a part of it as he, and she knew it. Under no circumstances could she undermine it by telling him she was carrying his brother's child; that Neville had been sneaking into their bed at night while he was working shifts. It would destroy him and his new-found success, alienate him from his newly discovered kin and, no doubt, end their marriage.

'Maybe I should go with you,' he said. 'I daresay Clara and her mother would like to meet me. It would be like adding the last piece to a jigsaw puzzle.'

'There's no need yet.' The truth was she didn't want him to accompany her. She needed to talk to Clara alone. Clara had always been her mentor when they worked together at George

Mason's. Now she had the urgent need to talk to her again. Clara was worldly. Henzey could confide. Clara knew the whole situation, and what Henzey wanted to tell her was only part of the same continuing story of Bessie Hipkiss. Only Clara would have the answers. 'I'll take you to meet them another time, Will,' she said. 'In any case, it would probably be more appropriate if you went with Neville.'

'Yes, I suppose it would,' he agreed. 'Good idea.'

Over the next few days Henzey's thoughts wavered between thankfulness that she was pregnant, and regret, to thankfulness again. She was so absorbed with her predicament and so profoundly conscience-stricken, that she really did not feel like celebrating Will's appointment with the same exuberance as he. He was high on a cloud, whereas she was bumping along the bottom of the sea. Only when she had sorted out in her own mind what she should do would she feel more settled. Whatever happened, she must protect Will. He must not lose what he had just been accorded.

So on Wednesday afternoon she walked to Monument Road and caught a tram that would take her via Smethwick and Oldbury to Dudley town and Clara's home. As she travelled through Smethwick's bustling town centre, between rows of shops with their awnings lowered, through Oldbury and Tividale and eternal acres of factories and tall chimneys, it struck her that Bessie Hipkiss might have travelled this very route, seeking Theo Newton after having been turned away by Will's and Neville's father. What a strange coincidence that Henzey herself was seeking moral support from Theo's kin, also carrying a bastard Worthington child.

She arrived, expected, shortly after two o'clock, for she had telephoned Clara on Monday from work to tell her she intended visiting her. The ritual of putting the kettle on to boil and the subsequent making of tea was strictly observed and, as they sat at

Clara's table, Henzey revealed that Will was Bessie Hipkiss's other missing son, and told her of the offer the Worthingtons had made to welcome him back into the family.

'But there's more, Clara. Nobody else knows, so you must swear to keep it a secret.'

'If you've any doubt about my ability to keep something quiet, then don't tell me,' Clara said. 'But you know I'd never divulge something you didn't want anybody else to know.'

'Oh, I know that . . '

'Here, have another piece of cake.'

'Thank you . . . That's why I'm going to tell you. I'm going to tell you anyway, because I don't know properly what I should do for the best. I feel too close to the problem to make a proper judgement. I'm frantic for some advice and you're the only person, apart from your mother, who knows this whole damn story from top to bottom. And I daren't tell her.'

'Well, what is it? What advice d'you want, Henzey?'

'The fact is, Clara, I'm pregnant.'

Clara smiled with pleasure at the news. 'But that's lovely, Henzey. Best news I've heard in a long time. You're pleased as Punch, I imagine. So what advice d'you need?'

Henzey nibbled the cake. 'I'm having Neville's child, not Will's.'

Clara gasped.

'When I tell you how it happened you'll never believe me.'

'It can only happen one way, Henzey.'

'Oh, I don't mean that. I mean, how it *came* to be Neville's child. I can scarcely believe it myself. You see, I thought Neville was Will at first . . .' Henzey explained. It took her about ten minutes.

'And you're absolutely certain it was not Will who came to your bed those nights?'

'It was not Will,' she said emphatically. 'It couldn't have been Will.'

'And you never discussed it with him?'

'How could I, Clara? It would have meant confessing I was having an affair – with his brother of all people. We never discussed anything the whole time it was going on. Nothing. I was too scared to open my mouth in case the conversation veered that way.'

Clara was convinced.

'So what should I do?' Henzey asked.

Her friend lifted the teapot thoughtfully and refilled their cups. 'You've got no choice as I see it, Henzey. If you want the child you must say nothing and have it as if it was Will's. Who's to say any different? It'll have the same family resemblance, the same Worthington blood. And look what an unholy mess there'd be if you told anybody any different.' She poured milk into the cups. 'Keep it to yourself, else everything will be ruined. Will need never be any the wiser.'

'I understand what you're saying, Clara, but . . .'

'But nothing. Women are passing off lovers' babies all the time as their husbands'.' She spooned sugar into her own cup and began to stir it. 'Oh, you'd be amazed, Henzey. Believe me. I could name three women already, not counting yourself, that I know of. You certainly wouldn't be alone. I know you're a decent and honest girl and that you want to be honourable but, in this, neither honesty nor honour is the best policy, take my word. Let your conscience get used to the lie and live with it contentedly.'

'Do you honestly think so?'

'I know so. It's funny, but that day you brought Neville to see Mother and me, I saw the way he looked at you. I thought then that he'd got his eye on you. Mother remarked on it as well after you'd gone. She reckons he must be a chip off the old block.'

'So what does that make Will, I wonder? He's totally different. They just look alike.'

'Tell me, though, Henzey. Do you feel any resentment towards Neville for taking advantage of you in the first place?' She sipped her tea, peering over the top of her cup intently.

Henzey allowed herself a laugh. 'Not now. The only resentment I feel is towards Will, for refusing to start a family. He's frightened silly that what happened to his first wife would happen to me. But childbirth doesn't scare me, Clara, and I can't make him understand that . . . I've wanted a baby ever since we got married and now I'm having one. That makes me very happy. It sort of makes up for the guilt.'

'Oh, don't feel guilty, Henzey. You didn't know it was Neville the first time. You had no idea.'

'I just felt it was my fault. I actually thought it was my fault that Neville fancied me. Now I feel guilty at not being able to tell Will the truth. I'm still cheating on him in that way.'

'Ignore it. Never ever confess. Whatever happens, Will can't take your baby away from you.'

'No he can't, can he? Oh, Clara, I'm ever so glad I came to see you. You've helped straighten me out no end. I feel a lot happier now. Thank you.'

'Just don't go blabbing it. If ever you feel the inclination to confess to Will, remember I warned you not to.'

'Have no fear, Clara . . . You haven't got any plums, have you?'

It was nearing four o'clock when Henzey left Clara. She felt that a huge weight had been lifted from her shoulders and thanked God for Clara's clarity of thought. It had been her intention to visit Lizzie, her mother, as well, while she was in Dudley, but time was pressing on and she must get home. As she approached the tram stop, the tram she had hoped to catch was leaving so, rather than wait for the next, she decided to catch the bus. It travelled a different route, along the Birmingham New Road, and entered the city via Hagley Road and Broad Street.

As Henzey stood up to get off at her stop by the Oratory in Hagley Road, she naturally looked in the direction of Wessex House on the opposite side. She could see Eunice in her wheelchair, a shawl wrapped around her, leaning forward, tending to some plant or other in the front garden. Then, suddenly, Henzey caught sight of the wheelchair tipping up, throwing Eunice forward onto the ground. Somehow, she must have leaned too far forward.

Before the bus had drawn to a halt, Henzey had jumped off it and, dodging the traffic, ran to help. As she ran down the drive she could see that Eunice was alone, lying on the path, struggling to shove the wheelchair away, since it had ended up on top of her.

She called out: 'Eunice, Eunice, hang on.'

When she reached her, Eunice looked shaken but seemed otherwise unhurt. At once Henzey uprighted the wheelchair and set about lifting Eunice back into it, with no thought for her own condition. But, thankfully, the gardener appeared, having heard Eunice's frantic cries. He ran towards them and effortlessly lifted her back into the wheelchair while Henzey steadied it.

Eunice thanked them both and assured them that she was unhurt. The gardener went about his business.

'Henzey, how can I thank you enough? It's so fortunate that you suddenly appeared. Heaven sent, I should say.'

'I was just getting off the bus, Eunice. I happened to see you tumble so I ran over straight away.'

'Goodness knows how long I might have lain there if you hadn't.' She dusted herself off and then laughed. 'I must have looked an absolute picture. Neville would have howled.'

'I'm sure he would not, Eunice. Are you sure you're all right?'

'I'll be fine when my pulse rate has slowed down a bit. Take me inside, please, Henzey, would you? I'll get Lilian to make us a pot of tea – if you have time.'

'All right. I reckon I've got time before Will gets home.' She pushed Eunice and her wheelchair round the rear of the house towards the ramp.

'Oh, it won't hurt him to wait a little while. How is he? Has he got used to the idea of being a director of Worthington's yet?'

'He seems to be getting used to it quickly enough. He can hardly wait to begin. He's bubbling with enthusiasm.'

'Wonderful news. And you, Henzey? I bet it was all a bit of shock, eh?'

'You'll never know how much, Eunice.'

They went inside and Eunice called Lilian, requesting that pot of tea for two and some biscuits. In the drawing-room, Eunice invited Henzey to sit down.

'It's rather special for me, too, you know, Henzey,' Eunice remarked. 'I now have a brother-in-law and a sister-in-law. Something I never had before. I intend to enjoy them, too, and see them as often as possible.'

Henzey smiled. 'I hadn't thought about it from that point of view,' she confessed. 'But yes, it'll be quite a change for you as well.'

'But we've had more time to get used to the idea than you have, my dear. Time when we considered what best to do.'

'I expect it must have been a big decision to offer Will such a generous welcome into the family.'

'It's simply what Neville had always intended. He's a very noble person in some ways . . . if not in others. I must say, though, that he's shown me far more nobility in the past than perhaps I deserve. Nowadays I'm thankful he did. Frankly I don't know how I would survive without him.'

Henzey did not reply. She felt an illogical pang of remorse at Eunice's open admission of dependency, as if she had some strange preconception that Henzey might want to lure Neville away.

'How are the children?' Henzey asked instead, turning the subject.

'The children,' Eunice answered, and her tone was strangely nostalgic, as if recalling them from far-off days. 'Oh, they're well. And back at school again, thank goodness. They'll be home very soon, I expect. And what of your own endeavours for a child, Henzey? Any luck yet?'

Henzey blushed under Eunice's scrutinising eyes. 'It's early days but I think there might be a chance,' she admitted.

'Then if it is early days, forgive me if I don't congratulate you, my dear. It might be premature to do so. Where is that woman with the tea?'

'Actually, I am fairly sure . . .'

'Fairly sure? The only one I was sure about, Henzey, almost from the moment I conceived her, was Kitty. She was a mistake. A dreadful mistake.'

At that moment Lilian entered the room carrying a tray. She set it down on an occasional table before them and left. Eunice lifted the lid of the pot and gave the contents a stir.

'But you love her?' Henzey prompted.

'I love her with all my heart. Frederic loves her . . . And even Neville loves her, in his way . . .' The comment begged Henzey's next question.

'I don't understand, Eunice. Why should Neville not love her?'

'Because quite frankly, my dear, Kitty is not Neville's daughter.'

Henzey gasped. 'Not Neville's daughter?' Of course, Kitty must be the daughter of that Harris Channon. Yet somehow, Henzey had the distinct impression that the affair with him had ended long before Kitty was even conceived. Henzey wondered whether she should be frank and admit that Neville had told her all about him. She decided, however, to admit nothing.

'I'm surprised he hasn't told you, of all people, Henzey,' Eunice said knowingly. 'And yet, maybe it wouldn't suit his purpose to do so.'

'Tell me what, Eunice?'

'Quite frankly, my dear, I hesitate to say because I fear that all I shall gain from you will be contempt. And I do so want your respect . . . No. More than that, Henzey, I would value your kinship and your friendship. I don't want to jeopardise either.'

'I'm sure it wouldn't come to that, Eunice,' Henzey urged.

Perhaps it was time to suggest she'd had a vague idea that Eunice had had an affair. 'We all make mistakes, don't we? I mean, if you've had an affair . . . Who am I to judge?'

'Two affairs, actually. But they happened a while ago, when I was fit and well. The first time I was a fool, Henzey. The second time I was an even a bigger fool. I think there's a bit of the slut in all us women, don't you?'

Henzey tried to shrug off the flush that was reddening her cheeks. 'Maybe so.'

'Yes, well I must have been a bigger slut than any woman living. I had a happy marriage once; a husband who would have died for me. But one man was not enough. I wanted to know what it would be like to lie with other men – to be really depraved – to do things you would never demean yourself to do with a loving husband, nor indeed expect him to do. I did it all with the first affair. He was as depraved as me and I was addicted to him. He wanted me to leave Neville, get divorced and marry him. I didn't realise he was after my money until he discovered I'd used it all bailing out Worthington Commercials. He was off quicker than a gunshot.

'Naturally enough, that affair ruined my marriage. Neville tried to warn me that I was being a fool, to give him up before it was too late. But of course, I knew better. My marriage counted for nothing in my eyes. Oh, there's nothing more sad nor more illogical than a woman who's obsessed. Maybe you know that already, Henzey.'

'I'll pour, if you like, Eunice. Milk and sugar?'

'Please. The second affair was different. It was just after the Wall Street Crash and I knew that the man was desperately seeking wealth to replace what he'd lost in the Crash. He was an upstart and, if he could have lured me away, he would have done, I believe. But I just strung him along for the hell of it. He was younger than me, handsome . . . very handsome in fact. I enjoyed his bedding me, but this time I was in control – or I thought I was – till I realised he'd deliberately made me pregnant to secure me and the money he thought I'd got . . . Does that sound a familiar story, Henzey?'

Henzey stopped what she was doing with some consternation and looked into Eunice's eyes. They seemed honest, vulnerable, and her expression was one of anxiety; anxiety lest she should alienate Henzey, perhaps. But Henzey was not certain what familiar story Eunice was referring to, so she merely gave a quizzical look.

'You see, Henzey,' she continued, 'that second man was your old friend, Billy Witts.'

Henzey almost dropped the milk jug. She replaced it on the tray, trembling, and tried to collect her thoughts. 'Billy Witts? But . . . You're saying that Billy Witts is Kitty's father?'

'Just so . . . Kin to no Worthington, I admit. So . . . now you can see just how much of a fool I've been. Consider yourself very fortunate, Henzey, my dear, that you were no greater victim of Billy Witts. You were well rid of him.'

'But, Eunice, he did the same to Nellie Dewsbury and married her.'

'I know. A double indemnity, what? As I said, Henzey – a familiar story.'

'I'm absolutely flabbergasted. How did you start seeing him?'

'The first time I met him he was with you. We all had dinner together, you remember? I recall now how Neville was very taken with you. Anyway, while you and he talked, Billy was showing an interest in me and, frankly, I was flattered. Some time afterwards he telephoned me and we arranged to meet. By this time there was no possibility of a full reconciliation with Neville, though of course we continued to live together. So I thought, what the hell? Billy and I very quickly became lovers . . . Oh, I apologise unreservedly, Henzey, for being responsible for him two-timing you.'

'Good God, Eunice. He wasn't just two-timing. I thought after that he was only two-timing me with Nellie Dewsbury. It appears he was three-timing all of us.' She laughed, aware that the passing of time had enabled her to laugh about him. It was actually quite funny now. What a pathetic cad he was.

Eunice laughed, too, feeling a growing affinity with her sister-in-law. 'So there, I've made a clean breast of it. I needed to tell you, and your passing by this afternoon has afforded me the perfect opportunity. If I've ruined our friendship it was a risk I had to take. But I hope I have not. At least, I don't think I have.'

'Oh, Eunice, I admire you all the more for telling me. I think, if anything, it might bring us closer.'

'I do hope so. But learn by it, Henzey. If you ever find yourself in a similar position – carrying another man's child – never confess it. Never.'

Henzey was startled again by Eunice's words but tried to show no outward change in her expression. It was almost as if the woman knew of her predicament.

'I confessed mine to Neville,' she went on. 'But I had to. You see, Neville and I had had no marital relations since the start of my first affair. And while he was supportive to a degree – he had to be, really, on account of the money and my standing in the firm – he bitterly resented it. And I think deep down he resents Kitty, though he tries to play the affectionate father. After all, the child is not to be blamed. If he could have killed Billy Witts I think he would have gladly done so.'

'At the time, Eunice, Neville would have had to have joined the queue. My mother would have been first in it, I can tell you.'

'I look forward to meeting your mother some time, Henzey. But please – what I've told you is in strict confidence. I'd appreciate you not breathing a word of it to Will.'

'Oh, don't worry, Eunice. What he's not told he won't grieve about.'

Chapter Twenty-Seven

Neville's seaside cottage was idyllic. Henzey and Will arrived at Bognor Regis during the early afternoon of Saturday and took a taxi to the cottage, which overlooked the English Channel at Middleton-on-Sea. As Will paid the driver and sought the key from his pocket, Henzey stood and peered beyond the cottage at the grey sea, a vast sheet of steel with white, rippled edges. She might even be able to find time to paint some watercolours. She had attempted no seascapes before and relished the challenge, spurred by the sight of a yacht, regaled with a tall, white sail, rocking to and fro as it tacked against the afternoon onshore wind.

The cottage was a modern three-bedroom affair, rendered white on the outside and with a hipped roof. There was a bathroom, a fine kitchen and a garage that housed a small motor launch on a trailer. Yes, there was a boat, as Neville had promised, but without a car to tow the trailer to the sea they would be unable to use it; an easy oversight on his part. In the hallway, a telephone was installed; essential for Neville, who would no doubt get business calls even when taking a holiday there.

Henzey unpacked and they settled themselves in, to enjoy the comfort and seclusion of the place and the panoramic sea view through the wide French window of the sitting-room. They ate, and later found a pub where they had a drink before going back and sleeping soundly till well after nine the next morning.

The weather was set fair for the latter half of September, but the days were getting shorter. On the Monday they walked into Bognor Regis, ate lunch at a restaurant and toured the shops in the afternoon. After the walk back, they retired to bed early again. Next morning, Tuesday, Henzey experienced her first real morning sickness. There was no doubt about it now. She was well and truly pregnant. But she collected her thoughts, bravely faced breakfast with Will, and uttered not a word about it.

On the Wednesday morning she was sick again, but could not face breakfast this time. Nor could she face going out. So she stayed at home while Will explored the coastline around Middleton by himself. It was at about half past two in the afternoon that the telephone rang. The operator said there was a long distance call for her. A strong Birmingham accent rose above the crackles.

'Henzey, is that you?'

'It is. Who's that?'

'Sidney Joel from Lucas's.'

'Sidney! This is a surprise. Is this a social call?'

'I wish it was, bab, but it ain't. I need to speak to His Nibs.'

'He's not here. Shall I give him a message? He'll be about an hour, I imagine.'

'Ask him to ring me at the works, if ya would. There's a God-almighty flap on here. Fur an' feathers flyin' everywhere.'

'Oh, no,' she sighed. 'I'll tell him. I'll get him to put a call through as soon as he gets back. He shouldn't be too long.'

Henzey returned to the back porch where she had been sitting reading a book. She drew her cardigan around her shoulders, sat back in the deckchair and began to read again. In the couple of weeks since she had seen Clara Maitland and Eunice Worthington, she had assimilated much. She had learned a great deal about womankind and women's wiles; how they would lie and deceive to protect their interests. Men were no match for women when it came to guile.

She could not concentrate on her book so she put it down. Her eyes were skating over the words, not absorbing them. Her mind was otherwise engaged, contemplating Will, Neville, Eunice, Clara and herself. She looked out across the sea glittering in the bright, afternoon sunshine. Towards the horizon she could see the unmistakable shape and colour of a battleship ploughing the smooth waters of the English Channel, and a private yacht incongruously sailing in the opposite direction closer to the shore. In the couple of weeks since Clara had advised her never to confess to carrying Neville's child, she had given it a great deal of thought. It ran directly against her nature to deceive, but she had deceived and she accepted without question that she must never tell Will the truth. He must never be in any doubt that the child she was carrying was his. Only Clara knew the reality and Clara would divulge nothing. Henzey believed that Eunice might have an inkling, since she offered advice similar to Clara's, with no prompting. Yet there was no hint of condemnation; only a sort of camaraderie in the way she spoke, of all girls together. Even if Eunice at some future time were ungracious enough to ask openly whether the child was Will's, she would follow her advice and, with a suitable look of indignation, say, 'Of course it is'.

In the matter of her feelings toward Will, she was confused. He was still the same kind, serious and often intense person with whom she had fallen in love and whom she loved still, but she was no longer *in love* with him in the romantic sense. He had refused to oblige her in her most ardent wish. That, she believed, was unforgivable. Thus, her feelings of resentment were increasing inexorably. Since marital relations had resumed she had allowed sex once or twice but with little enthusiasm, even though he had ceased to use any protection now. In any case her coolness, it seemed, had discouraged him from bothering her anymore. He was still preoccupied with his unexpected good fortune and planning how to tackle his new appointment with the 'family firm'.

She had seen nothing of Neville since that last evening they'd spent as his guests; that fateful night when Will had been shocked by the knowledge that he was a Worthington. Yet Neville had been haunting her. She had come to regard him as a sensual, passionate equal. No wonder she had always been drawn to him. When they first met, years ago, and he'd talked about lovemaking that made you breathless and exhausted, she hadn't a clue what he'd meant. It sounded appealing nonetheless, but having experienced it at first hand with him, she understood perfectly. The memory of it lingered in her heart and the consequence was growing in her belly.

When she recalled making love with Neville on those delicious nights, she knew without question it could not have been Will. It could never have been Will, even though, in the darkness of the bedroom, she believed it was at first. Will had never been that ardent, that hungry for her. He'd never made her squirm and cry out with such intense pleasure as Neville had. Will was never so vital; he was relatively inhibited, reserved, though never lacking in care for all his comparative repression.

She accepted that she would never be loved like that again. A pity, in a way, that she had ever experienced it. It gave meaning to one of her mother's sayings: that what you've never had you never miss. But she'd had it, and she could admit to herself at least that she missed it. She would always miss it now. If only Will would love her like that. Maybe she could teach him, but then it would not be spontaneous; it had to come from the heart, naturally, not just from the loins. With these wild notions galloping through her head she reckoned there must be in her, after all, something of the slut Eunice had talked about; a wanton, wayward inclination to be depraved; to wriggle like an eel all night long with a man till her body ached. Or was it Mother Nature simply urging her to do her stuff and reproduce, to maintain the species?

The sound of her name jolted her from her thoughts.

'I'm back, love. Do you fancy a drink of something? I'm parched.'

'Please.' She got up from her deckchair and went inside to stand leaning against the French window. 'There was a call for you on the telephone.'

'Oh?' He placed on the table a folded newspaper he'd bought. 'Who from?'

'From Lucas's. It was Sidney Joel. There's a flap on or something. I said you'd call him back.'

Will went out to the kitchen for a bottle of lemonade and two glasses, and she heard him slam the pantry door in frustration. 'Can't they sort anything out themselves in my department, for God's sake? Why do they need to bother me? I'm on holiday, dammit!'

'I daresay a simple phone call will sort it out, Will,' she called.

He came back into the living-room. 'Anyway, how did they get this number? I didn't leave it. I didn't even know there was a phone here till we arrived.'

He went into the hallway to make his telephone call and, after a few seconds, she heard him give the operator Lucas's telephone number. Henzey poured herself some lemonade and went back outside, clutching her glass. She sat down, placed it on the table beside her and picked up her book again. Again, the written words said nothing to her. She could hear Will's voice. He sounded annoyed but she could not hear what he was saying. It was another ten minutes before he came and stood at the French window looking onto the porch.

'I've got to go back, Henzey,' he said apologetically.

'Oh, no! I can't believe it. We've only been here five minutes. What's wrong?'

'There's a problem with one of the jobs for Worthington Commercials. One of the prototypes. It's packed up again. Nobody can fathom it. Worthington are working to a tight schedule and they're adamant it's got to be put right this week. Responsibility's down to me. I'll have to go back and sort it out. I am sorry, love.'

She slammed her book down angrily and stood up. 'Well I suppose I'd better start packing. When are we leaving?'

'There's no need for you to come, my love. You might as well stay here. Hopefully I'll be back next day. I'm having my holiday by hook or by crook . . . So are you.'

'I'm not staying here on my own, Will. I don't know a soul. I'd be bored to death on my own.'

'Oh, you've got your book. There's a wireless in the living-room. You could go for walks. You could paint. You said you wanted to paint. The weather's due to stay fine. Relax. Enjoy it. In any case, I'd fixed a surprise for you.'

'A surprise? Well you'd better unfix it, I suppose. I'd rather go back with you. We can always come back here afterwards.'

'All right.' He looked pleased that she wanted to return home with him. 'We'll get the train in the morning. By the way, it was Neville who gave Sidney this telephone number.'

'I assumed as much when you said you didn't even know there was a phone here.'

'He certainly intends to have his pound of flesh.'

'Oh well. If he wants you back there, Will, you can hardly refuse.'

'I know. That's the problem.' Will picked up his newspaper. 'Come on, let's go out on the porch and relax. That's what we're here for. I'll worry about Lucas's and Worthington's tomorrow.' He sat down and read with mounting horror Hitler's latest decrees. 'Perhaps it's for the best I go back.'

Henzey looked up from her book. 'What makes you say that?'

'Look at this.' He tapped the article in the paper with the back of his hand.

'There's got to be war sooner or later.'

'Talk of war scares me, Will.'

'It scares everybody. Nobody wants it, but sooner or later . . . That maniac Hitler can't be allowed to get away with what he's doing.'

'How can *you* do anything? It's up to the politicians.'

'I can do my bit, Henzey. This Worthington job is for military trucks. I'll consider it my pre-war contribution, helping to put a stop to his crazy antics by getting the damn things right.'

They fell silent, reading, for an hour or more.

'What time shall we eat?' Will asked eventually.

'Are you hungry?'

'Yes, I'm a bit peckish now.'

'I'll go and get it ready. I thought a nice ham and cheese salad . . .'

'Fine.'

She stood up, then hesitated, standing at the back of his deckchair, looking out across the sea. 'Will, I think I might stay here after all,' she said lightly. 'If you're only going to be away a night or two, it seems pointless packing everything then lugging it all back again.'

'But we wouldn't have to pack, if you think about it. We could leave it all here.'

'Yes, I suppose so . . . All the same, I think I'll stay. I wouldn't be a hindrance then. You don't mind, do you?'

'No, course not. It's what I suggested in the first place.'

'I'll stay here then.' She turned and went inside.

Will left early the following morning, apologising again for having to go. He said he'd try to be back next day but, if he was going to be delayed, he would telephone. To occupy herself, Henzey cleaned the cottage from one end through to the other, thinking the whole time of her new situation, how it might affect Will, and how Will's new situation would affect them both. They had been presented with a God-sent opportunity to be happy and prosperous beyond their wildest dreams. It would be a tragedy to squander it by allowing her secret to ruin their marriage. It would be a further tragedy to bankrupt this promising new way of life as fully fledged members of the Worthington family, before it had even begun.

But what had been done could not be undone. And what had been done she did not regret. It just had to remain hidden.

Of course, it had occurred to her that Will's being called back to Lucas's might be a genuine panic requiring his expertise; but, on the other hand, it smacked of interference from Neville. She was ashamed to admit to herself that that very notion had perversely urged her to remain at Middleton, while Will conscientiously returned to Birmingham. Perhaps Neville had deliberately engineered Will's return to get him out of the way.

Henzey ate some lunch and decided to stroll along the sands towards Bognor. The weather was fine and dry and she reckoned that as long as she took a cardigan to keep warm from the sea breeze, the exercise would do her good. She would be able to ponder things more; and the more time she had to think the easier it was to come to terms with everything. So she walked for an hour and a half, barefoot most of the way, across the sand and the shingle. The lines of breakwaters jutting out of the beach made a graphic pattern and she decided that at some time she must capture it on paper.

When she returned to Middleton, her legs aching from the exertion of walking on shingle, she put on her shoes and strolled up Sea Lane towards the village in search of a café, happy to be on firmer ground again. She could have a cup of tea before returning to the cottage. She bought fresh vegetables from a greengrocer and meat from a butcher. She was tired by now but her appetite was huge, and back at the house she ate heartily, alone with her thoughts.

Outside, the evening sun was lending a deepening yellow glow as it started its spectacular descent through a lattice of cyan and magenta clouds. It was worth capturing. If only she had the ability to capture it in watercolours. Hurriedly, she scooped up her paints, brushes and a sheet of textured watercolour paper from the dozen or so she'd brought, filled a mug with water and began painting. The relaxation that drawing and painting always brought her was so soothing. It concentrated her mind on her subject, so that it seldom wandered. Worries evaded her while she painted. And by the time the light had faded, rendering further work impossible, she realised she had pondered little about herself, about Will, or even Neville.

But that realisation triggered off again thoughts of Neville. What if he had fixed things after all to ensure that Will was away? What if he called on her tonight? Her heart started pounding at the thought.

She left her watercolour taped to the table to dry flat, collected her paints together and washed her brushes. She put some milk to boil on the hob and made herself a mug of cocoa, which she took to bed along with her book. She tried to read again but recurrent thoughts of Neville and the possibility of his invading her bed again that night ensured that she absorbed little. If he wanted to come she could do nothing to prevent it. If he wanted to come she would welcome it. If he was going to come, she hoped it would be soon . . . before she fell asleep.

However, it was morning that arrived, not Neville. Henzey opened her eyes and realised she had spent the night alone. She was relieved, yet at the same time bitterly disappointed. She stretched and yawned, turned over and closed her eyes again. Why hadn't he come? It was a heaven-sent opportunity. Perhaps he would come today. Perhaps he would make sure that Will was detained another day or two and come today?

She could not rest. She slid out of bed in her night-gown and went to the bathroom. When she was dressed she wandered to the French window. How different the light was now to how it had been last evening. She glanced at her painting. The rich oranges, yellows and vibrant reds of her sunset were in stark contrast to the pale, misty blue of this morning. Nature used such an unyielding method of characterising its phases. Perhaps she should sit down now and paint the same scene by this flat, indifferent light. A real artist would. But where was the inspiration? No wonder artists painted sunsets. So, instead, she went to the kitchen, boiled the kettle and made herself some breakfast.

It was shortly after ten o'clock when the telephone rang.

'It'll take a miracle for me to get back today,' Will said. 'Shall you be all right?'

'I'll be fine.'

'What have you been doing?'

'Oh, I did some cleaning, then I went for a long walk along the beach. After tea I did a watercolour — I'm quite pleased with it as well. I had an early night . . .'

'And have I got a surprise for you,' he exclaimed, interrupting her.

'You mean as well as the one you already mentioned?'

'Yes, two surprises.' He laughed, and she thought how bright he sounded.

'I can't wait.'

'It'll be worth the wait, I can tell you. I'd better go, love. Looks like I won't be back till tomorrow.'

'Have you seen Neville?' She tried to make it sound like an afterthought.

'Yes, I saw him yesterday. But I'll tell you about that when I see you. He's travelling to London today.'

'To London? Oh.' Her heart thumped. What if he'd told Will a lie? 'Well, I'd better let you go then, Will. I'll see you when I see you. Bye.'

'Bye, darling.'

She did not like herself much for thinking it, but the likelihood of Neville coming to see her when she was alone in his cottage and not going to London, as he had evidently told Will, thrilled her. London had to be an excuse; his excuse to get away. So he was coming to see her, to be with her, to make love to her once more; and her desire to make love to him was growing inexorably.

The more she thought about it the more certain she was that this whole situation was just a ploy. So certain was she, that she began holding conversations with Neville inside her head; conversations that reflected the circumstances and time of his arrival. She imagined it first to be at about teatime; he would say sorry for detaining Will in Birmingham, smile knowingly, then whisk her off to some restaurant or other before they made love. He might arrive before that, take her out in his boat for the afternoon and contrive to make love to her on some deserted beach as the sun went down. He might simply be his old self, before those midnight visitations, uncertain of her, uncertain of himself, anxious that she should know how he felt, but reticent about forcing himself upon her for fear of rebuttal. And these thoughts made her heart pound with anticipation.

Something had been in the back of her mind, however, struggling to surface into coherent logic. And it was at this time that those thoughts took shape. It had been with complete and utter surprise that she had learned of Eunice's affair with Billy Witts. It had surprised her even more to learn that her beautiful, lovely daughter, Kitty, was actually Billy's child. She might have had a child like that herself if only Billy had . . .

So how much of Neville's scheming and passing himself off as Will had been driven by a perverse desire for revenge? Just how deep and sincere was his confession of love that afternoon in the shade of the trees on the approach to the golf course?

Now he'd taken his revenge, if revenge it was. But Billy Witts wasn't suffering because of it; Eunice wasn't grieving either, or certainly didn't seem to be. Henzey herself wasn't tormented emotionally. She was directly affected, but for her the outcome had been positive: she was expecting a child; Neville's, yes, but a child she'd yearned for these long months. It would be an illegitimate child but nobody else would know that. The only person to be adversely affected, though thank God he was blissfully ignorant of it, was Will himself. Who, therefore, was being punished?

Nobody.

So Henzey dismissed the notion and took a leisurely bath. As she lay in its soothing warmth she realised with some surprise the ease with which she had accepted her lot. She was astounded at the ease with which she found herself already deceiving the husband she loved – or thought she loved. The feelings of guilt had disappeared long since, the last mere traces dispersed in the late summer breezes of the south coast. She felt at peace with herself as she lay back in the soft, luxuriously warm water. She was eager to talk to Neville again, ready to be open and frank with him.

She gently prodded her wet belly. It was harder and slightly more rounded than normal, though of course, her condition would not be obvious to anyone else for some time. What was it about her, she wondered, that had driven Neville to such lengths to have her? Was it her looks, her figure, her voice, her demeanour? She had no wealth; it could not have been that. Fine looks, she had, and she was aware of it, but never had she consciously exploited them to lure a man. She had only ever been interested in one man at a time. More than one would have complicated life too much, as indeed it was doing now.

She realised Neville Worthington was totally occupying her thoughts. Just thinking about him brought a lump to her throat, made her yearn for him again. Oh, it was wrong, she knew, so against all her principles, but she no longer had control over what she felt.

She pulled the plug out of the bath, reached for her towel, stood up and dried herself. She pulled on her dressing-gown and went into the bedroom where she sat in front of her own reflection in the mirror of the dressing table. If Neville did intend to come to her this must be the very last time. It could not go on. It must not be allowed to go on. But she could not forego such an opportunity today, under such ideally romantic circum-stances. He had opened her eyes to lovemaking. One more encounter could do no further damage. The damage, if indeed it could be construed as such, had already been done.

So she readied herself for his arrival in a haze of sensual daydreaming. She applied her make-up with extra diligence and did her hair with extra care. She chose underwear that was alluring and a dress that, without being pretentious, showed her figure off beautifully. And, when she was ready, she awaited him in the living-room.

At one o'clock in the afternoon she decided she was hungry but decided to allow him another fifteen minutes, for if he intended to arrive for lunch she wanted an appetite so she could enjoy the food. But half past one rolled round and he had not arrived.

So she ate alone.

By half past four in the afternoon he still had not arrived and she was hungry again. It was too late to be taken out for afternoon tea, so she polished off a lemon curd tart with a cup of tea.

What if he did not come at all? What if he was going to London after all? She would feel a complete fool. But, thankfully, she would appear a fool only to herself. What if he was apprehensive of coming? What if it hadn't even crossed his mind to come? She had not really pondered that. After all, they had not had the opportunity to discuss what had gone on so privately in their lives. He had no idea how she now craved to be with him; and indeed, he might be more than a little surprised to learn of it.

She tried to shove such negative thoughts to the back of her mind. Of course he would come. It was a heaven-sent opportunity, brilliantly engineered. He would not throw away such a chance; the first since those hot, steamy nights of July and August. He would arrive in plenty of time to take her out to dinner. Most likely, he would already have reserved a table at a swish restaurant in Bognor Regis or Littlehampton, or even Worthing.

At seven o'clock, he still had not arrived. Perhaps in another hour . . . Henzey inspected her dress. It was creased now from sitting about all day in it; hardly suitable for going out to dinner. So she went to the bedroom and opened the wardrobe to remind herself what other dresses she had brought with her. There was one which would do just nicely for dinner out. It was not an evening dress – she had not expected to be taken out to dinner – but it was a plain, navy-blue day dress with the hemline just above the ankle. It would suffice. It would have to suffice. So she took off the one she was wearing and put this fresh one on. Her heart jumped when she thought she heard a car, and she peered out of the bedroom window overlooking the road. But it turned out to be a motor boat chugging along the coast at the back of the cottage. She sighed with disappointment but adjusted the dress, her hair, and touched up her make-up.

By eight o'clock she was ravenously hungry and still there was no sign of Neville. She would give him till half past eight and then she would have to eat. She went outside on the porch and breathed the seaside smells of the late summer twilight and felt an awful ache in her heart, which she knew was her longing for him.

She stayed on the porch till half past eight, caring not that she was growing colder, till hunger summoned her to the kitchen to make a ham and tomato sandwich with a smear of mustard. So the true, overwhelming affection that Neville had bestowed on her in his many masquerades was to be denied her this day in its unmasked guise. It was certain now that he would not come. Perhaps she had been over-confident that she still appealed to him. He had had his fun. He had achieved what he had set out to do. He had had her. His appetite had been sated. Why should he complicate matters? Why take further risks?

She could scarcely believe her own disappointment. It was as bitter as a bereavement. Her ardent desire to experience again what they had experienced before, and savour his love for what it was, was to be denied. It was criminal that he should avoid such a wonderful opportunity. And yet maybe it was no more than she deserved. No doubt it was for the best. She could ill afford to lose her head. It was important to keep both feet planted firmly on the ground. Will was still her husband; he still idolised her; and she him, in her own diminishing way.

If Neville had not arrived by nine o'clock she would know for certain he was not about to. She would know by then that she'd been deluding herself. As the minute hand of the clock wound its way lethargically round its face, her hopes faded altogether. He would not come now. Definitely not. So she went back into the bedroom and undressed. When she had put on her dressing-gown she went to the kitchen, poured a glass of sherry and sat sipping it till half past ten, attempting to read her book, absorbing only the odd paragraph, re-reading the parts she had not digested first time. Then, disconsolately, she retired to bed.

He was on her mind constantly and she doubted whether she would sleep. She panted for him, longing to be his. Her eyes were closed. Alone in the darkness, but warm in the big bed, she remembered those former nights, how happy and content she was while he was with her. She re-lived their lovemaking, vigorous, vocal; the sweat from their bodies running together in the exertion, mixing, infusing like some erotic cocktail. She ached for him intolerably. Why had he let her down when she was so sure he would come? If only he knew how much she wanted him now. If only he knew how high her emotions were running for him.

A sound woke her. She must have fallen asleep after all. It was a key turning in a lock. Suddenly she was wide awake. She sat bolt upright. What if it was a burglar? She heard the front door open and close, and her heart began thumping hard and fast like a bass drum beating out a tango as she heard his footsteps in the hall. She dared to smile to herself and sighed with overpowering joy as she snuggled back down in the bed.

He was here. He had come to her at last; just like he had before. Of course, it *had* to be just like before, in the middle of the night.

The bedroom door opened and she pretended to be asleep.

She heard him take off his jacket, his tie. He loosened his cuff-links and his collar, undid his shirt and his trousers, and she heard them all in their turn fall to the floor with a faint swish. Of course, she might yet be wrong, she knew. It might yet be Will returned. She would know soon enough.

He slid into bed alongside her and she sensed the chill from his body at her back. He must have been aware of it, too, since he lay still for a while, collecting her warmth, unwilling to allow his cold skin to touch her, for that would spoil the moment. Still feigning sleep, but eager to hold him, she tossed, turning towards him. He drew her naked body to him and she snuggled up to him as submissively as a kitten. Her heart was hammering hot blood through her veins, more pronounced than it had ever been before. With her eyes still closed she blindly turned her face up to his and felt the warmth of his breath as he bent his head to find her lips. Instinctively she opened her mouth and her tongue probed his with such urgency that he flinched in surprise. His leg parted her thighs and she savoured the bliss of contact as the whole length of their bodies touched. And then she knew; she knew for certain that this was not Will in the darkness. This was Neville. Her arms were around him, her eyes were shut and her lips were smiling, though she was trembling, trembling all over.

She whispered aloud, pleading, 'Make love to me, my sweetheart. Make love to me with all your heart and soul.'

He responded by smothering her body for ages with sensual kisses, caressing her with clever fingers till she thought she must surely burst with desire. At last he settled upon her; and when she was actually weeping with longing, he entered her. Her hands gripped his buttocks and she moaned with pleasure as she pulled him hard into her with such sweet, deep relief; and those little cries of pleasure settled into a rhythm in time with the rocking of their bodies.

*　　*　　*

'I knew you'd come to me,' she said, wiping the smear of perspiration from her brow with the back of her hand.

Starlight penetrated the darkness through the open curtains.

'I wouldn't have missed it for the world,' he replied, his hands behind his head, as he lay back on the pillow. Then he drew her to him again, and she lay with her cheek against his shoulder, smiling to herself with utter contentment.

'I didn't know what time you'd get here, though . . . D'you know? I got all dressed up ready for dinner. I thought you'd take me out to dinner first. I fancied being wooed for once.'

They laughed together like conspirators.

'Wooed? . . . You really are a kitten, Henzey . . .'

'Yes, I fancied being wooed properly.'

'If only I'd known. But do you know how long it takes to get down here? I left the office at six.'

'Then I'm glad you didn't leave it any later.'

'So am I.'

She snuggled up to him again, her arm around his waist, still smiling to herself. Thank God he'd come. It had to be the very last time, but thank God for this opportunity. It would provide one more memory to add to her precious store. She hugged him and he hugged her in return.

'This can't go on, you know.' The tone of her whisper was poignant. 'You know it can't go on, seeing each other like this.'

He laughed. 'Actually, if you think about it, it can. It can go on just as long as we want it to. And I want it to.'

It was such a relief to hear him say it. She wanted to as well, of course, but how could they maintain this charade? It would be the ruin of both of them.

'Well, I wonder just how long you'll want to. Not so long as you think, I bet.'

'Why do you say that? I'll always want you.'

'Not when my belly's big. Not when I'm all fat and ugly and you can't get near me.'

He raised his head up from the pillow and rested it on his

411

arm. The fingers of his free hand glided sensually across her stomach to her triangle of hair, arousing himself again. 'You'll always be beautiful to me, Henzey . . . and desirable.'

'Oh, I bet.'

'Anyway, if you're saying you're pregnant, I only have your word for it. I'm not so sure. I think we ought to make absolutely certain.'

He held her in his arms and their lips met again in the darkness. Instinctively she offered herself by drawing him onto her, and again they made love. Then, both fell into deep, contented sleep.

Henzey awoke to the sound of somebody hammering the front door knocker. She opened her eyes and, to her surprise, discovered tears quivering on her long lashes. It was the dream she'd had of herself and Neville in an emotional parting, and the subsequent weeping. She knew that long after the snow falls of winter had been melted by the spring sunshine, long after the bluebell carpets of May had faded, long after the baby that was theirs had been born, they would still remember those nights and yearn for them again. Desire would seize them and there would be no greater pain than that which they would inevitably feel at having to deny it. But it would have to be endured.

She heard the knocking again and jumped out of bed, grabbing her dressing-gown. Her heart was in her mouth. What the hell was the time? Surely it couldn't be Will returned? Not this early? Even allowing for over-sleeping it could surely not be later than nine o'clock? Please, God, don't let it be Will. Not with Neville lying naked in her bed. Please, please, God, let it be anybody but Will.

Trembling, and yet strangely reconciled to an imminent showdown, she padded through the hall to the front door. The by-now familiar queasiness of morning sickness was urging her to vomit but she resisted it. She turned the catch and opened the door about four inches, ready to face whatever retribution fate was about to hurl at her.

'Hello, our Henzey. Aren't you dressed yet? You do look pale.'

'Mother! Jesse! What on earth are you doing here? I . . . I . . .'

Lizzie smiled expectantly. 'Well, aren't you going to ask us in?'

Henzey wished desperately for a very large hole to open up in the floor and swallow her wholesale. She was well and truly compromised. What else could she do but open the door? 'You'd better come in.'

'You seem surprised to see us.'

'I am a bit . . .'

'Didn't Will tell you we were coming?'

'Not in as many words.'

'That's a nice, new car outside on the road,' Jesse commented as he lugged a suitcase in with him. 'You must be comin' up in the world if you can afford a car like that.'

'The car?' Neither her mother nor Jesse noted any significance in the look of apprehension that clouded her face.

'That maroon car. Beautiful motor car. A Swallow SSI, or I'm a monkey's uncle. You don't see many o' that colour about. Will said he fancied a Swallow, but I never thought . . .'

Henzey looked at him open-mouthed for what seemed an age, her mind racing but getting nowhere. A *maroon* Swallow? Neville had a black Swallow. Burning with curiosity she peered outside and saw the brand-new maroon car parked on the road.

'Put your things down here for a minute,' she said, becoming increasingly confused by the second. 'Mom, the kitchen's through there. Put the kettle on, will you? I'll just go and get dressed.'

A maroon Swallow . . . A *maroon* Swallow? She scurried to her bedroom apprehensively and closed the door shut. The urge to vomit she'd felt only a minute ago had left her. Now she just felt hot and she was perspiring. She peered intently at the man lying in her bed just as he was rousing himself.

He opened his eyes and smiled. 'Good morning, Petal,' he said brightly. 'What got you up?'

She stared at him hard, not knowing whether to laugh or cry, hardly knowing whether to scream with relief or frustration, still doubting whether good fortune could smile on her sufficiently benignly to make this person Will. She was still too confused to be absolutely certain who it was. 'Oh, it was just somebody at the door,' she said experimentally, endeavouring to sound unemotional.

'At this time in the morning? . . . Ha! I didn't think they'd get here this early.' He rubbed his eyes, then ran his fingers through his hair. 'They must have travelled down last night and took digs in a boarding house overnight.'

'Who?' Her level voice concealed the ferment inside her head. 'Who are you talking about?'

'Who do you think? Your mother and Jesse. We're not expecting anybody else, are we?'

Tears stung her eyes. Impetuously, she picked up the pillow she'd been lying on and beat him over the head with it several times till she felt her strength draining from her. God, he deserved to be punished for the agony he'd put her through.

He was amused by her animated response and, laughing, he held his arms above his head to fend off the blows. 'What's the matter?' he chuckled. 'Didn't you want them to come? I told you I had a surprise for you.'

But *he* was by far the greater surprise.

'And the other surprise, I suppose, is that new maroon car outside?' Another rain of blows from the pillow.

'Ouch! Pack it in, Henzey,' he chortled. 'Have you seen it already then? Have you been outside to see it already? Neville got it for me. It's a company car.'

She threw the pillow down onto the bed, her eyes glazed with tears, and slumped face down onto the mattress, trying to come to terms with this unexpected twist. Her breath was coming in gasps from the exertion of bashing him. 'Will Parish, you are an absolute swine,' she sobbed. But she was laughing as well now and unable to stem the swirling torrent of criss-crossed emotions. She was as yet unable to grasp fully the implications of what was happening.

'I thought you'd like your mother to come,' he said. 'Hey, there's no need to cry. They're not as bad as all that. I quite like them, you know, even if you're evidently not so keen . . . What's got into you?'

She flung her arms around him and tears rolled down her cheeks uncontrollably. He held her tight, stroking her hair, unable to fathom out why she was sobbing and laughing by turn so intensely. It was such an unremarkable occasion, after all.

'Oh, Will, it's . . . it's the most fantastic . . .' Her voice, faltering through her weeping, ensured she could not finish her sentence. 'Oh, I couldn't be happier . . . Thank you . . . But why didn't you bring them with you last night?'

'Two reasons. First, I didn't feel that confident about driving – especially all that way – and in the dark. And second, I wanted us to be alone last night.'

'I can't understand why you even bothered to come last night. You could've waited till this morning and driven in daylight.'

'And miss the chance of sneaking into bed with you in the middle of the night again? Lord above, it's the only way I seem to be able to get any passion out of you since you threatened to cut off my supply.'

She thought her heart would stop beating. She lifted her head and looked at him with consternation through her flood of tears. 'Passion? What d'you mean, passion?'

'Oh, come on, Henzey. First you deprive me of my conjugal rights, then when I leave my shift one night to come home and make amends and tell you all right we'll try for a baby, despite a poorly stomach, despite being racked with anxiety over your unhappiness, you just overwhelm me with passion. And it's been the same ever since – every every time I've done it. You know it has.'

'Wait a minute . . . You mean, you agree? You agree we should start a family?'

'I said so. Weeks ago. God, where have you been all this time? You've been so obsessed. Don't you remember anything? Sometimes I swear you've been going doolally tap.'

Henzey swallowed hard and looked at him in disbelief, trying to assimilate this information as quickly as she could before she made a serious *faux pas*. But she could not help smiling. 'I thought . . . You know, I thought I'd dreamed it – you sneaking back home at night,' she said, and she scanned her memory, trying to recall whether she'd said anything last night that might incriminate herself, such as calling him Neville. 'So how many times did you do that? How many times did you leave your shift?'

He laughed again at her apparent bewilderment, blissfully unaware of the reason for it. 'I'm not telling you,' he teased. 'How many times did you dream it?'

'More than once,' she replied ambiguously.

'More than once? Well, lucky you.'

'But how many times did you leave your shift? I want to know . . . It's not funny, Will.'

'Yes it is, and I'm not telling you. All I'll say is that it was as often as I thought I could get away with it.'

'Oh, Will.'

'You must admit, though, Henzey – since then our love-making's been a bit off. That's why I thought I'd try again last night to catch you in bed late. I drove down here like a madman crazed with lust. But it worked, didn't it? . . . Why can't you be like that every night, Henzey?'

She sighed. She could. Well . . . maybe she could. 'You'd only get fed up with it.'

So she had loved Will as ardently as she thought she had loved Neville; and he her. What a turn-up. What a love match this had turned out to be. A surge of relief swept through her, cleansing her, purging her. Never had she experienced such exquisite feelings of release. The very last thing she could have hoped for was deliverance from her nightmare. She was carrying Will's child after all. And, just as important, Will had been the same sensual, passionate equal as herself, given the chance. She would settle for that. She would happily settle for that.

'Henzey, the kettle's boiled,' Lizzie called from the kitchen. 'Where's the blasted teapot?'

Henzey grabbed her pillow and hit him again, more playfully now. 'Will Parish, if my mother and Jesse weren't in the kitchen right now I'd . . . I'd . . .' She stopped suddenly and swallowed hard. 'Oh, God . . . I feel sick now.'

'Sick? Does that mean *I've* got to go and find the blasted teapot for them?'